# The Legend of Susej

## An Un-Christian Novel

Jeffrey Schmidt

PublishAmerica
Baltimore

© 2007 by Jeffrey Schmidt.
All rights reserved. No part of this book may be reproduced, stored in a retrieval system or transmitted in any form or by any means without the prior written permission of the publishers, except by a reviewer who may quote brief passages in a review to be printed in a newspaper, magazine or journal.

First printing

All characters appearing in this work are fictitious. Any resemblance to real persons, living or dead, is purely coincidental.

ISBN: 1-4241-7230-6
PUBLISHED BY PUBLISHAMERICA, LLLP
www.publishamerica.com
Baltimore

Printed in the United States of America

To Bob,
Jeffrey Schmidt
2007

# One

The penthouse on the 110th floor of the Bio-Med Building in New York City was Darius Celosi's earthly salvation. It was his reward for a life, up to then, of deprivation, perseverance and hard work. It was here that after years of denial and avoidance he realized reclusive achievement.

The penthouse was the eminent reward for Bio-Med's "top of the ladder" executives who lived there in total isolation above a fetid society, all their necessities provided without having to leave the edifice. All the penthouses, apartments and suites which were a part of the complex were designed for eye-pleasing beauty to instill a sense of pride in the executives, as if they were not a part of the connivance and coercion of management, but instead it sought to convey an aura of grandeur in tune with the constructive aspects of the human spirit and thereby encourage the free flow of creativity and energy.

But it was more than that. From this lofty place, one was high above the turbulence and violence of the street, its stagnating pollution unseen, as well as the pathetic homelessness, the sheer desperation of the masses of a muddling society without purpose, direction or hope. More importantly, one would not be constantly threatened by zombie-like creatures stumbling through the streets and back alleys or the savage packs of demented youths ravaging the remnants of a devastated city.

So the high achievers were blessed with their own living space of modern architecture and Martha Stewart elegance, a deceptively satisfying accomplishment which they, in total naïveté, believed to be a result of their own superior performance. Yet, like so many of the generation before them, they were unknowingly on the edge; just an economic downturn, a CEO's decision, or a corporate buyout away from the abyss that was society.

Celosi sat in a deep-cushioned settee in front of a panoramic picture window dominating the penthouse and felt a deep sense of satisfaction and, more importantly, he felt secure. At the end of a twelve-hour work day, he was able to retire to his own space, to be by himself and his own thoughts, unhampered by management's imperatives or coworker's intrusions.

As it was still light outside, he rose and walked to the window, pausing at a comfortable distance. He suffered from fear of heights all his life but had learned to deal with that affliction by avoidance. A couple of feet from the glass he could peer down without seeing the street below but was able to appreciate the broad view of the Hudson River and eastern New Jersey as if it were an artist's surrealistic impression of a modern landscape, cosmopolitan and abstract, while unseen directly below was the black jungle of the city. Day was ending and the clouds, wafting by with tinges of red from a sun receding somewhere to the west, seemed to share his solitude and disdain for the urban.

But vertigo was not the only affliction troubling to Celosi when he was assigned to the top-floor penthouse. He was also badly conflicted by his associations with the smooth-talking, well-educated bluestockings who always said the right thing and by their very manner, whether charming or confronting, seemed mocking or condescending. However, driven by insecurity and ambition, he overcame any overt response to their incivility through sheer determination and abnegation.

He returned to his settee after making himself a brandy Alexander and settled in comfortably, and his mind, uncluttered now that he was alone, began to dance with serendipitous thoughts. He enjoyed the creativity of his mind when he was free to do so and the brandy may have added to that. He felt elation at his sense of freedom, a freedom that accrued to a mellowing of mind and body. He made a second brandy. The clouds were fading to darkness and his emotional connection with them would soon be broken. Then gradually, the mellowness he felt became what he would describe as an all consuming smoothness, everything he did and felt was casual and coordinated as his thoughts floated effortlessly, unfettered by restraint.

But then as always, the free-thinking mood became jangled, suddenly amok with undisciplined ideation, a cluster of the unimaginable and the nonsensical. He struggled to return to rationality but unsuccessfully. A third brandy helped not a bit. Neither did a fourth. Desperate for lucidity, he punched in his satellite radio. Tuned to Satellite NEWS, the announcer was relating that "several thousand environmental protestors stormed the offices of Sedgeway Protocol, the largest corporate conglomerate responsible for food production and distribution in the world, but were met by police and the national guard, who shot and killed 325 of them and wounding another 430 under the authority of the Domestic Terrorist Act of 2012." The announcer was vague regarding the nature of the complaint of the protestors but assured listeners that all precaution had been taken in order to avoid bloodshed but the unreasonable demands leaders of the outlaw assemblage got out of hand. Celosi quickly tuned to Satellite GOD.

In a syrupy overly animated voice, the host was quoting from the Bible "'...God said to them, Be fruitful and multiply: fill the earth and subdue it; have dominion over the fish of the sea, over the birds of the air, and over every living thing that moves on the earth...'" He punched in the visual revealing a non-descriptive thin man, looking older than his voice, impeccably dressed. He flipped off the visual. *That must be one hell of a coincidence,* Celosi thought of the ironic contrast of the two messages. Then reasoned, *Maybe not.* Mercifully, Christian music began to fill the room. Celosi always found Christian music formless and repetitious, but relaxing; at least it was palatable compared to the vicious, driving, social-issues emphasis of modern rock.

All too soon, the room began to rotate and Celosi, anticipating his usual whirling emotional meltdown, bracing against the inevitable scramble of lights and shadows, wrapped both arms abreast and collapsed into the deep pillowed recess of his couch and attempted to force lucidity into his brain. But to no avail; he lacked the introspection to understand his own emotional Babel; he was too self-absorbed to build personal relationships in order to develop self-understanding and maturity; he was too phlegmatic to contemplate viable alternatives to his inner self; and he was too removed from human compassion and empathy to appreciate his own potential for humaneness.

It was insurmountable. He made a gasping inhale and struggling to his feet, he stumbled toward his bedroom using his hands on furniture to steady himself and, lurching to his unmade bed, cast himself askew, his head now spinning with the sewage of his bereavement melted into morbid abyss.

It was discomfiture equal to any pain, whether mental or physical. He passed out piteously. Sleep—one of God's great blessings.

Darius Celosi was born and raised in Albuquerque, New Mexico, the oldest of eight children born to a common laborer, Mateo Celosi, an immigrant from Juarez, Mexico, the son of an East Indian oil executive killed in an auto accident when Mateo was an infant. Mateo never attended formal school as a result of his father's death and was functionally illiterate. But he did learn to value hard work and after he moved to the United States, he gained the reputation as a hard and willing worker and was never unemployed. Because of that very factor he was considered a good catch by the ladies frequenting Cantina Azteca every Saturday night and he eventually was to marry Maria Gomez, a second-generation Mexican-American beauty coveted by the local young men for her bearing and upbringing.

Both Maria and Mateo were Catholic and the marriage was one of strong commitment. Children were always received with great anticipation and loved equally by the parents. Darius was born after a difficult breech birth and as a consequence was spindly and often ill with a variety of ailments. He would seem that he would have to pursue academic endeavors from the very beginning and when he attended elementary school, it seemed that he had at least a moderate capacity for such work.

In the primary grades Darius had the ability to read and comprehend far beyond his years and he would forego play and entertainment to pursue his studies; in fact, it became an immeasurable pride to him. He had a disdain for physical work, a necessity in a family in which all members contributed in an effort to survive the hard times of depression America. He particularly resented working in the outside summer heat or winter cold or with brothers and their chaotic bickering and what he felt was false camaraderie. His deliverance from these family tasks came when his mother, although with only a moderate education, viewed education as an imperative, proclaimed that any of her children who would spend serious time reading would be credited with work time in family chores, equal hour for hour. Darius flourished. He would always recall that first winter day after that edict, sitting comfortably in his bedroom, warm and left to his own resources. His newly found freedom did not set well with his siblings, which concerned him not in the least.

When in high school, Darius met one Timothy Berqoise. Top of his class but still somewhat of a casual free spirit, Berqoise had an uncanny ability to read two or three books in a single evening with perfect comprehension and it was something that he did almost effortlessly. Darius, although not particularly competitive, was stimulated to improve his own reading ability accordingly. But it was not that simple. By attempting to read faster, Darius began to lose comprehension and recall. He subsequently took a course in speed reading but by skimming over words or trying to eliminate unnecessary words or trying to read with his "third ear," he lost meaning as well as a feel for the flow of words. Then in one of life's funny little ironies, he found out something important about Berqoise and life—and himself.

Berqoise had on one occasion demonstrated to Darius that he had a photographic memory, something that Darius had thought to be a myth. But it was exactly that—a memory with perfect photocopy recall. Timothy had Darius open a magazine to a page randomly, the first time being the *AMA*

*Journal*, and Timothy would look at it for a second or two and his mind would seem to go "zap" and he would register the whole page in his mind at which time he would return the magazine to Darius to read and then, as a demonstration to Darius, he recited the page perfectly. This was deeply disturbing to Darius, who immediately knew that he could never match that performance.

However, as Darius got to know Timothy, he discovered something that he thought to be very strange about him, and that was that Timothy had absolutely no sense of logic and lacked even a novice ability to reason. In fact, many of his personal relationships were counterproductive and alienating and, as the two boys progressed through high school, Timothy became increasingly self-destructive, and perhaps inevitably, his own worst enemy. This, of course, gave Darius a renewed sense of self, particularly as he watched, without undue concern, as Timothy slowly destructed until his once-great academic potential had been exuded, eliminating him from any chance of high achievement. So, it became aware to Darius that there was no assurance that reading in itself was the ultimate end. The reader must have other assets to complete scholarly accomplishment, particularly determinant aspiration, focus, realistic concepts and self-discipline.

The second great lesson Darius received from reading was quite by accident. One day, during his junior year of high school, Darius found himself without any reading material. He ventured into a used book store and browsed for an hour or so but unable to find anything he was interested in reading, he bought an old used copy of a college-level textbook on the philosophies of the world. Once at home, he found it very abstract, difficult reading and requiring the constant use of a dictionary. In fact, he was tempted to give up, but that had never been an alternative to him before and he had no intention of allowing that to happen now. At one point in the book, Darius, frustrated, put the book down and then starting over, began to read from the very beginning of the chapter with forced concentration, moving on only when he was sure that he comprehended the full meaning expressed in the text. It took him to a level of concentration that he had never experienced before and on that level, required an inordinate amount of time for him to complete the reading, but he conquered the material.

Out of that experience he came to realize the power of quintessence and that it was essential to understanding the most perfect manifestation of quality. Furthermore, when he returned to simpler reading material, he noted that he read with increased speed and comprehension—very simply, he had never tested himself before. Suddenly, it came to him, unlike the norm of his generation, that we all must read within our ability and our innate ability for learning, that we all have different abilities and that the power of concentration was in itself more of a gift than was a quick unschooled mind. So it was that he would have never realized that he was undisciplined except for this challenge.

There had long been resentment of Darius among his brothers as they surmised that his treatment from their parents was preferential and unfair. That was further aggravated by Darius's aloof and alienated attitude toward his siblings. He had tired of their squabbling and bickering, not to mention their endless interest in mindless electronic games and time-wasting entertainment. He was impatient with what he regarded as their petit problems and overreaction to the normal events in life which he felt should be put into perspective and dealt with inherently. How often during the routine and habit of everyday life he had caught himself admonishing one of them in their criticism of him, "Just learn to live with it and go on with your life."

Darius's growing tendency to be remote as a family member was viewed by his parents as a result of his deep involvement in his studies and was accepted as a trade-off with the loss of involvement in the family coil as the price to be paid for academic success which they reasoned would ideally benefit the family in the long term.

One particularly frosty school day, while preparing for school in what his brothers referred to as "his own little world," Darius became aware that the youngest sibling, Jamie, nine years younger than himself, was crying hysterically alone in his bedroom. Darius had to pass that room and in trying to slip by, he saw young Jamie huddled on the corner of his bed, blankets over his head, wailing uncontrollably as if terrified by some terrible macabre threat. Almost casually, Darius asked what the matter was, a question he almost instantly regretted.

"Doesn't the sky ever end?" Jamie wailed despondently. "I mean, like, it just goes on and on forever, but if it did end what would be the end and then what would be after that?"

Unsympathetic, Darius responded, "Why worry about something you can't do anything about? I mean, like you are warm and safe here on earth, why worry about it?"

"Cuz, I need to know, there has to be a reason for the way things are and I want to understand it and it scares me," said Jamie, breathing out the words between sobs.

Darius smiled at the situation and wondered why Jamie, the youngest and most protected of the children, was so insecure. "The sky doesn't necessarily go on and on; in fact, there now are some theories that space is curved."

"Waa," Jamie sobbed, "that doesn't help."

Maria entered the room, cuddled up beside Jamie and cushioned his head to her neck. "You go on, Darius, go to school, we'll be all right."

Darius stood in the doorway for a few seconds and an unfamiliar feeling flickered in his brain, perhaps it was pity or compassion for his young brother but it was fleeting and he quickly suppressed it.

At the age of sixteen, Celosi entered the University of New Mexico. He eschewed the social life of college although had he chosen to he could have balanced books and play quite well without hindering his academic performance. The few associations that he did have were much like himself, high academic achievers but social lightweights and not inclined to change or grow. With a major in business administration, he found his courses easy and in an effort to keep busy, he took non-major courses that looked tempting. One such course was a fledgling research study in biotechnology that opened him up to previously unexamined interests. It was an independent study program that so inspired him that he applied for and was accepted for an internship in the summer of his graduate year at Bio-tech Incorporated, a laboratory in Landover, Maryland.

Celosi felt quite independent in school as he had a full scholarship and felt that he was paying his own way. Once he worked in Landover, it broke ties with his family, even as extrinsic as they may have been. Being away from the dank smell of a congested house, constant squabbling and personal grievances, never-ending financial problems, the interruptions of unapologetic siblings, household chores and the occasional drunkenness and aggressive behavior was an uplifting experience for Celosi. Most importantly, he came to appreciate just what a position in a large growing corporation could offer him.

After a brief tantalizing taste of corporate life, Celosi returned to the university for his graduate year, now more determined than ever to make his mark in the corporate world. He knew from his internship that if he could achieve a high position in a corporate hierarchy, he would have the material benefits and prestige to make life comfortable as well as providing with a sanctuary of preferred isolation, and he desperately wanted to leave behind capricious roommates, casserole meals, the din of telephones, televisions and radios, sloppy garbage-can-filled alleys, and the irritability of others. Simply, he wanted his own space, and success within a corporate system would provide that.

## JEFFREY SCHMIDT

Upon completing his master's degree in 2026, he received an entry-level position with Bio-Med, the largest medical research corporation in the world. His initial assignment was disappointing, certainly nothing like what he had anticipated from his summer at Bio-tech. From the beginning, there was tension and competitiveness among the young trainees and it was a disconcerting atmosphere, but for Celosi, there was no turning back. Such dedication paid off for him, as during that first year, the new recruits had thinned out as the demands imposed upon them were overwhelming, even those used to long hours and difficult tasks. By year's end, he had been given his own office and received permanent status.

As the exemplar Bio-Med employee, Celosi was neither amiable nor social toward coworkers, but he maintained a professional demeanor when working with them. In addition, in an effort to improve his work skills as well as his standing, he took all in-house training available, volunteered for outside projects, took on-line college courses and read updated material in scientific and technical journals.

He maintained a respectful attitude toward the research scientists in the Bio-Med laboratories and was able to converse on a sophisticated level with them. In return, they were impressed with his knowledge of research matters and they regarded him as an individual on his way to the top, which, of course, made his supervisors nervous.

He drove himself beyond the limits of normal endurance but, if he wavered or felt his resolve slipping, he had only to remember his poverty-level existence with his family in Albuquerque or, even more directly, to remind himself of the choking acidity of the air or the pitiful souls that inhabited the nightmarish streets below him.

As much as he felt satisfaction with his achievement at Bio-Med, he was too cautious to assume that he had permanent security and, correspondingly, he was vigilant toward unforeseen occurrences. So it was not unexpected to him, considering the world-wide depression and a recumbent stock market, that Bio-Med lost over a billion dollars in fiscal 2030. On the Dow averages, it had been a down year with medical and technical stocks the big losers. Competition had been fierce in those industries with various organizations investing heavily in research and development—costly but necessary expenditures.

It was during this impending financial crisis that a new company, Lenex Mega-Systems, small and sinewy and working on a meager budget, began producing new and innovating computer systems. Industry newsletters hailed their products as the most radical and advanced components on the market.

Unfortunately, the play-pen era of computers was history. Much of the market had dissolved and certainly, there was no market for electronic games or virtual reality once so popular. Simply, computers had run their course. Without consumer interest, Lenex products seemed unavailing.

But it took a charged mind like Celosi to see a connection between Bio-Med and Lenex. He was aware that Bio-Med was mired in an unchanging discipline, hanging on to a losing proposition, and competing with corporations that were essentially all selling the same products and services under different names. At the same time, Lenex, although without direct competition, had no demand on its products. It was obvious, Bio-Med needed to update its operation and Lenex needed a partnership that would meet its need for a demand.

Celosi's proposal of a buy-out of Lenex to the board of directors was initially met with little or no enthusiasm. But it was recognized by the board that a buy-out could be accomplished with relative ease considering the inevitable financial position into which Lenex had been floundering. In fact, once the idea of a planned buy-out had been presented, the concept gained steam and enthusiasm began to thrive within the board. Even before a formal report had been prepared for the board, initial contacts with Lenex, whose management was relatively inexperienced and unsophisticated, were encouraging, hinting of a desperate monetary shortfall in their operation. In fact, it came to light that Lenex was so close to bankruptcy that a tenuous offer of the buy-out, initially to assess the potential range of buy-out, was met with discreet enthusiasm by Lenex administrators.

Celosi literally drove himself night and day to formulate a comprehensive agreement acceptable to both companies, and in doing so, was developing inner capacities as a mediator, his role varying from authoritarian to manipulative persuader and he allocated no responsibility as he checked every line, rough-drafted, edited, rewrote, communicated with all involved parties and thus coordinated the physical merger of the two companies.

But what was so important to him and stimulated his interest in Lennex was their potential for innovative electronic designs being developed by them and which could be used to enhance Bio-Med's overall operation. He had been aware from the outset with Bio-Med that profit was being cut by the use of over a thousand scientists working in the medical laboratories, many of them on projects and research that would not bring profit to the corporation having never been evaluated beforehand—there was no way to do so before the fact—but only after their marketability was tested in the market itself.

Therefore, it was with great curiosity that he ran across and discovered a software program designed by Lennex titled The Census Probe Analytic Simulation, a program with the capacity of evaluating large populations, feeding the data into a data bank and then producing statistical information on the population at large. It was just what Bio-Med needed in order to cut their operation and work force to bare bones and eliminate programs that were economically not profitable considering demographics.

In examining Lennex, he saw that there was disorganization and a lack of experienced management and even that many of their most talented computer engineers were working at cross purposes. But he did like the potential and he knew that there was brilliance in their creativity. He sought out one Clarence McNiff, a nerdy thin-faced youth with all the appearances of a high school social outcast but the creator of the CPAS program, which was still in the developmental stage.

On his best days, McNiff would be called a seedy dresser, his hair was openly rebellious and he possessed an outrageously large Adam's apple. He was essentially without expression and referred to others as "dude" or occasionally, "man," unless he had disdain for them and then it was "dink." His life was computers or what he called "spy-ware." He had no knowledge of the outside world and no social life to speak of, so totally consumed was he in his work.

At their initial meeting, Celosi sat stiffly at a table across from McNiff and opened with, "Clarence, how are you doing?"

"Okay," Clarence nodded.

A long moment turned awkward and Celosi, who had planned to offer light patter to start, suddenly felt uncomfortable—it would be years before he would learn the wrinkles of conversation.

"I want to discuss with you on the CPAS program that you developed."

"It is still in the early stages of development but we don't entirely know how it works," McNiff responded.

McNiff opened what appeared to be a computer play book to a marked page. Celosi smiled to himself that the use of a tea bag for a book marker was noticeably eccentric.

Celosi started, "I understand that your program collects demographic information very accurately and that it can be used to modify operations—particularly of a corporation like ours which is essentially involved in demographic commonalities. The way it stands now we are growing in size but not profit. Expenditures toward realizing profit from this growth just have not been realized. Too much of our research, our insurance and our public service programs have not made us money, or even paid for themselves, so we need to eliminate the waste and optimize our operation and your intelligence-gathering program could certainly help us achieve that."

"I don't see it as intelligence—the information is so mundane."

"Well, that may be so, but I see this as some kind of a beginning and it could lead to something big—maybe something sinister, but I hope not. Nevertheless, it can provide us with information that we can use to make important changes in our structure, and this is information that we can't get from Gallup or other polling organizations."

Offering a rare pleasant but suppressed expression, McNiff replied that he was happy his program would be of value to someone—anyone.

"Can you give me an idea how it works, I mean, like, there's no report or article in print about it in any of the scientific quarterlies, is there?" Celosi asked.

"No, it's too new, but I don't do that kind of stuff anyway. But, here it is. We seek out people with computers who are mainstream America and we plug in our software which will target their computers. When they initially start their computers, they are of course looking directly into the screen and at that instant a laser-like ray penetrates the pupil of their eyes. It is quick, like a nanosecond, and they never notice it, or rarely notice it. The ray bounces back to our computer after having scarfed up all this information within each individual."

Celosi looking confused countered, "How does it get this information?"

McNiff increasing in intensity, "The computer-generated rays that are what we call esurient, in other words, starved and will devour anything, any kind of info. It's a concept that has been around for a while but the info they picked up before was useless stuff, like ball scores. Anyway, the way we set it up, the ray enters the eye and goes directly to the brain where it encounters encephalon liquid which is really not a liquid but electronic waves, and then it returns. We put into a computer which reads the results and then it goes into the database for the particular group to which that person is assigned."

"You mean that you invade these peoples' privacy?" asked Celosi, a little in awe.

"Sure, if the feds knew that we were doing it, they would make a ban and outlaw it and then only they could do it, which they would—if they knew about it. Of course, they have removed so many business regulations we feel free to do what we want."

15

"What about selecting a research study group, it seems that there would be a lot of work and research to that, I mean, to identify a group norm."

"Wrong. That's the easy part. Remember when the feds tried to give everyone a personal ID number? Well, that number for most people became their bank numbers, their e-mail address, just about used in every way possible. So we don't even know the person we are contacting—we just have an ID number."

Thinking he saw a glitch, Celosi challenged, "But that hardly gives you a demographic group. We can't inquire whether the overall population at large needs a given pharmaceutical drug and are able to pay for them; we have to target people in the loop, people with resources, in other words, essentially the middle class."

"That is where it really got simple. When the feds went to personal IDs, they expected everyone to sign up. But our research shows that people in the underground economy did not sign up, the homeless did not sign up, the drug dealers and junkies did not sign up and the criminals did not sign up. They all saw it as something that was against their interests and provided them with nothing. So, what we have on our computers is a well-defined demographic group which represents the economic middle class, and I would think those are the very people that you would want info on, in other words, consumers, and to think that it was all done for us—thank you very much, feds."

Celosi was quiet for a moment and then softly asked, "How does the ray garner this information and what is the information?"

"First of all, the liquid gives us a genetic rundown on the individual, what age they will contract what illness. The AMA has similar info but their data is based upon studies in the past—what we are dealing with is the future, and with the environmental destruction and general livability of the planet, that is undergoing constant change.

"Furthermore, we can even predict political opinion from our methods."

"How can that be?"

"We live in a culture where people who read and grow and mature are rare; most are products of their upbringing and research tells us that they do not change much during their lifetimes. There is enough physical info and particularly genetic info in each individual tested to make an accurate assessment—people cooperate by fitting into categories and they are very predictable. We call it bio-tech assessment and I would think that if the government got hold of it they could use it divisively."

"But," Celosi mused, "it just doesn't figure. I mean, I see where you could pull up one's gene pool and that would create some medical predictability on that person, but even if you could break it down so fine as to give information on cell structure, it wouldn't give you an impression of one's philosophy or political beliefs—those are determined by intellectual inquiry which is developed later in life."

"That's what one would logically think," McNiff answered, "but we were disturbed by some things that didn't figure out, so we got a large group of volunteers whose ID numbers we had used. We didn't know their names and could not fit them to anything specific outside their read-outs. They each filled out a questionnaire and from that we could put them in one of two groups and then made up a graph chart. The ones who were what we called over-structured, that is, brought up in a strict belief system, were dogmatic due to religious rigidity and political indoctrination at a young age with a belief system that was continually being reinforced, had a very flat line on our Confabulation and Social Comprehension Scale graph studies. On the other hand, those with a more open and diverse upbringing had great variation on the chart; in fact, some of them tended to be quite serendipitous. Then, of course, there were those in the middle who couldn't be identified with either reading, nevertheless, they were quite predictable."

"When you were in contact with these people, did any of them express outrage and accuse you of spying or invading their private space?"

"Not many; we pretty well convinced them that we did this as a group study and there was no personal interest."

"But there could be eventually."

"Sure, this is only the beginning and it has great potential for mischief."

"Have you contacted any federal agencies regarding your methods and findings?" Celosi inquired.

"Sure, we contacted the CDC and the AMA, but they weren't interested or they thought we were kooks. You may remember that about ten years ago—I am told—regulating computers became such an overburdening to the feds that they simply gave up. We thought the CDC would be interested in our work when we discovered in many gene pools a predisposition for a degenerative disease of the muscles which, as far as we know, has not inflicted anyone, but nevertheless, is in their genes and surely one day many will get ill and it might even become an epidemic."

"So, what did they say in response?"

"Very simply, there was no evidence and that our methods were shoddy and until there is an actual disease, they consider it a non-issue. We admit that the whole thing is arguable at this point, but we believe that there is enough evidence to warrant investigation. Also, many of our findings were compatible with studies by social statistic research groups which gave us confidence—stuff like percentage numbers on stress, obesity, cholesterol, hypertension and so on. We knew we were onto something."

Celosi, pushing his chair away from the table to signal a closing of the conversation added, "Well, we would certainly be interested in your findings and subsequent investigation. I mean, can you imagine what a breakthrough it would be to find a cure for a disease before it inflicted anyone?"

"Quodlibet, man."

"What's that mean?"

"Whatever in Latin."

"Oh."

It can now be recorded that scarcely three months after the amalgamation between Bio-Med and Lenex was proposed, the two companies, each on the edge of bankruptcy, joined together in economic matrimony. Bio-Med retained its name; Lenex became an ancillary.

With the merger there was a euphoric reaction by all involved and a celebration was scheduled for the concentration room of Bio-Med Headquarters on the evening following the signing of the legal agreement and contract. That day, an exhausted Celosi returned to his apartment with the intention of catching some sleep before the party. He undressed partially and he slid under the sheets feeling the coolness of satin slipping by his thighs. He awoke two days later.


For his part Celosi was named man of the year by the corporate board of directors, an unofficial commendation, but nevertheless, highly appreciated. With the achievement came a hefty raise, membership on the board of directors, a vice-president's chair, his own extension, and above all, a key to a penthouse on the 110th floor of the new Bio-Med Building. Celosi had arrived.

# Two

Whenever there is a major change in any capacious organization, be it a mega-corporation or governmental agency, there is little understanding of the abstruse purpose of the main mover and shaker by those within the organization who are working toward a noble goal. That is one reason that negative consequences are never anticipated beforehand and then afterward when they are realized, the organization never concedes a mistake. However, in the case of matters concerning public health issues, those in the medical and support industries feel a moral obligation to address the public good. This, of course, may for some be nothing more than lip service, but for others, there is a deep respect for the integrity of the medical community.

So it was, a year after the Bio-Med-Lenex marriage that a new physical impairment, the Alford syndrome, came to light. It was named after the first case, a John Alford of Nashville, Tennessee. The syndrome was symptomatic of ALS in that there was muscular weakness and tremors. But it had been preceded by a period of amentia, a temporary confusional insanity and also differed from ALS as all the symptoms came and went but their return was marked by an increased intensity.

The initial response by the planning and assignment board of Bio-Med was to refer the illness as a new project for the stem cell and embryonic research division, but after review of that decision, the project was rejected. This, of course was met with fervent outrage by the more personally involved. That all resulted in an appeal to the board of directors to hold a closed meeting on the subject.

The meeting was held within three days of the rejection and literally filled the concentration room of Bio-Med with advocates for the research. It was a noisy and at times there were eloquent oratories. The issue boiled down as to "whether we are altruistic or consumed by greed and insouciance." Management allowed the opposition advocates to spill out their venom and energy and it was all quite dramatic and enlightening but in the end, a very affable Darius Celosi calmly approached the podium and in a dominating presence that caused all to look upon him with new respect. But his comments were timeless and all heard before. "The bottom line," he started in a marginalized voice, "is that there is no argument; this is what we have to do to stay solvent. The proposed research for a single case cannot be justified on a cost basis. It simply will never pay us off." Then, looking directly at some specific individuals, he added, "When we downsized and lost fellow employees, we did it for the same reason. I don't recall any altruism then. As for Alford's syndrome, we don't know how prevalent it will be, there is too much to be determined before we can call on research and its expenditures, Alford's syndrome may even be related to Lou Gehrig's disease and there certainly has been plenty of research in that malady. We can't get all weepy about what we can and cannot do to stay competitive but, in the future, for example, we will have to cut research in parasitology or geriatrics and transfer those resources to something like cosmetic surgery where the return is. That's a fact of life."

All board members were present, six Chinese, two Indians, a Pakistani and the only American-born member other than Celosi, John Whitman, the chairman, applauded enthusiastically.

That unfortunate meeting which occurred on a bitter gray autumn afternoon was a fatal blow to any future dictum by Bio-Med that would move the corporation in the direction of concern for the human condition being their primary goal. The air had been cleared, workers went back to work— "Bottom-line Celosi" had spoken. Bio-Med, which had gone through a few years of retrenchment, lay-offs and down-sizing, had become a pure, competitive, business entity. The board had easily gone along with Celosi's pronouncements and employees could only shrug at a decision that was out of their hands from the onset although it grievously violated their ethics.

The position taken by Celosi gave him begrudging respect and that, with his aloofness, set him apart from his fellow executives. Yet, he wondered to himself, "Are we all from the same mold?" as he shuddered when he found himself repeating shop-worn office humor that was neither funny nor clever.

But his temptation to become involved in the stock market—didn't all executives have a stock portfolio?—was impossible to overcome. Almost daily he had gone over Wall Street reports, over-analyzing stock value and performance and ruminating how and why he would buy or sell specific stock as if he had psychic insight into their capricious gyrations. So he made the plunge. At first hesitant, none of his clever moves came to mind when faced with the actual pressure of putting money on the line. He became increasingly conservative and unable to generate any new ideas on the long-sought understanding of the mysteries of the market, conceding to the common practice of sitting at his laptop and typing in "1,000 shares" of some over-valued stock that had been in positive territory for the previous year but in which the return was modest.

Despite himself, he found himself habitually standing by the lithium-tinged Gatorade dispenser with other staff relating the daily stock news and returns. Each of them expressed their buys in a hushed whisper as if a treasured secret but then burst into boisterous hilarity over unexpected and sudden losses.

Back at his desk, Celosi did not feel the smugness of the others. Somehow until now, the self-regulating little voice within him had been muted, but then he felt shame as if he were looking into an accusing reflection pool and that feeling exposed him to his own weaknesses and the old self-doubts and insecurity returned like a nagging bad dream. He had played the corporate executive and found it unbecoming.

Typical of his mind-set, he recognized the emotional ogre and swooped it into a safe hiding place in the catacombs of his mind. Free of the emotional confusion, he would recommit to his work.

It came to be that his social friend at Bio-Med was one John Buckman, an individual very much unlike Celosi whose special talent was his quiet charm and sociality. He had been hired as a liaison between Bio-Med, Lenex and the various research laboratories located in upstate New York. Initially, Celosi saw Buckman as emotionally distant like himself, but had misread that trait. In actuality, Buckman's quiet tendency was not emotional restraint but his preoccupation and concentration on his work and when that was not the issue, he could be personable and eventually became Celosi's closest friend; perhaps his only friend.

Buckman, square of face with harsh but handsome features, carried a shock of black curly hair wisped into a loose ponytail behind his head. He was average height and had the air of an individual possessing an amplitude of worldly experience. As much of his contact involved him personally with research labs, he dressed casually and during his contacts with Bio-Med executives who saw themselves as the loftiest of the lofty, they tended to be quietly disapproving of his dress and appearance, themselves being inclined to overspend to be ostentatiously fashionable.

Celosi and Buckman would have never become friends except that their professional responsibilities drew them together. To his surprise, Celosi found Buckman to be approachable and he did not feel the usual discomfort during conversation with him. He even caught himself discussing trivial things and even moved toward personal discussion in order to gain some minimum level of understanding and affirmation. Even those hidden goblins of his dark side began to move to the center.

This was a god-send for Celosi as it was a time that he was having personal difficulties beyond his normal uptightness. His family had been dependent on him, particularly after he was making a good salary. Mateo was receiving workman's compensation for alleged on-the-job injuries when, in actuality, he was simply worn out from overwork. This had come at a time when all the children were maturing or were matured but were still all living at home in the old five-room wood-frame house built in the 1970s. The nation had been in a prolonged depression and the family, out of necessity, had hung together in desperation. All the children worked, most for less than minimum wage, and even Maria had taken a part-time job as a house maid. College had not become an option for the children reaching adulthood; college in America had become a possibility for only the wealthy and everyone else would be cast into the chaotic morass of neo-modern society. Mateo had begun to drink out of inactivity and frustration and despite a reputation for gentleness, he became a mean drunk. This was the burden upon Celosi and it began to wear on him.

So much of Celosi's compensation for his position within the corporation was in remunerations—the penthouse, all services and utilities paid, groceries paid for and delivered, a safe haven above a debauched society. It was a package so inclusive that he received, or needed, very little in monetary payment. So it was understandable that his contribution to family diminished. But the family remained loyal to their eldest and reasoned that in the long run he would contribute to the family's welfare. Maria and Mateo were outspoken of his achievements but among the children there was an unspoken resentment of having been abandoned. That, in itself, was one issue as the family had keen memory of sacrifice and hardships that had drained them in putting Darius through college at a time when there was a rising political climate against minorities and the social programs that helped the disadvantaged. Racism had once again raised its head in a society that was becoming increasingly envenomed.

Celosi initially had a difficult time separating himself from his family—he had always at least given lip service to family and family values. But the demands of his newfound social experience required a certain persona in conflict with traditional values and much of what he earned could not be doled out independent of his lifestyle at Bio-Med and the little money he had left during the month would have been little aid to his family. Despite his attempts to deny the obvious, he was nonplused by the conflict. Enter John Buckman.

Since Buckman's daily routine included contacts at three university research laboratories with which Bio-Med had contracts and Lenex, he needed to report the results of these contacts and the expedition of that research and thus he ended every day at headquarters in the Bio-Med Building. This of course gave Buckman and Celosi an opportunity to socialize, an uncommon thing for the latter, who despite himself now saw Buckman as casual and approachable. It was a coincidence that they both were letting down emotionally about the same time each day and it was a natural development that the two would get together a few days a week at Celosi's penthouse on the top floor. The apartment was modestly but comfortably furnished showing the relaxed and the slightly mussed lifestyle of a bachelor.

As both men were unmarried, time was not an issue. Celosi had always been a non-drinker but after a brief and disastrous affair with drugs, he decided to become more conventional with his social tastes. Hard liquor was distasteful to him; in fact, it sickened him—he did develop a contemptuous relationship with brandy—and although beer was bitter to the taste, he found it the lesser of the various evils but had to acquire a tolerance for ale through a daily practiced ritual of drinking. It was a habit not lost on Buckman and together the two would spend hours imbibing in beer and conversation.

Buckman had always been the rough-and-tumble type who could certainly take care of himself. His talent for making people feel at ease was what made him a good liaison for Bio-Med, but it was his wit and physical toughness that gave him ability to function in the chaos of the street. Yet, in Celosi's empyrean refuge, Buckman found a haven of tranquility and recovery.

It was during one of these meetings that Buckman first revealed to Celosi that he too had lived in New Mexico. Somewhat taken back, Celosi pressed for details. "It was kind of a whim," Buckman indicated. "I was eighteen and living in New York with my father and I ran into a friend of my father who offered me a job in which I could work in a place called Cuba, New Mexico, on a natural gas pipeline…"

"I think Mobil Oil had an operation up there," Celosi interjected.

"Yeah, that was it," Buckman continued. "I thought that it would be cool to see the west and a different lifestyle so I took the job—kind of sight unseen. But it worked out, it was easy work—all I had to do was make the rounds of the wells every day and record the production of each well. The wells were strong—about 10,000 PSI at well head which means that they were strong and required little maintenance. Cuba is located in the southern end of the Rocky Mountains and in the winter I ran my route on cross-country skis and if there was ever a mechanical problem I couldn't fix, I'd call for a company copter and a mechanic."

"Sounds like an ideal job for the right person," Celosi offered.

"I loved the rural life and the job made me feel like a rugged individualist. And then there was the town. It had a population of four hundred and they were all Apaches. I really got into that. I was learning the language and I volunteered some at the grammar school. Actually, I thought that I had found my place in life and I would stay there."

"So, why did you leave?"

Buckman looked into the distance for a second or two and then said, "One day my father called and said that it was about time that I continued my education. I think that because I was supporting myself for the first time he thought that he was losing his hold on me. He appealed to my ego, I guess, he said that I was made for better things, that I had a destiny to fill and this was a dead end for me. He said that if I didn't get away I'd end up marrying a squaw and then I'd be stuck for life."

"Do you regret leaving?" Celosi asked getting a little closer to his own dilemma.

Buckman was quiet for a long time and then in a subdued voice said, "That was the happiest time of my life but I didn't realize it at the time, I had nothing to compare it to. You know, he may have been right; I've never married but I could have easily fallen into that down there. There is something special about those women—the Indians, the Mexicans, the half-breeds—they get to you in a different way than white women, they touch you deep inside—like a wolf—you know what I mean?"

"Do you wish that you were still there?"

"No, not now anyway. Father was right, I would have never accomplished anything down there. I would have been just another worker. And you can't look back. You have to strive for higher accomplishment, onward and upward as they say, your worth as an individual is measured by what you achieve and what you possess."

"But is not happiness an important goal?" Celosi asked. "And isn't loyalty to one's family paramount?"

Buckman was quick to respond, "No, sentimentalities of life are luxuries an upwardly mobile person cannot afford—at least as he is climbing the ladder to the top. And mankind cannot be held back by mushy feelings about family, the downtrodden or the poor. That weighs us all down. The irony is that you can't help them nor do you need them—what they will face is their fate, now that's not up to you."

Celosi mused a moment and then said, "No matter how hard I try, poverty always seems to be a step behind in my mind. I left Albuquerque to get away from it but my family is still dependent on me and it stresses me because I am caught in the middle."

"Look," Buckman said, "times are tough and what you give your family will never be enough, they'll always want more. You have a once-in-a-lifetime opportunity here, so don't blow it. You will be replaced if you don't keep your eye on the ball and you will never get another chance like this. And one of the rules of the game is don't bring any baggage with you. Your family will either make it or not—probably not—but once you make it big and you career is over, you can always go back and make amends."

Celosi felt a sense of relief. Is this what he had been seeking all the time? Some justification of what he had been unconsciously thinking? There was nowhere else to go with this; the issue had hit a wall. Buckman was outspoken and spared no feelings, but damn it, he made perfect sense. Why should one risk his only chance of success?

So the spirit of the braceros and the trabajadores who had for decades sent a large percent of their income home to Mexico was lost on Celosi, and with it he lost the vestige of an old family culture that had been the way of life in the west. Celosi felt a new energy within himself, a new dedication to himself and his life-goal. He felt that he had been set free.

# Three

It was most chilling, that telephone call. Even the flashing intercom light seemed ominous.

Celosi did not recognize the voice at first. It was too shrill and accelerated to be Buckman. But it was Buckman. He had called in to Celosi from his automobile on his way to headquarters and in a frenetic voice said, "I'm on my way in but traffic is heavy and I'll be late, but I gotta talk to you…important…some damn kids set fire to a garbage truck just for fun and all lanes were closed for a while. I'm moving now but I want you to call me…but from somewhere else." The latter was a code expression between the two meaning that Bio-Med telephones were monitored and this information should not be shared.

Buckman hung up without further message. The always infallible Buckman was suddenly fallible, Celosi thought. *This must be critical,* he thought.

Celosi waited a few minutes and then walked out to the reception counter. "I'm going out for a few minutes," he said motioning to the robo-receptionist.

"I'm sorry but I must have destination and reason for the record," she responded.

"I'm going over to supply, I need an echo transmitter," he lied.

Once in the hall, Celosi went to the Bio-Med elevator, dubbed "the med jet" by coworkers, and in three seconds he was nine floors down where a balcony overlooking the city was used by employees addicted to smoking. Once outside he began to fumble for his cell phone and then he saw it—the Bio-Med eye-spy copter, no bigger than a lunch box but equipped with a camera and sound recorder, hovering busily under its whirling blades, focusing on him as if it were a personal thing between the two. Obviously, the copter had been requested by security on the assumption that his conversation with Buckman needed to be assessed as a potential threat to the agency's security.

He pretended an unconcerned aloofness and feigned an interest in looking down on the city, fighting his perennial fear of height at the same time. He could see the north section of the city through brackish clouds and below, with a pressing east wind and an unusually high tide, the streets reflected a gleaming inundation by the Atlantic. He gave it little thought as the flooding had become an all too common factor in the lives of New Yorkers. He knew from experience that the subways would be closed, the sewers flooded and traffic snarled.

He walked back into the hallway, casually strolled the hall until he came to a janitor's closet. It was open. He entered and felt for his cell phone. At the rear of the room was a window. He drew toward the window and then peered out to look for the copter but was satisfied that it had not detected his presence in the closet. He quickly dialed Buckman's cell phone.

He heard Buckman answer and then ask, "You there?"

"Yeah, what's up?"

"Well, hang on to this one. We got a guy who works in computer research at Georgetown University by the name of Sinclair Waffleman—we call him Joe Waffle and today we had to send him home because he was fuckin' freaking out. I mean, this guy has an eccentric nature anyway but today he really got weird. He was talking all kinds of crazy shit, I mean, like futuristic stuff and using terms and expressions we never ever heard before and he said that the computer has the future history of man in it as if it had already happened."

"So, what do you make of it, overworked?"

"I don't think so; he has been in computers for forty years and he is perhaps the most knowledgeable expert in the field He never got a promotion to supervisor as he has virtually no social skills—or personality. He's like a computer himself—but that's Joe. What happened today was that a research scientist came to him and complained that he couldn't pull a needed math formula out of the computer. You see, these formulas are so complex that they are impossible to remember and it is very tedious typing them out so they are on computer, and then the only thing the researcher has to do is download the specific formula into his research project and it saves time. But suddenly this particular formula wasn't there and once we checked, others were missing too."

Celosi asked, "So aren't there these same formulas in the research manuals?"

"Sure," Buckman responded, "but that is time-consuming and then when the technician looked for his research manual, he couldn't find it."

"What program were these guys working on?"

"They were in programs in the degenerative disease and aging unit."

Celosi asked, "What specifically was the technician doing?"

"It involves embryonic stem cell procedures."

Celosi quickly seized on that. "That's interesting. Do you remember a few weeks ago there was a memo, allegedly from headquarters, that condemned embryonic stem cell research and with the surprising statement that that type of research has always provided negative results. It indicated that successful stem cell work uses stem cells from adult neural tissue, bone morrow, adipose tissue or from tissue around the umbilical cord or placenta and that these cells are more controllable in laboratory conditions. Recent studies, it said, showed great promise from stem cells obtained from these sources but that embryonic stem cell research had relatively poor results. And that was before the memo got into the moral issue involved. The memo spoke of liberal-leaning scientists and nefarious experimenters."

"Yeah, I remember somebody talking about that memo. But it wasn't signed or approved by the board of directors so it really wasn't company policy."

Celosi paused cautiously and then moved to the window, furtively scanning to the right, then the left but not seeing the eye-spy copter, continued, "But the bottom line is that despite the fact that the memo wasn't official, it still intimidated some workers—I remember that there was a couple of researchers who wanted off embryonic stem cell research projects and asked for reassignment. They brought up the moral issue as an excuse. It really freaked some people out."

Celosi walked back to the door and as if to depart and then stopped at the door and said, "Just to understand the whole thing, this guy Waffleman—can it really be that serious? If he has been around for forty years, maybe this could be the first symptoms of dementia or just plain burn-out."

"No, after he tried to figure out what had happened to the math formulas, he got frustrated and desperate because in his lifetime of working computers, he never failed to find the cause of a problem. But in this case when he couldn't find an answer, he began to surf around and that is when he got into this futuristic stuff and that really freaked him out. You have to realize this guy's mind-set—computers were always predictable and therefore non-threatening. So when he pulled up a few web sites and there was reference to things that will happen in the coming decade but in language of having already happened, it set him off. The super just told him to go home and didn't investigate any further."

"What do you make of it?"

"Well, I looked at the web site he was looking at and it didn't make any sense to me. So I went to surfing and found a medical site that stated that because of new procedures, there had been—past tense—a significant breakthrough in severed spine therapy in the year 2045—fifteen years from now."

"What do you make of that?" Celosi asked.

"Darius, I am going to have to pull off the road or I'll have an accident sure as hell."

"John, are you there?" Celosi asked after a moment of silence.

"Okay, I'm back. Here's what I did, Darius. I reversed the computer site I was on, I mean by that, I went back in time and found that I was getting data on the screen that had no way of being there. It couldn't have existed but it did—unless, of course, someone was setting this up somehow."

"What did you find when you went backwards, I mean, into the past?"

Buckman continued, "I found data and dates going back three centuries. This stuff is being made up by someone or the computers are creating it themselves. I didn't have time to study it to understand the context of it."

"What computer was Waffleman using?" Celosi asked.

"The Lenex Super-Mega Star Search computer," Buckman offered, "it's the newest model, it hasn't even been approved for sale yet."

"Did you investigate any further?'

"Yes, I did. I went fast forward to the past as I said, to the cutting edge, and the damn thing was compiling data faster than I could read it."

Celosi was silent for a moment and then said, "So what's the answer?"

"Well, you know Joe had a lot of pressure from researchers, that is geologists, anthropologists, medical researchers, historians and the like to help them fill in the blanks in research that had hit a wall—couldn't go any further. So Joe developed a new system for authenticating researched data that was incomplete. You see, if you lay out data on a geometric plane you will visually see the gaps in your research so it can't be documented. But to fill those gaps would be costly and time-consuming so Joe reasoned that the computers could predictably fill those gaps with what he called logical configuration. It's like averaging between two known factors. We checked a couple of test runs and they appeared to be accurate. So Joe ran it before the board of directors and they saw that it would save money and said to go ahead with it but that on each research report completed by logical configuration there should be an index to indicate that probability of accuracy on that particular report. It's something we couldn't do before they deregulated the industry."

"So you think that is a possibility?"

"All I know is that the computers are running by themselves and we can't stop them."

"So," Celosi reasoned, "we may be creating a lot of useless information because that data was not obtained through the scientific method?"

"That's right," Buckman answered. "The problem is that we deal with medical data and we have to ask ourselves if we are using data for medical treatment that is fraudulent."

Celosi cautioned, "I'm glad you called me first. Don't mention this to anyone. This is the old rock and a hard place thing—if we expose this and purge our computers it could bankrupt the company. At least until we know the specific nature of the beast, we had better keep quiet about it."

"Okay, but I'm too bummed out to work—I think I'll come over to your place. You going to be there?"

"I think so, I will take off early—I think I will feint a headache."

"Cool, I'll bring a six-pack."

"Bring a twelve-pack."

Celosi made several phone calls to conclude the business of the day and then, his last call was to Clarence McNiff. He seemed the one person eccentric enough to make sense out of the non-sensible. McNiff listened without comment as Celosi explained the situation through his earlier conversation with Buckman. Speaking in his usual flat expressionless tones, McNiff indicated he would look into the matter on his own time. His affect was so casual that Celosi suspected that he was not taking the matter seriously. But in a calm, apathetic manner typical of his obdurate generation, McNiff assured Celosi he would investigate the matter and promised an answer as soon as possible.

Once at the penthouse, Celosi and Buckman, expecting the usual tranquility and distance from an insane world, were distracted and unsettled, trying unsuccessfully to make sense out of the events of the day. Buckman, as if a cabal plotter, saw conspiracy and intrigue in every aspect of the events and in a short while his incessant prattling began to disturb the usually calm Celosi. Suddenly, Celosi saw his friend in a new light, not the steady, controlled personality who drove dangerous highways and fearlessly walked the bloody alleys and streets of New York City, but a very vulnerable individual whose security and appearance of personal strength was based on the stability of a culture that was itself inherently unstable except to the one percent at the top of the heap as it precariously brought order to their lives through plasticity and manipulation. The thought of his friend being less than the all-knowing hierophant that he had thought him to be gave Celosi pause and with it a sense of superiority but that was little consolation in light of the purported seriousness of the current situation.

The two men were fidgety and uncomfortable during the hours of the early evening. Then, abruptly, the phone rang with startling shrillness. Celosi had not been expecting any calls and he was certain that he would not hear from McNiff in regard to his investigation for several days. But it was McNiff and he had a lot to say.

Without a brew of warning, he launched into his investigative discoveries. "I thought that this was some kind of aberration or the result of some imponderable hacker," he said, "but it's bigger than that. In fact, it involves at least two methods of electronic invasion, both of an insidious nature, at counter purposes—meaning two opposed groups are involved—and undoubtedly for political advantage. Some of it is comprehensible and much of it very subtle—but it all boils down to one thing—it is blatant propaganda."

"How did you get onto this so quickly?" Celosi asked.

"Computers can tell stories—they are predictable and are meant to be used honestly. But if they are not, they can tell on you. It is just a matter of what to look for and I had some immediate suspicions based on recent events."

"So what did you find out?" Celosi asked impatiently.

"Do you remember when logical configuration was popularly used to complete undocumented or incomplete research studies?"

"Yeah."

"Well, that software program was used for several years and as long as that program was used properly, it was feasible and its use could be just justified. But the probability of its conclusions was increasingly open to question because a lot of the research uses of the program were inaccurate or poorly done and the results were an embarrassment yet businesses continued to make profit on the skewed results—and I think that there was some direct manipulation involved as well.

"So the use of the software was discontinued. But I found out today that a small software company in New Jersey took the same program and spiced it up and made it so that when it rewrote material it would give that material a biased slant in one direction or another and that leaning could vary from the slick to the crafty but all of it devious. And because it was illegal to use, it could only be used in a clandestine manner."

"Have you run across any examples of its use?"

"Yeah, lots of it. It appears that there is someone or some group of people rewriting all kinds of stuff and maybe with the intent of rewriting everything in the computers. As for Bio-Med, we have a closed system so no one from the outside can invade it, but there are a lot of researches and medical findings that have been or are being rewritten. So it has to be someone on the inside but there is no way to discern who it is. This of course gives rise to the preconceptual scientist—the new science of reaching a conclusion before doing research and then simply dismissing anything contrary to your preconceived notions. In other words, science has followed politics in manipulating facts."

"I can remember when that was a joke. What else have you found?" Celosi queried.

"There is a lot of historical rewriting going on all over the net. Today I pulled up the official United States Historical Record and Archives and took a look at it. Now this is a governmental system that cannot be invaded and anything put into the web site has to have governmental approval—so naturally whatever you read you would think would be factual. But reading this stuff, I would think that I don't know anything about American history. For example, I looked up a singular event in history—the death of Thomas Jefferson—as I had thought that all historians would be in agreement on that, but this is what I found and I copied it so I could read it to you accurately:

'In his last days, Jefferson was suffering from severe restriction of the urethra due to an enlarged prostrate. It was his cherished desire to see the fiftieth anniversary of his beloved country. But so great was his pain that he could not walk, lie down or stand up. But Jefferson was so determined to live to survive until the Fourth of July that he was willing to suffer through whatever agony he would have to face. He took an unknown amount of an opium derivative, laudanum, and improved to the point that he rode horseback about five miles a day. Yet, as the fourth approached he fell ill once more and on that date, he was in and out of coma. On the final day, July fourth, 1826, he lay in a huge canopied four-poster with family around him. He called for the Reverend Joshua Schoedigger of the Montecello Episcopal Church to his side.

'In the presence of that company, Jefferson expressed great guilt and anxiety over his failure to embrace the Lord during his lifetime and he renounced his atheism at that time with the fervent hope that he would be forgiven and would realize salvation. Family members became quite agitated when Jefferson began to screech and beg of the reverend for exculpation for his sins so that he would not enter the ether alone and without atonement to Jesus Christ. He further called Sally Hemings to his bedside and urged her to accept the Lord, seek redemption and thereafter live in spiritual prosperity with the Lord as her savior. After that he broke down sobbing and begging for atonement.'"

Buckman, listening with intensity over the speaker-phone, injected, "No one will buy that. Jefferson's distrust of religion is well known and one has to ask why such as episode on his final day, if true, did not come to light. No one is going to believe it."

McNiff answered, "Don't be so sure. There is not a lot of evidence out there any more either way. When the government started shutting down museums and libraries and burning books about ten years ago, most of the most compelling information on the revolution that was this country was lost. Furthermore, I don't think that you understand the cyber-geek generation. They don't read and they have disdain for academics, particularly history. Perhaps you remember a few years ago the cyber-guru Jonathon Decker revised an old shop-worn decree, changing it to 'I am one with the computer.' As much as people made fun of that, it connected with the young people. You talk to them and you realize that there is nothing going on upstairs. No innovation, no creativity and they are incapable of seeing incongruence in the system. Furthermore, I seriously think that their minds have been captured by cybernetics and they are incapable of thinking independently of their computers, therefore, it seems that they have been computerized, to coin an expression."

"But surely, there are those among them that retain an interest outside of the computer culture," offered Celosi.

"Not really," answered McNiff. "Here's how bad it is: in the colleges to graduate, you need to complete a course in social science and history. But the course consists of a single book, 1,600 pages in length, that covers those two subjects. I read the thing and it is so watered down that you get no real feel for history, or social science, for that matter. But upon taking tests after reading the book many students failed so miserably that thereafter they simply asked them to read the book and then sign a standard form that they had read it. Thus they had completed their requirement and, of course, they stopped reading the material altogether. Now these people are the best of the best—how pathetic is that?"

Buckman argued, "But aren't you of that generation? Surely, if you see the contradictions, then others do too."

"You don't know me," McNiff countered. "I play the geek because I need to be accepted by my peers. If I were more obviously compatible with guys like you they would reject me and I think that it is important to be on the inside and what I see is very discouraging and I would like to do something about it, but I don't know what."

"So what makes you different?" Celosi asked.

"I grew up in foster homes. I was treated alright but never completely accepted by anyone and certainly I received no emotional nourishment from these families, so I have always been an outsider but I also knew that I would have to keep that to myself. So I have always had this questioning mind but that brings up the question of how I knew what was right and I cannot answer that—but then maybe it is because I see so many people railing against each other that I thought the truth was somewhere in the middle. I saw my only chance in life to be academically superior and thus make myself available to the power elite as someone they could rely upon."

"So where does this leave us?" Celosi asked.

McNiff said, "We are pretty well up against it. Research several years ago by the American Association for the Advancement of Science showed through their studies that the high-tech revolution and wide use of computers in this country has given rise to a computer culture, and as a result, the mathematical number of voters unable to discern between fact and fiction has steadily increased until those voters represent an overwhelming majority. In fact, it was indicated that a two-second recondite message hidden in television entertainment could carry an impact as long-lasting and penetrating as any significant event in the listener's life. And, the politicos behind this collusion are spreading their gospel knowingly and with intent and as they have informed us in the past, they are creating their own reality and there is nothing that you can do about it other than learn to live with it. And that is not even considering those caught up in the virtual reality addiction—those people are like friggin' zombies.

"What is even more disconcerting is that the brain seems more impacted by controversial messages, or even worse, by messages that provoke emotional rather than rational responses. Even veritably negative or out and out deceptions have a high positive return for the presenter—or better, the propagandist. Unfortunately, politicians follow these trends with a calculating eye and subsequently modify their own messages and campaigns to coincide with the national obsession for fantasy. And what has predictably happened is that a conspiracy of politicos now controls every source of communication and they are scripting their ideology into the national cerebrum and have taken us over without a shot being fired."

*So came the death of democracy,* Celosi thought. *But that is beyond my control; I need to deal with the situation at hand—I can't save the world—if the country has an uncritical acceptance of a cataclysmic message—so be it.*

He sat back and absorbed all that had been said and then with a sense of satisfaction thought with a smile, *I have a plan.*

# Four

On March 1, 2030, the board of directors for Bio-Med Technologies convened in the Bio-Med conference room for the first quarterly meeting of the year. The ethnically diverse board was steeped in corporate protocol and their progress, as usual, characteristically measured in cautious accord.

The meeting commenced at nine in the morning when called to order by the chair, Johnson Whitman.

Whitman, an apple-pie handsome man, looked like a caricature of a 1930s Saturday afternoon matinee idol. His appearance gave no hint of his personality, which was somewhat of an enigma among his peers. They did know that he was a self-made millionaire several times over and with that there was the obvious implication that there was a determined but unseen driving force within his mental make-up.

The members diligently went through the agenda imaged on their laptops item by item. But they seemed to have an air of restlessness about them. Most of the items on the agenda were routine, received quick confirmation and the board moved on. The usual banter and camaraderie was missing and Whitman was devoid of his usual raffish jokes.

The board's new member, Darius Celosi, had agonized for several days over a decision to present the "Joe Waffle affair" to the board, knowing full well that they had been discussing rumors about the situation and finally, in a state of uncertainty, he went to Whitman himself to confer about the matter. An expressionless Whitman listened to him patiently, giving no hint of his feelings of a positive or negative response but then beseeched Celosi to give the information before open discussion under new business.

The item was presented and as Celosi read from a prepared statement, he felt not the expected astonishment from the group. Did they already know about the matter through rumors? How widespread were their suspicions and did Whitman set him up as some kind of a bearer of bad news?

The item went to open discussion. Every member had an opinion and there was no hesitation—they had all given the matter much thought as was indicated by the prepared statements presented. The consensus was that the corporation could not look back or rectify the situation. In the eyes of the board, whatever the consequences of using the newfound information for profit far outweighed the alternative which, considering the competitive hostility of the medical research business, might mean economic ruin and that was unacceptable. An excitable board agreed with that opinion to the man. Through the frenzied babble that ensued Whitman's voice could be heard calling the meeting to order.

All eyes turned toward Whitman, who until then had sat quietly through the proceedings. In sincere soft tones he began, "I want to backtrack for a moment to another subject because it is relative to this situation and undoubtedly will help us make a definite decision as both issues fall under the same reality. I don't mean to interrupt your presentation, Darius, but you'll see the intrinsic connection between your presentation and the subject matter I now bring to the table. And since the two matters are so closely related, one will help us make a decision on the other.

"It came to my attention last week—before I was even aware of the Waffle situation—that Monroe Psychological Laboratories was bringing into the market a new product called Self-counseling Analysis."

Whitman looked over the group and then continued, "This is a pretty daring project because it promises a lot and if you don't deliver, you will lose business integrity. But what we have found out is that this program—like the Joe Waffle situation—whether by design or accident, has discovered a resource computer program that explores the past. Monroe knows that it sounds like science fiction to the public; therefore, they have to be careful in marketing. But what this all boils down to is that we were not the first but if we don't take advantage of these same resources we could become history. So I see this as a superb challenge because, on the one hand, it would sound to consumers like fantasy time-travel but, on the other, this phenomena is quite real. I took the time before coming down here today to check with our accounting services and although the quarterly report is not due until next week, all indications are that we are marginal regarding profit for the quarter—a downtrend over the past year—and therefore we cannot delay on this opportunity and must move forward aggressively." (Whitman was not so bold as to repeat his oft-used cliché that the purpose of the new capitalism is to kill the wounded.)

At that point, Yeni Aballa, seated next to Celosi, spoke, "So, what's this program Self-counseling Analysis all about?"

Whitman looked down on his notes and said, "It's a program whereby the individual is connected through electronic intervention with himself when he is older. The emphasis here is upon maturity, in other words, the older self is in the growth stage of senescence when, through life's experiences, he is able to give advice and counsel to his young self, not as an authoritarian figure but as the only person from whom the youth could objectively trust and accept advice. We all know how the young reject advice from elders, but in this case the youth identifies with the self and thereby sees a nurturing father figure and because that father figure experienced the same problems in growing up, he can help the individual avoid the traps of youth. We don't know if the elder in this case is factual or not, but if it is accepted on face value it doesn't matter."

Whitman studied the board members for a moment and then continued, "This program involves a clever marketing scheme by Monroe. They have appealed to the pop-culture mentality and apparently successfully according to initial reports. The target group is eighteen to twenty-four and apparently really got off on the concept of meeting one's own self in later years and discussing personal matters, and few, if any, questioned the veracity of the program so caught up were they in their personal involvement and it fit right into the timely concerns of the youth, that is, identity crises, the father wound, cultural and peer conflict, high aspirations, low self-esteem, the whole works affecting that age group.

"In their infomercial shown on the national audio-visual communication, a sensitive young man came on and with worried demeanor wondered aloud where he was going in life. He was frustrated over attending college, working full-time having a tenuous relationship with his family as well as an ambiguous relationship with a girlfriend. He thinks that it is all too much for him and then a voice comes on and suggests in a soothing tone that the youth meet with an individual who has experienced the same problem in his youth and he understands the consequences of failure to make the right choices. Then the young man identifies that person as himself—only older and mature and who would be better for that young man than himself to explore mistakes and experiences that you might say that they share?

"So, in the next scene, the young man is facing a much older version of himself, man on man, and there are no trust issues or suspicion of manipulation. The older man's tone is fatherly, stern but sympathetic. He assumes the authoritative manner of a guru and uses sophisticated psychological terms to demonstrate his ability as a counselor. The young man responds almost with reverence and easily takes the advice to heart. In the final scene, the young man appears refreshed and renewed and with a new higher energy level tells the listeners, 'I've avoided serious mistakes in restructuring my life and have broken away from personal relationships that would have eventually been devastating to me. My life now is on the correct path and I owe it all to the counseling and a born-again attitude that I received from my own resources.'"

Celosi suddenly cut in to inquire, "How is the program working out?"

"First of all," Whitman responded, "the demand has been overwhelming, I mean, what kid would not have initial curiosity over meeting himself, although a computer simulated version of himself when he is older? Of course, it probably means more to a youth to see how he will eventually make out, but that information is only superficially revealed but that is the chance for the program to plug the youth into its message. In a survey of those taking the therapy, there are those who say it was meaningless, others say that they will probably make the same mistakes anyway, but there is a large majority who see validity in the program and feel that they have benefited.

"But here is the important thing to us and the national economy in general. The therapy is not designed after the traditional psychological theories, the Freudianism or the emotional verbomania that passed for treatment in the last century. Instead the program rejects all the chitter-chatter of that era as futile engagement that produced no benefit. But to look at the issue objectively, we are dealing with youth at a troubling time of their lives and it actually becomes a matter of survival; that is, how they survive within the system as it exists, not ideally how it should exist in someone's fantasy. In other words, the therapy is designed to coapt the individual within the economic-social system as it is, not as we wish it to be. Reality is how one responds to economic demands, how he gets along with coworkers, how he gives up egocentric pursuits to become one with the economic reality. So the father figure admonishes the youth to grow up and not waste time on seeking one's identity, whining about the emptiness of life or becoming involved in a meaningless lucubration of the meaning of life. I think the key here is that the word 'environment' is never used, instead they use 'reality' and that is how it should be. The word 'environment' is a sentimental and silly utopian abstraction and it has no purpose; meanwhile, this program appeals to what should be most important to youth and that is corporate achievement and overcoming autotheistic individualism."

"What methods do they use for treatment if they eschew traditional psychotherapy?" Celosi asked. "I mean, aren't we opting for fantasy over reality?"

Appreciating the opening, Whitman answered, "Their researchers found that traditional forms of therapy elicit self-pity and forms of self-delusion, all demeaning to the individual and destructive to his well-being. This therapy includes behavioral therapy which attempts to change destructive patterns of thinking by honing social skills—tested in the workplace—self-control and problem-solving strategies. Good behavior is rewarded by upward mobility in the corporate system, blended with cognitive therapy which boosts confidence and counters fear of failure by demonstrating how competent one is. All this is compatible with the underlying philosophy of the born-again creed which essentially says that a youth, at a time that he has demonstrated aberrant behavior and is unindustrious and directionless in the corporate scheme of things, is thereby subject to be reborn in the image of an enlightened corporate success."

Aballa, in a flush of condescension, said, "All these programs provide us with asset diversity, research modulation, corporate loyalty, but what is the impact on…"

"What the hell are you talking about?" Whitman roared. "Look, we are struggling for survival here. Monroe has thrown the gauntlet and they apparently feel it is necessary to go ahead with tenuous projects. And we don't have any choice ourselves. I want to get on with it and we have to get on with it no matter what the ramifications or if any project is actually valid, just as long as it works for us."

"But what about the ethics of it?" Aballa stammered.

"Wow," Whitman interrupted. "Ethics—there is a word you don't hear much anymore."

The board became restless and uncomfortable and Whitman called a recess before deliberation on their own version of a self-counseling treatment program. Upon returning to the table, the board was quick to approve a proposal for exploring, schematizing and developing their duplication of the Monroe self-counseling project which included a more aggressive father figure message. Upon passage, the board felt relief and they relaxed into feckless chatter. As a reward for their unanimity, Whitman invited the board to his townhouse apartment for lunch—a rare treat.

The board and a few research supervisors met in an informal meeting shortly after lunch to hear the finish of Celosi's presentation. Ties were absent, shirt collars open and there was an air of informality. Coffee cups littered the desk along with the occasional Coke. A robo-steno prepared to record the meeting on a laptop. Despite the casual setting, the group was attentive.

Whitman watched as Celosi returned to the podium, a confident and persuasive individual, quite different from the uncertain hesitant young man of a few months ago. When first hired, based upon an excellent academic record at New Mexico, he was a thin and paled-faced, wearing an ill-fitting basket-weave jacket over a rumpled pastel shirt, slacks that could not hold a press, a wilted bow tie and athletic socks in loafers. His presentation then was that of a first-year junior college instructor whose speech was uninteresting and flavorless, hardly something to inspire rapt attention, unless of course, one was terribly interested in the subject in which most were not.

But now, by contrast, Whitman could see that Celosi had come a long way in a short time. His manner was dominating; his dialogue personable. He had impeccable dress even when others present were in more comfortable mode. His personal presence and style were impressive. As he began, his words were precise and commanded attention. There was no hesitation or miscues. Whitman was proud of the personal growth of his fledgling.

The subject of the Joe Waffle affair had been on Celosi's mind for a long time and having mulled over its possibilities, he was well-prepared for his presentation. The matter had impacted him and he could think of little else; but at the same time, he recognized that it was an outstanding opportunity, albeit, one fraught with danger.

Celosi quickly outlined what everyone already knew and then he touched on unknown possibilities of medical breakthroughs being forwarded by the unguided, runaway computers that offered untested advances in stem cell research, cloning, degenerative diseases, genetically modified organisms, genetics and even vaccine for various forms of cancer and he emphasized that "we are only scratching the surface." Then he cautioned, "We must always be cautious of public opinion, so that the validity of our research is never questioned, and in that regard there must be tight rein on the media and politicians."

He warned rather emphatically that there would be hidden traps, that all employees must think as one to direct all efforts toward the welfare and advancement of the corporation and there must be vigilance of the columnists and investigators who would undermine "our" efforts through the manipulation of public opinion, and do so as if it were a public service.

"In order to avoid that," he went on, "we should contact our political friends in D.C. and have them direct the main television channels to refer to our research as exciting with promising breakthroughs and rejecting any pejorative comments about the research as yellow journalism and a detriment to medical progress." He went on to suggest that any negative investigating reports by independent channels or newspapers be referred to as those desperately seeking a sensationalist story.

He continued saying that any appearance of a cover-up of information would be damaging. "So, if there are leaks, the best policy is to react without visible concern and to avoid any deliberate contact with the media—allow our spokesmen to handle all inquiries; they are well-schooled for that. The advantage that we have is that the public is so apathetic about things that should concern them, they are no threat."

In the case of very complex medical procedures or research that would appear unexplainable and might impact the media negatively, Celosi offered two responses, the first of which was the twelve-men response, in which it was intimated that "the matter in question was of such profound complexity that there are perhaps only twelve scientists in the world that can even understand the issue and they are all in agreement and as they are dedicated scientists and are of such high integrity that it would be to the interest of the common good that we accept their opinions on the matter without question."

The second scheme is what Celosi detailed as his one-on-one response. In this dodge, Celosi recalled how before the turn of the century, the environmental movement was gaining momentum and becoming a serious threat to corporate capitalism. The environmentalists would provide the testimony of, say, two thousand scientists proclaiming, for example, that global warming had become a dire threat to the earth and the future of civilization. Obviously, any legislation enacted as a result would be harmful to business encroachment on the environment so, in response, the business interests would locate a scientist or two who would dispel with disdain and ridicule the environmentalist position as a "liberal conspiracy" and a "made-up issue." Of course, the fact that only one or two scientists held that position went unnoticed by an unknowledgeable public that only witnessed what they thought was two equal sides on the issue, thereby neutralizing the issue out as the media debate on the subject was, to appearances, one on one—a numerical standoff.

Celosi then shifted to the matter at hand—the unexplored and unverified data now being produced by computers working as if on their own and at an alarming rate. He conceded that no one knew the force that was driving the computers but he did know that the computers were uncovering useful if not entirely understood information. Initial research into the phenomenon revealed medically useful data but the scientific community would demand affirmation of such discoveries "but we need time to do that."

"The problem would arise that there are people who have nothing better to do than cause havoc with other people's achievements," he continued. "And such individuals would refer to Bio-Med's research accomplishments as 'audacious inquisition,' 'careless exploitation,' or 'rakish predacity,'" he stated, and "they would accuse the researchers of not being in control of their experiments but slaves to them. The whole scientific community would be adrift on an uncharted course and much of the information available to them would be lost.

"Therefore," he continued after a pause, "we must take the high road, we will have to maintain righteous posture; that is, establish high standards for ourselves and keep our research feasible and beyond question. If we cannot do so in the laboratory, we must do so in appearance. We must emphasize to the press and public our commitment to the principles of the scientific method of research. I admit that this is emergent but we must play for time. The research of our computer discoveries will be very time-consuming but were are one hundred percent convinced that we will be able to verify all that has come out of our research at this time."

He went on to explain that the first impression in the public mind, whether true or contrived, would be an impression that would dominate all subsequent information presented to the public. It would be simple imprinting and nothing would entirely undo that first impression, at least in the mind of the great unread. "Add to that," he theorized, "the incessant use of tabloid newspapers, right-wing talk shows, and a series of factual books would present our view for public perusal." Then he smiled wistfully and said, "We have on our side, several mainstream news moderators able to subtly sway argument to give countenance to our position."

Then, breaking eye contact with his audience, he said, in emoted seriousness, "This may appear subterfuge to you but let me assure you that it is completely necessary. At this point in time, our industry and its future are extremely vulnerable because of what we don't know in regard to computer breakthroughs, so we can leave nothing to chance and we must, therefore, take unusual risks to get us through this uncertain time. We have put these computers in motion and now they delve into the unknown, divulging unexplored intelligence, and since we were the creators of those systems and have set them on their course, we must have faith in ourselves and the course we have set. Fortunately, the news media are engrossed in political crises, corruption, crime, financial chaos, and other things and medical news or research does not receive very much attention. That is to our advantage."

At the conclusion of Celosi's remarks, Whitman arose and, as usual, was the appearance of corporate aproposity and presence. He strode to the podium without Celosi's transitory opening. Although that was unnecessary under the circumstances, Whitman had always demanded strict adherence to protocol. But, with a quick glance from Celosi, he was forgiven. Whitman was a humorless man and he was not about to initiate his remarks with banal drollery or commentary; but, he did have everyone's attention.

He began, "As you know, this is a very exciting time and every day will bring new discovery and challenge. We will all be tested. Your input will be invaluable and it must be emphasized that this is a team effort and thus we must all be in sync and working together. This is going to be sensitive stuff and there will be little room for error. If, at any time, you are unsure of anything, simply contact the appropriate reference or myself. Even slight errors of judgment may have dire consequences.

"As you are aware, the information supplied to us by our Star Search Computer Systems may be the greatest discovery in the history of man and can bring the greatest benefits to mankind—far beyond what he has ever imagined. So, we have embarked upon this journey, an enterprise to make available for consumption radical new medical programs that will enhance the human condition and aid its progress through the ages. To accomplish this, we have prepared to invest over a billion dollars. Our initial plan is to hire 250 new lab researchers to be assigned to Syracuse, NYU and Georgetown medical facilities. There will be also a hundred new on-staff physicians at those same three sites. There will also be openings within the company for inspectors, supervisors and advisors. And we are looking at 250 new programmers once we get this effort underway.

"To say that this a very exciting time, is, of course, an understatement. We do know that this is very big, very big. We have explored inner space, outer space, the future, the past, and now, a dimension that we really don't understand.

"Currently, we are beginning to look at potential research findings transmitted to us by this new dimension including before unknown data in biochemistry, cloning, transplant surgery, demographics of communicable diseases, microscopic technology, presage of fetus of prehistory, robotic investigators, nanotechnology, DNA data, and many others too numerous to mention. In our planned studies, there will be obvious spin-offs that will put us in the position of being the general watchdog of community health matters.

"It will be incumbent upon us, before we initiate research and study into these various issues, that we understand the legal ramifications involved as well as our moral obligations to national health. These are matters to be studied and reported on by our legal experts."

Then Whitman took a step back, scanned his notes and modulated his presentation to one of adroit dramatization. All present knew that this was the big finish—Whitman always had a big finish!

"We must strive to keep our research pure and beyond question and ask only the highest standards of ourselves. For it is with great humility that we accept this calling to lead man, the wanderer of the universe, in his great quest of the challenges of the unexplored and, in so doing, we will guide an intellectual revolution that will render him an efficacious crusader of his culture and genre. In the past, it has been prophesied that a great bright light would come at a time of total darkness and it would bring an awakening and order to utter chaos and a quickening of our resolve for exploration and celestial achievement. To maintain such discipline, there must be urgent confederacy and dedication instilled in those who toil so thanklessly in the terrine world of seemingly worthless drudge. We must realize that only a very collaborative effort will achieve the unachievable. We cannot extricate ourselves from mundane tasks but must see such as a striving for glorious accomplishment for the common good. To set ourselves on this momentous course, we must imbue ourselves with the resolve of a core belief system that is annealed by the blood and sacrifice of those before us and sanctified by scientific authenticity. This core belief will not endorse or perpetuate unscientific fantasy but will be empowered with the recognition of the genius of man and that he himself has been divinely chosen and directed to a destination within the universe and, thus empowered, he would achieve what the Gods of Olympus themselves would not have even dared to dream."

There was a light smattering of applause.

# Five

The first week of July 2030 began Bio-Med's Project Featherstone, a program to evaluate data material and formulate programs resulting from the Star Search 21 Computer findings, all this amid great anticipation and high excitement. But the week's exhilaration suddenly gave way to despair almost before it had begun.

In that week, three things happened that put the program in serious doubt if not in jeopardy. The program, which had been named after an obscure social science professor at Columbia University who introduced and popularized a radical philosophy that there was no God and that man was the supreme ruler of the universe, had an immediate crisis time when expectations and enthusiasm were running high.

The first incident involved a program being set up by a programmer, Linda Chastain, but which resulted in a setback which would affect the whole industry.

Chastain was a sluggish-appearing young woman, not obese but heavy to the point that her facial features were flaccid and whatever teenage cuteness she once possessed was lost in porkish shapelessness.

She never dated, had no friends as far as anyone knew and seemed to have no leisure-time hobbies or interests. She was characterized by fellow workers as only an average talent but she made up for any lacking she may have had with an incredible energy for work. It was her intention to appear indispensable to her employers and toward that goal, she applied herself diligently to her assignments and in particular, strived to develop the first Featherstone operational program to be approved by the directors of the project, even before Star Search 21 went on-line. Thus, she worked night and day starting several weeks before the official start of the project on futurity research to develop a program that would predict the future medical history of an unborn fetus with one hundred percent accuracy—an obvious advantage during a potential lifetime.

## THE LEGEND OF SUSEJ

On the morning of Featherstone, day one, Chastain waited patiently in almost intoxicated anticipation before her computer waiting for the work area to fill with coworkers and then, with intense fanfare, she pressed the key to reveal the premier product of Featherstone. Nothing happened. She pressed the key again. It did not respond. Her moment of glory was lost as one by one other programmers turned away having lost interest. She checked her hard drive. Nothing. She examined her CD. Again nothing. Visibly angered, she began punching keys with great force, putting her considerable weight behind each stroke. Nothing came forth.

Other programmers thought that the matter only involved a computer malfunction but when the situation persisted, a computer tech was called in to examine the computer. Still, the window stared back blankly. A second Star Search 21 computer was assembled in the office and once installed, the tech attempted to bring up the same menu used by Chastain. But that computer too refused to bring up the program by window or printer.

By the end of the day, consternation was spreading throughout the work force. Theories of the malfunction ranged from industrial sabotage to providential intervention. By late afternoon a Problematic Emergency Research team was assembled and a meeting was scheduled for the next morning.

The first day of the ambitious Featherstone Project had been an utter disaster and as well, the overly ambitious Chastain was left a nervous wreck.

A very somber PERT met the next morning before regular work hours in order to seek a solution to the Star Search mystery and to remedy the malfunction. Some members diddled the keyboard with eyebrows raised in serious contemplation. No ideas came forth. After muddling through the possibilities, a very stressed and agitated John Whitman announced that he would put in a call to an old friend and consultant, Dr. Leonard Haven, a professor of computer science at Hofstra University and one of the original developers of the Star Search system. Dr. Havens was arguably the leading mind in the field of computerology. Whitman excused himself to compose a fax to the good professor indicating the urgency of the situation. PERT thereupon adjourned with a scheduled meeting for the following morning. All staff was advised that the problem was technical and would be absolved.

The professor responded almost immediately and advised that the problem had caught him by surprise but he thought that if he gave the dilemma a night's consideration he could unravel the puzzle. He scheduled a personal call for Whitman for the next morning.

On Tuesday, the second day of Project Featherstone, at 9:45 AM, Whitman, a picture of nervous anxiety, reached for the telephone with trembling hand upon advise from the robo-steno that Dr. Haven was returning his call. Whitman was with Darius Celosi at the time and put the call on speaker-phone.

Dr. Haven said in opening the conversation, "I read your fax and it appears you have a unique problem but after a little thought, I recalled something from when we were developing the program that is the crux of the matter."

Whitman answered, "Thank God, we need answers. We haven't set up a production schedule as yet because we are still in research mode, but even at that, we are getting seriously behind."

Haven said, "Well, it won't be all that easy to reconcile things and you'll have to do a lot of homework but it will be worth it."

Whitman said, "That's okay, we'll do whatever we must to get this thing back on track."

"Well, this is how I see it," Haven said. "Your Star Search Computer is not responding because it was been programmed not to. Let me explain. When we built the Star Search system, the engineers added something called an Ethics Probe. The Ethics Probe is a system that is designed to insure the integrity of the computer itself. That is because in cases involving very sophisticated computers that can create undocumented data, the federal government wanted a corrective system so that surreptitious data would not be accepted or further processed. Therefore the Ethics Probe was installed in all new computers that the squeamish in the computer industry insultingly refers to as subterfuge."

"But we didn't compromise the integrity of the computer," Whitman shouted with Celosi nodding in agreement.

"Ah, but you did. If you want to explore data and even create programs using that data, that is acceptable. But you must understand that the computer itself will review the data and if the proposed program resulting from your research is unacceptable, the computer will shut down—permanently or until the problem has been rectified. You may ask what constitutes unacceptable. Very simply, the computer is programmed to coordinate with natural law. That is not natural law—I mean, like the environment—but natural law within a computerized system and, surprisingly, ethics are involved. The computer does not want you to come up with results that are too far-out or not possible within the probabilities of computerized natural law."

"But," Whitman protested, "there was nothing in the operations manual that warned us of this—this is a complete surprise to us. Why were we not advised?"

"Because," Haven continued, "it is a real big deal. The government wanted it to come up if there was a significant violation of ethics so it would impact everyone severely and that it would also expose those who are cheating. And this an old law—dating back to the days of governmental regulation and lofty moralism."

Whitman, sadly, "So we are stuck." Then after a thought he said, "Can't we do anything like dismantle the Ethics Probe?"

Havens answered, "The Ethics Probe is permanent and cannot be changed—unless you change the law. That would be a hard sell for most of us. What you have to do—and with your connections there is a distinct possibility you can pull it off—is this: Go to the legislature and convince them of the potential of futuristic research and how it could benefit mankind in numerous ways. In other words, appeal to their compassion and sense of benevolence and you can even put pressure on them through the media; that is, if they don't remove the law, then you can say that they are hindering human progress. So, all you would be doing, in a sense, would be to give the computer system more flexibility in determining ethics violation while keeping in mind that the research itself is for the good us all—particularly the bottom line."

A thoughtful Whitman said, "That doesn't sound easy, I mean, removing an established authority."

"But, look at it this way," Havens said, "these legislators are hard-pressed. They need answers and they need to prove their worth. They have been gridlocked for years and they are scared of their constituents. They are unable to show anything for their time in the legislature and they need to be part of something positive and the appearance of doing something useful. So if you can convince them of the authenticity of your program—and believe me, they want to believe you—you can sell it to them."

Celosi interjected, "It seems amazing that a machine can actually have ethical concerns. I mean, will they seriously buy that?"

Havens answered, "Ethics to a computer are not significantly different from that of humans, but it is based on the premise that there is no vacuum in nature and that it is essential that all things comply to electronic natural law. It must all fit and everything must be in sequence and accounted for. So if man, in his desire to create something to fit his particular perspective, does not comply to electronic natural law, the computer will reject it in order to keep the system pure. On the other hand, if you develop a process and it seems to work, you must then do the research to justify it ethically. That may not seem expedient but for the computer it completes the cosmos and the research itself becomes not a vehicle of discovery but one of verification; and thereby man and computer maintain a symbiotic relationship—one of trust and affirmation."

Celosi replied, "But it would seem a stretch to a bunch of dumb politicians that computers can go into such a sophisticated dimension."

"Not so," Havens offered, "these politicians are not stupid, they know what's going on with these computers and they know how sophisticated they have become. But that is not the issue here. What you have to do here is give them an example of how an action on their part will give a positive result. For example, show statistics that demonstrate that Alzheimer's disease represents a number of patients nationally that takes over half the federal medical budget to care for them but that Star Search has revealed a method of treatment that may reduce that amount by half and that every day we delay in implementing this program, it costs us millions of dollars. That will certainly put pressure on the legislature to act, particularly if that argument gets out to the press."

Whitman responded urgently, "Okay, Darius will draw up a memo to the Central Committee of the Republican Party…"

"Whoa," Celosi interrupted. "Didn't you hear the news this morning? The Republican Party met last night and officially changed their name to the Evangelical Party."

"Jesus, why did they do that?"

Celosi answered, "Because they could, I mean, like, eighty percent of the Republican enrolment are fundamentalist Christians. And besides, there has been widespread discontent in the party because the Christians want to get rid of a lot of Republican bad baggage."

"Get rid of Republican baggage? The party has been projecting the fundamentalist agenda for years."

"That's right, but the public doesn't pay attention to that kind of stuff so they will buy the argument that their shortcomings were due to Republican incompetence."

"Alright," Whitman said, "that will work for us. In fact, the evangelicals owe us big time and this will help us push our hype. Make sure to use today's date and address the memo to the Evangelical Party—they will think that we are really on top of things."

So the Chastain affair was absolved rather quietly and with the problem perhaps went the last vestige of governmental control of corporate expedition. It became what Whitman was to rejoice as a "new beginning."

But in that fateful week, a second disaster struck the business organization as it was attempting to return to composure by treating the Chastain crisis as nothing more than a simple computer glitch subsequently presenting to the world that it had been corrected "quite matter-of-factly" by routine adjustment as was stated distinctly in the organization's weekly newsletter. The second problem was unrelated to the first but had a devastating psychological impact upon Bio-Med personnel.

It was that Bio-Med employed a programmer by the name of Paul Luftus, a bookish individual working on communicable disease research. He had been in the corporation for five years and was a quiet unassuming individual pretty much unknown to his fellow employees. Because his leisure time was spent reading or studying, he rarely socialized and when past-dimension data became available on Bio-Med computers, he began researching and categorizing the information on his own during his evenings. He had been working an historical paper—his first love—and the availability of the historical documents—whether manufactured or real—seemed to fit into his historical thesis. By the time that Featherstone was in process, he had a rough draft ready for his publisher, *American Legacy Quarterly*, a left-wing periodical known for agitating status quo organizations and which, on more than one occasion, had been threatened with being shut down by the government for the inflammatory and revolutionary rhetoric of their articles.

Luftus was advised by his publisher that as his work was non-fiction and, considering the Chastain matter, it would have to be carefully footnoted and authenticity thereby established. Luftus suddenly feared his work as virtually useless. But he still believed that he had a solid paper and although he conceded that without documentation it would be controversial—not necessarily a bad thing—but the letters, essays, diaries and obscure books which now had to be documented had given it life.

Out of desperation, Luftus submitted his paper to computer blogs, obscure or even illegal newspapers, left-leaning radio talk shows and even some very unsavory web sites. To his surprise, his paper caused an immediate stir, on occasion entering the mainstream media although usually in a nefarious context. But what was even more of a surprise was that the essay struck a nerve with a surprisingly large and apparently unknown segment of the population that was unorganized and totally unaware that there was, within their demographic population, a common unified belief, a belief related not only to philosophical concepts but in their very survival in a world that was becoming increasingly alien to them.

Luftus had been an history major at Stanford University but, unable to find work in that academic field, he matriculated to San Jose State University where he earned a second degree in computer science and upon completing his studies found temporary work in Silicon Valley before landing a position with the west coast branch of Bio-Med.

Although working in the medical research field, Luftus remained faithful to his love of history and began work on a collection of essays on American history. He had become an admirer of historian Richard Hofstater and as such, he developed a belief that American history up to the twentieth century and beyond was a myth imposed by a monopolistic capitalistic system that manipulated the citizenry by propagandizing all aspects of the national culture. He came to believe, for example, upon study of the early writers on Puritanism, the Puritans were hardly puritanical, that being a moniker put on them by an over-zealous business community concerned by the influence of that church on American culture which they found threatening to the economic system as, in their interpretation of that church's leanings, they found it too economically restrictive.

Similarly, Luftus viewed the early regulatory movement of the 1700s as one of the best examples of democracy. He saw that movement, spawned in the vacuum of a lawless frontier, as the most logical and democratic of institutions and he particularly applauded its organization, structure and dedication to the principles of democracy. Yet, he was to sadly relate, when the regulators became too effective, idealistic and perhaps too righteous when they took on corrupt and greedy big business, they were attacked as being vigilantes and "taking the law in their own hands." The pejorative stuck and when the Ku Klux Klan used their name and techniques in the 1920s to extend racism, the propaganda imbued the movement with the murky stigma of sedition.

As to the rightist-leaning historical accounts available on the internet which were having a jarring impact on the technological industry as well as the pop culture, Luftus saw it as a ruse imposed upon the public by an aggressive public promotion of political propaganda and by which he was not only able to discern but which he used to help identify the ideology and method and thereby he was able to dramatize its very delusive nature.

Throughout American history, Luftus maintained, corporate business kept a steady drumbeat against the middle class and what he considered basic American values. However, he argued, periodic depressions interrupted the march of capitalism and brought the country back to economic balance in order to right itself. The business elite realized that their one deniable obstacle was the Constitution itself. No viable political candidate could ever attack the Constitution; however, they did come to believe that they could overcome its limitations on their power by ethereal assailment on the core beliefs of the people although they be at odds with original American ideals and the Constitution. It was conceivable, they reasoned, that a whole society could have schizoid tendencies, that is, split into two diametrically opposed concepts on all issues, at war with each reality, but in the unsophisticated public mind, quite real.

The failure of corporate capitalism to establish a monopoly after the Reconstruction period, the 1800s period of the semipiractical "robber barons," the 1920s when the top five percent received one third of the nation's income or the salutary 1950s, according to Luftus, they strengthened their resolve after an election defeat in 1964 in a strategy that appealed to populism. But more than that, the corporate prescription for success realized the necessity of having dedicated political allies equally bent on unseating the well-established middle-class representation that was dominating American politics at that time. Thus there occurred, in Luftus' theory, an unlikely marriage of the corporations, Christian fundamentalists and right-wing fanatics. Many of the time-honored values and ideological precepts of these groups were at odds with each other but what held them together was their common disdain for what they deemed a runaway government that had no concern for the issues important to them. Unfortunately, the movement took on a personal and emotional cadence and despite previous studies in history suggesting that such appeals to populism are inherently unstable, the movement only seemed to grow in force and sheer numbers.

At this point, Luftus seemed to abandon historical analysis for psycho-historic analysis. Although he was not schooled in psychology, there was much written about the dynamics of political and social life of the day, albeit, most of it suppressed by the government and media. Nevertheless, Luftus found that the work done in that regard fit well into the political mind-set of the day giving it impetus and misguided but emphatic direction.

At the root of this psychological phenomenon was what has been termed acute egophrenic disorder, a pathology not inflicting individuals but whole cultures. Now, in retrospect it would appear the all the dictatorships in history may have been similarly afflicted. It became dangerous in large populations due to its tendency to feed upon itself. This form of psychosis—if we can call it psychosis as those inflicted appear so normal—is particularly endemic in religious populations when followers believe that they are righteous and because they are righteous they recognize no argument against them and they are adamantly in denial of their own dark side. But like all of us, they have a dark side which they disown by projecting their dark side onto others—others "out there." By this projection they don't recognize the evil in themselves but they see their own shadow reflected in others. Luftus pointed out that the great C.G. Jung understood this condition and said regarding it, "The psychological rule says that when an inner situation is not made conscious, it happens outside, as fate. That is to say, when the individual remains undivided (not in touch with both the light and dark parts of themselves) and does not become conscious of his inner opposite, the world must perforce act out the conflict torn into opposing halves."

At the root of this psychological process there is an inability for self-examination, an unwillingness to feel guilt, sin or shame, as if one would be exposed to the world that one is a failure and shamed and that is threatening to the self-concept. Without self-reflection, the true self, which includes the hidden dark side, is protected. Its replacement is the shallow and superficial religious self that is buoyed up by constant piety and religious exclamations but also, to give the religious self continuity and involvement, there must be the challenge of fighting evil both within the religious and political silhouettes, sort of like fighting insensate windmills, and what has long astonished onlookers was that the two elements, religion and politics, are hardly distinguishable from each other.

When the leaders of such a dynamic are hiding a great lie, which is in itself very intoxicating to the followers, it has a very mesmerizing effect upon them and they tend to reinforce their own pathology and thus aid the leader in projecting his lie. Luftus again quotes Jung on this point, "Nothing has such a convincing effect as a lie one invents and believes himself." An individual so afflicted with the disease appears charming and convincing, the classical appearance of a sociopath. But therein lies the danger, according to the thesis of Luftus, the dark side is thus hidden by charm and cordiality and so conceivable and acceptable is the psychosis that it replicates itself within the culture and even its failures or shortcomings are totally ignored as irrelevant.

Luftus concludes that this collective psychosis, once it is out of control, is eventually self-destructive as the numbers of the population so affected increase exponentially and have become so accepted in the mainstream that even mental health agencies are victim of it. When a people fall victim to the disease as individuals they are unable to recognize their sickness and, at the same time are unable to appreciate their projections and, in fact, they exorcise their own dark side by expending great amounts of energy toward defeating those upon whom they have projected their dark side. It is a disease which could be simply called ignorance but those so stricken when criticized or condemned actually see their accusers as being insane.

Of course, Luftus' thesis was nothing new as it had been the subject of discourse by historians for many years and even egophrenia had been discussed by the psychiatric community for an equal time. But it was the first time any writer put the two together in a comprehensive study showing the causal effect between the two. Additionally, Luftus was employed by the largest biomedical complex in the world which gave the essay impact of exaggerated importance. But because fundamental Christians rose in common outcry against the paper, even before it was published, it was summarily rejected by mainstream sources. However, once on the internet, it was eagerly accepted by the underground community which not only accepted the premise of the works but printed it throughout the subterranean communication system and it became the apostolate revelation of their mantra.

The coworkers of Luftus felt betrayed although they had no emotional connection with this distant and reserved man and as a result he was to feel denigration and rejection at work. That however, was of small consequence as the administration of Bio-Med mulled the situation over very briefly once the author of the essay was identified and then quickly they dismissed Luftus because of "substandard performance." Coworkers and administrators alike were amazed that Luftus did not understand that such contemptuous undertaking would result in his dismissal from the corporation. But for Luftus there were moral issues which had always intruded upon his composure bringing about introspection and a questioning of the whole sociopolitical structure of his employer. He had never done anything in his life that would remotely be considered bravery. He had never stood up to anything, anyone or a cause that was important. He had never spoken out in defense of a minority nor had he expressed empathy for anyone less fortunate than himself. He did not rationalize others' failure to achieve but then he never made any effort toward aiding the less favored. But he saw the direction of an out-of-control system and he wondered if he did not come forth, who would? This and his guilt had caused him to act.

A benumbed Luftus retreated into the underground community as there simply was nowhere else to go. Although fearful of the violence and constant strife he had thought typified that community, he was shocked at its organization and realistic complexity. The violence of the street was simply that, individuals rejecting both the system of the elitists and the underground—they preferred their chaotic lifestyle and would not change if they could. He immediately found employment for an underground newspaper and for a salary dreadfully low. But there were compensations. He was given a cot in a storage room for sleeping and there was a common cooking area. His main assets were a bicycle and a respirator. He had few other needs. The most serious shortcoming he felt was the lack of purified air fed into elitist buildings but that too would be something he would adjust to, and thus the respirator for emergencies. But most importantly, he found in that community, a sense of family. On his first day, a very young and personable girl showed him around the work premises and introduced him to very congenial employees. His leisure time was also to meet radical change; no longer was he subjected to the glitzy diversions he had known, for now what leisure time there was available to him was imbued in the simple fascination of abstruse candlelight conversation. So he was exposed to a new reality—whereas he had known competitiveness, he now felt cooperation; he had known aloofness, he now felt care; he had known alienation, he now felt companionship; he had known uncompromised ideology, he now felt intellectual freedom; he had known ruthlessness, he now felt gentleness; and, he had known meanness, he now felt love of fellow man. He could not remember being happier—he was experiencing soul. And deep inside there was a profound satisfaction that for once, he had spoken up at great risk to himself.

The third calamity to befall Bio-Med during that disastrous week occurred on Friday when the staff felt relief that nothing else could go wrong; but late in the day came word that Joe Waffle, who had been sent home after his unnerving encounter with the ghosts of the past on his Star Search exploration, began to hallucinate and subsequently became totally incoherent. The episode had resulted in his involuntary retirement from the corporation but the very first week of his retirement revealed that Waffle could not take care of himself and was, in fact, in a catatonic state and was placed in the psychiatric ward of a local hospital for evaluation.

According to the subsequent report, Waffle was suffering from an increasingly common affliction particular to, although empirically less severe than the symptoms experienced by him, the computer industry called "symbiotic psychosis." This was defined as a condition in which the victim, usually a long-term computer operator, developed a strong symbiotic relationship with computers and that relationship made his human relationships so tenuous that he sought emotional fulfillment in the medulla of the computer, identifying so closely he gave up his humanity, and did so gradually but apparently willingly. Those knowing Waffle—or perhaps more realistically, not knowing him at all—could easily see that relationship and that in itself caused consternation within a staff that could easily identify with his condition.

While being evaluated, it was determined that Waffle could not take care of himself, was virtually unresponsive to all stimuli and although not dangerous to himself or others, would be placed in a nursing home for the rest of his days. The episode put a pall over the assemblage at Bio-Med after an already devastating week. Ironically, they had had no compassion for Waffle before, but his condition caused abnormal anxiety over employees subjecting themselves to hectic self-examination to the point of hysteria.

Such was the shallowness of the structure on which the medical industry, the afflicted and society now depended.

# Six

The 2030 National Republican Convention was held at Convention Center, Cornerstone Christian Casino (play for Jesus) in Las Vegas, Nevada, as it had been for the previous five years. A jubilant noisy crowd of party faithful anticipating the emotionally provoking official ceremony of changing the party name were gradually silenced by Pastor Orwell Rubin of Trinity Church, Miami, Florida, as he prepared to present the convocation for the proceedings.

Reporters to the event could not recall any difference in the bestowal from previous clerics giving the spoken word—they always seemed the same in appearance, tone and message; and that message, given before a solid mass of political zealots, oblivious to the message, was televised nationally as had been all Republican observances and was identical to that given every year for as long as anyone could remember.

Pastor Rubin waited patiently for the hush that was to follow the din of political revelry and, leaning forward, staring through bifocal glasses at the crowd and then in operatic somber tones glanced down to read his message (why this shop-worn conferment had never been memorized remained a mystery) which he delivered in an overly dramatized devotional voice.

The fact that the convention setting and the prayer projected to viewers a political entity seemed not to bother the good pastor at all.

"Oh dear God," he commenced, "we come here today as your messengers. The words we speak are yours. We have been called by you as your disciples and we deliver your word to a waiting and joyous world. We have been enlightened, energized and empowered by you and we carry your meaning and we know in our hearts that our political agenda is from and of you. We know now that political beliefs and religious beliefs cannot be bifurcated and all political messages must be unequivocal. We ask for your continued guidance so that we become the beacon of the world."

As the pastor spoke, a slow spontaneous rhythm began building into a crescendo pulsing with such vitality that Rubin could hardly be heard, his voice rising in pitch as well as volume but nevertheless, his last few words were lost. It mattered not—the aggregation had come to feverish gospel level as it seemed to be far more of a victory celebration rather than a sacred statement of faith.

The convocation was followed by a military honor guard and a band performed a Sousa march before the singing of the national anthem, which was sung with such verve as to make it appear to be a spiritual call to crusade. Although the convention was undifferentiated from conventions of the past, this one degenerated into a combination of a Saturday night hoe-down and a Sunday morning gospel meeting. But there was one important difference in this convention.

It was to be the last convention for the Republican Party for the first order of business would be the ceremonial and formal enactment of changing the party name to the Evangelical Party of the United States of America, a change that would presumptionally suggest to an incognizant public that it would include a significant change in philosophy and leadership—but it would not. It would be a change in name only, for the movers and shakers of faith were already well integrated within the party.

This was an anticipated event, an obvious result of political opportunism and to appearance, quickly accomplished, while in actuality, the seeds of insurrection were a long time coming and had required precise planning and the fanatical dedication of ecclesiastical foot soldiers.

The keynote speaker of the convention was the Reverend Billy Hallowed, long an itinerant preacher of inspiring messages (which coincidently brought him great wealth) and currently the president of the Evangelical Counsel of U.S. Governmental Policy. The reverend's introduction brought forth an insurmountable gush of emotion, the result of a victory so long coming that the theopathic fervor could not be denied. It went on and on.

Obviously pleased, the reverend leaned forward on the podium before an immense crowd of brethren standing, most of them tearfully, crowded into an auditorium built to accommodate half their number. Hallowed did not call for order, instead basking in the glory of their adulation, their pent-up emotions and their politico-religious triumph, he smiled as if in reward. There was no time schedule to be adhered to—so uncommitted had been the convention committee to procedure or agenda.

Slowly the emotion began to subside but periodic bursts of cheer interrupted the reverend, causing him to pause with spurts laughter obviously enjoying the spectacle. Finally, there was a hush that allowed him to speak. "God has given us a great victory today," he began. "Glory be to God." Again applause and cheers drowned him out.

At last, he began his prepared speech. "We have achieved a historic political victory this evening—a result of God's will. It could not be any other way for he has spoken and has said that there will be no political entity before us. We have to put the turmoil and indecision of the past few years behind us as now that we have severed our ties with a political party that detoured the imposition of biblical truth. Now we can go forth in the belief that biblical truth will become the governing reality of our governmental system. Never again will we be subverted from our dedicated divine entrustment.

"And with this dedication there must be an awareness of past failings and recognizing such failings there must be, on our part, a constant emphasis on effort to purify our faith and maintain biblical truth. We have long acknowledged the phenomena of the monastic cycle in which idealistic movements produced great organizations of devotion and discipline only to deteriorate as they turned to God in time of need but when things went well, they forgot God and those movements were then without spirituality.

"In the sixth century, religieux Bendictines, in helping to provide for the impoverished, cleared forest and seeded lands, but several centuries later the abbeys had ceased to be spiritual institutions becoming instead collegiate sinecures at the mercy of cultural predications. Similarly, Dominicans, Jesuits and Franciscans have demonstrated periods of great devotion and discipline but then drifted toward apathy and indulgence.

"In avoiding such pitfalls of the past, we must maintain a strict political discipline that will abjure the evasive doctrines and solutions of political excursionists and maintain a system that, no matter how difficult it may be, is pure in its concept of a literal interpretation of the Bible. Our failures in recent years have not been a result of our belief system but rather the failure of our politicians to follow our belief to consummation. We must be aware that decadence drives out discipline and the failures we have experienced were caused by the timidity of our politicians to carry out the intention of God as related in the Bible to its fullest. In the future there must be no compromise in our government, we must forcefully reject the sins of Satan—there must be no homosexual acceptance in our society, no sodomy, no stem cell research, no abortion, no permissive behavior of any kind, no incestuous sexual practices, no activist judges, in fact, we plan to reject anything that smells of the decadence of liberal diabolism. So I say to the world, 'We are back and we intend to stay.'"

The convention erupted into a single voice of unrestrained exuberance, a bellowing of the release of decades of political denigration, collective self-doubt and ideological derision. "They need this—we all need this," Hallowed whispered to himself, "I'll give them all the time they need." The emotional outburst continued unabated for what appeared to be a full ten minutes, but once the crowd had purged the visceral tension of anxiety, rejection and ridicule imposed upon them during their deathless struggle, quietude passed over them.

Hallowed continued his speech but after the peak of frenzy there was little attention paid to his utterances. Speakers followed Hallowed to the podium in seemingly endless procession, their messages lost on a murmuring assemblage that had lost focus but nevertheless politely responded to all presentations. It seemed that each and every scheduled speaker was determined to have his moment in the spotlight of this glorious occasion and accordingly, emoted with great energy and acumen.

The scheduled formal transfer of the party name was brief and equally as emotional as Hollowed's inspirational speech. What was actually said in the ceremony was obliterated by the noisy enthusiasm of those in attendance but was concluded when a convention-wide banner was unfurled from the ceiling to reveal the party appellation—"The Evangelical Party of the United States of America." That, of course, received a prolonged frenzied ovation; and even then, at the conclusion of the convention, many of the attendees stood transfixed at their time of historical affirmation; simply, they had been a part of a long consecrated struggle and they did not want the acknowledgment of victory to end. But then they began to dissipate, moving slowly into the casino gambling area, many of them shapelessly obese people who, once they started to move, seemed to glide along effortlessly carried by their own momentum. The Cornerstone Christian Casino would do well with this generous ecstatic congregation this evening.

The following morning, the collusive *Rebel Voice*, the New York-based newspaper that became the most read periodical after the government took control of the internet, featured an editorial by columnist Gary Freeman regarding the festive convention of the previous evening:

"Last night a miracle happened in Las Vegas. Thousands of Christians marched into the Cornerstone Christian Casino Convention Center and a scant three hours later traipsed out, converted to Evangelicals. The celebration thereof seemed to convey that something of great historical significance had occurred. But, indeed, it had not. So, instead, I call them the party of irony.

"The so-called change of party was nothing but a name change that was little more than symbolism. To imply any political importance to this is ludicrous. This the same group of extremists that have had their way with the Republican Party for the past thirty years and now want an out for their poor governance. They would want you to believe that they are breaking away from bad governance, but the truth of the matter is that they were the bad governance and now they want us to believe that it was them other guys and they want to start fresh with their same old agenda which somehow they attempt to claim is different—a new beginning that they want us to believe.

"It is irony that the Evangelicals who disdain scientific inquiry championed the imposition of scientific bio-tech identification numbers for all citizens so that they could keep track of them and know everything about them.

"It is ironic that the Evangelicals who preach peace have provoked and encouraged the environmental and oil wars that have devastated the earth over the past thirty years.

"They speak of democracy but subjugate the masses through despotic politics and electronic monitoring.

"They rage about 'responsibility' but have none when it comes to acknowledging their own shortcomings and failures.

"They wax piously over God's creations and flawless design, but are cruel and uncaring about the condition of the earth which they claim was put here for their use.

"They bellow long and loud about the priorities of capitalism but were sure to dismantle middle-class entrepreneurship.

"They speak of freedom but through electronic control they thwart thoughts not their own.

"They have compassion for children who recite biblical passages but not for those reciting from the Koran.

"They promote foreign missions and charity but are protective of their own wealth and materialism.

"They denounce fornication but hide their own licentious behavior from the world.

"They make much fuss about compassion for the poor but have little actual concern for anyone other than themselves and they destroyed Social Security—the last hope for many.

"They abhor vice but applaud the fact that a large segment of the population is addicted to virtual reality—the new opium of the masses—and therefore are not an issue in politics nor are they a threat to become invasive in society.

"In summary, they speak as Christians but nothing about them is remotely Christian. They have attempted to convince us that they propose a government of biblical righteousness and that would represent good governance. But it will not and the Evangelicals would like us to excuse and forgive the self-promoting schemes that have practically destroyed this nation in the past thirty years. While calling themselves fiscally responsible, they have squandered trillions of dollars on projects that benefit only them; they called for limited government but government has grown to big brotherhood. They have created a two-tiered economy—that of the elite and that of those who struggle daily for survival. They have brought back the debtor prison. They have brought back slave labor. They have returned to an era of racism and class conflict. They have initiated wars that they justify as God's wars. They are paranoid individuals who complain that everyone is out to get them, yet they have destroyed those beneath them. The bald fact is, they are responsible for what we have endured for the past thirty years and any attempt by them to lay that blame on a political party that has not actually been in existence for the last three decades is nothing less than a cheap cop-out.

"What happened last night in Las Vegas will change nothing—we can only expect more of the same. It was a shameful performance, a performance of the powerful who have no clue of the damage they are doing. They seek only to extend and consolidate power. Now they will return to their sanctuaries in their economic protectorates around the world. Sadly, they know not what they do—nor do they care."

Paul Luftus had been working for two weeks, fourteen hours a day, in the tiny print shop in the underground society when Linda Lefevre, whom he knew not at all, approached him as he sat at his desk and, touching his sleeve, said, "You are scheduled for a day off and I would like to show you around this morning." Luftus had found the job rewarding; the hours were long but there was no stress or demands, the workplace was relaxed and, unlike his days at Bio-Med, there was a prevailing honesty among those in which he had contact. As much as he loved his work, he conceded that a day off would be nice. He accepted.

Linda Lefevre was perhaps forty-three years and one time may have been a ravishing beauty, beauty that had been replaced by a face etched with indomitable strength and a glowing inner presence. Her manner was soft and appealing, her method personable and she continually touched others during conversation. When the economy crashed in 2019, it killed her husband and left her and her two children destitute but she persevered and rose from the loss and now she was totally dedicated to the underground society—called the Mole People by a hostile government—which had helped her fight depression and economic poverty and she undisputedly accepted the death of her husband as being responsible for her awakening and the resulting emotional enrichment that brought her a deep compassion for others.

Lefevre suggested a trip to Central Park to which Luftus accepted without giving it much thought although it was not something that he would do on his own. Of course, he had been to the park before on occasion but did not really consider himself a park person; nevertheless, he found Lefevre captivating and, as he would find later, the experience would be very enlightening. Arm in arm they moved from the building in anticipation of their special day.

The rear door of the print shop opened to a long alley between two buildings of four stories and the alley being lengthy, about four hundred yards to a side street where he could see occasional pedestrian traffic. The alley had no obstacles, no dumpsters, nor garbage cans and litter. As she apparently sensed his thoughts she said, "This alley is part of our domain so we keep it cleaned up." Then as they commenced to walk the alley, she instructed him, "Let's walk in the middle of the alley. Since the city has been deteriorating and, as a result of pollution, the mortar that holds the bricks or stone together in the buildings has been breaking down and subsequently, sometimes bricks come loose and fall and even entire mason walls have been known to come down. So it's safer in the middle but keep looking upward."

The alley protected the two from the wind of an easterner but once they reached the street and turned to the right, they were met by a stiff chilling breeze carrying a briny odor. The street was littered with debris of every possible description and Luftus had to reach down to remove a wind-blown piece of newspaper from where it had plastered itself on his thigh. He had never been on the street before—it had always been considered too dangerous—always viewing it from atop a building but now, actually on the street it seemed worse than he had imagined. There were few people there, and, if he were to venture a guess, they were the homeless, drunks and drug dealers. None of them looked particularly threatening but still, he asked if it was dangerous to walk the streets by themselves to which she casually replied, "I have my whistle; if there was a threat, I'd whistle for help. Do you remember those Hispanic guys standing around in the foyer the day you started? Well, they are our protection, they are called karatecas. They are very good. Everyone in our society has a job, or at least contributes, and that is what they do. They are our bodyguards and they have such a reputation that even the most dangerous street-zombies stay away from us. The street people are dangerous, of course, but they give us our space. At first when you go out it's scary. They have open sores, smell terrible, babble incessantly, many of them are psychotic and they can be very aggressive. On the other hand, they are not organized as the government thinks—they are simply people trying in their way to survive. Unfortunately most of them are so demented that they cannot make it so they just roam the streets looking for any opportunity."

He was beginning to feel better about this adventure and observed her as one who knew exactly what she was doing. The two walked down the street that was nameless, only because the street name sign had been run over and carried off long ago. At a corner a few straggled souls waited for the bus to Central Park. There the two stood starkly exposed to the elements among a group of individuals whom he could not imagine as more disgusting. Yet his companion seemed quite comfortable in their presence. She was one of those individuals who found joy in everything and she talked so easily with those waiting on the corner—small unimportant banter—but the tone and easy sensitivity in her voice showed her natural empathy.

Finally, the bus turned a far corner with group's spontaneous, "There it is." Obviously well-worn brakes screeched through a long slowing process, the driver bumping the tires against the curb to help stop the vehicle. The door's compressed-air system seemed to fail at first and then burst open with a great gush and the giddy group caught up in anticipation of a day, mounted the vehicle. Luftus and his escort were politely the last to board. As she passed to the passenger aisle, she gently brushed the driver's wrist with her fingertips. He smiled in acknowledgment.

"Don't we have to pay?" Luftus asked once they were seated.

She answered, "We don't use money in the underground, at least not very much."

"But how does the bus pay for itself?"

"The bus driver gets his necessities from the underground. He gets food, shelter and clothing. The bus was abandoned as too old and we simply took possession of it and fixed it up. We have mechanics and maintenance people who keep it running. It is run on wood alcohol which is produced upstate and we reimburse the farmers by supplying them with farm laborers."

His immediate thought was that it was a precarious system.

"But there is something more important than just the trade-offs for service," she continued, "and that is what we discovered when left to our own resources after the economic collapse, and that is the essence of any society is the work itself and not material reward. Does not the soul mean more than food and the body than clothing? We have found that giving to others is such a deep spiritual reward—that is something that was lost in our society. But to experience that spiritual reward we must have love among us and subsequently happy are those conscious of their spiritual need and once we acknowledge that we must always act in harmony with that knowledge we will understand that happiness comes from giving and serving, not from selfishness."

"That sounds idealistic but I doubt that it would work over a period of time," he countered.

The bus bumped along a degraded street, dodging potholes as Lefevre stared into the remains of a once-proud city. "You see, we have come to believe—I use the phrase 'come to believe' because it implies that we learned this through empirical experience—that this gentle spiritual quality is the nature of the human species and can be achieved through self-analysis and self-knowledge. The other side of human behavior is the learned evil that leads to egoism, materialism and assault upon other cultures or beliefs and even their personal relationships within their own culture is at odds with what we feel is the natural love for one's fellow man."

He said, "But there are bad people out there and you just have to be able to fight them off to protect yourself."

"We don't believe that," she said. "Peace is a commitment that you have to adhere to. It's simple, if you abhor war, then you don't create armies. If you understand our society's inculcations of gentleness and non-resistance in the literal sense you identify with peace and strongly condemn war for its bloodshed. Likewise, if you abhor adultery, you refuse to dwell on improper yearnings and tear them out of your mind, then you will overcome the potential problem of immoral behavior."

"But you can't live on love, I mean you give and feel rewarded but how do you feed yourselves, how do you get money?" he asked.

"A long time ago someone said that money handlers are the source of all evil and even in my lifetime I have experienced that. There are money lenders who have good intentions but when the economic situation requires them to demand exorbitant profit and they resort to devious methods to make that profit, the good intentions are long forgotten. Our system is a barter system and it was not just thought up by someone who said, 'Let's try a barter system.' You must remember that the underground culture started when we were all cast into the economic wilderness without any assets or hope and the tendency was to resort to violence. But instead we began to work—any work, maybe just to keep one's mind busy. And, I think it was the women who led the way. One just said one day, 'I can't live in this filth' and she began to scrub a wall. Then we all started working—at something, anything. Pretty soon we started trading services and then we found that food was available for the services we could provide and then a system of barter and exchange came out of it and the important thing we learned was that a spiritualism transcended and we realized our love and commitment to one another and we would not hesitate to surrender our soul in behalf of our comrades. Then when we all realized this we condemned government and we had our identification microchips removed surgically—I think that the government body counters wonder why so many people are at the bottom of a sewer."

"But don't you think that an economy benefits from the profit and organization of business?" he asked.

She responded, "Every politician and every administration that we have ever had has orated that social and economic problems can be overcome by economic expansion—they always say that. But it never does. A small town brings in a box company to relieve unemployment and stimulate the economy and they end up with more unemployment than ever, more people, housing problems, more pollution, more congestion and then they say we need more business. Do they actually think that economic expansion is limitless? The way we live supplies only our needs, not our material desires, and we don't impose on others and particularly the environment—we have given up so much of our natural world."

"Aren't afraid you will be victimized by cunning people taking advantage of your system?" he offered.

"That's one of the redeeming things about the underground. That is you develop this ability to communicate which is awesome and, in interacting with people you come to know about them, their feelings, their intentions and if their purpose is nefarious you will know in plenty of time. You see, the truth is in their eyes, the eyes show their soul and we know them and if they persist in untruthfulness, they will be ostracized."

He thought about what she had said and then took a pause to look around him. He recognized the bus as a Ford Motor Van, perhaps twenty years old, which was about the time they were first made. It could carry about thirty passengers and was now about two-thirds full. He noticed that rust spots had been sanded and primed and that the frame of more than two seats had been repaired by welding. For a moment, he listened to the engine. He thought he heard an occasional miss and he noticed that when the driver backed off the accelerator, there would be backfire. Then he took note of the other passengers. A scruffy lot, their clothing looked as if taken from a YMCA lost and found or been retrieved from a Salvation Army grab bag. Nevertheless, they were happy and garrulous, so caught up in the festivity of a simple trip to the park that he began to wonder if he had not missed something.

Sooner than he expected, the bus ground to a halt at the edge of the expansive but dried brown lawn of Central Park. Passengers began to file out in order but she hesitated to talk to a person who appeared to be retarded. He continued off the bus then walked a few paces to his own claim of space away from what he considered to be rabble where he turned to face the bus to wait for her.

Presently, she was at the door and with a spring in her step, bounced to the ground, missing one step altogether. It was the first time that he was able to look at her objectively. He saw a captivating woman with an exquisite smile and encompassing warmth. He saw black hair hanging in a tight cluster from an off-white Grosgrain trim straw hat with blue ribbon trim, extending over her should to below her neck, a White Stag ski jacket, cropped pea-green pants and sheep-lined after-ski ankle boots. Not exactly stylish but eye-catching.

She caught up to him and they walked along in silence for a while and then she said, "What is so special about this place is the sense of space. I think that Americans have always known space, the early frontier and all that and it is a need we have—I know that I have to get out at least once a week."

Suddenly, before he could reply, she bent over to look at something on the sidewalk. There had been a hard driving rain for a few minutes the night before and she found a huge night crawler struggling on the bare, almost dry, sidewalk. She picked it up and held it up for him to see, a vibrant healthy night crawler wriggling in rejection to the warmth of her hand. Then as she opened her palm, it stretched out and began to move to somewhere else—anywhere else. She said, "Isn't he beautiful—one of nature's gorgeous creatures." She carried the worm to a nearby tree where grass had not been mowed and had grown high. There she deposited him with gentleness and wiped her fingers with a tissue.

"I hope that the rise of the seas will not kill all these creatures with salt water—city flooding is getting more common," she said wistfully.

This was not of his world, he had never experienced what he was now exposed to and he did not know to respond, so he remained silent. She seemed to understand.

They walked without talking for several minutes and then in observing a couple of shady-looking young men he mentioned that he had heard that the park could be a dangerous place—that there were gangs roving about. She nodded and said, "It can be dangerous but as long as one leaves the park before it is dark there should be no problem. After dark, they come out in great numbers—we call them park rangers. They are young people, dopers mainly and when they come out they build camp fires and they dance and sing and just party. But what is of concern are those hanging out on the fringes of the group—blank-faced young men and you don't know what they are thinking. And then late at night the party gets rough and that's when they go looking for trouble. Even the Karatecas that patrol the park during the day won't go there at night."

"Have any of them come to you people for help—like when they hit bottom and get desperate?" he asked.

"Oh, yes, we have taken care of a few. We must spiritually forgive them and give them our assistance—you know, kind of a symbolic washing of the feet."

"Washing of the feet?" he queried. "What does that mean?"

"It's like paying homage to a brother. Washing of the feet shows humility, that you are not above tending to your fellow man and see him as an equal."

"How do they respond? Usually when druggies hit bottom and you offer them help they will go along until they are able to leave and then it's goodbye."

She thought about what she had said and then added, "Yeah, that usually happens; in fact, I don't think we have ever rehabilitated one, but maybe they just were not ready. Anyway our door is always open to them. Besides, because of that they know about us and hold no rancor toward us—we just stay out of their territory at night. Some of them had good jobs once but lost them in the crash. That isolated them. Like anyone else they need connection with others to have strength. Their peers have all shut down spiritually so there is no connection. But if they can forge a connection with us there they are welcome and can be saved."

He could not contain his curiosity about her any longer and asked, "You said that your husband died as a result of the economic crash—how is that so?"

She grasped his arm and steered him toward a path through some semi-deciduous trees. After a few minutes of silence and when he thought that she was going to totally ignore his question, she said, "He committed suicide. He was a corporate lawyer and had prestige and made good money. Now I have to admit that he was a bit arrogant. But his identity was his job and when the corporation merged and he was cut loose, he lost his sense of identity and when he found out there were no jobs available to him, he was devastated. He just couldn't handle it."

"So, what did you do?" he asked.

"Well, naturally I thought that it was the end of the world. But I had two kids still at home and I had to provide for them so when I found the underground community, I had food and shelter and work. They brought me in as a coordinator. That sounds pretty fancy-shmancy, but it is just about scheduling everything and then making sure everyone carries through on their assignments. Everyone is cooperative and that makes it easy, but then I had to pick up the slack—like washing dishes, doing laundry, babysitting, stuff like that when there is a time conflict or someone is late."

"So, how did you adjust?"

"Actually, quite well. You know, when I was married we were terribly in debt and most of it was the result of ostentatious spending. I took a job at Chinamart to help out but the hard part was worrying about paying off credit cards and bank loans—I don't think I ever got a night's sleep worrying about it."

"And you find your life now more satisfactory?" he asked.

She had her answer thought out in advance. "You have to look at the whole picture," she said. "At first, life in the underground was scary; I knew no one, the work was hard, we didn't know if it would work, yet we had no alternative. But then because your work has meaning—survival—a spirituality imbues your mind and the whole thing ties together, love of each other, work with a purpose, the commonality of us all, the communal effort and the sense of achievement when we feel successful and there is progress. Happy are those conscious of their spiritual need."

"But it was such a far different situation from your married life. I would think that it would be overwhelming and then living in an abandoned apartment with the windows blown out, graffiti on the walls and filth on the floors."

She answered, "We pick up our torture stake and face the world's harshest conditions and that is because we no longer live for ourselves but live in unity and love and what we burden is what we accept in exchange for our soul. You know, in the past three decades, people found that they had nothing to follow, no exemplar, no standards of behavior, nothing to believe in. I remember when religion became politicized and people began dropping out because they were asked to respond emotionally to political imposition but not spiritually to matters of the soul—the churches failed them. Young people, desperate for direction and stability, found it in computers which they believed were rooted in electronic truth and could be relied upon. But then came rumors that the government was revising much data, even rewriting historical records or scientific findings while at the same time limiting user input.

"We believe in a fourth dimension which is the profound thought necessary to understand the supernal and to entice deep communication. But the government has used the concept of a fourth dimension to promote themselves and they have done it through control of the computers as they revise data to prove their cause. They have even appealed to extremism in proclaiming that their belief system will resurrect those who have died and suffered in the past. That was a devastating blow to people who had no other belief system and were lost."

"So why would they find salvation in your spirituality?" he asked.

"I think because it is a real experience. You mentioned the abandoned apartments that street people moved into and what bad shape they were in. Well, I experienced that and the simple act of cleaning and decorating anew turns you on to the sacredness one finds in real work, work that has purpose and is for the common good. In previous days, money was made by manipulating numbers and wasn't actually earned and because people were so far removed from any real work and were dependent on a mindless system, they lost focus on matters of personal belief. They had the freedom to do that but what they lost was an imperative to behave and believe in an ethereal way. Their minds were vacant and without direction."

They walked in silence for a few minutes and then she said, "Our system is beginning to grow and expand. You may not appreciate all the work it took to get this far. All those three- and four-story buildings you see around our neighborhood have small farming tracts and greenhouses on their roofs. It took a lot of labor to pack dirt and supplies up there. And when they harvest, some women work all night canning. But surprisingly, we now actually have a surplus of food and that is quite comforting. In addition, there is more leisure time and many are beginning to start small business ventures. And then, there is our food source upstate—most of it is grown by horse-farmers. They use no modern methods, horses are used for plowing and other things, they are easy to maintain, they reproduce and need only about an acre a year to strive. The farmers operate very cheaply and produce more than corporate farms per acre and when they supply us with food all they ask is that in the future we produce a few simple things they need and that, we are beginning to do. So the system is growing, the future looks bright—why, we even have a doctor, a man of great ideals who barters his services only because he is a believer."

She paused to look at a rare spectacle, an itinerant bird of unfamiliar species flitting about a leafless tree. "Poor thing," she murmured. "It's the first bird I have seen in weeks." They had been walking for over two hours, in a large arc and in noting the time said, "We have got to start back, the bus will be there for us in about thirty minutes. But he won't leave until he knows that everyone he brought is on board."

With a bemused smile she took his hand and began swinging it between them. She felt a little guilty that she had been lecturing him. But, of course, that is what she meant to do.

He finally broke a look of deep thought and asked her, "Don't you have a leader, someone who inspires you, someone of deep faith who believes as you do to lead you?"

"No, at least, not now," she answered. "But there will be someone," she added. "He will come and we will know him and he will know us," she said softly, "and he will bring restoration of all things necessary to life."

# Seven

John Maynard Stacy was born to a socially prominent family and grew up on an elm-tree-lined street in Western Springs, Illinois, a suburb of Chicago, where he lived in an old Dutch Colonial home built by his grandfather in 1910. He was raised with all the social and material advantages that wealth could bestow; but, to his credit, he was multi-talented, had a good work ethic, and had what women praised as "devastating good looks." Many of his aunts, uncles and cousins lived within a few blocks radius and thus, as the family was close-knit, he was exposed to a nourishing family environment that gave him ample opportunity for emotional growth. Just across the street from the Stacy residence was a city lot that had been put into lawn and became the hub of youth activities in the neighborhood. The congregate social interaction of family school and play activity forged in Stacy a very outgoing young man who was a joy to be with and obviously possessed leadership capabilities. With all the trappings of success, he became every mother's favorite son.

Having been a participant in Little League, Boy Scouts, Pop Warner football, high school sports, church activities and charity groups, he developed an affinity for any type of social organization. As a benefactor of public schools, a private academy and private tutoring, he came to appreciate educational pursuit and as he was intellectually gifted, he began to demonstrate ability as an orator as early as middle school. At one point during high school, a coach spoke of him as having the ability to become a professional athlete in two sports although one might suspect that such exhortation was merely an attempt to inspire lofty performance; nevertheless, his interest in sports waned rather early as he increasingly turned to law and politics, which became a consuming passion to him. He attended the University of Illinois, graduating with honors in 2002 and then matriculated to the University of California's Boult Law School, again graduating with honors. Upon completion of his studies, he was immediately hired, before he passed the bar, as a field attorney for the California Rural Legal Assistance, an eye-opening experience for a young man having grown up in an upper-class Midwestern community.

As a field attorney, his first assignment was to defend a young single mother of two, who was to be taken off state welfare if the allegation that she was living with a man not the father of her children could be proven. The woman resided in Meridian, a small community of a few hundred in California's Central Valley, and Stacy, upon investigating the case, could find not one witness who supported the state's contention that she was cohabitating in violation of the state statute. He thought it would be an easy case to win, but how wrong he was. The state had no evidence other than the fact that a male friend of the welfare recipient parked his pickup truck in front of the woman's apartment every night. Stacy easily contended that the man lived in an apartment directly across the street from the woman and he asked pointedly, "Where else would he park his truck?" To his shock and amazement, the jury, a conglomeration of soap-opera addicts who could not wait for the trial to end so that they could get back to their preferred activity, found the defendant guilty, which undoubtedly satisfied their personal prejudice toward welfare cheats who drove their Cadillac to the supermarket adorned in fur. Stacy was unable to reconcile the loss but more importantly, he was personally chagrined as to how the defendant and her children, now cut off from any source of income, would survive.

After two years as a rural attorney and having passed the state bar examination, Stacy was hired as a prosecuting attorney by the City of San Francisco where he established a reputation as a fair-minded but tough representative of the criminal justice system and where he practiced for eight years. If nothing else, what Stacy drew from his first ten years of employment as an attorney was an appreciation for the diversity and the problematic segments of American society. Coming into the field of law from a privileged background, he had ascribed to the traditional upper-class consensus that the poor and down-trodden received their fate because of lack of talent and incentive. But then he saw too many things that undercut this belief of deserved subordination. He saw much unfairness that made justification of rigorously held preconceptions of guilt; he saw a complexity in cases that confused even the most astute jurist who then sought a simplified solution; he saw a justice system so overwhelmed by the volume of cases that a quick fix would become commonplace; and he witnessed a creeping and insidious ideology that threatened fairness and justice. He wanted desperately to change all that.

From the beginning, Stacy had a deep respect for the Republican Party and what it stood for. In his view of the political spectrum, he recognized an obligation of the party to assist the hungry, the elderly, to combat racism and inequality, to improve education and to provide adequate health care for everyone; but, he saw the role of the Democratic Party which claimed to be champion of those issues as more likely to promote blind proposals that gave no thought to unintended consequences while it was the purpose of the Republican Party to guide and shape those processes with the specific intention of maintaining the integrity and values of America. But Stacy knew almost from the beginning that he would never be able to do so as an elected leader. He was a realist and he knew from observation that he would never he a viable candidate for an important office for, despite an optimistic upbringing and as an individual with almost unlimited assets, Stacy had one flaw that he recognized as the debitum naturae of a political career and that was that he was physically short. Too many times he watched as political candidates of angular stature easily overcame those of abbreviated size, their intellectual capacities strained but unimportant to their constituents. Stacy did not intend to face an under-educated Hollywood actor posturing in such a manner as to make much of his height and masculine presence while betraying the very purpose of intellectual discourse.

As of Stacy's political realization of his limitation, he sought to fashion for himself a positive role within the party in which he could promote his agenda and strengthen and guide the party and that was as a president-maker. In that dream, Stacy identified with James Madison, the nation's first president-maker and an ardent supporter of Thomas Jefferson. Madison, like Stacy, was short and, like Stacy, recognized that it would unjustly limit his political career. Unfortunately, Madison had the additional flaw that he did not meet strangers easily; in fact, he was described as "mute, cold and repulsive" in such situations, which prompted Washington Irving's contempt of him as a "withered little applejohn."

A concern for the integrity of the party had initially drawn Stacy into activism after having witnessed a deterioration of a party that was capitulating leadership to the corporations at the expense of the common good. That was augmented by an insipient anti-intellectualism, a deep concern for Stacy. He had always believed that the roots of Republicanism were from Protestantism, where the arena for political debate was shaped by Puritan thinkers. The Massachusetts Bay had great faith in the value of learning and the intellect and Stacy, as a youth, had memorized several lines from Moses Coit Tyler which he repeated to himself almost daily thereafter: "In its inception New England was not an agricultural center, nor a manufacturing community, nor a trading community: it was a thinking community; an arena and a mart for ideas; its characteristic organ being not the hand, nor the heart, nor the pocket, but the brain…" The short phrase, "a mart for ideas," impressed Stacy as a youth and stayed with him and that became what he believed that the Republican Party could become again—a marketplace for ideas essential to dealing with the wrenching problems of the day and like the Puritan Church of the 1800s, he felt that all members of the church could become, and should be, intellectuals by following in the footsteps of men like Jonathon Edwards, the revivalist of the Great Awakening who brought together the piety and intellectualism of New England with the creativity and passion of modern times; and, that is exactly what Stacy would ask of the party, to bring an intellectual revival to rebuild the heart and soul of the Republican Party.

In 2015, at the age of thirty-five, Stacy was elected chairman of the Cook County, Illinois, Republican Party, a highly sought after post that was well-contested but won by Stacy due his charisma and personal popularity that made him acceptable to all diverse segments of the party. As chair, he wasted no time in implementing a plan designed to improve the Republican image and performance at a time when lesser men would have played a sedentary role at the beginning of their term. His initial plan had been well thought out in advance and included individual membership participation in interactive groups, diversified economic and business seminars, direct involvement on school boards, PTA projects, volunteer tutoring, public forums, being available for conferences with "everyday people," studying new models of political participation for policy development and methods of analysis and to work with urban renewal and police agencies.

The plan appeared overly ambitious and received outraged responses from some of the party elite not used to being active and thereby alluding to the concept as naïve and bureaucratic, and that sentiment included those who believed that the plan by itself was subterfuge designed to divide the party. But Stacy's strong character, apparent good intentions and good will toward all party members convinced a majority to support his strategy.

Within just a few months, party meetings began to exhibit a new spirit and energy. Meetings were more confrontational but at the same time, more constructive. Ideas came forth with a new enthusiasm for creativity, something long absent in the immediate past and with it topics on the agenda for discussion were more diverse and more pertinent to the problems of the day. With these changes came an uncharacteristic tendency for members to look within themselves to understand previously unexamined strengths and weaknesses and this new attitude began to flow outward to party faithful. A true revolution was in the making.

There were those who thought that Stacy was moving too fast and that the well-entrenched right wing would resist passionately. But even the anti-intellectual segment of the party was caught off guard by the enthusiasm of the faithful Stacy followers responding to the call, and although that call for a new intellectualism had a limited appeal, it was tinged with an emotional zeal that had a galvanizing effect upon the party. Furthermore, Stacy's attempt at amelioration brought national acclaim elevating his name into the spotlight as an important news-maker. *Newsweek* and *Time* wrote glowingly of his political and moral leadership while the latter named him Man of the Year. As a result, the party's media image improved dramatically as newspaper captions identified him as a "new rising star," and a "genius political power broker."

In the summer of 2017, Stacy was elected chairman of the National Central Committee of the Republican Party and, as one newspaper opined, "While he is at the top of his game." Actually, it had been a tenuous vote and it was as if the party had held its collective breath in an instant before there were second thoughts or time to carry out political espionage. But the election had been so swift there had been little time for opposition, but unfortunately, the eventual backlash, initially in the form of e-mails and blog protestations, was at first muted but lying in wait and Stacy's victory was only to be a brief moment of militant success.

In September, a triumphant Stacy gave his acceptance speech in Washington, D.C., before a Republican Convention in a speech lauded by syndicated columnists and intellectuals who viewed it as an almost miraculous turnabout from the fatuous and temporal political address to which they had become so used to during the previous decade. They had so come to expect the protracted and predictable style typical of the times that they were shocked into rapt attention by the substance of the speech and awed by its candor.

Stacy stood before his audience, strong and confident, a distinguished figure with a powerful delivery and a profound message. He immediately launched into a laundry list of failures of both political parties and, for their part, the Republicans had to accept their share of the blame: high unemployment, preemptive wars, high crime rate, homelessness had become an overwhelming problem, forty percent of the population was starving or undernourished while twenty percent were obese, many public schools had closed due to lack of funding, there was violence and chaos in the streets, the national debt was untenable, foreign countries owned more of America than did our own citizens, ninety percent of individuals going outside needed inhalers in order to breathe, entire species of animals were facing extinction, America's farmers were unable to feed our population, the nation's infrastructure had broken down and oil was $200 a barrel, which brought economic havoc and had cast American into a post-industrial stone age.

In the hush after he had completed his indictment, a voice could be heard to bellow, "Traitor."

Stacy, a master of patience, paused and answered, "No, I am not a traitor, sir. I believe in my party and I believe in America. But these things have to be said. We have been the party in power and these issues must be addressed. For too long we have relied upon denial and trivialization of our problems through jingoistic thinking, blind dogmatism, material greed, censorship, blatant propaganda, a pandering media and ignorance, and it is simply cataclysmic to democracy. For us to reclaim our party, we must subject ourselves both individually and as an organization to critical self-analysis and through that process, come to understand our failings and once we do that we can rebuild a conservative party that can justify its existence in this great country. Let me point out that a conservative is a subtle synthesis of reverence, traditionalism, distaste for the material, high morality, moderation, peacefulness and the intellectual spirit and, most importantly, a conservative has a feeling of deep respect tinged with awe for authority, history, the law, legal institutions and traditional values."

Stacy went on to say that a belief system was not enough—only empirical evidence could prove success or failure and, in that regard, "it appears that we have been a colossal failure and the reason is obvious—we have strayed from traditional principles." He then outlined the principles abandoned by the party as the distrust of big government gave way to the creation of super agencies, fiscal responsibility gave way to frivolous spending, avoidance of foreign entanglements was ignored for nation-building and a commitment to democracy became a commitment to one-party rule, theocracy and a unicameral congress.

"It must be essential," Stacy continued, "that the conservative be a man on a mission, that he demand the most of himself, that he pledge to defend his community, protect the rights of individuals, raise the level of public discourse and defy arbitrary power."

Then without trepidation, Stacy took on the factious hallmark of the contemporary Republicans, as he pointed out the governmental objective of serving the people had become lost in subservience to the demands of corporations and if corporate profit purveyors continued to dominate our political life, the democratic infrastructure would break down.

"The task is difficult," he said, ending his remarks, "it will be a massive undertaking and it must be within each of us to recommit to conservative principles with the dedication to the common good. Allow me to end with a quote from Ralph Waldo Emerson in which he said, 'It is one of the most beautiful compensations in life that no man can sincerely help another without helping himself.'"

The speech took forty-five minutes and upon conclusion the applause was polite but restrained with an occasion extemporaneous burst of enthusiasm.

On the Sunday morning following Stacy's acceptance speech, an itinerant preacher by the name of Lester Scroggins gave an historic first sermon before the congregation of a small South Carolina rural Baptist church. Scroggins, a small man, thin and gawky with a perpetual look of surprise on his face, seemed to have been worn haggard by nervousness and spoke in a high-pitched penetrating voice that would cause crows to put to wing.

He claimed to be a self-made man. Always an outsider, he knew that he would have to lift himself up by his own resources. He was virtually friendless in high school. He excelled at nothing and did not like to study. At one time he found enough courage to ask a gorgeous classmate for a date but she laughed at him. She was not a rude or mean-spirited person; simply, his request had caught her by surprise, his approach was so awkward and appearance so unusual that she was genuinely amused and her laughter was sincere, a point not lost on Scoggins, who withdrew in humiliation. The rejection became a mark that he never forgot nor was he to forgive her or any other woman for her indiscretion. The event walled into an already angry disposition and the motivation that moved him to some kind of success in life. It was shortly after the ultimate rejection that Scroggins quit school and became a common laborer. While so employed, he took a correspondence course in the ministry and upon receiving a certificate of completion he could preach in the ministry— at least, that is what his certificate indicated.

His first sermon, offered for no fee, was instantly appealing to a fundamentalist congregation as Scroggins instinctually touched the emotional buttons that brought forth evangelistic passion. His opening statement became a standard one-liner for Scroggins as he addressed the crowd and said, "Other than the Bible, I haven't read any book since high school and damn few before then." He then launched into an attack upon established religions and elite academics and he spoke of the common preacher with a calling and a message to be delivered from God and Scroggins came to know that he had connected with this flock as he knew them to be simple uneducated folk. He reiterated that "we need no other books" and the important thing is not how one interprets the Bible but having a personal relationship with God and "the proper emotion, inner conviction and relationship to God makes us the true believers."

For Scoggins, the work of conversion of laymen without orthodox study could lead to a correct interpretation of the word of God and this would call for a popular crusader, not a learned theologian who would be too caught up in theological dissertations to see the light of truth shining through. In attacking the elitist of the establishment, Scroggins was at first cautious but even in that first sermon he sensed a seething emotional response rise from within the flock and he intensified the attack. "What can be more distressing," he asked, "than the arrogance of the learned elite and their pompous posturing as their idealism and erudition interferes with our daily lives and our ability to communicate with God directly."

The sermon was short but when it was over, the congregation was on their feet cheering. Scroggins had struck a nerve. By the following week the word had gotten out Scroggins was the new start of the evangelical movement. By the following week there was a schedule of appearances for Scroggins at two hundred Sunday morning sermons and Wednesday night meetings, scheduled over several months. These appearances by Scroggins would be financed by the action committee of the Evangelical Party of America.

The message subsequently carried to the various congregations was nothing new; it had been a standard representation and had been part of the weekly fodder in many churches in the South for decades. But what made Scroggins' presentation so impressive to the evangelists was the physical dynamics of the speech itself—the raw energy, his high-pitched piercing voice, the breathtaking emotion of the words and, above all, his incredible belief in his mission. One lifelong churchgoer, himself a minister, reported that Scroggins gave him "goose bumps" and "touched my soul."

Scroggins became famous instantly, being in demand all over the South, and his successes were drawing the attention, if not serious concern, of many church leaders. Scroggins represented an area that many of them had thought was behind them and would not come before them again. Two months after his initial sermon, Scroggins appeared on the televised show *The Protestant*

*Hour* with a panel of six ministers from various Protestant churches. He listened patiently while the panel indirectly and then directly challenged his emotional oratory from the pulpit and deplored his attack upon an educated ministry, most culture and all science.

When he was able to reply, Scroggins; response was vintage Dwight L. Moody, evangelist from the nineteenth century. Speaking in slow, measured rhythm with strong tone, he said, "Aside from the Bible I read almost nothing. I have one rule about books. I do not read any book unless it helps me understand THE book. Novels? They are flashy...I have no taste for them, no desire to read them: but if I did I would not do it. The theater? You say that it is part of one's education to see good plays. Let that education go to the four winds. Culture? It is all right in its place, but to speak of it before a man is born of God is the height of madness. Learning? An encumbrance to a man of spirit: I would rather have zeal without knowledge; and there is a great deal of knowledge without zeal. Science? It has become a threat to religion rather than a means for the discovery and glorification of God. It is a great deal easier to believe that man was made after the image of God than to believe, as some young men and women are being taught, that he is the offspring of a monkey."

It was lost on the panel that the speech had been lifted from Moody, the famed evangelical revival preacher, and that without the quote, Scroggins, left to his own intellect, might have floundered badly. But he had reasoned that anything is fair in the pursuit of righteousness and now he had pulled off a coup. His explanation was well received by followers and he knew what those on the panel did not know and that is that populism is an incredibly powerful force and to resist it is futile.

# Eight

The American symbol of the second decade was the personal respirator, a modern version of the inhaler. At the beginning of the decade, a few respirators were seen on the streets of big cities, usually worn by victims of emphysema or allergies. But by the late teens, eighty percent of the population used, or at least carried a respirator out of doors. The government encouraged the practice to avoid "irritation" which was blamed on "environmental factors."

But in reality, the use of respirators was a response due to the increasingly poor quality of air from industrial pollution in the cities and, to a lesser degree, the rural areas as well. By mid-decade, the quality of air was so poor that there was hardly enough oxygen in the air to provide an individual walking briskly with enough energy to maintain a rapid pace, and thus many runners and walkers carried inhalers, respirators or even oxygen bottles on their person. The atmosphere had undergone degradation to the point that one could detect a pungent smell upon inhaling, a development that came on so gradually that it went unnoticed until people began to just accept it passively as a natural condition.

The public took this occurrence sardonically, blaming it on nature, and jokes became rampant on the subject and there was an implication—started by the media—that one was to be considered a coward for complaining. Subsequently, consumer oxygen became one of the most successful industries of the time. Upper-class apartments and better businesses had commercial oxygen pumped into their edifices while the lower classes used artificial means to insulate their homes—mostly unsuccessfully—against the invasion of pollution. Unfortunately, much of what was being peddled as fresh air was merely recycled air.

The effect upon public health was catastrophic as pollution became the leading cause of lung cancer and lung disease and the leading cause of death in the United States. On high-alert days when there was government-approved but illegal "sky dumping," the atmosphere would be of such acidity that in the involuntary action of inhaling one would experience resistance from the natural defense mechanism of the body so that the individual would need to resort to forced breathing, a frightening experience that could be emotionally devastating and eventually bring about severe depression in the individual.

Americans attempted to take the aerial crisis in stride, casually portraying a can-do jocular attitude with feigned unconcern. Respirators became subject to graphic or floral design, many highly individualized which became a national fad encouraged by business and government alike. The basic design for respirators became mask-like to give a more face-fitting configuration and space for creative decoration.

This was not lost on purveyors of woman's fashion. They designed and displayed new individualized "rators" flouting the current high fashion of the day which became reminiscent of the provocative masks worn at gala balls during the Renaissance. Women began to wear rator-masks on the streets and, invariably wearing revealing clothing, showing only their cosmetically enhanced eyebrows and long multicolored eyelashes over rator-masks, adding an aura of mystery about them. It brought a new dimension to courting and sexual play. The most popular rator was Avante's Moon Glow, which offered the "innate luminosity of 18kt gold, the understated glimmer of matte finish and the subtle texture of hand hammering conspired to create crescents alight with moon glow." Other rators extremely popular, their name implying their features, were the Wish-Upon-the-Stars (featuring diamonds), Stormy Sky (includes a blue chalcedony "raindrop"), the Finger Full of Pearls, the Champagne, the Sapphire Spectrum and the Eternal Love.

Of course, humor and whimsy followed suit. Disney characters were popular and the Spiderman, the never-forgotten hero of yesteryear, became a rage. For men, Darth Vader inhalers were most in demand, complete with exaggerated sound of breathing. A fashion accessory worn by nearly all women was the rator compact, usually worn on the belt or pinned to that area and it was always quite chic. The Moon Glow compact, the most prestigious, was all in black except for the famous logo of a full moon in inlaid pearl.

But there was also a deeper and more sinister effect of the inhalers upon the public. With the other miseries befalling the country, Americans knew instinctively whether they were willing to admit it or not, that living for each day with no thought of tomorrow would assure that each tomorrow would certainly be worse. Environmental defilement had become so profound that even the most dedicated environmental organizations had gone out of business or had become advisory services, giving up on activism. A few of the more abstruse individuals refused to give up the fight for environment protection and had become militant. They had become so dedicated to their cause that there was no option for them and unfortunately resorted to violence. Except for a few furtive individuals, the military made short work of them as the high-tech police methods were beyond anything that they could deal with. The "database for radical dissidents" could accurately single out those with a philosophical disposition for environmental activism whether they had been active or merely had the sympathy for environmentalism—it did not matter. Thus, once identified, lack of illegal act or suspicion of illegal act notwithstanding, the individual would face life in incarceration per the American Security Act of 2012.

The symbolism of the respirator was at the forefront of a media commenting on the culture of that era, not as if it were the most pressing problem facing America, but because it was the one issue Americans could confront with a show of defiance, an ostentatious challenge to the forces of evil, an overcompensation for the denigrated feeling of powerlessness. To laugh in the face of a perilous threat was both denial and false bravado, an American characteristic derived from the adventurism of the Mid-east wars.

A crisis of more serious proportion had been brewing for some fifty years and was about to erupt—the calamitous and deliberate neglect of the nation's infrastructure created by an economic blind spot in the bureaucracy. At the century mark, a scientific survey of the infrastructure on which the economic system was so dependent determined that in order that the nation's business be able to maintain itself at only an acceptable level—not considering future population growth intrusion—the structural system would require repair and restoration in the amount of 1.4 trillion dollars. If they had acted at that time, it would have been cheap at that price. But they did not. The recommendation was ignored without debate as tax breaks, security measures, military outlays and a poor economy decimated the federal budget. There were modest attempts at the state level toward rebuilding the decaying system but floundering state budgets hindered those efforts.

America was awakened from its indifference on April 1, 2017, when a 5.1 earthquake shook the San Francisco area at 9:32 AM. The quake was centered near Hayward and was not particularly thought to be serious at first, with little reported damage. But in the next hour, water taps would not flow and flushed toilets would not fill. The Hetch-Hetchy Water System had collapsed and within the next twenty-four hours, eighty-seven percent of the population of the San Francisco Bay area were without water.

The antiquated Hetch-Hetchy Project extended 167 miles from Yosemite to San Francisco's North Beach, was eighty-five years old and never been properly maintained. It included twenty-one reservoirs, twenty-five water tanks, two treatment plants, twenty-three pump stations, forty miles of tunnels and 1,470 miles of mains. The entire system, primitive and rotting, had been predicted to be unserviceable some twenty years before.

When the quake was first felt there seemed to be minimal damage thanks in large part to a city initiative in 2003 and the ensuing reclamation project that prevented a catastrophic collapse. Nevertheless reports filtered in indicating rupture and tunnel collapses occurred so evenly throughout the aqueduct that it produced the same effect as a massive failure of the system and 2.4 million people were without water. The resulting flood in rural areas drew little attention from a nation already weary of constant news reports around the globe of tsunamis, earthquakes, train wrecks, floods, droughts, warfare and terrorism.

First impression of San Franciscans was that the event was nothing more than a giant inconvenience. A substitute emergency water delivery system was begun and water was moved by pipe and rail from the Sacramento and American rivers. Then a week later, the Calaveras Dam suddenly ruptured, inundating the countryside with loss of life and substantial residential property damage. The Silicon Valley computer and electronic industries were devastated and a gloom descended on San Francisco.

The national reaction to the Hetch-Hetchy catastrophe was mixed. Some sensationalistic commentators and columnists gleefully implied that the arrogant attitude of San Franciscans dispossessed them toward indifference on such mundane things as the maintenance of public utilities. But such vivid explanation satisfied only those reluctant to deal with such costly issues or those emotional lions always seeking fault in others but never solution.

But as a result of the disaster, city managers and state officials nationwide became nervous and set out to survey their own facilities with full knowledge that benign neglect had been factored into their system as well. Fortunately, the Hetch-Hetchy system was unique and there was no water authority in any other state that was similar. But even with that, a high level of unconcern of public utilities, transit lines, rails, freeway systems, turnpikes, bridges, airports, schools, public buildings, and sewer systems had existed throughout the nation for an extended time and needed to be addressed.

It was not by coincidence that some 700 toxic dams nationwide were being eroded from within by toxins and that, as there was nowhere to dispose of the wastes, at least one dam a month collapsed under its load during a five-year period. Unlike dams holding non-toxic water which could be lowered to safe levels if structural weakness was detected, toxic dams had been maintained at maximum level for decades while awaiting a place to transfer toxins to be worked out. Already in the twentieth century, such methods as "sky disposal," and "underground burial" had been tried but found to be too damaging to the environment, even by an administration unsympathetic to environmental concerns.

As if by spooky coincidence, four toxic dams blew open within thirty days of the Hetch-Hetchy disaster although the events were obviously unrelated. The corporate media conveniently spaced the stories and placed them on back pages so as not to cause panic and the actual news accounts of the failures were not linked to specific causes or circumstances.

The most sensational dam failure occurred a full year after Hetch-Hetchy when an eighty-five-foot-high toxic dam at French Gulch, Nevada, used for mining wastes and filled with hydrogen sulfide and other residuum, split open a few minutes after midnight and drenched the town of 535 people. At the base of the dam lay a long arroyo, less than a mile long, that ran perpendicular to the retaining wall of the dam and pointed directly at the town like a loaded shotgun. On the night of the collapse, the dam released its chemical gunk which roared down the canyon at a high rate of speed, gaining momentum as it went, only spreading out and lowering its depth as it hit the town with an incredible roar. One hundred and twenty-five people died instantly in their sleep and a couple hundred more who were to suffer from burns and lung damage wished that they had as well.

The Gory Bucket Saloon, located on high ground in the center of town, was inundated, the slush rising to a little over ankle depth at floor level as grizzly old hard-rock miners rested their boots on bar rungs and continued to guzzle beer with the casual logic that they would have to wait until the flood was over before they could deal with the devastation.

Next to the Gory Bucket was a three-story house of prostitution, the House of the Rising Son. Both legally and socially accepted in the county, the Son was the economic and social center of French Gulch. As the only building over a story in height, residents flocked to the brothel at the onset of the flood as water raged through the first floor but spared the Spartan bedrooms on the second and third floors. The working girls of the Son blinked curiously as schoolteachers, housewives, a banker (whom they knew quite well) the elderly, a church cleric, schoolchildren, non-school children and businessmen, all in various stages of dress and undress, proceeded to the protection of those upper-story rooms of the commercial gymnastics center as water gurgled relentlessly below them. If the men of French Gulch knew all the working girls by their first names, a certain suggestion of personal intimacy, surely their wives and children would now have that same pleasure.

The French Gulch disaster did not receive much press from the corporate media as the news sources did not carry the story for days and then newspapers relegated the story to a back page as per usual. For most citizens, knowledge of the tragedy was so delayed that they knew nothing about it until an investigation by the State of Nevada convened, but by then readers with little information were unable to put the investigation into perspective. As for the town itself, the residents surviving the ordeal had no economic life to return to and simply moved away and within a year French Gulch was just another quaint Nevada ghost town, its aura giving arcane hints of the ghosts that haunted its soul.

The condition of the national infrastructure was little better. As the population had lived with a gradually deteriorating situation for many years, there was an anesthetized acceptance of the condition of the infrastructure, something that they simply "had to learn to live with." But to augment that indifference to reality, the government financed and encouraged both glitzy and lurid forms of entertainment and video games in order to lure the citizenry into a steadfast complacency.

Live with it they did. There was a concerted effort to put to use every old and worn structure in some manner and there was, as usual, an effort to accommodate businesses as there was a continued reluctance to give up on the old saw that the common good was served by economic expansion. The only issue of the public addressed by the government was the critical situation of public transportation. As for the infrastructure itself, safety precautions were imposed only in the most desperate cases as repairs and maintenance were severely limited by calumnious budget crises. In a last-gap attempt to maintain bridges, the structures were inspected, their conditions reported and weight restrictions for use were posted. Freeways had become hopelessly clogged even during the traditional times of light usage and no longer could the working person rely on a schedule that was dependent upon a viable freeway system. Freeway repair had become piecemeal, giving the once-proud expressways a look of patchwork desperation, the resulting effect being rough and bumpy travel forcing the reduction of speed and limiting heavy commercial usage. The cost to commerce was in the billions.

If the machinery of civilization was in disrepair, the population suffered accordingly. The elderly were in a disaster mode. Most were homeless and few, if any, could afford needed medication. Ten million were afflicted with Alzheimer's and received substandard care. There was only three people working for every individual retired or out of work, and social security, once the salvation of the working classes, had been expunged by the ragtag tinkering of politicians who convinced the public of their concern for the well-being of the system while their actions were disastrous. Nursing homes, unless they were very expensive and were designed for the ultra-rich, ceased to exist and were replaced by state institutions reminiscent of shoddy nineteenth-century mental institutions. Many families attempted to keep their aged in the family home, straining budgets and relationships. Still, seniors were dying at the highest rate in history, many after excruciating pain and suffering.

In one of the eeriest statistics of the day, a research report stated that fifty-two percent of all Americans suffer from some type of mental illness. Most of those individuals were marginally functional but few were hospitalized as a result of the high costs of treatment and the U.S. standards for what was considered normal behavior had been lowered drastically and predictably, bizarre behavior had become so commonplace that what had once been viewed as unorthodox had become the common norm. Simply put, if one were not a danger to himself or others—all other factors of behavior considered irrelevant—hospitalization or intervention was not deemed necessary.

During this time of our history, the unemployment rate was a staggering twenty-four percent; but even that was a statistical departure—the actual rate was much higher. The official figure may have been significantly higher. Frighteningly, many economists believed that the number of workers needed to run the country was only ten percent of the total work force and some administration officials were determined to achieve that figure. The attempt by politicians to meet that number was applauded as a triumph of automation and business-driven planning. But what of those unable to support themselves? The rough estimate was that half the unemployed population was not statistically counted although an increasing number was marginally employed in an underground economy. Homelessness was in the millions—six out of every hundred were without a roof over their heads. Who did these people include? The elderly, the emotionally troubled, the disabled, those too ill to work, the unemployable and the retarded. Still, the historical rhetoric of self-sufficiency and individual high aspiration persisted.

One may ask how the working members of America were surviving. Poorly would be the answer. Many employed were so mentally ill they should not have been working at all as they were victimized by extreme stress, excessive work hours, innumerable problems in their personal lives and stimulus overload. Had the minds of the workers been allowed to focus on mode-specific tasks and given ample time for recuperation, there could have been a healthy work force. But the constant demands of high-tech application required multi-tasking, a sensory plethora of dangerous consequences that brought dissociation and confusion. The resulting stress released chemical byproducts damaging to the portion of the brain responsible for problem-solving, reasoning and sophisticated thought processes essential to high-tech operation. There were no complains from workers however, so willing were they to comply to management demands made of them because of their awareness of cadres of eager young workers more than willing to give in to any demands of potential employers.

There had been no attempt by any organized political group, even the most liberal leaning, to overcome this abject assault on labor by corporate business. It would have been political suicide by any mainstream organization or media source that had once led in indoctrinating the country with this pernicious ideology to now take a noble stand on behalf of labor.

In addition to the social/economic woes that had befallen the country, the long-debated issue of global warming became heated after decades of being relegated to a non-issue by corporate propaganda and religious artifice. Whereas the issue in itself had low appeal to the masses, natural disasters and the slow, steady deterioration of the planet lifted it to prime concern. Scientific predictions had always been causative and seemingly related to personal bias; but, that began to change when scientists were clearly able to document evidence that global temperatures caused rainy seasons to be wetter than usual, dry seasons to be drier than usual, had brought a new ice age to Europe and that violent storm patterns caused irreparable damage severely impacting world food supplies.

As had been predicted for decades, the rising sea levels were beginning to lap at New York City and Tokyo while surging high tides and blasting storm fronts had wiped out ocean island communities and were invading the lowlands of Bangladesh and the Netherlands. The atoll of Tuvalu had long been abandoned and remains of those islands could no longer be seen and the Alaskan town of Kilileena had to be rebuilt at another locale at great expense to the taxpayer. The preference of the populace toward waterfront property at the beginning of the century drew large numbers to coastal communities and then when mother nature began to nibble away at those beautiful shores, the populace began to pull back and with the continued influx of those drawn by the dream of ocean views and seaside lifestyle, there was a compression of the multitudes with devastating consequences. In addition, floods had killed or rendered homeless millions of people while droughts virtually destroyed all life in large geographical areas, areas growing in size by the encroaching desertification.

In the American Middle-West, tornados literally came in packs and instead of the usual brief touchdown, they would continue to ravage an area for several days, destroying whole communities with such regularity that it became infeasible to rebuild and it became commonplace for many individuals, living among the debris of storm violence, to construct shacks and shanties out of the twisted remains and live a more primitive existence than those living in third-world countries.

With overpopulation and a scarcity of land, people moved relentlessly into economically productive areas, further impeding efforts toward environmental protection. Laws and law enforcement had become dim memory in national history, allowing for the growth of large disorderly masses of people without culture or direction, muddling about in hopeless confusion, its homeless conglomerations fermenting a cult of lawlessness and primitive survival.

In the second decade of the century, the population growth of the world began to slow and as the total world population approached nine billion, it was believed by many scientists that for the first time in known world history, the mortality rate exceeded the birth rate. However, as the population was in constant motion, a fluid quality confusing population trends, census-taking and the demography tracking became hopelessly confused. Many lauded the decrease in sheer numbers seemly to imply that mankind was finally coming to grips with its most serious dilemma. Others however, saw the decrease as proof that the earth could no longer sustain such large numbers and that the figures really represented an unnecessary and tragic loss of life resulting not from man's self-control but from the very environmental degradation that man allowed to prevail.

It was during those first two decades that the ocean levels rose six inches and scientists predicted that ocean levels would rise another foot and a half by the end of the century and then the inundation of New Orleans one summer morning brought home to a nation not inclined to pay attention to such matters, the seriousness of the threat to the world. The presidential administration snorted in response that the current sea level was zero as it had always been and would always be. Other than the flippant observation that "perhaps the mountains are shrinking," the administration had no explanation why the oceans appeared to be rising. Despite overwhelming evidence to the contrary, the government continued to ignore ecological degradation. And the disasters mounted.

If the problems facing America were not serious enough, a new economic crisis was brewing, a residual of the mechanism set up by globalization when the International Monetary Fund and the World Bank began to aggressively pressure the United States for not being ideologically committed to the new world order. The United States had always enthusiastically gone along with the concept of globalization, particularly when money flowing into the country from exploited third-world countries enhanced the national treasury committing its military and intelligence agencies to collection and enforcement of payment, but with the extended economic depression and mounting debt, America began to turn inward; although high-ranking public officials continued to align with the global order.

In itself, this was serious enough, but the minions of the new world order became concerned with the menacing threat to socialism in those countries with a proclivity for community-based programs and social cooperation used as methods to stabilize and encourage economic growth in their own countries; acts, according to global purists, that would undermine a system reliant upon homogenous "free trade." The canards of globalnality claimed great success in organizing the world economy while attacking countries like Chile and Venezuela with sanctions for acting in methods benefiting their own people and were nominalized as "failed economies." The situation was exacerbated by the all-consuming environmental wars being waged by the super-powers as well as the environmental degradation that was draining the resources needed to fuel the super- economies. The zealots of globalization believed ardently in a free economy without exception or modification and would use any means of enforcing compliance of those tenets on others, including military intervention. In those countries where the results of globalization were mixed or less than satisfactory, the purists argued that the politicians of those countries had not completely accepted the free trade philosophy or, they had not given it sufficient time or engagement for it to work and those more seriously in defiance were referred to as rebels against the concept and relegated to the status of rogue nations.

The Americans had always presented a face of willing cooperation with the internationalists and the American connection, often referred to as the "iron triangle," a coalition of government, military and big business seemingly steadfast in its commitment to global pursuits, gradually seemed to waver in that commitment. As lauded as the triangle was for its political intrigue, it had been increasingly unsuccessful in its global goals or overcoming the limitations imposed on it by democracy without duplicity of an economically driven media and religion, a power base so extensive and interconnected that it dominated all aspects of American life.

The American power-brokers, flag-wavers all, utilized patriotism to achieve their economic goals but gradually that patriotism wore thin and their demeanor toward internationalism, the position of the administration, weakened when the American economy faltered and they were not then hesitant to quietly pursue non-global solutions to internal problems and stringently enforce cumbersome demands upon their own people as surely as they would do to any third-world country. The inevitable rift was not lost on the political pols and the resulting political polarization coursed through shifting political sands and brought the beginning of new political entrenchment.

Although the federal government maintained a free-market philosophy, the individual states preserved, or drifted to, elements considered socialistic, a sort of a cautious insurance against the free market's unpredicted results that had an destabilizing effect upon regional economies. Pro-globalization thinkers lambasted those who they condemned for "wanting it both ways." As the division between the United States and the new world order became more serious, there was a new urgency in keeping the American free market in power. Failure to do so would have been a crippling blow to globalization, and the stakes were so high, the methods of cohesion and political manipulation were without limit. The ensuing political conflict consumed the time and energy which could have been better used to overcome the severe problems already facing America; but instead, the nation set out on a destructive obsession of a we-versus-them mentality.

So this was the chaotic state of affairs in the United States when John Maynard Stacy took the chair of the Central Committee of the Republican Party, a position that he accepted with a deep sense of mission and humility. He understood the depth of the challenge it represented and that the ideological goal he sought to achieve was so out of line with the party's Weltanschauung that what he would attempt to achieve was nothing short of revolutionary in concept. The national events that had radicalized the nation to this point made it so that the Bill of Rights appeared to be an extremist's devotion.

What Stacy failed to grasp was that he inherited a party so deeply divided over issues that were so mutually contradictory that there was virtually no possibility of negotiation or compromise. He had a belief in his own ability and purpose of mission but he failed to comprehend the depth of the forces against him and the silent forces that sidled within the dark domain of collusion. He was confident enough to march forward as the champion of idealism but he was not cynical enough to suspect conspiracy or calculated betrayal.

Stacy believed that he was saving democracy. The Republican right wing believed they were saving souls.

# Nine

The first obligation of John Maynard Stacy as chairman of the Republican Central Committee was his attendance of a party commending his selection as chair that was held at the Republican Headquarters in Washington, D.C. It was a role that he particularly enjoyed as he genuinely liked people, had an easy manner with those he did not know and therefore was very approachable, but more importantly, there would be at the occasion many from within the party with whom he had an uneasy alliance as they did not know him personally, did not fully understand his activism and therefore this would be his opportunity to present his case to them.

The party gave him a running start as chair, an opportunity to mend party fences and to establish a solid base for understanding by building trust through blunt honesty. As serious as that goal sounded, the party atmosphere was gay and cordial and Stacy was certain that he could overcome the superficiality of the moment, even in that gossamer setting, and create honest dialog impressing the attendees with his straightforwardness. Walls could be broken down and rebuilt by mutually shared goals by committed party members, he felt, and he knew that he needed to use this opportunity to get off to an aggressive start and alleviate the stress that tore at his party.

As Stacy entered the cotillion room, he moved through an enthusiastic reception line of shakers and movers, a face in the background caught his eye. Stopping short, he disposed himself to seek the identity of that face with its besetting familiarity with which he could not put a name. A memory flashed forward. Of course, it was Anthony Ermantrout, once a very close college friend and roommate but with whom he had lost contact during the past twenty years.

Stacy made his way to his old friend and the next few minutes were lost to vigorous hugs and heartfelt salutations. Finally, Ermantrout managed, "I had to come see you and congratulate you on your accomplishment—very impressive!" Stacy, unable to be overheard in the din, motioned to his longtime friend to get a drink and meet him in the closest thing to a quiet place, a spot just behind the dais.

After what seemed an endless session of fraternal backslapping ritual, Stacy was able to make his way, drink in hand, to Ermantrout. The joy of the meeting of two old friends for the first time in twenty years was cut short by a mood swing when Ermantrout, in awkward directness, asked, "Are you sure that this is what you want to do to yourself?"

Caught off guard, Stacy uttered, "Pardon me?"

Trying to be heard over the party but not wanting to be overheard by others, Ermantrout raised his voice with a loud hushed quality—not exactly his intention—he said, "You are really setting yourself up, my friend, I know that you have always strived for the top, but these cannibals will eat you up."

Falling into the same serious tone but trying to smile to shrug it off, Stacy replied, "You're just being a little cynical, aren't you?"

"Well, maybe you are just a little naïve, John," Ermantrout retorted.

Stacy started to explain, "Look, this political party is not so divided as it is rudderless. We need to get direction and an agenda and to do that, we need to pull together with common goals, a genuine conservative agenda and then together we can…"

"John," Ermantrout cut in, "it's not that easy. Look around you. These people seem to be comrades and they are pleasant and reassuring right now— but they are ruthless; and in my opinion, they are committed to a sinister ideology and toward achieving that, there is nothing they will not do. Look at them right now—What do you think they are doing? Study them with their happy cocktails and smiley faces. I'll tell you, they are undermining you at this very moment—even before you can get started. For many of them, there is too much at stake and they are not going to give you a chance to take it away from them. They will listen to you and they will nod approvingly, but to them it is just rhetoric—political rhetoric—they have all heard it before and for so long that they truly believe that there is no connect between what a politician says and what he actually believes. And in response, they will tell you what they think that you want you to hear but watch out, my friend."

"So soon a party turns sour," Stacy thought out loud. He had not be prepared for this onslaught and almost felt resentful toward his friend but knew from their personal history that Ermantrout was sincere and had his interest at heart. Then after mulling over the comments and trying to keep the conversation civil, Stacy said, "Look, I'm no ivory tower idealist, I know the realities of life and politics."

"But," Ermantrout countered, "you are bringing an outdated belief system to the table in an effort to revive that belief system and it is something that they just don't believe in anymore; just listen to what they are saying…"

"Like what?"

"Okay," Said Ermantrout. "I have heard you say repeatedly that we are in jeopardy of losing our democracy and you want to revive and make it the cornerstone of our country again—God knows the Democrats won't use it. But if you listen to what the power brokers of the Republican Party are saying over and over again to anyone who bothers to listen, 'America is not a democracy but a constitutional republic' and no one replies, no one challenges them. It's as if no one is paying any attention, or cares. And by repeating it again and again, pretty soon it is like planted memory, it's in our unconscious and we don't question it. They have made this decision long ago and it is not something they are going to debate and certainly they will not retreat from their position—they know that they cannot survive in a democracy. These people are very radical and your political philosophy is alien to them and when they don't get their way, they can be very dangerous."

Frustrated, Stacy tried to ease away from the subject by asking Ermantrout about his personal plans for the future. "I am going into private practice as an attorney. As you know, I was the mayor of Castabol, South Carolina, for eight years, and that is why I am concerned about you. From my first day in office, there was a clandestine movement against me and after a couple of years, it became overt—crank calls in the middle of the night, indirect, and then later, direct threats, constant undermining of my programs and even threats on my children at school. It all seemed silly because this was a relatively low-level political position and I made it clear that I had no further political ambition. I tried to negotiate with these people but they were steadfast and uncompromising and when I didn't go along with them, they came after me with vengeance. Frankly, I got tired of the stress and worry—it really wears you down. I probably would have been reelected but it just was not worth it—I had a life. And you know what? They think that they are righteous—they deny their dark side and since they talk to God, everything that they say and do is from God and that makes it alright no matter how evil it may be."

"Who are these people? Everyone uses the expression 'they,' but who are they?"

"Just your middling right-wing kooks," Ermantrout answered.

"You mean the Democrats were right when they complained of a right-wing conspiracy?" Stacy asked, feeling a little perplexed.

"No, they were overstating it; it was not a conspiracy as such because it wasn't or isn't organized. These people are of the same mind-set, the same basic ideology and the same emotional make-up and so by appearances, they are all in sync, marching to the same drummer as if they were organized and then it only takes some unscrupulous opportunist to plant a suggestion to which they all respond as if on cue. Do you remember when our government was so frustrated with the Al Qaida and we tried to destroy their infrastructure but couldn't because they had none? They had no formal organization—they were effective because they all thought alike. Activist groups like that need no organization. They are inner-directed and all respond the same way to like situations."

"So, what is it that these people want?" Stacy asked.

With biting disdain, Ermantrout answered, "I don't think that they even know themselves. Their objectives, beliefs and methods seem to change with each situation but, as always, it has the appearance of being coordinated. But I do know this: they are committed and fanatical and nothing will get in their way and they have a natural connect with the most evil assailments that one could imagine. And look at all the liberal politicians throughout our recent history who died in mysterious plane crashes, investigative reporters who committed suicide or radio or television commentators who were inexplicably fired from their jobs. I'm worried that you are in over your head."

Sadly Stacy responded, "I would have never believed that that could happen here."

The two men stood silently for a moment in the harsh light behind the dais and then Ermantrout said in trembling breathlessness, "My grandfather was an infantryman in the Third Division in Germany in World War II. When he came home after the war, he was very disturbed; in fact, he had two or three psychiatric hospitalizations in the following years. When asked about the war, Grandpa wouldn't say anything. But later when he did talk about the war, he was obsessed with one aspect of front-line action in which certain battle-hardened G.I.s would move through German residential neighborhoods, looking for women, then when they would find one, they would rape her and then kill her. It was justified because she was the 'enemy.' One day Grandpa told that story—as if to purge the guilt from his mind—at a family dinner but as he concluded the story, he was interrupted by an aunt who shouted, 'my country would never do such a thing' and she stomped out of the house and never spoke to Grandpa after that. And he never spoke of those atrocities again—that is a fact of life in this country, truth is just not tolerated."

Then Stacy said, "I'm sure that those things happen in war but I not sure how that is relevant to what we are discussing."

"It is relevant this way: it is an example how we set a goal and then when we are caught up in accomplishing that goal, the goal is obliterated and the activity itself becomes paramount. In other words, we set out to rid the world of tyranny and in that pursuit we commit acts worthy of a tyrant ourselves. To call an innocent German hausfrau 'the enemy' is crass in itself—in this case it was just a selfish rationalization for one's own self-gratification and yet, there are those who will refuse to believe that righteous people could do such a thing."

Just then a senator, getting an early start on drinking and with a young woman who looked as if she were made of shiny plastic in tow, grabbed Stacy by the arm congratulating him on his new position while Ermantrout, stressed and drawn, blinked out at the crowded assemblage. After a few minutes of depthless banter, the senator and girlfriend giggled their way into the crowd.

The timing of the interruption dampened an already funereal encounter; the two men stepped back emotionally and welcomed the respite to collect themselves and per chance change the course of their discussion. Then Ermantrout said stoically, "Perhaps you had better tend to your social obligations."

The rest of the evening Stacy drifted, congenial but troubled, through the patronage. Not comfortable with his feelings, he tried to be more outgoing than was his nature and that made him feel awkward—he always felt awkward when he attempted to contrive his feelings. He found himself studying body language and looking for hidden meaning in conversation. That night which should have been his night, a night to rejoice in pride and accomplishment, had become a laborious obligation.

Stacy arose the following morning early for a meeting with the president at the White House, a meeting that had been arranged by the president on very short notice. He awoke groggy and irritable and because of that irritability, he surmised that the president had called for a meeting so unexpectedly soon that it would not afford Stacy the time or preparation to be ready for such an important meeting despite the fact that it had been emphasized to him that the meeting would be casual. He had met the president on two previous occasions and had worked with him indirectly on several projects over the years. Nevertheless, the two men had never had an in-depth talk and had no feel for one another. Stacy had stayed too late at the party and as he pulled himself together this morning, he felt a lack of energy, unusual for him, and he remembered an aide's admonition that once you are in the high-stakes political game, the whirlwind never stops.

Stacy was escorted to the White House by civil service agents. The president had penciled in a half-hour meeting at 9 AM with another half hour optional if it was deemed necessary.

In passing through the foyer leading into the Oval Office, Stacy was taken back by an oil painting on the wall to his right. He recognized the painting, an original, as *Midnight of Medina*, by the new age painter Cirilius. The oil was of a man, from the back, standing in near darkness, his arms spread downward, his body illuminated by two moons has he stared upward at them as if in prayer or giving thanks. The moons were blurry, an effort by the painter to have the viewer's eyes descend to the man and the planet, both well-defined and typically of Cirilius, the darkened landscape was subtle and demanded close study. Upon examination, Stacy could see that the place was not only alien but an antediluvian planet. The mountains, buttes and other geographical formations were craggy and austere, the broad valley forested and the river meandered through the heart of the picture reflecting in the moonlight.

"So what is the painter saying there?" Stacy turned to see the president standing behind him.

Without any formality, Stacy answered, "I think that the man is looking at the planet for the first time—perhaps he has just landed there—and he is initially encouraged by what he sees, but still he is concerned about its resources and whether it is inhabitable."

"Very perceptive," the president said. "Actually, there is real history here. You see, there actually is a Medina. In the Andromeda constellation! There was a project a couple of years ago which was very hush-hush—we were going to explore Medina with the eventual intention of colonizing it. You know that the earth is overcrowded and it is just common sense that we carry our civilization to another place for a rebirth. That would extend our culture, relieve population pressure on earth and we felt that it was God's will that we do that. So Cirilius was commissioned to do the painting which became emblematic of the project."

"So, what happened to the project?"

"Well, the effort was well under way—we had developed a nuclear spaceship capable of the speed of light—186,000 miles an hour—and we had researched Medina and its sun, the star Havoc, and at first it seemed suitable for earth exploration. Its day is about twenty-four and a half hours, its year is slightly longer than ours and—it has one moon, not two—its moon created a planet rhythm much like our own. But it would take our spacecraft twenty-six years to get to Medina and that would make our astronauts too old to explore and develop the planet so we had to put the project on hold until scientists could invent some type of suspended animation to sustain the youth of the astronauts for the voyage. Then a satellite exploration vehicle got within a million miles of Medina and probed the atmosphere. The report said that Medina was a dead rock, its mountains rounded, its valleys filled with silt and what was once rivers cut straight through the valleys like canals. In other words, there probably had been a civilization there but they used up all their resources and the planet died. So, we are in the market for a new planet."

"Is this a high-priority project?" Stacy asked.

"No. Armageddon is imminent and then our savior will remove all the faithful to the heavenly domain."

Stacy responded with a furrowed bow but before he could speak, the president took him by the arm and escorted him to the Oval Office which was followed by a quick, vigorous and light conversation. Secret Service agents remained outside the office while two aides stood a short distance from the president and his guest, one of the aides overtly studying Stacy.

In this interlude, Stacy had the opportunity to observe the president and he was shocked how aged he had become since elected. The president was by nature a very slim, handsome, photogenic man and most of his media images were from file photos approved by White House staff. But here in this revealing light, Stacy saw a man with a double chin, heavy jowls, dark circles under his eyes and he appeared not to have any muscle tone in his entire body. The two men, normally comfortable with others, talked easily at first almost as if longtime friends. But Stacy knew the president was very orthodox and could be pugnacious and the president knew Stacy as an uncompromising idealist; but both men, in their egoistic confidence, thought their own approach as the advantage.

Suddenly, interrupting Stacey's light banter, the president cut in, "I assumed that you have prepared an agenda as chair of the party."

Previously prepared but nevertheless caught off guard, Stacy responded, "My agenda has received much media scrutiny and, generally, those reports are accurate."

The president answered, "Well, on the surface they seem a bit idealistic and I just don't know how you would plan to implement it—it's not as easy as simply stating your case and our current policies are so engaged as to discourage diverse options."

"But that is what leadership is all about—you have to implant new ideas, nurture them along through education and the media and then organize to implement the ideas."

The president replied, "You have never been in an elected office. You must realize that to accomplish anything and to do that you must have the blessings of the electorate as well as longevity; and therefore, you have to do what is acceptable to remain in office, otherwise you could be out on your ear. It's a political balancing act—you give some to get some. And take in account that recent studies show that over fifty percent of the public actually cannot distinguish between fact or fantasy and that, my friend, like it or not, will influence political rhetoric."

The meeting was already beginning to lose its congeniality. Stacy frowned at the president's comment and said, "Leadership is hard to define. One cannot be a leader for no reason—there must be purpose and passion, but unfortunately much of today's leadership today is built upon superficial imaging and lacks substance. In other words, some character imitating a cowboy will look better to the low-brow political junkies than a gentle but thoughtful intellectual."

If that repartee stung the president he chose not to show it. "You have to do what you have to do under the circumstance. It is essential to present to the public a persona that they can identify with and to do anything less would be self-defeating and just why would you do that? You have to realize that many of our citizens are childlike—they respond to politicians as if they were fictional characters on TV."

To that Stacey said, "But what is at stake here is democracy and that requires an astute search for the truth no matter where it takes us. Truth may change or bring down the political system peacefully; but, if we fail to honor the truth and if the truth is withheld too long from the people, it could eventually lead to a catastrophic breakdown of the government."

The president said forcefully, "Democracy is a fable. As a form of government it is emerged in the totality of the system and by its own ineptitude can be disrupted by mob interference or quixotic dreamer. Truth is reality and many cannot handle reality."

"But," Stacey shot back, "if there is peril in our future, we must recognize it before it is upon us and while we can do something about it—then only the truth can save us."

The president snorted, "Political and social scientists have long argued that the successful politician must not only be deceptive but must be such an accomplished liar in order to be effective and maintain the sophisticated balance that is the modern nation. Uninformed people cannot be trusted to make decisions. The long-term crisis in the Middle East began in the 1950s when our administration surreptitiously overtaxed the American people on oil to make a pay-off to Iran in exchange for the oil. It was illegal and deceitful—but a good call."

Stacey said, "Perhaps the whole fiasco in the Middle East could have been prevented from the start by honesty."

"Look," the president said growing impatient, "change is inevitable, and you can do one of three things with it: you can be passive; you can try to retrain it; or, you can adapt to it. I chose the latter."

"But sir," Stacy protested, "you are moving the country away from cherished values."

"Like what?"

Speaking in measured softness to lighten the impact Stacy said, "Well, I remember when our party championed this nation as English speaking only. Now the language most taught in our schools is not English but Chinese. This has been encouraged and condoned by your administration and has robbed the people of a sense of identity."

The president almost erupted, "That only makes sense. The Chinese are the leading economic power in the world. Their economy dwarfs ours and we can't fight that—it's a simple matter of numbers and it was always inevitable. We must get along with them and to do that we must be able to communicate with them. Eighty percent of our policemen are Chinese. They are excellent cops—they do everything by the letter. American cops want two hundred thousand dollars a year—Chinese will work for about one tenth of that. But Americans must learn their language so that we can communicate with them—we must all learn to get along."

"But that is the problem—your administration has given into them on every issue and as much as you think we are co-partners with them, they are calling all the shots."

The president shot back, "I'll admit that they are running things in the world, but they have attained that position and they deserve it and any military engagement between our countries would be disastrous. Besides they have wholeheartedly embraced Christianity and so, like us, they follow the Bible and our savior, Jesus Christ."

Stacy interjected, "I've heard that the Chinese Communists allow Christianity among their people but the actual number of Chinese embracing Christianity is rather miniscule, in other words, it's just a political ruse."

"You can interpret that any way you like," the president responded, "but the fact is that those who accept our Savior will be saved and when the end comes government affiliations will be unimportant."

Stacy retorted, "There are a huge list of critical issues befalling this country that are simply not being addressed. To give a few examples: Our military is made up of mercenaries and they are beginning to pose a serious threat to our nation; China owns more of our country than we do; every dime we pay toward our national debt goes to interest and what happens when they demand payment on the principle?; the environment has virtually collapsed and even the corporate farmers are going under; the streets are full of homeless; our youth are uneducated; there is a growing underground that could be a threat to our stability; all our institutions are breaking down or are totally ineffective; we backed away from protecting Taiwan and let the Chinese have it without a fight and now no one trusts us; the list goes on and on—the infrastructure, lack of transportation, the depression and lack of jobs—and none of these issues are being looked at."

Fitfully the president said, "All this does not matter, the Bible said that the world would come to an end and that there would be Armageddon, the last decisive battle between the forces of good and evil fought before Judgment day, and all the signs we see now point to that and, compared to that epic event, nothing else matters. I mean why worry about our grandchildren having to pay off our debt when we'll all have met our maker? Today we are fast approaching the end of the economic, social and political systems of the world. How do we know that? Because Jesus Christ foretold a series of world developments that would provide a sign indicating that God's day of reckoning is near. Like a volcano that rumbles, smokes, and spits out cinders, that composite sign includes great wars, earthquakes, famines, and pestilences—all of which have ravaged the world on an unprecedented scale. But the good news of God's kingdom will be preached in all the civilized nations; and then, the end will come."

Stacy asked, "Even if that is so and a select number of individuals are saved, what about the others—do they just perish?"

"The true believers will be saved. All others have the freedom of choice and if they choose not to accept Our Lord Jesus Christ as their Savior, that's up to them and they will perish. They have had ample time to accept biblical truth. But prior to Armagedden, God could send his son, Jesus Christ, to us and through his leadership and guidance we could restore the earth to its previous state—and cause natural disasters to cease—and we could become a world of believers and we could submit to his word and if that is God's plan we must be prepared for that and be aware of the sign that tell us that his return is imminent and that will be a glorious day. But we must be patient and continue to believe that such is inevitable."

"So, that's our plan—to wait for the return of Jesus?"

"Amen."

"Let me see," Stacy mused, "your administration says two things: one, that we have a free-market economy in which we must not tamper because whatever the market does is according to free-market law; and, two, Jesus is coming to make things all right. And other than that everything else is ignored."

"Well, I wouldn't put it that crudely but it is true—I have spoken directly to God," the president said.

"And what about the underground movement, they appear viable," Stacy added.

"We call them the Mole People," the president said.

"Demeaning them is of no use, they are peaceful, hardworking people and they are developing a growing economy I hear based upon real supply and demand and they have a deep spirituality," Stacy said.

The president responded sternly, "But they are against us and whether they are peaceful or not they mean to covertly overthrow us and so we see them as terrorists and that is the very purpose of Homeland Security—to thwart insurgency in our own country."

Then Stacy said, "But they are trying to come to accord with the administration through democratic negotiation. And in a peripheral matter, and I don't mean put this on your administration—previous administrations have done no better—but genetically modified foods have become a significant threat to health, the environment and the global food supply and yet, you have done nothing in that regard."

The president replied, "As for the Mole People, it is their choice as I said, as to whether they will accept our God. They chose not to and that is their problem; as for the genetically modified foods, that has been determined by the forces of the free-market economy and we don't meddle in that—liberal meddling has always caused chaos."

Stacy continued to argue but the president grew impatient and began to lecture, "If you are going to be a positive influence in politics in this country, remember the 'morning in America' theme. You must inspire. You cannot keep whining about problems. That's what the Democrats did and now they are history. People do not want to hear negative things—you have to say things that reassure them, make them feel secure, feel uplifted. You must remember that there are no problems—that would be admitting that you made mistakes. Righteous people do not make mistakes because they are led by God and accordingly, your message must stir the soul."

"Do you know" Stacy asked, "that eighty percent of the population is entwined in virtual reality games on their computers and that half of those are seriously addicted, in some cases causing death, and that your politicians just pass it off as a way of keeping the population under control and out of government business?"

The president then declared the meeting over. It had last twenty-four minutes.

High Mass of the St Thomas the Apostle Church of Los Angeles on the seventh Sunday after trinity was held at 10:30 AM. The prelude included two pieces from Esquisses Byzantines—Rosace and Campanile. These pieces were followed by parish announcements, the opening hymn, asperges, the greeting and several other rituals and hymns before the Reverend Ivan Davis quietly proceeded to the podium for the sermon of the day.

Ritually clad in a light rose-colored vestment, Davis was smallish, about forty in years with black neatly-trimmed hair, and the only distinguishing feature of his face were unusually heavy eyebrows. More importantly, he was a paradox. His personality was gentle and subdued and his voice, stressing a rich British accent, was very soft. But in his face one could see sincerity and deep commitment to his faith and humanity.

Davis had been ordained by the Church of Wales. His formative years were in the Baptist tradition which laid the groundwork for diversity in the Christian experience. He completed postgraduate work at Cambridge and was confirmed an Angelican. He service on the Board of Education of the diocese of London, promoted an AIDS project and was a hospital chaplain. His commitment to good works was best expressed in the church credo, "To be a holy place where love is found. Where all are named and where hearts are freed to change the world."

Upon reaching the podium, where behind him an elegant apse portrayed a stained-glass image of Jesus Christ, Davis gave pause and then looked down sternly at the large silent congregation and began to speak. Very soon his internal energy, articulation and charisma became apparent:

"The world into which Jesus and his followers were born was a world in which people were divided into camps: There were privileged citizens of the great Roman Empire and those who were forced to live under her rule, but were granted no special rights. There were those who spoke classical Greek, the highly educated, and those who spoke their native tongues. And there were may other social distinctions... For St. Paul the author of our lesson from Ephesians, there was also another one: There were the Jews, God's 'chosen people' to whom God had been revealed and to whom all the promises of Hebrew Scripture had been made; and the Gentiles, that is, everyone else, the pagan idolaters. From this perspective, the Jews were 'us,' and the Gentiles were clearly 'them.'

"Some things don't seem to change much. There seems to be something deep in human nature that makes us want to divide the world into 'us' and 'them' and that causes us to choose up sides, draw dividing lines, and build walls. We do it all the time in so many ways: In many places it is about the color of your skin or ethnic make-up. In other places it's about whether you are Christian or Moslem or a Shiite Moslem, or whether you are a Protestant Christian or a Catholic Christian; or among us Angelicans, whether you are an Evangelical or an Anglo-Catholic. Sometimes it's whether you are an immigrant or native; or labor vs. management; Democrat vs. Republican; and animal rights activist, or like shopping for furs on Rodeo Drive. Other times it's whether you are gay or straight, or if you live in east West Hollywood, or West Hollywood.

"It's a world differentiating 'us' vs. 'them.' It's about who is a stranger or 'strange' to us, because they are not like us, or do not agree with us. We humans are good at building walls to keep ourselves 'safe' and to keep strangers out.

"It also strikes me that any religion, and I include our own Christian tradition in this, can carry a potential—I use my words carefully here—to breed profoundly misguided and inhuman convictions that result in bigotry and then act in ways that have no regard for the sanctity of God-given human life. It is an unfortunate enduring fact that unscrupulous, opportunistic and autocratic power-hungry leaders will seize upon this vice in human character and use it brazenly to promote their own selfish agenda without thought for the common good or consideration of socially destructive consequences. But the strange feature of religions is also this: they have the potential to inspire and nurture the most altruistic, humane and profoundly selfless convictions and then act with kindliness and generosity.

"They say that the causes of the defeat of the Japanese Army in World War II was complex. But one of the major reasons was integrity. The Imperial

Japanese High Command had emphasized to their officers that if they were ever captured by the allies they would be treated with utter brutality, torture and a blatant disregard for human dignity. The Japanese officers were horrified and went to most extraordinary lengths not to be captured. But some of them were captured and they were not tortured or brutalized and they came to realize that they had been lied to. Eventually the Japanese High Command itself, which had swallowed its own propaganda, began to realize the truth and that fascism is evil and must necessarily lie and is always intrinsically murderous.

"These revelations do not provide answers to the complex questions about suffering and why devout and goodly Christians and nuns and monks are murdered today, why a young baby has leukemia or why the unrighteous and wicked prosper. But it does provide a framework of understanding and we must use that framework like a template to analyze and evaluate the forces of evil be they seemingly acceptable in our culture as it is just comfortable to go along with easy compliance. And in analyzing, as Christians, the forces that affect our lives we must be objective and subject our own government to that template of justice and goodness for we are governed by the same frailty that have typified despotism throughout human history. We continue to exhort enthusiasm for a radical cause through the hackneyed propagandized rhetoric of 'freedom' or 'human rights' when in actuality, we surrendered those principles years ago and to win them back at this stage of our history would be a monumental task worth undertaking. But this framework of which I am speaking is a way of seeing that allows us to ask questions, to protest and demonstrate, to voice despair, to utter prayer and anger and tell the story. To put it bluntly, the more we are aware of God's presence, the fact of evil and suffering, the more vulnerable we become and then moral disorder will hurt us more, not less. This is wisdom, which is more than explanation or intuitive penetration, it is knowing the scope of the tragedy and yet praying, protesting, speaking out, challenging and acting…"

A sudden shattering at the once-magnificent portal, the threshold of the church, interrupted the sermon with an explosion of bright morning light from outside flooding into that beautiful divine cathedral, disrupting the congregation into confusion; many had been so focused on the reverend that they continued to seek his words while others, shocked by the outrage, turned in their seats and froze at the sight of six burly uniformed FBI agents marching sternly to the rector.

The lead agent thrust a paper at the good reverend and when the rector refused to acknowledge it, he was slammed onto the podium. Surrounded, Davis, knew the drill, they would keep him off balance, even cause him to collapse into a fall or stumble into furnishings to make him look like an incompetent stumbling drunk. But he countered their jabs and shoves with soft parries and kept his feet. This angered some of them and they responded with roughness. The lead agent shouted in the deathly silence of the church, "You are under arrest for blasphemy and insurrection under the authority of the Patriot Act." Davis had been through this all before and he was practiced. He had protested the environmental wars and the oil wars as well as other persecutions by the government and as he was led toward the entrance to that Episcopal church, he held his head high as if he were leading the way.

There was a moaning murmur from a congregation in helpless confusion after having just lost their source of strength. Then, the assistant rector moved cautiously to the podium, searched through papers spread before him and then finding the last page of the reverend's sermon, continued, "This wisdom is not to anaesthetize us to suffering or resigning our responsibility, but to facing up to our duty and taking seriously our vocation: to work together, pray together and steward together the gifts that God has given to us in this place. All this in the presence of Christ who is the Wisdom of God, the beauty of God and the mystery of God the eternal Father, Son and Holy Spirit. Amen."

# Ten

    G.H. Houten was a self-made man—there was absolutely nothing natural about him. At the age of sixty-three he had become a paleoanthropologist and to provide an image compatible with that occupation, he reinvented himself. All his life he had been one of those nondescript fellows you could meet one day and then not be able to pick him out of a crowd the following day. But now with a professional appearance to project to the world, he created a tenuous facsimile of what a world-class anthropologist might look like and certainly an appearance that would set him apart from his peers should he have the good fortune to benefit from a group photograph in some prestigious professional publication or, more luckily, in a popular news weekly.
    He had a receding hairline and he knew that there was nothing he could do about that. But from there down he went to work. He enhanced his impression with oval eyeglasses that were tilted outward from the top and secured to his lapel with a thin silver chain. Actually he only needed reading glasses but their presence gave him such an intellectual look that he kept them on all the time. Then he developed a rich flowing mustache and beneath that a well trimmed and pointed goatee. To complete the assemblage, he wore what might appear to one to be a laboratory smock but in actuality it was an expensive outer garment designed to give the very appearance of how a laboratory scientist might look to others. Then to achieve the image, he incorporated in his language a subtle but undefinable accent that sounded suspiciously like a poor imitation of Sigmund Freud. His makeover was complete and would never be without it and even acquaintances failed to recognize him at first.
    Houten was the son of an Assembly of God minister and as one of six children was lost in the family reciprocity. His father was rigid but unlike many inexorable fathers, he was gentle and communicative with his children. He would attempt to deal with childhood issues and religious issues with firm conviction and the fact that there would be no compromise or alternatives to

expectations did not change his method of child rearing. Under the father's influence, Houten became a devout Christian and the father's gentle confrontation and strong character impressed him so that he completed study at a seminary and dedicated himself to a life of serving his belief and in doing so tried to emulate his father's care and method as much as possible. But there was something missing—there was inexplicably, an absence of self and fulfillment. He offered nothing out of the ordinary to his God, there was no higher expectation and he would leave no legacy and this troubled him greatly. As a person of modest talent and one who had never shown any promise of being anything but a normal average-as-you-can-get human being, he desperately had within his heart a compulsion for achievement, to leave a mark and show his God some accomplishment above and beyond the normal piety that would set him apart from all others and prove to his God a great worthiness.

It was a time in which the debate between creationism and evolution dominated much of the intellectual dialog in the church and secular society. As nonsensical as the issue was, it had become a black hole of reasoning, sucking the more vital issues in which society should have been focused for a whirlwind of confrontation that could neither be proven nor dispelled. As a young minister, Houten plunged himself into the debate, cautiously at first, although he knew little of the studies of anthropology or the cosmos. He initially made the mistake of projecting a mind-set of a rigid faith-based belief system onto the evolutionists, claiming that they were, like himself (although he would not admit it), manipulating facts to fit their own preconceptions. This made him appear more ignorant of the issues than he already was and for a young man of faltering self-confidence, this was devastating. He knew that he could make his point before his peers and that would be applauded and thereafter to remain within his own arena and his circumscribed philosophy would be safe and comfortable. But more importantly, he knew that he needed more than that. He needed to venture into the thought and interaction that was threatening to him—it was something he had to do for himself and his God.

After the death of his father, Houten became reverend of his church and surprisingly to him, gave him an unexpected sense of freeness. He thus began to present sermons that challenged his flock far beyond the mundane and predictably traditional sermons offered by his father year after year, and his weekly presentation, at first a hesitant, uncertain allocution, progressed to attain a high level of eloquence and natural flow. Thus Houten began to realize a new self and that personal growth could and would lead to his becoming a more effective servant of his lord. During this period, he kept participation in the evolution debate in his thoughts and prayers and then one day, almost as a crashing pronouncement from the Almighty Himself, Houten realized his calling—his legacy, his place in life and his tribute to his Lord would be that he would rise up to confront the false doctrine of evolution, that he, G.H. Houten, would battle Satan as few before him had done and that he would strive forward to gloriously strike down the evil that challenged biblical creation and led so many astray.

One day, inconspicuously, Houten was in a beginning course in anthropology at Southern Methodist University's Human Studies Department. In taking the course, he was unaware of his laden skepticism on the subject or that it would effect his understanding the subject he was undertaking. His reasoning was simple and that was that he must understand and know the enemy, for was it not a great Chinese general who once said that a military leader who did not know his enemy would suffer defeat. But that inbred hostility led to immediate disassociation with the instructor, particularly when Houten announced on his first day in class that he was an evangelistic preacher.

Almost immediately, he began to observe flaws and gaps in evolutionary theory and pointed out such discrepancies. But that was the response of a neophyte and he was soon to know an intellectual dressing down. During his study, he was introduced to Paranthropus, a predecessor to man whose name erroneously meant "akin to man." Paranthropus had appeared in anthropological history later than more advanced types and thus the mistake was made initially that he was on a higher plane of development than he actually was. In his studies on this pre-man ape, Houten gleefully discovered that the Paranthropus had been on Earth for a million years and had not evolved one iota, giving Houten the ammunition he needed to reject evolutionary theory; when he offered his opinion in a loud and bellicose manner, the instructor very politely suggested that if he read on, he would be exposed to the theoretical explanation that evolutionary change in pre-man was dependent upon the particular type being studied having used tools, as it was always evident in human development that tools were always the element that brought stability, consistent food supply and a change of lifestyle that would bring about evolutionary change. It was a graphic and humiliating experience for Houten and a mistake he would never make again.

As he studied anthropology, he came to understand the draw that it had on those that studied the subject in depth and he felt its mesmerizing effect and its seduction, a strong inner pull that frightened him. Was he to succumb to the wiles of this spiritless speculation that enhanced human curiosity but was deathless to celestial understanding? For the first time he could sense the strong connection to this secular belief by the mere touching or holding of an artifact of antiquity and that it would produce an emotional connection of the student to the pathetic forerunners of human civilization whose only purpose was to survive in a hostile world. He constantly made subtle attempts to raise the specter of doubt to others but was met with silent but admonitory glances. Furthermore, his steadfast refusal to surrender conviction to this discipline not only lost him respect of his peers but threatened his very understanding of the subject, undermining that which he had set out to accomplish. Failure at this early phase of the game would produce nothing of value—Houten knew that he had to grow and expand intellectually while retaining the rigid dogma of the spiritual realm. It forced him to bifurcate his thinking, to attain a protracted duality of the mind, to huddle religious conviction in some far antrum of his being where it would rest undisturbed and intact until the call to rise to pronouncement would be issued by ecclesiastical summons. Conjointly, he would maintain his intellectual curiosity as if it were a thing apart as one might study to be a lawyer in order to obtain a high level of employment while having no innate interest in law. It were as if Houten had joined the enemy in order to undermine the enemy. It was an engaging compromise that he found necessary and which caused him no guilt or apprehension as he knew that he had to understand that enemy before he could confront their philosophical fortress.

Thus Houten's newfound duality allowed him to press to a venerable goal without the strain of inner conflict and once so inspired, he did so with tremendous inner conviction and dedication. Although this first attempt at academic quest was uncertain and brought apprehension initially, he engaged himself so fully in his studies thereafter that it became a virtual lifestyle to him. In order to become a full-time student, he found it necessary to approach the elders of his church to convince them that his project, although it would take him from many of his official duties, was to the direct interest of the congregation as well as an ambitious effort to scour the beliefs of the secular scientists castigating the literal tenets of the Bible. Houten never realized until then the persuasion of his oratory or how easily the elders could be swayed by such venal rhetoric. Not that he felt any guilt or later, remorse, over his education being paid for by the church—his mission justified such expenditure so lofty were his expectations of evangelistic accomplishment. To smooth the impact of his part-time absences he asked that Shepard Hobson, a willing young man of modest abilities, be placed in the role as his assistant and that he be involved in the day-to-day operation of the church and congregational activities. Hobson viewed the request as an opportunity and full-heartedly sought acceptance of the request. The elders accepted in good spirit with the understanding that Houten would continue to be available for Sunday's sermons and maintain supervisory contact with his neophyte cleric.

Houten's undergraduate studies went well as he maintain high scholastic achievement and, without conferring with the elders who had failed to address the longevity of Houten's sabbatical, he commenced graduate school. By continuing his Sunday sermons at the church, he maintained contact and influence with a congregation on which he was dependent for his very livelihood. But upon receiving his master's degree in anthropology, he felt intellectually unsatisfied and yet, he knew that he had tested the patience of the church's elder and thus spent a summer without academic study to mend fences with conflicting church members. But Hobson was performing well and although underpaid, he seemed committed to continuing his role in the church. Then, Houten was accepted on a scholarship in the newly founded Evangelical School for Advanced Study in New Orleans, Louisiana, with the goal of receiving a PhD in paleoanthropology. The conflict between church and furthering his education was easily bridged by Houten—his pursuit of higher learning by now superceded everything else and if the elders failed to approve he rationalized that it would be their loss. But the elders, without leadership of their own and confused by pervasive argument, conceded to a compromise whereas Houten would come home to preach each Sunday but would be relieved of all other clerical duties. For This he received reduced pay but that was unimportant in light of his scholarship.

During his first year in New Orleans, Houten began to consider several topics for his thesis which would direct and organize his studies for the next three years. He had considered several possibilities but when he began to read extensively about an exiting new concept, the anthropic connection, a conceptualization of the universe that was compatible with Christianity and the Intellectual Design Hypothesis, he enthusiastically seized upon the notion that God created the structure of the carbon atom, which He designed to support the existence of all organic molecules. There was obviously no direct evidence to support or deny such a hypothesis, but the magnificent interaction and chemical balance was compelling logic that the universe with its overwhelming complexity was organized to a specific plan for human existence while in a universe that was random and not organized for purpose by the creator, such organization would not be observed as it would be impossible.

On the night of Houten's discovery of the potential magnitude of the anthropic connection argument, ecstatic and inspired, he returned to his one-room quarters energized that he had found a new stratagem to accomplish his calling—the destruction of the iniquitous theories of evolution. In his simple austere apartment setting, a bed, a hot plate, a desk, a table and two chairs and piles of books stacked askew, he sat entranced by the potential of his undertaking. Was he up to it or was he in over his head? Anthropology had led him to the cosmos and now, would the cosmos lead him to divine revelation? He dropped to his knees and prayed to his Lord for guidance or a sign of confirmation. The following morning he arose as usual, set water on the hot plate for coffee and went to his favorite place where two large windows came together to make a corner with a small diner table and a chair that allowed him to sit before a small well-kept garden of rock, a single fir tree, an artificial pond and a variety of perennials separated by expanses of bark dust. Here, every morning, he had his private time, a time to compose himself and allow his mind to wander through the infinity of space and dimension. For Houten, it was a pleasant time, one of renewal and reinvigoration, and a time to allow the brain, every bit as torn and bruised as the physical body incurs from the devastation of life, to heal. He would cautiously sip hot coffee and always muse to himself, "I could sit here forever."

Then suddenly he noticed something unusual about the golden poppies with their unruly spacing, the older plants stringy and scraggy while the fresh blooms of the new seedlings beamed upward like the uplifting bright faces of little moppets. Then he sat back in a single lurch, startled to see in the midst of the golden flock, several beautiful orbs of sterling white poppies. "They weren't there yesterday," he gasped.

Was this the sign from God that he was looking for? The message was unmistakable and could not be denied in the way it was given. There could be no other explanation other than that those sterling poppies, golden and fleecy, were of divine creation, a harbinger of the intellectual crusade to overcome Darwinism because that belief had relegated biblical teaching to an ancient myth to many of the young people as it had for many and the Bible was no longer viewed as divine revelation but rather an errant product of the evolution of Israelite culture. God was ordering Houten to involve himself, mind, heart and soul in the crusade to destroy those satanic teachings.

Thus inspired by a personal message from God, Houten was anxious to return to the confrontation with the evolutionists but he knew empirically the futility of the biblical explanation of the creation of life as it was easily debunked by naturalists and that the explanation, dependent upon theologic interpretation but never scientific interpretation, did not use the scientific method of investigation and therefore was not considered a science.

Instead, Houten was determined to develop comprehensive research that would appeal to logic and become inexorable in its conclusions that sees the universe with structural consistency and that when all the facts are put before us, both religious and scientific, we will then look at the make-up of the universe and any logical person would come to the inescapable conclusion that the universe was made with a specific purpose and that the very structure itself was obviously designed for the existence and perpetuation of man. Then Houten would turn to the basic innate need of man for a belief system to regulate human behavior—a need contingent upon the affirmation of God. But, Houten would maintain, even if we were to eliminate both religion and science from the argument and then independently examine all the current knowledge on the subject, the evidence would be conclusive of creationism, based not upon theology but the facts that allow us to draw a picture of a universe made for one purpose. It was as if science had discovered a cocoon but initially had no idea what had lived in it or what it was used for. Scientific inquiry would study the cocoon and seek a purpose for its structure and existence and then would be able to put together an accurate description of a moth and there could be no argument as to what creature depended upon that vehicle for its existence, or the basic purpose of the cocoon itself.

In his argument Houten would point out that the carbon atom, which would appear to be ideally designed to perpetuate and support all organic molecules, was the essence of all living things. This explanation rejects the "chance" hypothesis of Darwinism but allows that God specifically made the carbon atom so life would be born and flourish. Thus Houten introduces the anthropic connection into his philosophical thinking and he further argues that if the world was made up of an arbitrary mix, why would it be so systemized? Wouldn't the world, if composed without specific structural purpose but left to chance, simply break down without purpose or direction? Thus Houten would make the astronomical leap from anthropology to cosmology with the explanation that the logic of creation cannot be detoured by scientific dividing lines because there are no limitations to the intellectual capacity of the mind when motivated by God's behest.

As Houten progressed toward his doctoral goal, unexpected circumstances began to happen that gave his life almost supernatural distinction. He became an instant celebrity on the campus, doors began to open up for him and he was not beyond being a blatant opportunist. He found out, happily, that he was in demand as a speaker at numerous churches that would pay for his presentations. He was seen by evangelical churches as the leading authority on intellectual design and that his new ideas on the subject as well as the anthropic connection struck the Christian community as if it were the enlightenment. His name became known throughout the Southern states and he even felt the elation of one who perceives that others viewed him with awe. This brought to him a smug sense of intellectual self-confidence but, unfortunately, it also gave him a false acumen of infallibility.

While reading a scientific journal one day, Houten ran across a sentence which included a reference to "the evolution of the human mind." The piece was not written specifically on that subject—it was only the momentary thought of the author—but caught Houten's attention as perhaps little else would have and he had to ask himself, "Do these people really believe that?" So he shifted his direction of study to include what eventually turned out to be a new area of controversy between religion and science. But it was a controversy on which religion—at least then—could argue on a par with science as the concepts on both sides of the argument were imponderable and therefore unproved. Thus, Houten had strayed into a field of his advantage as his call for reasoned thinking and down-to-earth logic appealed to the populist mentality, particularly in light of the fact that there was no direct scientific evidence to dispute such logic.

Even before completion of his doctorate Houten was the most published religious writer in the country and it was without hesitation that he began to write articles that the human mind as created by God was perfect, capable of profound and expanding thought and had been designed in the image of God's great intellect. Houten's theory was immediately challenged by scientists who claimed that in analyzing DNA samples throughout the world, they had discovered two genetic varieties unique to the human brain which did not exist in humans thousands of years ago. The scientists admitted that they did not know what the variants' functions were but that they might improve cognitive ability. The scientists also admitted that they assumed a change rate in the human brain over a period of time and that led them to the ancestral gene.

The scientific response to Houten's thesis brought out the best in him. In a strongly worded rebuttal before an Assembly of God congregation in

Chicago, Illinois, on the following Sunday, he appealed to the emotional depths of the assemblage when he roared that "God did not create the world and then withdraw and stand idly by. He had created a perfect brain in man and no force can improve or alter what God has created." He went on to preach that man's perfectly formed brain was always capable of the great things we see in humans today. "They were always capable of that," he emphasized. "But it must be understood," he went on, "that life in the days of Jesus was comparatively simple and the great potential of the human brain was not in use because of the lack of complexity in their lives. So, in a sense, the human brain was in dormancy. But as civilization advanced and became more complicated, there was an awakening within the brain in order to understand and deal with this new complexity. But that was not created by evolution but was a melioration response designed into the brain in order that God's people could function on an equivalence with a changing world—change dictated by God's plan. And, we must understand that the man's intellectual vitality is the essential ingredient to that plan—it is more important than anything else on earth. And we must also remember that our God is an active God and that through creation he will not allow man to falter but He will make facilitated changes to affirm man's role in the Godly scheme of things."

Houten went on to relate many examples of young individuals showing brilliance and talent in music, mathematics, science and other disciplines when there was no reason to predict that that particular individual had the innate intelligence, parental encouragement or the genetic composition for such accomplishment. Obviously, to Houten that unforeseen ability was God-given and inert within the individual until awakened by a calling from the Lord and then, he concluded, "It is incumbent upon the individual that such talent be conducted in the works of the Lord and what cannot be forgotten here is that man will progress and one day seek God's glory for himself as he grows emotionally, intellectually and spiritually until he has overcome disquieting thoughts, realizes his purpose in the universe and becomes one the same as God."

Those few words brought great emotion to the congregation and perhaps more than just a few of them saw their own mentality in a new sphere. That short speech became the core belief of Houten's great work and one that was to elevate Christian intellectualism to its highest plane. But personally, Houten saw his advantage and that was, his base core believers would accept his theory as they accepted everything put before them no matter how absurd or outrageous, but the true advantage was that this new intellectualism appealed to anthropocentrism and egotism and that would attract the middle-of-the-roaders of marginal beliefs with disdain for traditional religion and its lack of selfism.

Houten poured himself into his writings, no longer concerned to impress those who paid his expenses. His dissertation was well-written and intelligent but still lacked the criteria of the scientific method but after much of his works were published in religious journals, he managed to get two into print in scientific publications and in both cases there was no editorial comment denigrating the works as either unscientific or a peripheral writing to the scientific community. However, a brief comment did point out that the author was a doctoral candidate at a Christian institution, stopping short of the suggestion that such writings would not have been approved as a thesis for an advanced degree in secular universities in scientific studies. Houten's writings had given him great prestige within the confines of his school but there was little reaction outside the school; the scientific community uncharacteristically seemed to ignore him, an occurrence that caused him some dismay as he had come to expect virulent criticism which he considered a badge of honor and which energized his growing number of followers.

Once he had completed his doctoral application, Houten was faced with setting a course for himself that would maximize his efforts toward his goal of short-circuiting Darwinism which outside of fundamentalist groups and political opportunists seemed to be a non-issue. Supreme Court decisions and governmental positions had made creationism the law of the land although that fact was generally lost on the public and largely ignored by scientists. But that was not enough for him. Scientific findings and new cosmic theories persisted as though the government mandate on creationism was of no particular consequence as individuals continued to perceive reality as they saw it and a large portion of the populace saw evolution as no threat to either them or their beliefs. This Houten abhorred and renewed his determined to return to his crusade as the great destroyer of the evil hypothesis.

Houten's doctoral dissertation was published and although enthusiastically accepted among evangelicals, received little response from the scientific community or the general public, a result that was very disappointing to him. But receiving his PhD and completion of the thesis did have a profound impact upon him personally. It gave him a sense of self he had never known; it was if all those early years of arrested emotional growth had been vindicated, that all the aspects of maturity and self-awareness had been reaped through his studies and intellectualizations, an awareness that gave him rise to consider that his calling was the divine course and must be continued. With his achievement, he gave the appearance of a new personality, so confident and verbal had he become. But with any change there can be a trade-off and that was even more obvious to those aware of subtle nuances in him as an old problem with suppressed anger and irascible impatience had replaced an otherwise gentle demeanor.

With this new self-concept, Houten began to exhibit a newly found personality; confident and outspoken, he spoke easily in front of others, even those with whom he was not acquainted—an entirely new experience for him as he had always been quite withdrawn and awkward and with this inner conversion came an obvious change of dress to a conservative but modish style complete with facial adaptations that moved him from nondescript to distinctive maturity. At that time, he was thrown into a melee of activity, attempting to integrate lectures, speeches, sermons and the expectations of the Evangelistic Counsel into a workable program and if that was not too encompassing, he began a cautious social life, an activity that included association with the opposite sex, which brought out an entrancing boyishness in him. As a person of stature within the evangelical community, he attracted much attention from the ladies of that faith and as much as he had always yearned for the physical attention of women, he gave it short shrift—a year or so—before he decided on marriage. The marital partner in this case was one Bridget Bordeau of Baton Rouge, Louisiana, a lady very active in the church and a "born again."

Bordeau had been married twice before and had a modest but reliable income as a result. Her first husband died and she divorced the second after a violent and drug-filled relationship had left her physically emaciated and emotionally impoverished. She sought condolence in the church although she had no religious history to speak of. She desperately sought help through several sources but it was not until she attended an Assembly of God congregation in New Orleans that she experienced the strong emotional draw that she was looking for. She had the appearance of being very attractive in her younger years, but now at forty-seven, her face was too broad for her bone structure although beautiful features were still evident in her middle-age facial configuration. She was perhaps a little heavy for her height but well-proportioned otherwise, but the outstanding feature she portrayed, not lost on Houten, was a large and shapely bust line. When the two married, he was sexually inexperienced while she was more than a little experienced; in fact, she had been sexually active before and after her marriages, which was discussed quite openly in the Assembly of God's ladies' gossip brigade. But in her relationship with her husband, Bridget was discreetly nurturing but not controlling, allowing him to believe that he was "teaching" her as she cleverly guided his efforts under the façade of submission. There were those in the church that believed that Bridget was immoral and that the relationship was doomed from the beginning, so different were the two. But Bridget was an active person and well supplemented her husband's career. She had worked several years as a book-keeper and had learned her trade well. Thus, she was able to organize her husband's work which she found in total disarray at the outset and she did so quite well, managing his activities so as to limit his stress and allow him to make the important decisions regarding conducting his affairs—with just a little prodding from her.

The first order of the day for the Houten-Bordeau team was to reinvent Houten and return him to the task of leading the crusade against Darwinism and the dictatorship of the sciences. During the four years of his doctoral studies, he seemed to have lost his passion—he had actually found the study of anthropology interesting and challenging and as always is a part of the anthropological disposition, he had increasingly come to exercise the creative mind-set essential to a thinker attempting to fill in presumptive explanations where evidence was weak or lacking but, he conceded, this was the one concession he made to the altar of academia, a trade-off that was necessary at the time.

It took but a brief time for him to reorient himself in time and purpose, for was it not these same scientists that created the myth of global warming which was made to influence national policy, or the idea that hurricanes and tornadoes are man-made, or that embryonic stem cells are essential to medical progress, or that fossil fuels demean wildlife and the environment and seeming other politically tinged positions that all began with an assault upon biblical literalism? With these protestations, the old Houten began to emerge but with a new vision of the battle and energetic dedication to its cause.

Bridget began to formulate a plan to start with a new vehicle to initiate a blueprint for action, a front organization, if you will. It would be relatively simple, not particularly demanding but structured without the worry of propriety. The name would be obvious—The Evangelical Anthropological Society of the United States of America or, simply the EAS. Bridget recognized and appreciated that fundamentalist Christians had bundles of money and, more importantly, were anxious to spend it on emotion-provoking issues relating to biblical permanency. The society would have a twelve-member board of directors—twelve was a good number—and all members would be important members of society with political influence and, at least two members should be well involved in the corporate media. The superficial purpose of the society would be that it would present itself as a think tank for intellectual discourse on creationism as a method of bringing Christianity to the public spectrum by media debate, discussion, lecture presentations and educational programming. Bridget needed to test the response to their proposed society and began making telephone calls to potential board members and money donors, and the reaction was indeed overwhelming—such enthusiasm she had never felt before and all seemed to be impelled by Houten and his work. After several successful telephone contacts, Bridget turned to her husband and said, "This is going to work; you're hot, baby." He blanched slightly at the reference and with a weak smile said under his breath, "I guess I need that kind of enthusiasm."

Putting the society together was going to be much easier than Bridget had thought; the potential members interviewed by telephone seemed to be in lockstep from the very outset and their enthusiasm was overwhelming. Houten made some of the calls himself in an effort to expedite the process of organization but he had a tendency to get in long-winded conversations despite Bridget's constant reminders that time and efficiency were of prime importance and she eventually restricted him to busy-work that would not get in her way. Bridget obviously had excellent organization skills and she went about her work not only as a professional but as one who felt that the present opportunity was a lifetime chance not only for her husband but herself as well. Not having been a member of a fundamentalist church for very long, she was surprised at how much the members thought and responded alike and how that made organization and a mission declaration relatively easy. In fact, willing participants in the governance of the society were beyond her expectations and made recruitment simple but personnel selection difficult.

Once the society was set up, it involved each board member in a weekly laptop meeting with other members and semi-annual in-person meetings in a designated city. All members selected for board participation were active church members and would have stringent requirements regarding intellectual contributions. They would be expected to lecture and teach in their immediate locale and in other ways to be active in the public forum. Most prominent board member was Paul J. Link, the president of Mega Media Inc., the largest conglomerate of television and newspapers in the world. His membership was imperative according to Houten, who appreciated the power of a friendly news source. Link was not only a devout Christian but he was a political right-wing pundit who was not beneath stirring the pot with a little spice that would induce a response from the readers and listeners that was not quite what one would call accurate reporting but tended to draw the more gullible in his particular ideological direction. If there was any question regarding such reporting brought up as to ethics, the standard and acceptable response within the church was that any method of conveying God's intent would be acceptable and that activist Christians must utilize whatever contrivance is deemed necessary to achieve the Christian mission.

The introductory society meeting occurred in January, 2031, in the conference room of Mega Media Inc. in New York City, much to the delight of Houten, who felt that the appearance of ascendancy and prestige rang from the confines of that lofty station and that such contiguity to an important source of power would imbue the society with the impact of consequentiality. Link was quickly elected chair of the group—the obvious choice—and under his leadership business moved almost too fast for some of the members who fell back on the tendency to vote favorably for any position that appeared to have a consensus. In looking at this group, Link could see, through a long practice of judgmental observation, that the group was a rag-tag conglomeration of rigid and unimaginative religious fanatics probably appointed as pay-off for persistent support and favored by their champion. But with that uninspiring thumbnail view of this pathetic parade of followers, Link knew instinctively that his task as leader would be simple and autocratic.

The first task, the formation of society rules and guidelines which were disposed of quickly by Link, who recommended the approval of the standards used by other such groups and which he described as "time-honored." The second motion of business was for a mission statement, an issue which traditionally got bogged down in debate in meetings of this sort but to Link's surprise, there was such homogeneity within the group that they adhered to the first proposal, presented by H.L. Houten, in toto. The mission said, in brevity, that the group had been formulated as a study, lecture and education group to advance Christianity and creationism through anthropological research and study.

The third issue of the meeting was to plan and approve the society's first project other than the customary speeches, lectures, televised presentations and educational forays. It was generally agreed that the project would involve anthropological digs in which relics would be categorized and recorded prior to evaluation by theological anthropologists approved by the Assembly of God

Church, which would oversee the entire operation. Toward that end, Houten was selected to put together a six-man team of experts and, depending on the eventual size of the operation, they would be able to gain the assistance of outside non-professionals for menial work. Houten, as a paleoanthropologist, would be in charge of the investigation from start to finish, would pick the site, obtain financial support, hire labor and organize, supervise the work in progress, integrate data from each specialist and publish its findings and conclusion. It was an assignment that he anticipated with relish.

The discussion on the project did take longer than Link imagined and that was mostly due to the staggering ignorance of many of the members bringing up inane issues not relevant to the discussion or to bringing into the argument some special patronage they thought that their particular church deserved or had earned. Ironically, that was exactly what Houten expected for himself, as for him it was the ultimate presentation for self-promotion but it was not evident to the attendees that his every constructive criticism, commentary, elaboration, clarification, or interpretation or was self-serving. Undoubtedly, Link was aware of this contrariety but seemed not to notice and gave the benefit of his attentiveness to his prodigy.

It was a forgone conclusion that the project would be in Iraq, were the world was created and civilization was born. Here at the confluence of the Tigris and Euphrates had been the Garden of Eden and it was near this geological site that the cities and empires from Genesis lay buried beneath the sifting sands and it was here that the first languages, writing, the concept of law, the idea of moral clarity and eventually, the first teachings of religion were created. Christians, long mired in the negativity of denial regarding archeology, had now become more sophisticated, and driven by their faith, eagerly sought to discover the mysteries of the Bible for they no longer feared scientific findings—they fervently believe that truth is on their side and interpretation of all cultural relics relative to biblical times would affirm the tenets of their faith. With that, biblical scholars had come to accept the new tools of archeology; DNA analysis for human and animal identification; chemical testing to evaluate the patina—a fine film on civilization's ornaments—for age and cultural identification; satellites to outline ancient towns buried beneath the desert sands; and, carbon dating to determine age of even the most minute residue found in relics. So then it would be here where the Dead Sea Scrolls were found; a Pontius Pilate inscription was located in Caesarea; the Calaphas Ossuary containing the bones of a priest from the time of Christ, was found in Jerusalem; the Qumran Ostracon, the Dead Sea community that wrote the scrolls, was located and unearthed; the Nag Hammadi Texts containing the Gnostic Gospels were found near the Nile; and, discovered was the Tel Dan inscription, proof that King David existed. The concept was intoxicating to the panel but what was not mentioned was the current appearance of the Iraq desert where thousands of professional and amateur archeologists had descended on the land to excavate in that relic-rich place, but not always for the right reason, for here the landscape was one of countless pock-like holes, most left uncovered, most dug by common shovels that sliced brutally through ancient tools and art objects, rendering them of little value to the digger who would then casually cast them aside but then triumphantly sell for a pittance whatever artifact he unearthed.

The fact that the probability of a successful dig was greatly diminished by the rape of the Middle East by amateur bone-diggers which not only reduced the possibility of making a find, but made the uncovering of pirated artifacts useless even if recovered later because their possession meant little once they had been taken out of context. Nevertheless, Houten in taking the floor, attempted to inspire the board toward this first project with an attack on his personal nemesis, science, with a withering denunciation that the discipline was designed to outrage the emotions of the faithful.

"Scientists," he began, "have been given a free rein in this country too long. They have become omnipotent in a public eye that believes that they are all-knowing and their theories cannot be questioned. And when they go to biblical lands, they unearth precious relics from the biblical times and arrogantly take possession of them and then interpret their existence from their own secular bias. They have maintained this practice for decades and having practically written God out of their findings; they have established a secular interpretation of biblical times that went unanswered. But their conclusions are antithetical to the evidence and when we read their reports and the interpretations of their findings, we are appalled by their persistent bias in favor of the ungodly. The fact is that if we found the same artifacts under the same circumstances in which they found them, we would analyze and interpret them differently and who is to say which advocacy carries the truth. But times are changing—scientists are on the defensive, they are in the periphery and even many of their own are now accepting creationism as the true foundation of the earth and humanity and they do this without impairing the progressive finds of science that aid humanity because by maintaining one's Christian integrity one does not detract from science but actually gives life and direction to a science that disallows the intellectual elitists to drift away from God's teachings.

"We Christians have failed our religion by our inactivity in the field of archeology. We have failed to do our homework while secularists have been allowed to build their case for evolution and all the while they have looked down on us as ignorant and therefore, our comments incomprehensible. But we must remember that in the field of archeological theories, that because there are huge historical gaps that cannot be explained or cannot be fit into their precious theories accurately, they speculate and interesting enough, their speculative fervor always authenticates their previously conceived theories. Would it not be acceptable by any reasonable person that any newfound piece of evidence would be subjected to the scrutiny of all belief systems and that no theory or conclusion resulting from the study without such consideration would be invalid. I therefore submit that anthropological findings and conclusions to date are invalid for that very reason. We have conducted surveys that tell us that over fifty percent of Americans believe that the Book of Revelations contains true prophecy; sixty-five percent believe that the faithful will be taken up to heaven in the Rapture; ninety percent believe in Satan; and, ninety-five percent believe that God created the universe. Those are staggering numbers and much of these beliefs are the result of biblical study and calling to God for counsel and understanding. If such overwhelming numbers of people—Christian and non-Christians were interviewed for the survey—believe as was stated, surely it only makes sense that the Christian perspective play an important role in the analysis and evaluation of biblical artifacts.

"Therefore, in conclusion, I propose not only an archeological expedition to the biblical lands, but that we eventually must expand our operation so that will come the day when we can reevaluate all previous archeological evidence and put them into context with new findings in which the books of Genesis, Kings and Chronicles wait beneath the sands of the desert for revelation. And with these findings we will one day have answers to all questions of faith, the Gospels, the creation, the great purpose of life and the myriad questions surrounding the Bible and the life of Jesus. We must remember that in archeology evidential findings are never certain and that is why our interpretation of evidence will lead us to the truth. This is the noblest of all causes."

The panel stood in muted clapping in appreciation of Houten's presentation and the project was approved unanimously. Houten was on his way—he would become the great dragon-slayer for fundamentalist Christians but in his singular mind-set he was not mindful that a sustained blow to science in archeological study would unerringly denigrate science in other areas of study—global warming, the oceans, the environment, medicine, the food supply or any of the things essential to the survival of man on this planet or that public opinion if won over would easily outmatch scientific evidence. But for Houten those were non-issues—for he believed in the Revelation and all other things were not relevant.

# Eleven

What Houten hated most about Iraq was the oppressive heat, an all-encompassing, stifling presence that penetrated his total being, pressing downward and inward on him with suffocating pressure and overwhelming him no matter where he was or what task he was involved in or even when he was merely trying to rest on his soft feather mattress in the tent that he and Bridget shared among the dozen tents of the Evangelical Anthropological Society's biblical exploration team. He longed for the mild climate that he had always lived in and appreciated the climate-controlled buildings of his work and studies. He had hardly noticed that when he came to Iraq he breathed easier, having to use his respirator much less than he did in the states, which may have been contributed to the dryness of the climate, but Houten had no inclination to praise anything about that god-forsaken country for he desultorily disregarded this one single positive aspect of that desert country without comment. Of course, there were other things that he despised about this work, the project and the geographic area. After organizing the expedition and some preliminary training, there was little for him to do other than supervising the work in progress, which was of little challenge so he engaged himself to work in the dig alongside the others. He found this extremely distasteful and his innate impatience and resulting aggravation became evident. He found the work boring, constant drudgery and incredibly uninteresting. More to the point was that it lacked the uplift and the constant high that he had known as a leader in the assault upon Darwinism; here he felt unappreciated, a virtual unknown, lost in a wilderness desert doing meaningless, trivial tasks that any fool could do and in the process, his value to his religion would be lost. As the leader of the dig, it was Houten's responsibility to reproduce in drawing all relics found and then record the sketch for a report and conclusion, but it was difficult to identify a given relic drawn by Houten, so crude were his reproductions despite that the sketch required of a find was so basically simple. Furthermore, his plotting and survey of dig sites was of poor quality and would probably not have been accepted in an undergraduate anthropology class. Despite his education and alleged anthropological expertise, he was not of the mentality of the professional anthropologist—he lacked the patience, the deep interest in the affairs and lifestyle of our ancestors, he lacked the curiosity and sensitivity to put evidence into historical context, he failed to recognize that time at a dig was enduring and that there was a timelessness about the discipline; he lacked the depth of soul of the archeologist who upon discovery would feel past cultures come to life before him; and, he lacked the canny imagination necessary to exhume the indescribable human connections spoken to anthropologists by things of the ages. These things did not matter to Houten because for him the world's existence and purpose had been determined and nothing would change that—no dig, no relic, no great discovery from the soil of the earth. Such could do nothing more than confirm what he already knew. He did not need evidence, for he spoke to God directly and knew the truth. Now he had come to accept that and experienced a nonpareil oneness with God.

In the spring of 2031, the Israel Anthropological Society, the single authority over all excavations in the Middle East, assigned the evangelical team to the El Al site near Nasiriya, a meadow-like mound only recently discovered by Israeli anthropologists. The initial explorations of the site found it rich in artifacts although there was no indication that there would be any biblical significance found there. The mound was rather low but flat, indicating some type of presence there, but was not high enough to suggest a presence of long duration. It was in the proximity of Um Al Agareb, an archeological site which had been devastated by thieves during the Iraqi War who left the vast desert floor with countless holes scattered endlessly about without any conformity or apparent plan, then selling the valuable relics for a few meager dollars each on the streets of Baghdad. The society had assigned six teams to the site, each with the same overall expectations and each placed in a position to unearth what was believed to be an important part of the town if that was what lay beneath the land. The first diggings went well as the evangelical team showed great enthusiasm for the project and believed that their labor would produce biblical manifestations despite preliminary results suggesting that tools and art forms found by the team were pre-biblical. Houten himself was even less enthused as he felt a crushing sense of rejection when the Israeli society had failed to see the American team as more important than other teams as the society randomly had issued assignments without any subjective considerations. Nevertheless, Houten applied himself to the task at hand as he had signed a two-year contract, the whole impact of which he rationalized away by believing that something, somehow, would intercede and that would redeem him.

Bridget Houten was another story. Brought to the camp as a service worker, she was nevertheless thrilled to be a part of the exploratory team. She was not a big player but felt it important that she play even a minor role in an event that she believed to be historically significant. Her husband was surprised at her drive and energy in running the camp and doing the numerous chores essential to keep it operative. When he had married Bridget he found her enigmatic and as a victim of persistent corruptive gossip within the church he had some doubts about her rehabilitation as a "born again" as, in all reality, he knew that such accomplishment can be temporary or a manipulative ploy as much as he wanted to believe otherwise. Even on the day of their wedding, he had doubts, not regarding her character, but he had only recently become active on the dating scene and as women had been drawn to him—probably because of his prestige within the church—this was a new and flattering experience as he saw himself unrealistically as a roguish romantic with his choice of the ladies so it fell that he had the audacity to consider, in his thoughts, at the last moment, of not marrying his fiancée as, very simply, he believed that he could do better.

But providence had smiled on Houten when he went through with the marriage (it is doubtful that he would have had the temerity to call off the wedding at the last moment) for Bridget became an important asset to the evangelical operation in Nasiriya and enhanced his performance as well. She had incredible energy, was the first up every morning and the last in bed every night. She was an excellent cook and extended personal chores and courtesies to all the team. She and her husband shared a nine-person tent which was large enough to feed the entire crew at one sitting. She decorated the tent with locally bought beads, artificial flowers, wall hangings, feather pillows and a surreal-appearing oil painting of Jesus painted by a ten-year-old Iraqi boy. She carried water into the field to the team all day long and made sure that everyone took their salt tablets regularly—she was indefatigable. What surprised Houten the most was that despite her grueling schedule, Bridget's lovemaking intensified, a fact that made his existence in this forlorn place bearable. But her most important role was that of counselor-pacifier for her poor husband. He was decimated by the 120-degree heat and finding the project beneath him and unnecessary, he complained constantly. But she was soothing and understanding for she had not gone through two tumultuous marriages for nothing or without learning anything about men and their childlike dispositions and the plastic solutions necessary to appease their pouting narcissism. She had completed a twelve-step program and knew the importance of complete honesty in personal relationships but she also knew that her husband's fragile ego would not always allow the truth so she was forced to permit selective untruths to salvage a tenuous psyche. It was a role that troubled her as it reminded her of the perplexities of her first marriage and she knew well that circumvention will ultimately fail by its own deception. Nevertheless, she continued to mother her old husband with the faint hope that somehow she could provide the therapy that would strengthen his floundering self-esteem.

Needless to say, Houten's emotional make-up and lack of focus was contrary to the intellectual energy and focus necessary to an archeologist to uncover an unknown way of life by recognizing subtle evidence lost in rock and soil for centuries. Fellow archeologists saw in him an individual strangely preoccupied and inattentive to detail but those characteristics became so imbued in his persona that it was merely dismissed by his coworkers as the peculiarities of an idiosyncratic personality. That is, until he met Jalaal Alzawri, known as Jay, an archeological graduate from Columbia University.

Alzawri was a tall well-built man in his early thirties who could easily have been the son every mother wanted. He was extremely handsome and that was enhanced by a personality comparable to a border collie with a go-fetch attitude. Women would be melted by his good looks but when he addressed them individually, they absolutely would have been at his mercy. But that was not his intention for he greeted all with the same joyous enthusiasm and dignity no matter what their stature in society may have been. He saw joy in everything and all living things. Always dressed in khaki short pants, sleeveless safari shirt and an incredibly beat-up slouch hat, he could be picked out of any crowd for his animation and energy.

He had been born in America to Iranian parents studying on scholarship; however, upon completing their education when their son was four years of age, the parents returned to Tehran to complete four years of government service as part of their obligatory agreement as their scholarship mandated. Alzarwi completed elementary and high school in Iran and as an excellent student was accepted at Columbia and moved to New York City where an uncle still resided. By then Alzarwi spoke four languages and his English was without accent. He had always wanted to be an archeologist since he was a child, his early exposure coming from a cousin who worked in the field and might be described as a mythomaniac who embellished the most mundane drudgery into glorious episodes of romanticized adventure. But Alzarwi was not bamboozled by the fantasized descriptions—he began to read diligently at a very young age on the subject and became quite knowledgeable—most of his written language assignments while in school were on the topic and teachers recognized his intense interest and knowledge in a subject that was rather esoteric for most of them. Upon completing his master's studies at Columbia, he forsook a PhD to go into the field as an archeologist, his plan being to get the most diverse field experience possible in as many cultures as was realistic and by the time he was thirty, he had worked digs at the Maidu and Miwok sites in California; Dordogne Valley, France; Siwalik Hills, India: Makapan Valley, Bechuanaland; and lesser known sites in Chile, Egypt and South Africa; but, it was his dream to one day be like Louis S.B. Leakey; that is, to be the world's leading authority on a specific site and a specific culture, such as Leakey's work in the Olduvai Gorge in Tanzania.

No two men could have been more unalike than Houten and Alzarwi in temperament, personality or professional aptitude and, it may have very well been Houten's worst nightmare when the two met. Houten had heard the Iranian's name on several occasions and the comments were positive—most descriptions of him were paradoxical as he was seen, on the one hand, as very vociferous and outgoing but, on the other, totally absorbed in his work. The teams had been in place at the site for about two weeks when, one day, Alzarwi's head popped up over the lip of Houten's dig, his grinning face and twinkling eyes engaging all members of the evangelical team except Houten, who was taken back by the intrusion.

"Finding anything?" Alzarwi blurted out in making the most inane opening he could think of.

"No…no, not so far, just routine," Houten responded looking down at his hands containing a trowel and a brush as if he did not know what they were.

"My name is Jay—I'm working just a few meters north of your dig."

"I am Dr. Houten."

"Actually, we are beginning to pull out a lot of stuff—we hit a level that is pretty rich in artifacts…you know, the usual stuff, shards of pottery, broken tools of some sort and there is some indication of fire. We don't know what it all means yet but it is getting quite interesting. I thought I'd take a break and come see you guys, I tend to forget time when I'm in a dig."

Houten lamented, "We have not come across anything worth mentioning yet but we are hopeful."

"Well, recovering artifacts from the past is interesting but the interpretations is what I really get into." Alzarwi paused and then added, "I have a good background in the biblical history of this area."

Houten replied, "That is God's purpose—to give us little signs to stimulate what is already in our God-given brains. It lies there dormant but we know the truth—we know. And speculation is not necessary."

"That is utter ridiculous," Alzarwi countered. "God doesn't tell us how to think. We have to analyze and interpret the data and we don't know where it will lead us."

"Are you a Christian?"

"No, I'm Muslim."

"I see."

Houten went back to the soil but used the trowel with a little more force than he had previously. Finally, he looked up to Alzarwi and said, "Don't you believe that if man is made in God's likeness, then he has the same brain capacity and knowledge except that it is undeveloped because man has not achieved that plane yet. I mean look at all the great inventions—men could not have made such discovery without prodding from God."

Alzarwi was not smiling anymore and answered, "Man has never invented anything—it has always been done through association with natural phenomenon. If God induced all progress, why did He not point out to the early farmers that the Euphrates River was the best place to plant crops as it had water, fertile soil and plenty of space. But man did not even know about seeds—I mean, how could he, how would he make the connection. That is why farming began in the foothills. There the first farmers were actually hunters—goat hunters. But they figured out that hunting goats would not produce a consistent food supply so they began to capture goats and pen them up and what they found out over a period of time, was that the goats having eaten wild emmer would eliminate their waste which contained emmer seeds and the following spring emmer would grow up in their pens and the hunters knew emmer to be edible. So there you had all the ingredients of primitive farming being demonstrated for them—seeds, fertilizer, moisture, good soil—and there was no revelation from God, no signals from the supernatural, no mandated instructions from the god of agronomy. It was all quite natural, all quite explainable. And, all this explains not only the expansion of a culture but the proliferation of language. When the goat hunters were just nomads their language probably consisted of only five hundred to six hundred words. There was no need for more; that is, until they discovered emmer and then quite suddenly they needed more vocabulary to go with their new economy and the language probably grew by a hundred percent in the first year and then there were new activities…you know, like goat's milk, and a new woman's role, in cooking and processing the emmer. Just think, cultural change and the expansion of language all because some nomadic goat-hunter saw a goat shit."

"But," Houten argued, "that is what is wrong with mankind today, we make all these suppositions and do not listen to the word of God. If we remained in the realm of God and followed the teachings of Jesus we would not have become so alienated from Him. When the Jews crossed the great wilderness, it was not because some natural phenomenon caused them to, it was because God commanded them to and then they eventually became shopkeepers and merchants, something entirely foreign to them when they were sheep-herders, and all that because it was God's plan for them."

Alzarwi responded almost casually, "See, that is what you guys always do, you can't debate the issue so you become irrelevant. I mean, like, what does the migration of Jews have to do with the mind of inventors? Particularly when the event that you describe is historical myth. We don't know for sure what prompted the Jews to migrate to the east, it was probably demographic pressure. We just don't know."

That night, Houten, upon retreating to the tent he shared with his wife, was disconsolate. It would be a hellacious night for poor Bridget, who would have to suffer through one of the worst episodes of morbid gloominess that she could ever recall. When he began to rail against Alzarwi, she suddenly understood. She had seen the young Iranian herself and admired him but she was too aware of her husband's eccentricities to mention Alzarwi by name and it was obvious to her that he shifted his focus from his usual complaints caused by chronic insecurity to a direct attack upon another individual; in this case, not an individual representing a direct threat to him but one who might inadvertently expose his emotional shortcomings. Bridget consoled him well into late night and after getting him to down a bowl of soup, she put him to bed much in the manner she had once put down her first child suffering through a particularly bad day. Fortunately, there would only be one more day of work and then Houten would be returning to the states for a previously scheduled lecture in Washington, D.C., and then, before he returned two days later, a visit with Paul Link.

Once airborne out of the Baghdad International Airport, Houten relaxed and the imposition of Jay Alzarwi was quickly forgotten. His mind began to return to the familiar and safe sphere in which he had always felt comfortable—the static equanimity of fundamental orthodoxy where everything had an answer or an explanation and there was no argument. Thus imbued with the self-righteousness of gospel, Houten came out of his gloom and had an overpowering need to pontificate. The young man seated next to him, a shy and introverted soul, seemed a good subject to be proselytized—he was young, inexperienced and, Houten reasoned, probably lacked religious training. Turning in his seat to face the youth, Houten asked, "Have you heard the truth?" Confused as to just what that meant, the young man silently shook his head in the negative and Houten, without hesitation, launched into an oft-repeated sermon. Although the young man was unsophisticated, he was intelligent and soon inconsistencies and contradictions to what he had been taught became apparent in Houten's bombast but there was no pause, no expected reply, no opportunity to question, just the steady drumbeat of evangelical discourse as the preacher, with great emotion and selective emphasis, rambled on through the tedious homily. Houten droned on through what seemed an eternity obviously listening to and being inspired by his own voice while the poor jaded young man had fallen fast asleep.

The following day, Houten gave a customary Houten speech at the Evangelical Governmental Policy Center in Washington, D.C., before about thirty thousand followers, but the speech was amazingly tired and mundane as he had given little thought to it other than a stereotypical sermon relying on the patent tried-and-true method of lecturing as that had always worked for him. It seemed absurd later that a speech before so many would be simply presented as a hackneyed plate of platitudes while his appearance before the single most powerful man in the media, Paul Link, would bring out the exaltation in him.

In returning to the states having only been gone a few short months, Houten immediately had noticed how acid the air seemed and he subsequently wheezed and sputtered his way through his speech; however, upon deplaning in Chicago's O'Hare Airport, he observed an improved respirator on sale and the number on display in the gift shop suggested that it was a hot item. Named the "Accelerator Mask," it was a plastic face mask molded to fit the average face and which, if held tightly to the skin to prevent unhealthy air from sifting in, would provide the wearer with a shot of pure oxygen, amphetamine and a medical lung stimulant, all by simply tweaking the nose, giving the wearer a sort of jump start when having breathing difficulty. Never one for popularized trinkets or must-have accessories, he saw the practicality in the mask and purchased one despite its exorbitant price. Later, in approaching Link's office in a darkened hall after a long elevator ride, he took a whiff from the mask and felt a decisive sense of relief in his breathing and then instantly hacking up globs of mucus. When he composed himself, he entered the office of the media giant, CEO of the only surviving media corporation in the world.

The meeting, a private conference with Link, occurred at 9:30 AM sharp at Link's office in Chicago. Houten was led into the mogul's office by a live female receptionist—an unusual arrangement considering that robo-escritoires had become so inexpensive and practical. He found the office to be surprisingly austere but functional. Link greeted him cordially without rising. His desk, uncluttered but expansive, was huge and solid black, causing Houten to wonder at its beauty—was it cobalt? Teak wood? Or just hard black plastic? But what was most intriguing was the shape of it edges. Starting downward in a slow slope, the slope descended sharply and then straightened out for a pause and then went into another steep decline giving the impression of a wave before it breaks. The desk was well polished and was an object that compelled one to run one's fingers over its exterior which Houten did, an uncommon thing for him to do, and then when Link eyed Houten feeling the sleekness of the desk, Houten quickly withdrew his hands as if he had been burned on a hot plate. The desk was placed in front of a large plate-glass window with an incredible view overlooking the city of Chicago and its environs. From there Link could look down from his aerie to see a wondrous view of Lake Michigan, Montrose Harbor, Northeast Illinois University (which he owned) and the John Kennedy Expressway. Link sat aboard a swivel chair on rollers and it had become almost commonplace for him to suddenly wheel around to the window at any time to this commanding view which gave him an exhilarating sense of power. When Houten commented on the view Link gloried with pride but Houten, never analytical regarding the nuances of human behavior, failed to see the connection, merely assuming that his patron simply enjoyed the landscape. Link was not one for formalities and he neither smoked nor drank himself and did not offer Houten coffee which he personally thought to be a distasteful waste of time.

Link had always been quite relaxed around individuals or groups and being not the least pretentious, had no hesitation about discussing his own mistakes or shortcomings—his openness and straightforward approach to life had made him the success that he became. In an amused mode he said to Houten, "Perhaps you are wondering why I have a real-live temp receptionist. Well, I bought this robo-recept from Prudhomme Electronics Outlet and she has a malfunction, so for the time being, I need a temp. I'll show you what I mean. Miss Prudhomme, will you come in here please?"

"YesMisterLinkwhatcanIdoforyou?"

"See what I mean?" said Link to Houten.

"Miss Prudhomme, I'd like you to meet H.L. Houten, a doctor of anthropology."

"IamgladtomakeyouracquaintanceDrHouten."

Houten, taken back to a few seconds to decipher her garbled phrase, answered, "I am pleased to meet you too, Miss Prudhomme."

Link chuckling to himself dismissed her with, "Thank you, Miss Prudhomme."

"What I called you here for," Link said getting down to the issue at hand, "is that we are beginning the have a problem and that is that I feel we are losing momentum in the Christian movement—there isn't the fervor, the excitement that there was several years ago and as you know, these people are like children, they have to constantly be stimulated with something new and exciting. You know we have done everything to draw their interest—we built the Christdome in Houston, we introduced rock and roll music to our meetings, food courts, a skateboard park, we brought in celebrity guest speakers, we gave them musical concerts and festivals—anything to reach the masses. But now it seems that that has been getting stale so we have to come up with something new. And not only is there a fear that we will lose the marginally secular-minded and the unchurched, but even those who have always been devout seem to be losing interest. Stealth evangelism has worked well but it has reached its limit and now we have to be inventive and I think that maybe we should go back to basics, so to speak. I think that maybe we should bring the displays of religious symbolism that we have purposely eschewed and that we should return to, and reemphasize, the Bible."

This was all unexpected to Houten, who had no inkling of any loss of interest by the followers, so he rather apologetically admitted that he had been out of touch and that his current work in the Middle East would preclude him from being directly involved. Link immediately assured Houten that his place in the scheme of things was essential by saying, "No, that is not the problem, you are just where we need you and I want you to stay on your project for the time being. But here is the problem with that: what you are doing is time-consuming and maybe—just maybe—you will make some kind of a breakthrough that will prove, once and for all, biblical permanency, but that is just the problem, time is of the essence and we are going to have to come up with something momentous—and soon."

Houten sadly conceded, "It is very slow work but at the same time, I am really a neophyte archeologist in the eyes of the Israeli anthropologists and they oversee the project and will question anything that I uncover, they will question its authenticity and most likely reject my conclusions, and, you know that there is a lot of politics involved in all of this as well."

"Look, I am behind you all the way, don't underestimate the power of the media. Come to us first and we will give you favorable press; in fact, keep us apprised of your activities and progress and we can do human interest articles covering your work as you go. But I can't emphasize enough—we need something big, something really big to wake up the followers and I know that you can do it."

"To do something of which you describe will take me out of the ordinary into something that is quite daring and maybe intrusive and I may need help, for example, legal assistance—you know, the Israelis have everything over there tied up and you just can't get something done without their approval and, I believe, they are quite distrustful and protective of what they consider their territory."

Sitting back with a self-satisfied smirk, Link said, "Don't worry, we have their number. We have the support of the president, the court and legislature and we have a lot of political clout in Israel so when push comes to shove, we'll get our way."

Then Houten added, "That is fine, but not only do we need help with the Israelis but here in this country, we need to convince our own people to believe in our program and its findings—that our findings are authentic. You remember the James Ossuary many years ago? The ossuary held the bones of Jesus' brother according to the inscription but, despite the fact that many anthropologists supported its authenticity, Israeli Antiquity Authorities called it a fraud. Despite our protest, the verdict was upheld by the courts and they ignored our pleadings that the ossuary was real and that the bones in it were, in fact, those of James."

Link said, "That couldn't happen now. The media is too strong for them and it is so important that we carry the word of Christ to the world and we will do that very thing. In addition, the base of Christian believers are almost desperate for something to reaffirm their faith and I know that they would show great exuberance toward anything that would renew their fervor. And once they are so inspired, no one could convince them otherwise and once you've got them on your side, you're home free."

"That is encouraging and gives me heart. You are very dedicated and I know I can count on your support and I'm sure this will lead to a new day in Christianity."

Link said, "Well, let's go for it, we'll proceed and see what we can find over there. I wish you the best and in the meantime, is there anything you need, or are you having any problems?"

"No," Houten answered. "The only thing there is a young archeologist who has been getting under my skin."

"Is he a godly man?"

Houten reflected on that for a moment and said, "No," softly.

"Is he an American?"

"Yes."

"In that case I can have him removed."

"That would be helpful."

"Okay, remember, we need something big, I can't overemphasize that."

Abruptly, the meeting was over without even a god-be-with-you and, as easily as he had been congenial before, Link was suddenly detached and into a businesslike disposition. After a brief goodbye, Houten made his departure and, as he left, he heard one last utterance from Miss Prudhomme, forlornly sitting in a corner as if rejected by her master, "GoodbyeDrHoutenandhaveagoodday."

The following Tuesday, Houten was back at the Nasiriya dig with new vigor that surprised his team and delighted Bridget, who felt that she might now be relieved of her nightly therapy sessions, at least, the exhausting, emotionally grinding pattern of his despondency. In categorizing and recording artifacts on the site, Houten commenced one of the most important aspects of excavation, stratigraphy, a system of determining the sequential cultural history of the site. In most sites, stratigraphy can only be detected through chemical or physical segregation of the materials after completion of the excavation; but, in this case, stratigraphic differences were obvious at the dig at the time of the excavation. That was a fortunate aspect of archeology in the Middle East that gave Houten a hands-on appreciation of the project. The stratification in the dig up to then revealed Bronze and Copper Age artifacts, at one point mixed, so to confuse the time sequence, and that was followed by several inches of a sod layer with humus stain which indicated a period of abandonment with later human occupation and that was followed by evidence of fire which may have destroyed the settlement completely. Initial findings preceding the fire were broken pottery and some shards of religious ornaments.

In the middle of the week, while working in the dig, Houten overheard the team discussing the transfer of Jay Alzarwi to another location. There was speculation as to why he would be reassigned but, in judging the popular archeologist's character, it was always assumed that it was for tactical reasons. Upon hearing the news, Houten kept working, offering no comment or outward reaction other than a faint cognitive smile. He heard the same speculation over and over through the rest of the week but it did not give him total satisfaction as, inevitably, there was the persistent little kicker that Alzarwi would be missed.

Bridget noticed a marked change in her husband as, after a lengthy period of practically ignoring ecclesiastic incantations, he suddenly had become prayerful, not only at the usual specified times, but any time of the day as if he was seeking guidance or a sign of reaffirmation of his current undertaking. There was also a great amount of time in meditation, something entirely new to Houten and which was a tip-off to Bridget that perhaps something rather significant was in the offing for her husband. She questioned him in that regard rather gingerly so as not to appear overly inquisitive or controlling, but his response was the old familiar technique of falling back upon biblical phrases that told absolutely her nothing. Whatever was happening with her husband, Bridget reasoned, it was positive and uplifting as she had never seen him as happy and animated for a long time, and she was not about to tamper with success.

Houten's behavior, however, was not just a period of adjustment, or possibly that he was finally maturing—as Bridget may have hoped—but rather it was really something more momentous than that, for Houten suddenly developed an intense interest in the world around him. Bridget, initially relieved, eventually began to feel alienation as her husband seemed emotionally distant in a behavior toward her that might best be described as bending to marital duty, but little more. Slowly she began to find that she had idle time, particularly in the evenings, and only then did she realize how time-consuming her husband's dependency had been and now, she plaintively reminisced of the closeness she had felt and she regretted the loss of intimacy that it held, the touching and fondling, the emotional sharing, her sense of belonging and having purpose and the confidence that they had in their being together. But for Bridget, this would not become a communal problem; she had the inner strength to shut off her husband's exclusion of her from soulful interaction, a situation she hoped was temporary and in which he may have rationalized their emotional separation as being the consequences of God's work.

For the first time Houten began to realize the quintessence of being an archeologist. He felt a connection with the past but not as a past described in thousands of years but as an awareness that made dig sites timeless and substantive and imbued the individual with a sameness of self in that those ancient walls were a part of all mankind and that gave the archeologist an emotional unity with those of the same heritage as those who have passed before. There is in the mind of the archeologist an unbreakable link and a persistent element of excitement in the origins of humanity and the realization that all of it—the ancient remains or the modern society—are within the same geological eye blink of time and that there is no great difference between man then or now, for modern man would behave as did our ancestors under the same circumstances and thus, is born the meditative mind of the inquisitorial intellect.

In his time off, Houten began to tour the Holy Land and the biblical deserts of the Middle East—not the customary guided tours, for he had done that before—where he would wander through straw-thatched market stalls called souq in Morocco; visited Qumran, believed to be the community where the Dead Sea Scrolls were written; saw the wilderness temple at Petra, Jordan, and the Roman ruins of Leptis Magna on the Libyan coast; he explored the Neanderthal burial site at Shanidar, Iraq; and he marveled at the massive statues that guard the cave temple of Abu Simbel in Egypt. He watched as pilgrims to Mecca kneeled before the Kaaba and read the Koran; he walked several miles of what was once a caravan trail used by Bedouin nomads near Khartoum; he witnessed the grim struggle for survival and the ancient rhythm of Arab farm life; he felt pity for desert farmers using a water device invented by Archimedes in the third century; he saw scarce pasturage and scant water and the families dependent upon those limited resources. He saw the ambivalence of attitudes, the threat to national identities, the erosion of traditional cultures and the shocking poverty, all a result of a nation's attempt to reconcile two opposing cultures—modern culture driven by the global economic exploitation and the static ancient practice of the poor scratching in the parched deserts of the earth for survival. Houten felt saddened by what he had seen and, as an individual always on the outside of social descent, he felt the unusual compulsion to address the unfairness and deliberate stratification of societies. But Houten himself was ever so much cloistered as he had ever been, the product of a rigid uncompromising belief that was more a cult than a religion and because of this inelasticity, he was unable to challenge injustice and oppression even as it distressed his sense of humanity. Instead, Houten would fall back on his time-honored solution to all problems and seek redemption in his interpretation of God.

Then Houten began to spend more and more time in Jerusalem, specifically Kibbutz Tzuba, where he wandered the hills and contemplated the anthropological past as the way of life there that changed little over the centuries. Iraq had become too dangerous, Houten thought, as the discovery possibilities had been limited not only by the threats of outlaws and Islamic insurgents, but there, in the relic-rich desert where the first laws and religion were recorded, the land had been crudely decimated by the poverty-stricken who recognized the value of nothing above and beyond their daily struggle for survival, their ultimate objective, the cheap sale of priceless artifacts on the black market. Kibbutz Tzuba was just a few miles from Jerusalem, its few citizens sheltered from modern society, a fact that they cherished in that they esteemed the old way. Here Houten traversed the hills of nectarine trees hiding the caverns and dens where the ancestors of the area's modern-day denizens had lived in feculent circumstances for generations in a singular economy that produced nothing—their foremost activity being that of tending their goat herds and that led them to virtually no need for invention or improvisation other than the trivial trade of items from the rare caravans proceeding through the area. The modern-day counterparts of the cave-dwellers live out a few meters from those archaistic grottos in mud and wood houses adorned with doors intricately hand-carved and latticed windows, the main difference in their respective cultures being that the early cave dwellers were polytheistic while their modern descendents believe in one god. The modern culture is multi-faceted but nothing in comparison to the high-tech mind-numbing progress of the world's big cities where people lived in a mind-set of virtual fantasy; while those of Kibbutz Tzuba, surprisingly, know little of their ancestors and retain no myths or legends connecting them with the past; and the abandoned caves have not been used in any meaningful sense other than as sanctuaries for itinerant herders occasionally being caught in violent storms.

# Twelve

Houten first saw the cave from about a quarter mile away. Of all the caves that he had seen and explored this one seemed to call to him and he heeded that call. The cave itself was located at the beginning of a steep wadi, somewhat hard to see and considering the difficulty in climbing to the spot, not necessarily inviting to the casual explorer but certainly compelling to an archeologist. Houten had been drawn to the area of the cave as it was in proximity with a cave in which there was a controversial claim of it being the ritual cave of John the Baptist, who was born in the area. It did not appear to Houten that the cave would have been used by herders as it was not easily accessible to the hills or lowlands where the flocks would roam; instead, it would be more suitable to an individual wanting to use it as a haven, a place of preferred isolation where one could meditate and be free to contemplate oneself and one's relationship to the world; or, an outlaw avoiding his fate in the hands of the law or whatever law existed. In approaching the place, the cave entrance was parallel to the wadi and therefore from below the entrance appeared to be at an angle and did not seem very large but once at the entrance, the explorer could see a large opening and the darkness within suggested that the cave was indeed of adequate size and once inside would be very adequate for several people. The floor initially sloped upward and then leveled off but what caught the attention of the archeologist was that unlike the caves that he had explored in the immediate area, this one did not appear natural to the geology of the area. It was as if it had been excavated for some specific purpose and, considering the overwhelming task that would be for a primitive effort, it would be unlikely that the cave was dug in ancient times. Yet there were no roads or any type of access to the place or any debris outside.

The slope of the floor continued about ten meters and then leveled off and broadened out, the resulting room one would surmise was used as a living quarters. The archeologist however deplored the shallow ceiling which did cause him to bang his head and was uncomfortably low but then, when he thought about it, the average height of a man in biblical times was about five feet four inches and thus such an individual would be quite comfortable in movement about the room. Houten then took a pen knife and cut into the floor of the cave, the floor appearing very hard and rock-like but which cut smoothly under the blade revealing several inches of debris that had accumulated in the cave giving the archeologist the impression that the cave was one of antiquity and exciting him that there would be recoverably artifacts in the main room. The room showed no sign of water seepage from outside and there was no other room or entrance but on the east wall there had been a mantle cut in rock and to appearances it was designed for the purpose of placing ornamentation of some kind. In returning to the entrance, Houten observed that brush and small trees had grown around the entrance and he wondered aloud how he had seen the cave at all from the distance and then, in examining ground in front of the cave, he detected subtle mounds of debris which may have been from a previous excavation of the interior room—matter to later be subjected to chemical analysis—and that apparently had caught his eye.

He exited the cave slowly, then turned and faced the cave, dropping to his knees and he began to pray. He asked for nothing, only offering thanks for his discovery. Reluctant to leave that beautiful place, its gentleness and solitude, he nevertheless withdrew and began the long descent to the pasture below after memorizing the geological features that would help him locate that precious place again. Once in the meadow, he turned and gave a final look upward at his find and then as he turned to go, heard a long sorrowful call, sort of an anguished wail, from above, and looking back saw the swirling mist of late day and, as the light played on that ghostly mass, he envisioned what appeared to be a nebulous figure, looking downward at him and seemly waving for him to come, an apparition that chilled his bones but challenged his soul. He took one step back toward the cave, blinked and in full concentration, stared up at that surreal spot but saw nothing. Again he dropped to his knees and asked forgiveness for his intrusion and asked for a sign of acceptance of his returning to the hallowed cave.

The following day, a Monday, Houten made a telephone call to the Israeli Archeological Society to advise that he would submit an application for excavating and interpreting the cave located in the vicinity of Kibbutz Tzuba and he proceeded to give the contact person the geographical coordinates of the location. After a brief interlude, she responded, "Oh, that is the Heinrich Cave."

"Heinrich?"

"Yes," she answered, "Eric Heinrich, a European—German probably—traveled all over the Middle East and eventually ended up in that cave where he lived for years—I think during the 1920s—as a recluse. He died and then sometime in the 1930s a team went to the cave and evaluated for possible archeological excavation."

"What was their conclusion?"

After an interval the woman said, "Well, the bottom of the page is rather scribbled long-hand that says—or I think it says—that the cave had some hieroglyphic inscriptions, there was shallow sediment covering the floor of the cave and there was some undated mashed pottery but the writer did not think that the cave offered promise as an archeological site." Houten thanked her and advised her that he would be submitting an application form for a professional excavation and then added the oft-repeated adage, "the loss of the past impoverishes the future."

Although returning to the dig in Nasiriya, Houten's heart was in Kibbutz Tzuba, and each weekend he would make the long trip to Israel in the team's Land Rover but he refrained from anything other than minor archeological exploration as not to disturb the long-neglected site for the future excavation. But the trips were nevertheless rewarding for him as he found a sense of peace and serenity he had never known. Perhaps that is what had kept Eric Heinrich there for so many years—an incredible sense of soul and oneness with God. Each work week, Houten would return as if refreshed and fellow workers found him to be congenial and, at times, even outgoing. Bridget was delighted with her husband's progress and she unapologetically approved his long absences and praised his work in his "search for the sacred."

Approval for the excavation of the Heinrich cave was not received from the Israeli Archeological Society until the following spring, and then it was a trivial matter through the auspices of Paul Link for a transfer of Houten's duties to the Heinrich site which included the hiring of three additional staff members, two to accompany Houten to the new site and one to replace him in Nasiriya. At Heinrich, Houten set up camp just above the wadi of the cave in a flat area, the camp including three separate tents in which the excavators would live and an extra larger tent where relics would be collected and chemically processed and recorded. Bridget of course would accompany her husband and immediately found that her duties had become so minimal that she requested that she assist the archeologists in any way possible. Houten, uneasy with his wife's previously unknown talent to do so many things well, was reluctant but conceded that as long as she accepted his supervision and did not do anything she was not qualified to do he would have menial duties for her.

Both the new hirelings were hand-picked by Houten himself. Both men were Christians—a must—and virtual neophytes in archeology and both were hired after being recommended by the *Biblical Archeology Review*. Other than that the two men were dissimilar.

Booth Crable was a young man intellectually adrift and because of that was more than a little willing to listen to advice and instruction and in doing so, never seem to question information or data being heaped upon him. He was the product of a very tyrannical father, a fundamentalist Christian, who suppressed his son's emotional development. Upon completing high school, he matriculated to college because it was expected of him but he had no inclination of a goal. He attended Macalester College in Minnesota and dutifully went through the motions as a student. Initially, he had not declared a major but found that social science courses were most to his liking or, maybe more accurately, were the easiest for him and then he drifted into anthropology. Upon receiving his bachelor's degree, he was suddenly in a panic as he simply had not thought out the course of his life and had no idea what he would do after graduation. He won respite when he was advised that he would qualify for a master's program. After completing his master's studies, Crable was accepted in an intern position working with disadvantaged and emotionally disturbed Ojibwa Indians in Northern Minnesota.

While so employed, he applied for several positions and eventually received a call from the *Biblical Archeology Review* for an entry-level position in Jerusalem.

Patrick Haggerty was another matter altogether. From a broken home, he was arrested and convicted of rape of a child in his home state of California and sentenced to the state juvenile institution at Preston where he was diagnosed as having sociopathic personality disorder. After his release in sixteen months he was thereafter legally categorized as a sexual offender although the victim in the case was almost sixteen and Haggerty was nineteen but the designation put an onus on his back requiring him to register wherever he moved so that he was under the constant scope of local law enforcement not to mention the critical eye of those living within proximity of his place of residence, a problem that cost him more than one job. Discussed with the embroilment of his correctional supervision, he drifted into a life of crime and drugs. A second incarceration for possession of drugs with intent to sell changed neither his attitude nor his need for easy money but a persistent judge, apparently seeing something positive in the youth, ordered him into a drug treatment and educational program. At the recommendation of a counselor, he chose a Christian program and to his surprise, he found that going along with the requisites of the treatment was quite easier than being on the streets. He eventually completed the program but was kept in treatment as an advisor in order to finance his continuing education. He completed a bachelor's degree in anthropology—why he chose anthropology he could never explain, even to himself. Upon graduation, his grades had been average, his name was submitted to the Evangelical Anthropological Society for employment with an outstanding recommendation from the *Biblical Archeology Review* staff.

In the early spring of 2032, when leaves were sprouting from dormant trees and migrating songbirds were noisily reconnoitering in the wadi once used by Eric Heinrich, Houten set up camp in a flat meadow area just above the top of the wadi within sight of the cave. It was a spot in which he could bring his Land Rover, and such access would greatly ease availability of supplies needed for the project and for daily subsistence. He placed three tents in a triangle, the larger tent being for himself and Bridget and would include a dining table. In the center of the triangle, he placed a larger tent which, supplied by a generator, would be a work place for processing relics and formulating reports and for leisure-time activities. He had two weeks to work in the cave with his wife as Haggerty and Crable would not be available for the time needed to close their affairs in the states and travel time to Jerusalem. In the meantime, Houten planned to complete the preliminary archeological requirements for the local archeological authority.

Standing directly in front of the site, Houten sketched out a cave wider than it was high, its upper ceiling forming a pointed arch, or an upside-down "V." The soil beneath the entrance did not appear to be natural formation but looked like small smooth mounds where previous diggers had dumped debris outside of the entrance. The width of the cave was twenty-three feet ten inches and the entrance height five feet six inches. Inside, the ceiling was a little higher, rising to an average of six feet; the width increased slightly and the depth of the cave was sixty-two feet not including a hole at the postern that was eighteen inches in diameter, and had no feasible explanation for its purpose. The site had previously been designed "1-Isr-34" by the Israeli authorities. In preparing the site for excavation, he began a grid system, first establishing a datum point, the control point from which all measurements are referenced. The actual excavation would focus on what he designated as "the room" where the entrance rise leveled off and it could easily be surmised that all aboriginal activities happened. Then in starting a grid system, he laid out two sets of parallel lines in the room, each of the sets intersecting the other at right angles. He then laid out the grid by driving wooden stakes running north to south at specific intervals, and then labeled the stakes preceding the preparation of a contour map, not essential in such a limited dig, but Houten wanted correct procedure to validate any findings. He then laid out individual excavation areas, each worker being assigned an equal space for which he would be responsible. Bridget was not assigned an area of her responsibility as Houten planned to have her process excavated soil material through a screen in the work tent prior to tagging and identifying each relic. Houten denied an offer of contract workers or even volunteers with the explanation that the site was small and that once they were up to full crew, the project would go smoothly.

On the first of June, Haggerty and Crable had arrived and were ready to proceed with their assigned duties. Houten, of course, met with the two men, not only for instruction but to evaluate them for their fitness to work within his program as he had not had a hands-on encounter with them prior to their acceptance by Link and his board of directors over the anthropological society. To his first impression, both men appeared acceptable on the surface. Crable was quiet but tense and seemed willing to accept direction and, most importantly to Houten, be quiescent about the program and subsequent findings. It was Houten's feeling that Crable would apply himself to his work and, as an unsure and somewhat insecure fellow, would probably never be any kind of problem to leadership. Haggerty on the other hand, always charming and smiling, never gave a clue as to his inner feelings and so remained an enigma to Houten. With a tendency toward being outspoken and outgoing, Haggerty nevertheless restrained himself and kept feelings to himself, something he was not necessarily accustomed to doing.

In their first meeting, Houten emphasized that "this undertaking is of tremendous significance" and that its successful completion could potentially advance Christianity in the world and that as workers on the project they would be the recipients of much praise and glory for their part in what he considered a divine revelation. He explained that he had been led to the spot by God, that he had spoken to God and that He called on the anthropologist to unveil the mysteries of this hallowed cave. To this Crable nodded in all seriousness, taking in every word as if they were the gospel. But Haggerty's eyes narrowed as Houten explained his personal relationship to God and a faint smile flirted on his lips for he knew the powerful advantage of religious rhetoric as an agent of manipulation and he knew a con when he heard one, but that was not a negative characteristic in Haggerty's value system; he knew that one must control his destiny and any device to achieve one's purpose, and therefore, he respected this preacher-anthropologist for having the élan to propel himself ahead of the common herd. Thus, Houten had a stronger advocate of his management style in the wink and a nod of Haggerty than he did in the compliant and apathetic Crable. So this rag-tag collection of craftsmen began their assault upon the glebe of the interior room of the Heinrich cave where they hoped to exhume the theological riches of a biblical past, held together more by their differences and common sense of purpose than by compatibility. Houten closed the meeting with a prolonged prayer so time-consuming that Haggerty had the feeling that once again in his short life he was being smothered to death by a lecherous old aunt with rotten teeth, bad breath and lived in an attic.

The dig began with ebullience, a buoyancy so unexpected that the team became almost giddy as they began their assault upon the meager cave, at last able to satisfy their anticipation with actual work. It seemed too easy for Bridget, at first waiting for the fresh release of material from the cave's floor where she would submit the tailings to a strainer in the work tent after segregating the material of each digger; but all too soon the soil began to flow in and even before noon of the first day Bridget felt overwhelmed and had to reorganize to simplify the procedure. Two things transpired the first day; one, the soil was much harder than originally thought; and two, the depth of the compacted soil was much deeper than estimated at first, which thrilled Houten to no end as he logically reasoned that the deeper the sediment, the more vast the history of the dig would be. A third thing about the cave floor, revealed several weeks later, was that the floor was not flat and straight but was comprised of waves, fissures and potholes, all of which had been filled and leveled by generations of human occupation.

The team used the unit-level method of excavation as there was anticipation that the site may show little stratigraphic variation. In this technique, sections are set up by the lines of the grid system then vertically excavated as a discrete unit, each section being completed before the archeologist goes on to the next section, this being done on separate levels of between six to twelve inches. This way stratification is easily noted and it is virtually impossible to lose the vertical location of any excavated artifact. The first level of excavation as was expected, revealed nothing as it was apparently occupied by generations who left little in the way of physical evidence of their existence there as they used reed basketry, cordage, animal skins and most objects of personal use were wooden—although there were fragments of animal bone—all of which would rot into the ground leaving no residue. In his pre-excavation summary of the site and why he picked that particular place, Houten noted that the Hebrews, nomadic herders, crossed the desert about 700 B.C.E. to the cities of Jerusalem where they worked the fields outside of these cities until much later when they became merchants. But, Houten reasoned there are always those individuals who refuse to assimilate and continue to live in their previous lifestyle in some disparate way; thus, many independent herders and their families may have sought sanctuary in the caves and rock shelters in the foothills above the deserts where they tended their flocks. But this particular cave, contended Houten, had been unique as it was well hidden behind vegetation and difficult for one to reach on a daily basis. Therefore, he felt that those occupying the site may have been extraordinary and might have used the cave to conceal unsanctioned purpose.

Crable proved to be a hard diligent worker who, once he put himself to the task, rarely looked up, never seeming to have any bodily needs and being totally engrossed in his work, conscientiously straining forward with a "scratcher"—a bent ice pick—and a toothbrush for tools, tirelessly delving into the solid soil mixture searching for form or meaning. Contrarily, Haggerty had a streak of laziness and insisted on taking interval breaks but covered himself quite well by a constant barrage of trivial banter as, in the long run, he had an ability to be productive and, in his egocentric way, added to the stability of the team. Bridget was always bubbly but resented being separated from the boys in the work tent but she knew that her work was essential as she enthusiastically prepared the relics—those few that she found—for interpretation. When she caught up or needed a break she would immediately drift into the cave where "her boys" were absorbed in their common labor and she would flit about asking questions, retrieving misplaced tools or checking site survey records for errors or completion. Houten himself was well engrossed in his work, a level of concentration unusual for him as he scanned every potential artifact, always analyzing or interpreting all artifactual data no matter how minute or seemingly unimportant. In the evenings, after a short dinner, he retreated to the work tent on unexplained mission but emphatic that he wanted to work and meditate alone, his simple explanation being that there was a plethora of written archeological material of the area that he must study which would open a wide range of interpretive possibilities and he needed to understand the non-material aspects of the local culture as well.

The first level of the dig revealed little and, as the team suspected, was probably used for nomadic herders for several generations but during that period there was little to identify the people or their culture. The first significant artifact found in the first level was an iron awl which was so consumed by rust that it might break under the slightest touch. Then there were buttons of bone, thin and oblong, apparently fastened to the garment by rawhide. At that first level, there were no art or religious artifacts. In the second level, there appeared potsherds and then some large fragments of pottery and scraps of parchment, the most outstanding of which would be transported to Tel Aviv to a laboratory for carbon dating. Houten had no apprehension that the results would be disappointing or counter to his expectations as he believed emphatically that he had been directed to this site by God and that Christians had nothing to fear from archeology as the truth was on their side. In addition, Houten believed that this place could become, one day, for Christians, the holiest place on earth.

Then, unceremoniously, Houten turned his attention to a powdery baked clay that had been observed the first day at the very surface of the dig but which he had initially neglected as simply being an aberration and unrelated to the archaic history of the cave. But with the use of a magnifying glass, he determined that the clay could be found ever so slightly in the circumference of the opening at the postern of the cave where it had been hardened into that aperture and, very likely, had disintegrated over a long period of time, being trampled under foot and ground into the floor soil during relatively recent times. He surmised that the baked clay had been used to seal the opening, possibly to hide something of immense importance. Exploring further, he found the hole sealed by a solid piece of heavy rock which had been cut to fit the opening tightly and was therefore, a significant barricade to whatever lurked behind. He was aware that at one time, occupants of the cave had cut a mantle in the cave out of solid stone and he thereby knew that they had the tools and technology to cut such a rock impediment so accurately as to fit the dimensions of the opening. This archeological mystery excited Houten to the core and, at first, he clawed frantically at the sides of the hole in an effort to loosen the rock barricading the passageway, but to no avail; the rock had been cut so precisely and then driven in under such force as to make the rock wall and the blockage impenetrable as if it were a single piece.

Houten spent most of the day attempting to circumvent the rock blocking the opening so assiduously. A thin screwdriver would not even penetrate the thin space between the wall and the square rock preventing entrance.

Chiseling the hard rock wall surrounding the block was ineffective and he even considered cutting an aperture in the block to insert a pin to which he could attach a cable to a fulcrum system that would supply enough pressure to drag the block outward but even that brought frustration as he could not effectively chip away enough rock to form any kind of a hold in the rock. Attempting to dig under the rock proved futile as the underlying rock beneath was the same density as that of the walls and was therefore impenetrable and, the rock blocking the entrance appeared to be so thick that prying or pulling it straight forward would cause it to bind, making it even more difficult to remove. That gave Houten two choices; one, to use hardened stone chisels with sledge hammers; or two, to hire and rig up a jackhammer which would require contracting an outside worker. He chose the latter, requiring a man coming from Tel Aviv but which could not be arranged for a week. The team continued to labor in the dig during the interval with exciting expectations lingering and then on the day of the event, the aft end of the dig was covered with canvas to protect against the debris caused by the jackhammer

The contracted worker appeared slow-moving and easy-going, which aggravated Houten to a frothy tension which he concealed not too well with the eventual result that the worker politely asked him to remain outside, diplomatically, to avoid dust and flying particles. In retreating from the cave, Houten made a request that the driller not cut the entrance rock as it might have symbolic biblical significance. Outside the cave, waiting for the worker to complete his task, Houten was in a fit of nervousness, repeatedly clenching his hands and exhibiting the facial grimaces of a thousand deaths. From inside came the clatter of the hammer while outside a compressed-air unit competed noisily with the hammer in supplying air to it. The darkened cave boiled with rock dust with the occasional fulgent flash of light from a screened lamp bouncing erratically above the hammer near the hub of the work. To Houten the process seemed to be endless and he was sure that he had incurred some kind of private hell that would last for an eternity. Then suddenly, the drilling stopped and someone turned off the compressor. After a few minutes, the driller came out with a rag over his head and his body covered with dust and announced, "I've got it out and the rock is still intact—didn't have to touch it. But I'll wait around and see what you think, you know, in case you need me some more."

In reentering the cave, Houten found the rock which had blocked the entrance set near the edge of the dig. The driller, after freeing it from the hole, had drug it some ten meters, maybe even turned it end over end, an impressive feat either way as the rock probably weighed over two hundred pounds and in addition that was awkward and difficult to grasp. The dust particles still hung in the air and were so dense at the opening that he could not see inside the chasm. Houten prodded inside briefly but felt nothing in a space the length of his arm; but still blinded by the dust, he retreated to the outside of the cave to wait for the soot to subside. Finally satisfied and relaxed, Houten paid the driller and thanked him for his expertise with obvious relief. With the emotional pressure suddenly removed, Houten became earthborn once again showing a blithesome inner energy and he began to socialize openly with his team although he did not know as yet the result of the driller's work or what had been accomplished—he put that in the hands of God and, unworried, he giddily anticipated what his exploration might reveal when he was able to return to the cave. The excavation of the rock blocking the tunnel had not been a momentous event to the driller or to the archeological team who found it only to be a minor inconvenience, but for Houten, the clangorous cannonade had been an earsplitting and demoralizing affront to his senses and a personality complex dependent upon tranquility. But not only was he mentally offended by the driller's work, but the resulting caustic dust attacked his allergy-prone respiratory system and filled his sensitive eyes with acidic tears, its gritty presence irritating the eyes' outer membrane. He decided on an early lunch break and the crew retreated to Houten's tent where Bridget prepared an unusually sumptuous noontime meal and, to go with the anomalous situation, Houten was unusually talkative and engaged.

Houten was hesitant in returning to the tunnel inside of the cave even after the air in the cave had cleared, perhaps apprehensive at that last moment—were his expectations too lofty?—that he would be disappointed in what he might find or, may not find. Then in a moment of determination, he entered the cavern, bent forward as he approached the small tunnel at the postern and looked hopefully within. He blinked at what he saw. It was beyond his most glorious conjecture and he gasped in awe and shock, for there covered with a thin coating of rock debris and dust sat an ossuary, rectangular from the front but oblong in length, nestled snug in the tunnel which obviously had been cut to size for the object, which first-century Jews used to store the bones of their dead. In examining the tunnel itself, Houten discovered that the tunnel had been cut much larger than the ossuary but that the floor and surrounding walls and ceiling enclosing the coffin were of white marble—probably from Rome—which suggested that the placement of such was to give religious importance to the ceremony of burial. With the help of Haggerty, each man extending an arm into the tunnel while lying prone before it, Houten was able to shake the ossuary loose from its prolonged confinement and scoot it forward to the entrance where the two secured a stronger grip and were able to extract it. Once the ossuary was pulled from the tunnel, Houten bent over it and to appearance was hyperventilating. Then the two men began to rejoice and Houten fell into a prayer of thanks. The box was of limestone and, unlike ossuaries common to Israel, it had no ornamentation on the outside although there was a single inscription which Houten believed was in Hebrew. The inscription was simple and without any symbolism of any kind. It seemed appropriate at that point that the two men honor the ossuary in some conscious manner rather than unceremoniously proceeding with an exploration of its content or meaning. With small hairbrushes used to clean or uncover relics, the two dusted the box in an almost ritualistic manner, the process painstakingly slow, an obvious show of reverence for the ossuary. Then suddenly the spell was broken when Houten announced, "Now we must open it and see what God has bestowed upon us. We need some kind of thin pry bars, I think."

Haggerty left and hurriedly returned with two thin screwdrivers, a stout hammer and a small pry bar. The two pried around the sloped lid gingerly with screwdrivers as if not wanting to damage their precious find but were unsuccessful as the lid was on so tight as to appear concretized. At this point, Haggerty placed the pry bar on the lips between the lid and the main body of the ossuary and tapped gently. There was no chipping as the lid's slender gap was either spreading or was receiving an indentation from the pry bar. Once Haggerty had pressed the pry bar into the space under the lid at four places, the two men went back to prying with their screwdrivers and then suddenly, the lid popped upward and then everything ceased as all were waiting for it to be opened and examined. Houten took a hairbrush and began to dust the lid, then he examined the gap between lid and ossuary and even the inscription on the side, all of which seemed so silly considering the enormity of the discovery—this sudden preoccupation with little details was as if he were putting off the inevitable opening of the ossuary and facing the possibility that it contained nothing of theological value. Growing impatient, Haggerty asked softly, "Aren't we going to open it up?"

Drawn into something that he appeared that he did not want to do, Houten hesitated but with no other recourse, he pried the lid upward with a screwdriver until he was able to grasp it and suddenly the ossuary sat exposed, its contents dry and withered and unrecognizable. A trace of a finger drawn across the contents revealed that a coating of fine residue covered the remnants but once cast aside revealed the unmistakable outline of human bones, the obvious thing that one would expect in an ossuary. Houten was loathe to touch the remains which he felt to be an intrusion on his part on the sanctity of burial and the beyond. So the open limestone box sat exposed but unexplored for the remainder of the day as Houten, uncertain of what he had found but humbled by its implication, was mesmerized into inaction. Returning to his tent, he said to his wife, "We have to think this out—what we should do next."

"But shouldn't we do just what professional archeologists would do and proceed by the book, I mean, examine and categorize the remains?" she asked demurely.

"I just feel that I am intruding—even though it is the will of God. I think that this is a very important find and I want to treat the remains with the respect and honor they deserve, not just like it is another primitive burial like those Indians that we used to dig up in California," he answered.

"Well, the inscription—the inscription of the outside may tell us who it is or, at least, give us an idea of who it is. Maybe we are getting excited about nothing."

"I know that many of the American teams use a retired archeologist who lives in Tel Aviv for reading inscriptions. I think it is in Hebrew. His name his Tellier and he is not affiliated with any university or the government."

"What difference does that make?" she asked.

"Well, if the Israeli government gets wind of this, they may confiscate what we found; I know that they have done that on many occasions in the past and once they know of its existence, we will never be able to get it out of the country."

"But will Dr. Tellier be discreet?"

"I've heard that he has been, otherwise no one would have used him."

So an excitable call was put through to a Dr. Tellier from a number that another American archeological team had given Houten on a crumpled slip of paper. There was the usual telephonic confusion, the wrong number but the right name and when the good doctor's residence was finally contacted, he was, of course, not available and the answering party was unable to commit him to a date. This was exacerbating to an already distraught Houten but by the next day Tellier was contacted and because of the distance he had to travel and other commitments, he could not make the trip to the cave site for a week. Thus the bleak ossuary sat in the rear of the cave unattended, a provocative entity awaiting its destiny.

In the next week, the evangelical team proceeded to the third level of the excavation in the Heinrich cave. At the second level, the diggers had found broken pottery and some religious ornaments and the excitement of the team grew. Then in the third level, Grable uncovered a piece of red potsherd which Houten, without much thought or consideration, identified as Roman pottery of about the first century. At that same level a man-made pool was unearthed, a pool Houten would point out could have been used by the cave's occupant for performing ritual cleansing or baptism. The team's excitement grew— things were beginning the fall into place to form an inspiring picture of the cave's biblical history.

On Thursday of the following week, Dr. Tellier, a small taciturn-looking man who never smiled nor did he have a predilection for formality, arrived at the camp at precisely seven in the morning. Professional in manner, he gave the impression that he had done all this before and was not terribly moved by opinion or speculation, wanting to get right to the matter for which he had traveled so far during a busy schedule. He was immediately led to the cave where he observed the ossuary, reflecting a peach hue in the early morning light. He was agitated that the box had not been taken to a more favorable work environment and expressed as much to which Houten attempted an answer but upon realizing that he had failed to think things out in that regard, stopped in the middle of a meek explanation as it was apparent that Tellier had no time for such meaningless banter. Thereupon, Haggerty and Crable lifted the box and carried it to the work tent where they hurriedly assembled a bench for its placement at the insistence of Dr. Tellier. Then with almost mechanical efficiency, Dr. Tellier inspected, measured, sketched, photographed and analyzed the box. He concluded that it was, in fact, an ossuary which would place its time of existence as during the first century and then he suggested that it should be taken to a laboratory for DNA analysis, carbon dating and chemical testing to evaluate the patina found on the limestone. Houten, who could restrain himself no longer, blurted out, "But, what about the inscription."

Dr. Tellier, ignoring the childlike impatience said, "There are two things about that. First, the inscription is not in Hebrew, but Aramaic—that is not terribly significant as many of the early era were bilingual. The other thing is that in looking at the ossuary without the advantage of laboratory verification, I'd say that the inscription is of a much later time than the ossuary itself and, the quality of the work is poor. Also, a third thing is that this is the only ossuary that I've seen that did not have artistic engraving on the outside but then perhaps there was some sort of pressure to get this thing into the ground."

"But what does the inscription say?"

"Well, it's brief, it simply says 'The Son of God Our Savior,'" Dr. Tellier stated.

"Hallelujah, it's Jesus, it's Jesus Christ's remains," Houten shouted.

Dr. Tellier, not believing this response from a professional archeologist, responded, "That certainly is a stretch. That inscription may just be a religious ideogram on the coffin of an anonymous corpse. You have a whole lot of investigating to do."

But an excited Houten interjected, "But I have spoken to God and he led me to this place—he wanted us to find His son."

Dr. Tellier, no longer professionally indifferent and unable to hide his skepticism, said bitterly, "I suppose that that is the only way that a group of archeological neophytes with only a few weeks in the field could ever discover anything so momentous."

Ignoring the barb, Houten said that such a breakthrough could strengthen the core base of the Christian church and reconcile dissenters.

Making direct eye contact with Houten, Dr. Tellier warned, "Be careful how you handle this. It is a sin to disturb Jewish graves and the Jews take that very seriously—there could be militancy, maybe violence."

Houten said, "We had that problem with Indians in the states—they thought they had some claim to the past but ancient burials belong to all mankind and the government has always been on our side on that issue."

Dr. Tellier was running late and had begun glancing at his watch periodically but paused to jot a few brief notes on a pad while hovering over the ossuary. Meanwhile, Houten gathered his flock and held a prayer of thanks for their discovery. Dr. Tellier, in realizing that the prayer might just go on and on, made his departure sub silentio.

Houten lost no time in having Bridget contact Paul Link's office in Chicago by e-mail to set up a conference call with the media magnate. The call came through the following day. Link seemed unresponsive at first but then when Houten explained the results of their excavation and that it might turn into the most important discovery for the Christian faith in history, Link suddenly came alive and Houten could almost see him come forward over his desk in enthusiasm for additional details. "You mean to say that you might have found the remains of Jesus buried in a cave in Israel?"

"I am more than sure that is what we have found. The time of burial is about the time of Jesus' death and the container—a limestone ossuary—was common practice at that time. We have examined bones in the box, there is a skull, a humerus, a femur, some smaller bones and an ankle bone with a perforation that could have been from a Roman spike used when he was crucified."

"That is unbelievable, we have to use this right now, we can't wait for any more investigation or analysis."

"That is why I called you, sir. I think that it is imperative that we get this thing to the states. I don't know how long before the Israelis get wind of this but I am afraid that they will try to confiscate it once they know about it. Furthermore, it would be just like them to put some secular anthropologists on it and they would make a conclusion that would deny the truth of what we have found. They have done it before."

"That is why we have to stay together on this. We know that if they get their hands on it they will claim no evidence that it is Jesus and that their consensus will be that it is a fake thereby causing a serious blow to our faith and the welfare of mankind as well."

Aware of the power of the man, Houten appealed to Link, saying, "Once we get this ossuary to the states, it will be safe from outside interference—we need to get it there."

"Don't worry," Link cautioned. "We get you an air force plane to fly it to the states, no customs, no inspection. I'll have an air force fighter jet at our instillation at the Tel Aviv Airport and he will be instructed to fly the ossuary to O'Hare Airport as soon as you bring it. There will be no record of it and the flight will be secretive. I will advise you of the particulars by e-mail as soon as I make arrangements. So you've done good work but I'll have to have you return here because you will be a hot item—we'll need you to be on our lecture circuit as soon as we can. First thing we will do with this is run headlines in our newspaper, *The Daily Evangelist*. Our Christian base will accept your findings on faith and they represent the moral majority in America and you will not be questioned on the validity of your discovery. Then, until we get a more substantive report from you, we will do daily reports on the subject and I know that our followers will follow your exploits carefully; and when we have more information, we will present verifiable evidence that we have found Jesus. The main thing is that we have to circumvent the skeptics and atheists who will attack anything that smacks of righteousness."

"We will be ready for the next step," Houten replied.

"Tell me," Link asked, "how is the general excavation coming, is there anything else exciting to tell?"

"Well, the team has uncovered Roman pottery shards of about the time of Christ and they have also uncovered a baptism pool—it's man-made and could have been used by Christ himself."

Link said, "Thank the team for me. They are doing a heck of a job and they will be rewarded for their effort. It sounds like the whole thing fits—a secluded cave, ceremonial pottery, a baptism pool, an ossuary hidden in a sealed cavern. It makes a great story."

"Yes, sir, this is all very exciting."

"One other thing," Link went on. "We are actually able to celebrate two things today. Yesterday the U.S. Congress enacted a new law whereby taxpayer money can no longer be used to pay for anthropological studies or archeological research. There isn't that much private funding for such study so the secularists will not be in a strong position to exert their bias. I can see in the future when all human studies come from faith-based organizations and I'll bet that within five years, all we know regarding human history and the human condition will be compatible with biblical literalism."

"Amen to that."

# Thirteen

The first week of October was a troubled week for the president of the United States. All economic indicators were significantly down. Not that that would be viewed as a negative by the population at large; to the contrary, they simply did not know—the media at the instigation of the administration had kept such damaging news from the public. But the president knew; and, after all the effort to appease the big business elite—the removal of constraints on business, tax breaks for corporations, the deletion of environmental regulations, the subsidizing of investments, no-bid construction contracts to favored companies, human trafficking to lower labor expenses, sectional wars to open business opportunities in foreign lands and legislative favoritism for corporations that virtually eliminated small businesses—the economy was faltering and the annihilation of the middle class reduced the consumer base so severely as to impact national corporations as only those businesses whose profits were produced through the global economic network would ultimately survive. All this was the result of a well-planned conspiracy; and now, the president's legacy would be that of a corporate conspirator, a go-along-no-matter-what-the-price stooge who had become the collusive trumpeter of big business in total disregard for the welfare of the masses.

"But," the president contemplated to himself, "is this not what has been called for by our God, a punitive God who considers those not rewarded by His divine blessing to be dissenters and thereby not worthy of His benefaction—do we acquiesce to what happens on earth as being God's will? That seems to be the key—not all that happens today on earth is God's will. God is not the source of what is bad. That is what He meant when he said 'Let your will be done.' In other words, each person is responsible for what they have willed and those who suffer accordingly deserve what they have brought upon themselves."

But that did not make the president feel any better. He knew, somewhere deep in his psyche, no matter how suppressed it may be, that surreptitiously he had tipped the scales of fair play and justice, and he did it because of the assurances and support of the church and the corporate powers and he gave them what they wanted in return and they praised him. But that praise seemed so shallow on this day. He thought back a moment about his reelection and how his party had scammed the country by introducing a virtual reality program so cheaply on the market that the tape was shown extensively throughout the country and although it was non-political to appearances, it carried subtle invasive episodes of false memory which unsuspecting voters would unknowingly draw upon in the privacy of their voting booths when there was no other outside stimuli from which they could make voting decisions. Then there was the incident when an aide interrupted him while he was talking to an oil painting in the Oval Office; the aide was discreet but then a few days later another aide caught him talking in tongues to a wall. Surely the two aides talked about their experiences and to what result the president knew not. Was he becoming senile? He knew he could not suddenly reverse course—the right wing would destroy him; but just maybe, if he could remain in power he could make some moderate changes that would help a suffering people. But he knew better—the right was totally uncompromising and would allow no change and they would take him down if he made such an unapproved effort.

While the president was engrossed in thought, a secretary brought a copy of the day's newspaper, *The Glory*, the country's leading periodical, and although he started to put it aside, the lead story in headline shouted at him, "Remains Found In Kibbutz Tzuba May Be Christ." Stunned, the president grasped the news and read hurriedly. The details told little that would embellish the story other than the name of the archeologist, his team and that the remains were now in a laboratory in Chicago for examination. He immediately had his secretary call the listed laboratory and requested all information and evidential findings be forwarded to the White House. Then the secretary began to receive numerous calls, all excitable but adding nothing to embellish the newspaper account. With this new and uplifting information, the president was drawn out of his dilemma and murmured to himself with a smile, "Now, isn't this a magnificent diversion?"

Paul Link had been true to his word to Houten for he immediately made the Kibbutz Tzuba evacuation discovery a major story, filling every newspaper published by his corporation and crowding out all other television programming. In addition, he made appeals to the editors of *Biblical Archeology Review* and

*The Evangelical Daily* to cover the story in full. By the next day, the cave discovery was the topic of all discourse in the country and in evaluating the public response to the newspaper accounts, there seemed to be little skepticism that the discovered remains were those of the Savior. Suddenly churches were inundated by the churchly and not so churchly as clerics could suddenly see for themselves the impact of the event upon an energized public—there was an emotional rally that championed Christian belief at a time that skepticism had been on the rise. One Catholic administrator called the information, even as yet unproven and lacking in details, "The most important contingency in human history."

Within the week, evangelicals were plying the White House with political requests and if the president had made mistakes in addressing their concerns and aspirations so openly in the past, he certainly now had misgivings about how he could extricate himself from their influence and political meddling. But the most persistent request—perhaps more accurately defined as an order—was the call for him to met with Lester Scroggins, who had become the leading evangelical hierophant and whose legions of followers had made him a legend within the evangelical web. The president had never met Scroggins, whom he epitomized as "a hayseed," and what he knew of him was distasteful and he found Scroggins' strident voice irritating and his preaching as a rambling and incoherent harangue; and, although the president's religious views had been described by moderates as "dreamlike and chimerical," the radicalism of Scroggins had allowed the president temporary acceptance as a moderate. Nevertheless, the pressure from an increasingly vocal segment of evangelicals was a drumbeat upon his administration and there was no way to avoid the meeting which he recognized it for what it was—a trap from which he could not escape.

The meeting with Scoggins had been arranged for a day in the week following the archeological findings from the Heinrich cave and the national mood at that time was one of frenzy as one would conclude that there was total acceptance within the country of the claims made by the evangelicals of the discovery. Paul Link and his media empire had done their job superbly. *Newsweek* and *Time* came out with cover stories and news channels on television—at times desperate for fillers to avoid the painful news of the day—spent exorbitant time on hashing and rehashing the events of the excavation in language which would suggest that the world would somehow he transformed into a wondrous place and the convergence of mankind would be foregoing. If the president anticipated an ingenuous and challenging meeting with Scroggins, he was correct.

In his meeting with the president, Scroggins was accompanied by one aide, one Newton Becker, who was presented to the president with little fanfare or explanation as to his role with the evangelical society or purpose for sitting in on the hearing. He sat attentive but unresponsive to the dialog between the two men yet there was an intelligence in his eyes that gave the president an appreciation for his presence. To the contrary, Scroggins was singular and aggressive, seemingly wanting to get into some sensitive debate that might rattle the president, as unnerving opponents had become a pastime for Scroggins.

For Scroggins, there was no warm-up of trivial banter leading up to the contentious statements that he had proposed in formulating his message to the president. Instead, he started off by advocating that the United States needed new leadership, that the current leadership was failing the country and would ultimately lead to its disaster. The president, in wanting to understand the cleric's criteria for such a personally offensive statement, discovered him to be an amazingly ignorant man with little ability to speak of things outside of his realm and that things had to be put to him in the simplest language in order to be understood. This was a serious disappointment to the president, who genuinely enjoyed people and acquiring a personal perspective of any given person by the nuances of his mind and the connotative meanings of his semantics. But there was nothing to be discovered in this man—he was shallow and uncomplicated and the frustration of the situation was that he possessed incredible political power while having no qualms about the chaos and destruction that his perceptions could evoke upon the nation. The president questioned the cleric as to just what he had in mind regarding a need for new leadership but the answer was vague in that he simply repeated an axiom that the country must follow a higher authority, an authority that would reestablish order and create a new dawn of Christianity in which all decisions made would be compatible with the will of God represented by that new higher authority. But in the same breath, Scroggins let slip the idea of there being, at the same time of this enlightenment, a purification of all the Christian believers in that there should be no tolerance of dissenters, heretics or anomalous evangelicals as defined by the National Association of Evangelicals. When asked by the president to define an acceptable follower, Scroggins defined an Evangelical as a believer who accepts that Jesus Christ is the Son of God, that the Bible is the Word of God and that one must be born again and anyone else must necessarily by excluded. The president began to argue that he was beholden to all citizens of the country but Scroggins instantly exhibited that trait peculiar to him in which he failed to hear the rebuttal let alone respond in terms of dialectic argument. So the meeting ended—the evangelist had insulted the president, who amazingly was very gracious when ending the confab. Thus Scroggins had said his piece and would depart the meet to awaiting press corps and his ecstatic followers who gloried in his presupposed humiliation of the president. But the cleric's aide, Newton Becker, remained behind.

"I must apologize for Reverend Scroggins' indelicate approach to issues," Becker opened.

"I guess that can be overlooked and forgiven—I have to just assume that he was caught up in the enthusiasm of his belief and that he had an unusual opportunity to express himself and just got carried away. But you remember that his followers were pressing for him to be appointed secretary of state based on his leadership at the head of the Evangelical Church. I do say that his first impression suggests that our overlooking his name for the position was correct."

Becker responded, "He does lack many of the ephemeral characteristics typical of civic servants but that is because he has such strong conviction and he doesn't mince words but speaks straight from the heart and that is not by definition a negative thing."

Ignoring the explanation, the president said, "I have a concern—he talks of purification of membership and I wonder if he plans to exclude many Christians he used to achieve his position, like, for example, the Catholics who were so politically important in the Evangelical rise to national power."

Becker retorted, "You must understand that the Evangelicals have been morphing as in the past decade, they have had to modify their worship to create a favorable image in the nation so as not to look too bizarre, in other words, they were told not to appear to be glassy-eyed heavenly fanatics. But now they feel free, with Reverend Scroggins' approval, to express their belief in demonic oppression, visions, territorial spirits, and voices from heaven. That is pure evangelism and they will not be denied any longer."

The president shot back, "Actually, we have seen plenty of that, jumping up and down or dancing during worship ceremonies, talking in tongues, out-of-touch emotionalism."

Becker answered, "That is what we call free-market faith, the natural response of individuals who only want to be themselves and express themselves in their belief."

The president let the moment cool by changing to a debatable reality, "The reverend speaks of new leadership—what's he mean by that?"

"That is why I am here; we don't want you to misinterpret what we intend and the reverend may have given a false impression. We are not speaking of a change of governance in any way, we are just seeking that higher authority upon which a leader can look for guidance and direction…"

"But who or what is this higher authority," the president interrupted, "and how are we to know if it is reliable?"

Becker responded, "For the past twenty years, Evangelicals have been going through a catharsis that we call the abreaction, or the cleansing of the church. For example, African-American Evangelicals have social concerns derived from the scriptures and the Angelical community does as well but their sermons are theological so the two do not have the same compelling justification. But in a free-market religion, we have come to recognize that social justice has been detrimental to our economy and that is why we pushed to have the legislature change the classification of poverty, homelessness, unemployed, disabled and put them all under 'indigence' and, in that category, we find that eighty-two percent of the population fall under indigent in that they do not contribute to our economy in any way or cannot support themselves."

"I suppose that is why we have a developing problem with the underground community—they feel disenfranchised," the president offered.

Becker quickly shot back, "They are satanic, evil people who slink around in the abandoned burnt-out hulks of our cities, pillaging, raping and spreading their hatred. They have no connection with the righteous and do not want to change their evil ways. They are part of the morass of evil, the encroaching destruction of mankind as Armageddon approaches, and that is why we seek divine leadership and the return of Jesus Christ."

"I agree with you that all the signs are there indicating a complete breakdown of society that would precede Armageddon, but just how do you propose that we seek divine leadership—is that not always a possibility for all of us, that is, it is within our hearts but it is up to us to visualize that authority through the scriptures and our relationship with God."

"It's not that simple anymore," Becker argued. "The true believers in this country could accept such authority through their church but the world has become too diverse, there are too many who would not accept the truth and, in fact, would come very militant about it. They have to experience an enlightenment, a rebirth of our Savior himself, and then they would believe it."

"So, you plan on waiting for the rebirth of Jesus?"

"Yes, but it is imminent."

The president leaned back in his chair and holding his hands together before his face, his elbows on the table asked, "How so?"

The moment had come for Becker and he uttered in the faith of his belief, "We have the DNA of Jesus, we have the technology to clone Him and we have the ability to bring him forth into this world as the most powerful, knowledgeable man in history."

"Where did you get the DNA, from those bones from that Israel archeological dig?"

"Yes, that is obvious."

"But that has not been verified through the scientific method."

"We have had a call from the American Anthropological Society for us to allow their scientists to evaluate the remains but we know that their bias is secular and that they plan to expose the remains as a fraud and we cannot let them do that. We know that it is Jesus and that knowledge is based upon faith, our people were led to Him by God and He entrusts us to behold Him. If you spoke directly to God you would be elated by the experience and you would have no doubt of the veracity of our message."

The president sat up intensely and then said, "What you might just be proposing is one gigantic hoax and the result upon the nation could be catastrophic. You may think that you have the advantage here, most are in your pocket—the congress, the Evangelical Church, the media—but what we must look at is the ultimate impact upon society."

Making eye contact with the president, Becker replied, "Reverend Scroggins is going on a crusade starting this week and he will be going all over the country; in fact, we can't schedule him fast enough, and what will become his stump speech will be for legislation to clone the remains of Jesus who will then become our spiritual leader and even as an infant his mere presence will enrapture mankind and inspire hope for the future."

"But," the president interrupted, "You people do not believe in cloning and you have always taken an uncompromising stand against it. How can you now violate such firmly held beliefs?"

"We do not intend to adopt cloning as a commonly used procedure," Becker answered, "but these are hard times and we need the guidance of the Almighty and it only stands to reason that we must seek Him out in any way that we can. What is God's belongs to God and what we propose will have His divine blessing in that this will return His living Son to us. There is no argument here. This is not hypocrisy—God and His followers do not have to answer for the same misalliance as the common herd for our purpose is divine and is sought by God. Furthermore, Reverend Scroggins will be drawing multitudes of believers and this will inundate the land and it will destroy anyone who dare stand in the way as no dissenters will survive its fury and it will bring us all together in glorious harmony forever."

"I'm just not sure," the president offered, "that all this is true—it could be nothing more than evangelical hype. I have appeased the church for years, always believing that one day they would be placated and thus satisfied. But now there appears to be no limit to the control they want to exercise or what they want, which oddly enough always seems to change."

"Our love of God has never changed and seeking His guidance and love has always been our destination and we have sought in different ways—I admit that it is sometimes contradictory—but our dedication has always stayed the same. But with your sudden reluctance to follow the Lord, one would question your devotedness and, in light of the immense following of Scroggins, you definitely could jeopardize your administration."

So the meeting of the minds ended on a sour note and the president started down an uncertain path with no formulated plan in mind—he had always moved spontaneously with the religious right but now with the threat of their abandonment of him he suddenly felt alone and without direction. Becker, on the other hand, proceeded to a well-laid-out and aggressive course of action as Reverend Scroggins would rouse the masses, Becker would be the political point man and Paul Link would glorify the message through the media. It was to become the perfect blueprint and they could not be stopped.

In the anxious years of the new threat of terrorism to the United States, a panicky population was once more willing to allow the deterioration of constitutional rights in exchange for what they believed was a guaranteed security and, in accepting the devices proposed by the government, the people's gullibility was stretched to include fantasy-born operations that would appear ludicrous to people of a more reasonable era. One would have expected that the worst of times would have brought out the best in our leaders or brilliance in our intellectuals. But one has only to study Napoleon's disastrous Russian Campaign of 1815 to study the breakdowns in group behavior—even a group well-trained and much experienced—in the face of ominous peril in which those threatened resorted to absurd attempts at saving themselves while rejecting lucid and practical responses to danger as, in a state of desperation, they were more than willing to believe a far-fetched and foolish tactic for survival.

In the first decade of the twenty-first century, the United States government was grossly incompetent in dealing with terrorism and yet, as desperate as the situation had become, there was a failure to enact countermeasures due to bureaucratic malaise and political stalemates. Posturing and temporal positioning produced a deaf ear to the practical but Congress responded to the exigent mind with the delusive schemes of the frenzied sermonizer.

It all seemed so appropriate to the unthinking when, in 2010, both houses of Congress passed, and the president subsequently signed, a bill creating a National Information Center which by its name appeared innocuous, but, beneath that benign heading, there was to be sinister repercussions. As the bill was seen as a panacea for all problems pertaining to terrorism and as the act itself was loosely written, application of it was without restraint or temperate debate. So a series of poorly conceived laws—certainly not given the test of constitutionality—were rammed through committee and approved by Congress with an unfeeling matter-of-factness. The initial phase of the bill included an identification number from all citizens of the United States and, like the Social Security Act of 1932, in which such numbers were registered and private protection was guaranteed. The act appeared harmless, particularly considering the dire threats of unknown intruders.

The second phase of the program involved taking identification numbers to the next logical step upward and that would be to add necessary and applicable information of the individual to assure proper classification of each citizen for security purposes. But whether by design or patriotic fervor, the project began to delve into the psychological aspects of individuals, inquiries that went far beyond what was considered necessary, even to the most bellicose security administrators. The computer industry had been salivating for such an opportunity and immediately demonstrated new computer models of unlimited memory that gobbled up information at an incredible rate and was capable of analysis and evaluation instantaneously. The psychologists and psychoanalysts working on the project were caught up in the fever and since restraint had not been emphasized, they were more than enthusiastic in turning up all the gray traits of peculiarity. It would seem obvious to all that they could become easily carried away with such recourse and take their inquest far beyond propriety or one's constitutional rights, an inevitable result of the lack of legislative judiciousness.

Those workers for the NIC began to develop theories of malfeasance and unexpectedly began to target certain types of individuals and then later, just certain individuals. This was to become one of the biggest legal and legislative controversies of the new century but debate of the subject was muted by the radical right and their allies in the White House.

The first director of NIC was Nickolai Frugmann, a squat little man with no neck and a flat shapeless face, his most prominent feature being squinty eyes, swollen and red from overwork. He wore incredibly thick glasses and was nicknamed "the mole" by coworkers who always noticed that he demonstrated the same myopic intensity whether he was working a case, reading the comics or eating from a sack lunch. He seemed to receive gleeful pleasure out of his career at the information center and it was suspected that he had a prurient interest in matters he should have been totally objective about. Furthermore, his relationships with fellow workers were at times strained or indifferent but, despite his lack of social skills, Frugmann was unanimously appointed director of the NIC by Congress.

Such a promotion was the reward for his work in developing a psychological theory that had permitted the agency to delve into the personal lives of citizens, singling out many as suspected terrorists and justifying the retention of citizens for what amounted to little more than physiognomy. What Frugmann had discovered—or thought he had discovered—was a personality type that would of itself justify the incarceration of an individual unfortunate enough to possess those certain personality traits. It was nothing more than the most inept profiling imaginable but the tenor of the times and the overriding concern for national security allowed this obvious flaw to be overlooked.

In his mind, Frugmann had always been a sort of yin/yang mentality as for every pro there was a con and for every principle there was there was a contradictory principle. From that simplicity came the concept that if there was an Authoritarian Personality, there must out of necessity be the exact opposite, the Anarchical Personality, and Frugmann set out through research methods and contrivance to prove it. An Anarchistic Personality, by Frugmann's definition, would be easily identifiable and fit into the purpose of NIC while providing a plan of action that would give direction and impetus to that federal agency.

It was mischievous and ill-conceived from the beginning and there was an ensuing debate as to whether Frugman understood his own ineptitude and was deceptive in covering himself or if he was merely intellectually challenged and was actually unaware of his limitations. Frugmann's inventory of the AP was a conglomeration of psychological traits that might more appropriately be reconciled to twisted childhood immaturity. This individual, he claimed, usually came from an unstructured family environment, was non-religious, had rebellious tendencies to the point of disruptive behavior, was low in self-esteem, had no sense of self-exploration, cast blame upon others, associated with radical groups, resented or rejected authority, was open to radical philosophies and tended to be violent. The fact that fifty percent of the current membership of the House of Representatives met those criteria impressed no one, and an administration eager to demonstrate its effort toward fighting terrorism embraced Frugmann's concepts in awarding him the directorship.

Due to Frugmann's authoritative philosophy, many citizens were jailed, some for over a year without knowing the charges against them with their lives placed in jeopardy from job loss, social rejection or stigma. Even lawyers who saw the issue as very dangerous were stunned by Frugmann's rabid public support and, as one administration spokesman pontificated, "Frugmann's research findings, although rejected by liberals, have proven essential to the safety of the nation and we are fortunate to have a man at the head of NIC who has the guts to do exactly what has to be done."

As a result of the Frugmann controversy, the embattled NIC became the central point of heated debate and when lawyers challenged not only the basis for even having a NIC but also Frugmann's theories which led to questionable incarcerations, they found that their defiance was thwarted by judges sympathetic to the administration. All this fueled an already growing resentment of government that now appeared to be approaching the point of open rebellion. The government answered the dissent by ordering investigations seemingly arranged to diminish the outcry against NIC but which added nothing substantive to the issues. The hearings closely followed along ideological lines as would be expected in which those opposed to NIC were flagrantly accused of being anti-American. The investigations were well spaced in time but were unnecessarily drawn out, perhaps in the hope that public interest would wane, but incarcerations had been such an affront to the traditional liberal concept of fairness and as the nation was so polarized, concern intensified.

Eventually, public pressure increased to the point that Senate investigators could no longer resist the call to put Frugmann before the public with an explanation of his theories and their importance to the program and why they were necessary to public security. His speech before the Senate was articulate and well thought out and undoubtedly would have carried the issue to a successful conclusion were it not for one adventitious factor and that was his personal appearance as, in a culture known for a short span of attention, the text of his comments were almost completely obliterated by his appearance. He sat there before the Senate committee, a grotesque gnome of a man with sloped shoulders and blinking squinty eyes and, no sooner had television viewers digested that impression of him, he began to speak in a whiny, high nasal pitch of which one writer commented that Frugmann reminded him of the story of an old silent screen idol who attempted to jump without forethought into his first talkie but once the public was exposed to his whimpering elocution, the former star's standing went from matinee idol to theatrical farce in a single afternoon. This idiosyncrasy obviously caught the administration off guard as they had grown used to Frugmann's whimsical eccentricity and crimped speech and were unaware of the impact he would have upon a public which had never previously viewed him.

The speech itself was lost on the populace, which was unfortunate. In his address to the Senate investigative committee, Frugmann did not attempt any scientific sleight of hand but tried to factually deal with legitimate concerns about public safety in the face of a threat that was imponderable and therefore, he required unusual and extreme means to overcome the menace to public security and, in his argument, he did not reject per se the arguments of his opponents but attempted to still the agitation by assuasive response, acknowledging the intrinsic value of their positions. In the end, he conceded that his theory may have not been scientifically persuasive, but was simply a method for recognizing potential troublemakers and thus protect the nation. Politically biased pundits, even those of the opposing viewpoint, applauded Frugmann's effort and reasoning for such extreme measures.

Perhaps Frugmann would have become a mere footnote in the history of those times, but as the Senate committee was pondering action in the case, out of the blue rode a gallant figure to save him from the fate he richly deserved, and that figure, as unimpressive in shape and form as Frugmann himself, was none other than the Very Reverend Scroggins, who entered the hearings on the last day without invite or being scheduled in, but with great fanfare. After a week of testimony from Frugmann and his particularly aggravating shrill voice, the presence of Scroggins and his aggressive, nervous presentation, gave a comical ambience to the affair as if some demented screen writer was deliberately inundating a theatrical setting with the worst actors he could find. But the senators, aware of the immense power of the leader of the evangelical movement, were respectful if not awed by the reverend. The message from Scroggins was simple: order in our society is necessary; the society is full of miscreants who need to be identified and removed; Frugmann is a great patriot and so much so, that he has been caught in the double helix of faith and duty to the nation and thus would take any measure that would secure our nation; that a nation cannot survive in disharmony and it is therefore essential that we all pull together and those unwilling to do that must get out; and, compatible with such effort, the Christians are in the process of purifying their own membership and, as the government is of the Christian faith, all citizens should be subject to open scrutiny as a nation cannot long endure under the disruptive influence of an evil minority. Scoggins concluded that Frugmann and his program were absolutely essential to America and his efforts in that regard were profoundly acceptable to the evangelicals.

So what had started as merely a bizarre week ended on the edge of insanity. The NIC emerge into the evangelical movement representing the most unlikely marriage between two adversarial philosophies, that of Frugmann, the great archfiend hound, and Reverend Scoggins, the great purveyor of souls; and, for the Senate committee, the marriage was an expeditious out for them, a release from a desperate dilemma for which there was no acceptable answer. Frugmann, at the insistence of Scoggins, became a Christian and a born-again Christian at that, and in the commission of his duties at NIC, he shifted his focus from those of supposed high-risk criminal behavior to the political malcontents, and particularly those spewing derisive discourse at the evangelical church or the breakdown of the traditional American value of the separation of church and state.

One October morning, a rather gloomy wind-blown day of drenching rain, the Senate committee for investigating proposed legislation to allow limited cloning for specific individuals met in the capital in Washington, DC, without the press being present at the request of the Senate leaders. The senators had been drawn into a hearing that they did not want—a lose-lose situation—and the only recourse they felt that they had to avoid deleterious consequences from the hearing would be to minimize the feedback to the public by disallowing media access as much as possible. After all, to the man, each had run for election as a fundamentalist Christian and now, at the insistence of Christian leaders, they were advocating a hypocritical position that only a few weeks before would have been blasphemous. In the anxious moments prior to the hearing, each pondered a way out of the dilemma; perhaps, they imagined, by some high-sounding ecclesiastical grandiloquence that would elevate that orator as a great redeemer of the tenets of his faith. But all knew that was a myth; such discourse would be insurrection—they had been herded down this path for so long, appeasing their own self-doubts by believing that each step along that disastrous path would be the last but, alas, they had all come to this dungeon of ignominy and there, mustered without recourse, intoning a common chant without depth or meaning, they had given up all that was gentle and equitable in the human spirit.

The first and only speaker on that day would be Darius Celosi, the new CEO of Bio-Med Inc., the largest medical and pharmaceutical research company in the world. Few of the senators knew Celosi by name or reputation but their symposium outline gave a thumbnail sketch of the sensational rising star of the business world and it presented him as a shockingly young man who by appearance looked even younger and considering his numerous achievements, a very brilliant young man. Celosi had salvaged a floundering company in which their profits were marginal in that competition had been so severe and threatening that drastic methods had to be applied—a chancy prospect in any business environment but Celosi courageously took that challenge and eventually destroyed his competition; and now, the triumphant Celosi won the federal contract for Operation Resurrection, a high-tech cloning process designed to return an extraordinary deceased individual or individuals to a state of government-validated renascence; and all he had to do was to demonstrate that such a process was a feasible possibility.

In his opening remarks, Celosi said, "As I have explained in section 1 of the symposium outline—on your desk before you—in the process of bringing a clone to full term as a human, biological research accompanied by innovative informational research has given us sufficient evidence to indicate that we can locate and process a deceased individual—particularly one of note where there has been sufficient post-mortem information—with reliable competence and justify the expenditure of funds in the pursuit of reclaiming that individual to return him or her to the threshold of social interaction for the benefit of the human community.

"The first step in this process is simply to remove the newborn infant from the surrogate mother who, incidentally, has had her genes blocked off from contaminating the fetus, and then the fetus is placed in an Accelerated Growth Module—or AGM—in an ideal nourishing environment for a rapid growth process that will speed the physical and emotional maturation of the infant to the point that we can expect the whole process to be completed in perhaps less than four years and maybe sooner than that; that is, to go from fetus to complete adulthood in that amount off time. The AGM, when you first see it from the outside, resembles a beached nuclear submarine but inside, it is a series of intricate chambers, the main chamber being the one in which the fetus will be raised and nurtured and which is afloat in a larger vacuum chamber. The environment that the scientists are emulating is that of a different time dimension in accordance with the Theory of Time Dimension Alternation. This hypothesis states that as we travel to the sun, time speeds up but if we move away from the sun or the earth for that matter, time, according to earth time, is relatively slower so—in a nutshell—if we start a process in one time dimension and then transfer an object to another time dimension then back to our dimension, the object benefits from whatever difference in time that we are trying to emulate.

"This change of time dimension is accomplished by creating differences by isolating the birth chamber from the gravitational pull of the earth and artificially increasing its speed in relation to the another dimension—so what we have created is a totally artificial time environment by manipulating speed and mass. The growth rate of a child in space or inner space is exactly the same as it would be on earth—in that milieu—but by earth time we find that much less time has transpired. So we have created an artificial time dimension by electronically increasing or decreasing speed and mass by computer-controlled mechanisms, and this accelerates growth incrementally according to our computer manipulations. Of course, we have been experimenting with this for some time and we are nearing perfection. We have put mice, rats, dogs and monkeys through the process and they have all matured quickly, in some cases, depending upon brain sophistication—or lack of—almost instantly.

"In our AGM system we have assembled a habitat that will nurture a child through scheduled growth cycles to promote a completely healthy child and then guide that child through those various stages of human development in order to produce a perfectly functional and emotionally stable human being. This is accomplished through electronically controlled monitors that because of time restraints perform the tasks of feeding and care at a space that to us on earth would seem feverish, but still this provides a level of care far beyond human capacity for such care. In other words, the care would be perfect and would nourish the perfect child.

"The monitors are the most important aspect of the AGM system. There are many monitors and each has a function in the process of raising a fetus to adulthood. The monitors in the infant stage of the program are obviously quite different from those in the later phases of development and after their duties are completed they are never used again in this specific project as subsequent monitors are increasingly sophisticated as are their duties but even those are used for a short phase and then replaced. To view the monitors at work is intriguing—it is like watching an old silent movie in which the actors buzz around in herky-jerky fast motion going about their unexplained tasks with almost comic-like seriousness.

"We know from a laboratory experiment conducted in the 1920s that a child cannot grow in a totally neutral environment as, in that experiment in which everything that the children came into contact had been sterilized and, on top of that, there was no human contact for the children in the laboratory, the children began to die. So, from that we knew that an infant needed touching and cuddling by a mother figure. Therefore, we created a mother surrogate monitor—called an Amah Simulate—and she was designed as the most loving, caring robot imaginable and she was so cuddlesome, sweet and nurturing that many of the scientists working on the project fell in love with her. (Laughter.) One even wanted to take her home at night. (Laughter.)But she is the most important monitor in the project and is responsible for jump-starting the child from the threshold of accelerated growth to about age three or, in AGM years, about seven months.

"In the early stages of the program, at the suggestion of our leading psychiatrist, it was planned to program negative characteristics into the monitors so that—in the words of the psychiatrist—'the child would not come out of the program without the negative life experiences that would help mold his character,' or in other words, prevent him from becoming a geek or a nerd. (Laughter.) The psychiatrists cited numerous studies and anecdotal examples that demonstrated a relationship between deprivation in the family environment and the development of positive traits in the individual. Most obvious was the example of a child reared in a poverty-stricken family who then overcame his material destitution and developed indefatigable drive and determination for achievement. However, we were besieged with communications from people of the cloth who complained bitterly about the prospects of such contrivance. They maintained that Jesus was reared by a loving, righteous pair without fault or remiss in what was the perfect family and that family environment produced the world's most perfect human. (Sustained applause.) In response, we dismissed the cognitive dissonance theory and its application in our program.

"The first stage of a child's development is called simulated motherhood and in that stage the electronic mother figure will provide the child with unconditional love in addition to other child-rearing activities. By bonding with the child there would be a cultivation of trust essential to that age. The surrogate mother was originally planned only for the first stage but consideration has been given to allowing her to continue the relationship with the child as long as it appears the child needs emotional support. Although the surrogate mother is the primary player at that age, during the first stage a second figure is introduced and that is the simulated father figure who plays a diminished but nevertheless important role but does help in protecting a fragile infant ego structure at a time the child will be increasingly drawn away from the mother figure. Hereafter, the mother plays a diminishing role while the father never plays a major role although his presence continues into the second stage of development.

"In the second phase of development, the simulated mother and father continue as influences but they have become minor players as the bantling is now exposed to the first peer interactions of his life. The peer simulators are designed to a virtual reality representing a conglomeration of personalities to be introduced gradually and in themselves are deliberately non-threatening but are contrived to draw the child out of the ego-involvement of early childhood to a cautious individualism. Then the peer influence becomes stronger as the child moves away from the narrow and restricting behavior of the mother-son relationship. In the later stages of that phase, a personality begins to emerge, friendships are formed and there is give and take between the child and his newly acquired peers. This phase, as trust has given the child security, promotes intimacy and the first stirrings of ambition and the beginnings of a personal sense of identity. If on schedule, at this point in his young life, the child will have the development of a fourteen-year-old emotionally and physically, but in actual time will be about six months old.

"The third phase is one of increasing difficulty for the child for it is the phase in which we attempt to achieve self-identity, autonomy, ambition, and general sociability in the adolescent. The mother and father simulators are mere shadows now in the drama but remain in the background for support and emotional security but other than that their work is done and they have little influence. The adolescent's peers from the previous stage have been phased out or, in some cases remain as minor players, as the simulators that now interact with the adolescent are a cross-section of society, and this might included the most despicable or the most noble of our society and will include the most accomplished and the most abject of our society and expose the child to the con man or the simple manipulator. In the face of these influences the adolescent must be reactive and develop a strong sense of self so that he can objectively analyze and examine the people around him. This is not to say that we will create the perfect human being, but that the learner will come to realize the full potential of what he can be within his ability—he will be what he was meant to be what his genes call for him to be. At the completion of this phase, the tyro will have developed his prevailing character and established a purpose in life.

"In the fourth phase, the young man will seek out the peer simulators he prefers as he sublimates his autonomy into an interactive state and from this point his internal strength and self-commitment will be his weapons against problematic situations of his own choosing. As an individual, he can be clever in his associations and avoid crisis and despair or he can be of such character and emotional strength as to be able to throw off the deprecation of the corrupt and deprived without impact to himself. On the other hand, the youth could be the victim as a dupe for no other reason than he has an inherent trait for which there is no control or correction—hopefully that will not be so. Also, during the phase, the youth will be able to order his own books and entertainment and at this time in a last-ditch effort to discover behavioral flaws, he will be the most studied human on the planet. At that time, there will be countless social scientists, psychiatrists and church clerics analyzing his behavior—complicated by the fact that the subject and those studying the subject will be in different time-space dimensions that require computer translation—and then evaluating that behavior and formulating an intervening program, if necessary.

"That concludes the youth's AGM training and development. He will be released thereupon into society for one year in which he will be monitored, counseled and given opportunity to adapt to environmental changes that are anticipated, and probably many that are not anticipated. The time in this post-graduate phase has been set at a year but would actually be determined by the youth's progress."

In his presentation, Celosi had calculated the scientific level of understanding of his audience to be plebian and accordingly, he designed his speech in generalities directed to the lay person and much of his explanations as vague and inconsequential. The question period that followed was benign and not challenging as Celosi mentally held his breath that there was no fop in the audience who would expose just how little he knew himself about the science of the project. Celosi was a businessman, not a scientist, but he had pulled it off effectively. Probably more surprising was that everyone present was implicitly aware that the subject of the cloning and the accelerated growth process was Jesus Christ but, as if this had become the most gigantic conspiracy in the history of the world, there was no mention of it, no questions directed toward the role of religion in the project or that many of the aspects of acceleration were violations of the tenets of the Christian faith. It was a grand gathering of clandestine subversives.

In the following weeks, the Senate and the House put together their versions of a law that would allow the cloning of a specific individual, and the language of that enactment had to be so that cloning, otherwise illegal, in this particular instance would leave the possibility of future cloning to the legislature on an individual basis if it were deemed necessary. Both versions avoided naming an individual in question and the language used in the two versions was convoluted and represented the most audacious sleight of rhetoric ever to come out of two houses used to mind-boggling prestidigitation. The scheme of a silent conspiracy was obvious and nothing would bring that to the fore more than the fact that there was shockingly little debate or controversy over the proposed law or its language. The cloning of the unnamed subject was left in the hands of the scientists by deliberate obviation causing one to suspect why the scientists that politicians had always found untrustworthy were suddenly acceptable as peer-conspirators. But there was much more to it than that; it was as if the politicians could not say His name, it was as if they could not verbally bring His goodness into their messy little games of manipulation as somewhere inside of each was a conscience that jostled the mind into awareness that if this man of peace and goodness were used for political advantage it would be blasphemous but, unfortunately, it was too late, for there comes a time when even a good man who has sold his soul to the material world has degenerated too far to rise in a resistance that would bring about even his own salvation.

On Christmas Eve, 2032, the Congress passed the Freedom of Resurrection Act, a law that would allow one individual to be cloned without criminalization for violation of federal law or the tenets of the Christian faith. With the completion of the business of the Congress there was no elation or sense of triumph; this most hallowed event was without ceremony or exuberance as each senator and representative was left to his own thoughts.

# Fourteen

The State of the Union Address in January 2033 attracted only eight percent of the television-viewing public, a figure compatible with that event's annual poor showing over the previous decade; but, the viewers who did tune in were shocked at how much the president had changed—perhaps deteriorated would be a better word—over the four years of his administration. They undoubtedly remembered the aggressive, arrogant, egomaniacal unabashed self-promoter striving for the highest office in the land and the eloquent promises and flamboyant declarations made by him without vacillation. They could recall the high energy level, the emotionalism, that exalted face so full of life and high expectation and the incredible ability of the man to connect with voters and at the same time, appear to remain above vicious political attacks and rabid name-calling which typified the politics of that era. Most of all, they remembered a man who could take the most difficult, complex issues and make them so simple and easy to explain—probably the single most important aspect of his campaign personality.

But to juxtapose that image with the current image before the cameras was to reveal a stunning comparative depiction of a man broken by the cataclysmic quagmire that had become America. Previously in his addresses, he appeared to be modest in his advocacy of Christianity, and at times even questioned many of the ecclesiastical proclamations made by over-exuberant clerics while parenthetically appealing to his political base—the religious right. Now however, standing before the cameras in slump-shouldered submission, a picture of depression, a once-handsome face blank and expressionless, dull eyes encircled by anxiety, he clung to his religion as if it were his last desperate hope, but his Christian pronouncements seemed of epitaphic expression rather than inspirational sermon. For too many years he and his party had submitted contrived numbers to the public to disguise a faltering economy and social chaos, and now, it was not going to work any longer for that phase of political hyperbole was of the past. His aides had dutifully warned him that the public had been rejecting of that approach for many years and now the deceit of the government had become so obvious and the people so skeptical, that open rebellion had become a distinct possibility, particularly with the rise of the underground economy and the Mole People, a new political force in the land.

So it was a disheveled president in a television appearance facing a small minority of Americans of mixed political opinion with absolutely no recourse as to their acceptance or rejection of the views put forth by the president that night; and that is unfortunate, for that night would come to the people the most honest and forthright major speech by an American politician in the twenty-first century—at least, up to a point. The president had never given a shoddy performance as a speaker and he had no intention of doing otherwise on this night and when he commenced to speak, the usual brilliant articulation that all expected came forth but yet, there was a sadness about it that no one had previously anticipated. Even political opponents of the president saw something that they would have never believed in that as he presented his speech, he maintained direct eye contact with the camera and was devoid of the theatrics so common to his addresses and so essential to his popularity among his political base and, unusual for him, his language was simple and without the subtle innuendos and blatant generalizations of past performances.

He started by admitting that each major city in the United States needed 6,000 tons of food delivered each day to adequately supply the nutritional needs of the people, but that as a result of bad weather, drought and a deteriorating infrastructure, only two-thirds of the expected amount was being delivered to the average city. Accordingly, the price of food had gone up as only the wealthier families were able to eat adequately and he sadly announced that there are over eighty-four million people in the country who go to bed undernourished every night. This was further complicated, he said, by the fact that foreign countries have faced such a crisis themselves that they will have to cut shipments to the US in order to feed their own people. He lamented that 30,000 people in the US died every day due to poverty and that there is more slavery throughout the US today than when all the slaves were taken from Africa at the time of the transatlantic slave trade. For the first time, a president admitted that the US ranked at the bottom of all industrialized nations in education, health care, care for the elderly, mortality rate, infant death rate; but led all nations in crime rate, homelessness and untreated disease.

Then the president went through a long list of disastrous revelations threatening the country, going through the list item by item, the least of which was the state of the national economy, usually the high point of any presidential speech whether the economy was something to brag upon or not—it just had always been that America was a market-directed economy, thus our inherent boasting right. The president explained that we had become insolvent, were unable to pay even the interest on our foreign loans and that our main debt was to China which was threatening legal action. The president had delayed such a course by threatening to nationalize; however, he never offered that particular threat again after an aide suggested that nationalization was something a communist regime would do—but never capitalism.

Item after item, the president laid it all out in what appeared to be the most humbling experience of any American president in history, and even the fevered political observers of the political left applauded and sighed that "Perhaps now we are going to do something about all this." However, an hour after the commencement of this disheartening theme, when all viewers had descended into a mindless funk, the president suddenly came alive with ardent smile and beguiling demeanor and leaning toward his audience uttered, "There is an answer, one that we have come to expect and all Christians will applaud." *New York Times* political writer Edmund Linnus recalled his feelings at that moment when, mesmerized by a grand presidential sermon, he suddenly came to reality and murmured to himself, "Oh, oh, we've been duped again. He really had me going there for a while—his sincerity seemed so sincere. I wonder what corporate scheme he is going to sell us this time."

But it was not a corporate scheme—it would be the coming together of all things good that would produce the perfect paradise here on earth as God intended. Thus began the core message of the president's speech as if golden rays from heaven were revealing a miracle of Biblical proportions and there the president stood in that light, radiant and beaming with the evangelical joy of an apocalyptic presentation to inspire mankind and heal the wounds and illnesses of the tragic human society:

"Someone far more powerful than mere mortal man has been charged with the responsibility of bringing about permanent change. Who is that, I must ask? It is Jesus Christ. He is described in the Bible as God's chief agent for salvation of the human family.

"He is now awaiting for God's appointed time to act. What exactly will he do? He will bring about the restoration of all things of which God spoke through the mouth of his holy prophets of old time. He will deliver the poor one crying for help, the afflicted one and whoever has no helper. He will deliver them from oppression and violence and He will redeem their soul; and, through Jesus

Christ, God promises to make wars cease to the extremity of the earth. He promises that no resident will say he is sick and the blind, the deaf, the lame and all those afflicted by disease will be restored to perfect health, and even those who have died in the past will benefit for He promises to bring back victims of injustice and oppression.

"Jesus Christ will not bring about a temporary or partial change for He will eliminate all barriers to a truly fair world. He will remove sin and imperfection and totally destroy Satan the Devil and all those who follow his bellicose course, and the distress and suffering that God temporarily permitted will not rise up again. This is what Jesus had in mind when he taught us to pray for God's kingdom to come and for God's will to take place.

"He will return us to a pure path that will follow the literacy of the Bible and we will all be saved and at that time there will be no dispute of the true path as all true believers will lead the way and the doubters will be so impressed by the happening that they will throw themselves on the ground and beg for forgiveness and redemption for their skepticism. That will lead to a new world order where all rejoice in the one God and thereafter there will always be negotiation and cooperation and man will thereafter live in peace and harmony.

"Now we call on Jesus to return to us and lead us out of this decadent hole of deceit and treachery. But we are not passive and have not merely thrown ourselves to His mercy and plead for his return; nay, we have taken the initiative and are preparing to return Jesus through every effort within our ability. Would God ask us to simply ask for his redemption and expect no explicit effort from us or would He expect more from us and since we have so many God-given methods to expedite the return of Jesus, is it not evident that He expects more from us than wailing and pleading? Has He not demanded that we make direct effort to provide conveyance for the return of Jesus?

"For several decades now we have sought solution to our perplexities through the application of computer technology but that has become the scientist's tar baby in that there are too many fingers probing and prying in it and somewhere along the way we have ignored whether the computer simulation of human behavior is in any way relevant to human behavior. It seems that we have given computers a life of their own and as such they have taken a path separate from the very beings that they are trying to simulate and out of awe for their existence, we taken the same path—one different from that demanded by God. In an effort to extricate ourselves from that dilemma we have falsely followed the disciplines of philosophers and social schemers, but that has only exacerbated our alienation from our God. And now, sadly, we find that we fell heir to the supposed problem-solving prowess that compelled the collective admiration of intellectuals to believe in the infallibility of computers without even addressing a concern as to whether such problems were even solvable or to the interest of mankind. At that time, there was no a priori reason for analyzing analogies between the human mind and the supposed human-simulating computer and that was our failure.

"Now has come the time that we must take back our sense of self and direct ourselves in way to reunite us with God and in doing so throw off the burden of an oppressive system compelled by mindless machines that perpetuate their own existence but ignore the needs, hopes and aspirations of human society. So it is incumbent upon us to call to Jesus to return to lead us and in doing so we call upon ourselves to take back the mantle of leadership. We need spiritual guidance at this time and the world has become so complex and the solutions so incredibly complicated that we fail to realize that many of these difficulties can simply be cast aside if we return to a simple spiritual existence rather than one that demands our time and energy to chase the windmills of an out-of-control technological fantasy. We must now realize that Jesus is of us and we are of Jesus and the two cannot be separated and how strikingly simple this is, but that obvious relationship has eluded us, for through our greed and materialism we've forgotten the truth. Therefore, I have proposed that we initiate a procedure that will bring our Savior to us through technological resources—ironically—and perhaps that would be the one positive result of our scientific revolution.

"We now have the ability, as incredible as it may seem, to bring an individual—any individual—who is deceased, back from the grave once we are able to recover and identify the remains of that individual. As you probably know from news accounts that an American archeological team recently uncovered the remains of our Savior in a cave long noted as a place he habituated when meditating, and those remains have positively been identified as that of Jesus. The circumstances of that discovery are so extraordinary that there is little doubt that divine intervention was involved by a compassionate God who felt the despair and torment of human society. That is, an act that defies any other explanation—considering the enormity of the situation—that the cave and grave existed for over two thousand years but went undiscovered for that period of time until He found a compelling need to return His Son to us. In itself, it is a glorious moment, but when He delivered to those brave archeologists His only Son, His love and care for humankind became apparent.

And we must ask why did God deliver His Son to Christian archeologists and not secular scientists? Because that very act emphasized the importance of the findings and that such discovery could not be entrusted in the hands of nonbelievers.

"So now I call upon the nation and our nation's resources to embark on a mission that I have named 'Operation Resurrection' because of the discovery by Christian archeologists in a remote darkened cave in Israel we have the DNA of Jesus and the means to clone and the means to speed the time of the growth of the reborn Savior to about one-fourth of usual, or about five years. This is of obvious importance because the momentous changes occurring on earth are mounting and we simply cannot wait any longer than necessary for our spiritual leader. The prepared DNA will be planted in a surrogate mother in vitro but she will not pass on her genes nor will she be a part of child-rearing—she will have no further contact with the child. Immediately after birth, the child will be placed in an Accelerated Growth Module, a space-age incubator that will allow perfectly normal growth of the child from infant to adulthood in significantly less time. The growth chamber has been designed to duplicate the space environment that would be found on the planet Mercury, which is only thirty-six million miles from the sun, has an eighty-eight-day year and has a much increased gravitational pull and a faster time dimension. This duplication is enacted by a computer-driven system that manipulates the gravitational-inertia field through control of mass and speed to produce a distortion of time that will provide us will the fast-running time necessary to speed the growth of a living being.

"Research and experimentation on time dimension began in the second decade of the century when scientists were actually pursuing solutions to aging and came to focus on theoretical thought, based on the concept that 'time is gravity' and therefore, to completely understand the phenomenon, it was necessary to research the acceleration of time as well as the reduction of time. From this equation came the hypothesis that given planet's aether subjugates the mass aggregate of the planet to its aether flows and therefore, time dimension of that planet is dependent upon the planet's density and aether capacity. To test this hypothesis, NASA developed a chamber within a vacuum chamber, the inner chamber equipped with a device called a 'whirling dervish' which is a weight on propellers whirled at an incredible speed, and the centrifugal force from that creates the chamber's weight independent of the density of the earth; and later, a second dervish was added and it was found that such a manipulation could controllably accelerate or reduce time of the chamber using the normal earth aether as a time-keeping reference. Since nature abhors a vacuum or chaos, the pressure of nature always seeks a balance and the dynamic masses—morphogenic fields in humans—and tries to match any change occurring in density or aether flow—so enters the human component into the equation. Experiments thereafter showed that a reduction in the aether field could induce tissue regeneration while an increased aether field could bring about accelerated growth. The time inside the chamber and outside the chamber would appear exactly the same to anyone in either place but because of the different time dimensions, they will be different. The only outside connect is flexi-hose which allows atmosphere to be pumped into the chamber. Of course, this is the primitive version of the chamber as the AGM will be quite sophisticated before a child would be introduced, not to mention unlimited testing and experimentation to determine reliability. While in the growth chamber, the child will be cared for by several simulation monitors; and, in addition to child-rearing activities, the monitors will be educating the young Savior in all academics available to prepare him for his role as the spiritual leader of this great nation and all of mankind.

"So, I say in conclusion, perhaps a new spirit is rising among us. If it is, let's trace its movement and pray that our own inner being may be sensitive to its guidance, for we are deeply in need of a new way beyond the darkness that seems so close around us."

The president had laid out the plan for cloning the King in layman's language and, satisfied that his proposal would be accepted by the public, particularly after a pre-speech onslaught by the media which presented the domestic situation as hopeless and the president's plan as the only reasonable alternative to continued retrogression, he fell into light banter and was almost giddy at times. He was the hero of the moment as he had, as usual, stacked the Capitol audience with evangelicals who applauded his every word and then, at the end, stood cheering for a full five minutes—the effect on television was impressive. The president ended his speech with the usual prayers, the wording of which suggested a complete capitulation to religious aspiration.

So it was done. What no president had ever dreamed possible had been said and once said, it seemed so easy, so reasonable—the president wondered why there had ever been any fear that such a proposal would not be acceptable to a Christian society. But as several scientists pointed out—not that anyone listened—the time dimension theory was uncertain and, unknown to the public, three individual newborns were tested and two perished and one was successfully terminated after completing the program but was determined to be mentally impaired although arguments were inconclusive as to whether it was a pre-existing condition. But scientists had approved of the program and the enthusiasm for it was so high that there was no likelihood of calmer judgment prevailing. Also not mentioned by the president was a weekly cost of one billion dollars for the operation of the AGM, which included about one thousand scientists to monitor the program. The whole concept was mind-boggling to a public worn out by an administration that had ignored disaster after disaster but suddenly came forward with a program that appeared more fantasy than political solution. And no one questioned whether a young Jesus would have even an inkling of wisdom or insight in the enormous problems facing the world at the time; but, in the realm of faith, faith had carried the day and there was no turning back.

The preparation for the return of the baby Jesus to earth was immense. But most of the scientific preparation was lost to the public view as it was difficult to understand and the media was under the impression that extensive coverage of scientific matters would have little appeal considering that the average American read on a sixth-grade level and had an attention span of about ten seconds when not playing video games. But what the media did do, thanks to their intemperate leader Paul Link, was to romanticize the project by daily front-page articles, filled with obvious exaggeration and veneration for the principle movers of the project, movers not necessarily representing the scientific community but consistently boasting their religious affiliations. These daily bombardments gave the public little insight into the scientific aspects of the venture but were designed to entice and gain their unquestioning approval. The clever Link, rather than explain in altogether simple terms that the AGM separated the growth capsule from the earth's gravity by vacuum and then created a Mercury-like environment by a balance of mass and aether influx, instead presented a series of graphs which demonstrated the procedure of Operation Resurrection by a confusing array of spatial coordinates. In addition he praised the use of the powerful Chinese Baoshan Centrifugal engines to create the incredible centrifugal force necessary to power the growth chamber. The average man on the street would subsequently claim that he understood the concepts in full. To say otherwise would be un-Christian.

However, the single event that drew the public's interest, as if it were an issue involving celebrities, was about who the surrogate mother would be and it was a daily feature in all the tabloids. The public seemed to rightly understand that the mother would not actually be a mother rather than a human incubator which was a pre-biblical concept as expressed by the Greek playwright

Aeschylus who wrote, "The mother of what is called her child is no parent of it, but nurse only of the young life that is sown in her." Up to the eighteenth century when embryology was in its infancy, it was common belief that the father was the child's only true parent while the mother's role was to stimulate growth. Oddly, as the preparation for the birth of Jesus, this was a sentiment that was quite comfortable with the clerics of the Evangelical church and considering the paternal bias of biblical times, there may very well have been an unmentioned acceptance of that doctrine in the Christian faith even in modern times.

Of course, when volunteers were requested for a surrogate mother, thousands responded and suddenly there was a monumental task of weeding them out. Medical experts and scientists stated that the only requirement for a surrogate mother would be that she be physically healthy as the most vital function of the mother is to provide a nutritional system to supply the embryo with the raw materials for growth. On the other hand, religious leaders had their own prerequisites, the first of which and the most important was the girl be a virgin. When the AGM program announced that each girl must be verified by a medical doctor, most of them withdrew their applications. The second requirement demanded by the clerics was that the mother be a Christian and, as such, must be evaluated by a select group of religious representatives. Those two simple requirements when approved by the governing body of the AGM project reduced the applicants to a workable lot and strangely enough those remaining were not diverse but one of the most homogenous groups of women one could imagine as all seemed to be the daughters of clergymen, babbled incessantly about religious matters when being examined by doctors, and all seemed to be named Grace, Chastity, Hope, Joy, Destiny or Mary. Mary was the favorite name.

From the very beginning, the leading candidate was one Mary Faretheewell, the melancholy daughter of the Reverend Jeremy Faretheewell, long a White House favorite among the clergymen to confer with the president or his staff on political-religious matters. Miss Mary, as she came to be known, giggled to the press that it had always been a goal in her life to advance the cause of Christianity in some way and this, she thought, would be "cool." Anyone looking at this maiden would probably safely predict that she was, in fact, a virgin as she was not, in any stretch of the imagination comely, nor was she middling, passable, or, as one pundit put it, she was "not unugly." History is uncertain how Miss Mary became the chosen one to be the surrogate mother of the clone officially designated as Jesus II. The selection process was much debated but when the final picks were presented to the selection committee—all healthy and fecund—a lottery system was set up and not surprisingly, Miss Mary won that trial with the obvious response from her supporters that the selection had been determined by the hand of God. Other selection methods were incorporated in an effort to show impartiality but Miss Mary was on a winning streak. The whole thing erupted into an emotional shoving match as detractors thought the choice should look a little more like the imagined mother of Jesus but the scientists and medics who were ready to imbue the pregnancy were growing impatient when it appeared that the verbal donnybrook would not produce a winner satisfactory to all segments of the decision-making process. So Miss Mary was to become the mother of the twenty-first-century Jesus, a decision obviously applauded by her father.

If what the selected maiden was about to accomplish was the most significant achievement in the history of mankind then the apparent irony was that Miss Mary was the most unremarkable female for accomplishing that feat and with it was a forgone conclusion that her father, now known as Reverend Jeremy, had a lot to do with her selection behind the scenes. Reverend Jeremy could now boast that he would be the grandfather of the Jesus child and he indicated great pride in his daughter. But many who knew him privately were aware of how denigrating and critical he had always been of his daughter as many suspected that he just plain did not like her. Mary herself was a pathetic child who could never please her father and had little to offer of herself so she attempted to become the most devout of the pious. She was described by observers as dim-witted and one wag commented that "you could bounce a golf ball off her head and she would not blink." Physically, Mary was vaguely feminine-looking with wide hips that would ensure an easy birth and she was extremely healthy—perhaps about fifty pounds too healthy. She always wore sack-like dresses which she stated was due to her extreme modesty. She claimed to have resisted all sexual temptation and after the birth of the Jesus child, she contended that she would remain celibate for the rest of her life. During a media interview, Mary launched into a virtual religious revival and began to pontificate as interviewers vainly attempted to have her answer specific questions, and it was noted that her use of English was so poor that one wondered just what it was that she studied in all those years of home schooling.

On a gloomy day in March of that year, Miss Mary and her father were escorted to the AGM in Colorado Springs, Colorado, for the in vitro process and with the understanding that she would remain at the center for the entire period of her pregnancy for the protection of the child (in all subsequent reports Jesus II was referred to as "the child" but never "her child") as well for the protection of Mary herself. Mary had in her mind an impression of the AGM as having the appearance of a nuclear submarine, an impression put forth by news accounts but once inside she was shocked by the extensively plush underground complex beneath that structure. The first morning was spent in orientation, which her father was allowed to attend, and he was characteristically abrasive during that formality. In the afternoon Mary was shown her room for the next nine months, a room that was modest but had all the modern conveniences, many of which were unfamiliar to her. But she was pleased and particularly in that for the first time in her life she would not have to suffer the inquisitorial meddling of her father for an extended period of time. She was also pleasantly surprised to be informed that upon delivery of the child, she would become eligible for a federal pension, which pleased her to no end since, as an individual with absolutely no talent, she had faced an uncertain future. She knew from experience that her father would assail such money as "a government handout" but she had this one single thing that was hers and she was determined to hang on to it.

The following morning Mary was scheduled to begin the in vitro process of which she knew nothing. When she was seated on the examining table she resisted the use of the stirrups which were new to her as she had never been to a gynecologist and was totally unfamiliar with such procedure, referring to the stirrups as obscene and depraved. The matter traumatized Mary so badly that she had to be given a sedative. She subsequently was given two days to pull herself together emotionally and, after much counseling and the support of female nurses, Mary demonstrated the bravery to face the stirrups. A major crisis had been diverted. Actually, the doctors found Mary to be pleasant and cooperative. She had a little girl's high voice and became quite inquisitive but that revealed an incredible ignorance about even common matters. The medical team found that they liked her and they noted that she had unsatisfied emotional needs and was almost desperate for attention and support. When Mary was informed that she would be the most medically monitored pregnant female in history, she responded with zeal for a process that most would consider a crashing bore.

When Mary was asked to disrobe, she resisted initially then concurred modestly. A doctor noted in his report that Mary actually had a "nice" figure but that it was hidden by layers of fat which he concluded to himself was her method of avoiding the certain conflict that she must have had over her father's inability to accept her sexuality, a speculation based on a single meeting with the rigid and recalcitrant Reverend Jeremy. Mary was examined and then as she appeared to be an adequate specimen for the procedure and as she was beginning her menstrual cycle, she was given fertility drugs to stimulate the ripening of several eggs. During that week the normally restrained Mary made mild attempts at sociability with nurses and interns and she even left her room to roam the halls of the underground structure and attendants and maintenance men recalled later seeing the childlike Mary, mute and alone, taking all in with wide-eyed curiosity and during those forays her face seemed to developed a gentle softness and was almost pretty. She made some cautious friendships among the medical personnel who felt her need for companionship as, despite years of rejection, she began to develop the beginnings of trust and to test intimacy.

After the ninth day, Mary underwent ultrasound tests that verified the ripening of the eggs in her ovaries; then, immediately after ovulation, the ripe eggs were removed by ultrasound-guided needle aspiration through the abdomen. The eggs were then mixed with an organic substance which included a sample of the world's most precious DNA. Subsequently, after about forty hours, the eggs were examined and it was verified that they had been fertilized and the eggs were placed in Mary's uterus. The in vitro process had been completed and the rest of the process would be up to Mary, but thereafter, she would be under constant monitoring; and, despite what she had expressed was the most important event in her life, she became quite casual about the whole thing while showing vivid interest in the world around her. Both her mental state and physical appearance improved during the pregnancy as she drifted into an easy attitude of openness and sociability and, as her self-awareness improved, she became more realistic regarding her purpose for being at the AGM and her role there. One doctor, noticing the change, commented, "Our little girl is growing up."

During the pregnancy, Mary had a relatively easy time. In the first trimester she experienced little nausea or vomiting and she did not feel unusually tired as was typical of that stage of pregnancy. The second trimester was uneventful and typically during the third, she needed more rest and easily became overheated and sweaty and she was experiencing what the doctors called an easy pregnancy. But what was at first a concern of the medical staff and called for daily contact with a psychiatrist was the fact that at the onset, Mary was an immature little girl, somewhat withdrawn and of such low self-esteem and that was a concern as research studies had shown that a mother's mental state and attitude could adversely effect the baby's mental state and subsequent development. This was explained to Mary but eventually became a non-issue when the doctor saw rapid and positive changes in Mary's personality as tests showed that she was maturing and would be a positive influence on the unborn child, this undoubtedly a result of her association with the professional medical staff.

The team psychologist completed a report on the adjustment of Mary to the AGM pre-natal program with the following summary: "Mary Faretheewell came to us as a woebegone child, tightly wound, self-alienated little creature from an upbringing of an uncompromisingly rigid Christian sect that was more punitive than benevolent and more controlling than compassionate. From the beginning she was subjected to her father's view of reality at too tender of an age, and to a reality that saw the natural world as hostile and evil and all redemption was to be found in Biblical prophecy and so she was condemned to a life of drudgery and hoped-for miracles. But what she was denied was exposure to the magical world of fantasy so essential in a young girl's development so she did not search for flying horses in the sky, see pixies among the flowers or dream of a white knight coming to her window and because she lacked such a wonderful episode in her young life, she did not learn the intimate beauty of fairy tales and the human spirit, she did not learn about inner beauty or fairness or courage, or heroism or bravery, and she never learned to use her imagination. Therefore, she did not experience a natural transition from childhood, an easing into sheer reality that would accept her innocence and trustfulness. Instead, she only knew the stark, cold reality of rejection and ridicule and she sought redress in the riddles of religion. When Mary came to us, we felt her despair but she did not understand it and when she saw others in a happy state, she felt inadequate. But there was a spark within Mary, a suppressed discord and curiosity about the self, and in coming to AGM, she was unexpectedly in a social environment that would encourage and promote self-exploration. It was heart-rending to see how staff nurses touched her emotionally and although extremely hesitant at first, it was a thrill to see her approach a staff member inquisitively, something that she had previously been incapable of doing. But what was most significant was that Mary was learning trust, the primary building block of her development, and when she was physically touched by personnel, she responded with such warmth and acceptance as so needy had been this desperate little elf that she actually took chances that would have previously exposed her to denigration. The growth of Mary while here has been monumental and it is sad and tragic that under the circumstances for which she is here, she will be unable to raise her child as we feel now that she would be a wonderful mother. Our hearts go out to this girl and we wonder with despair what will be her future after she returns to her parents."

On Christmas Day in New York City, high water in the Atlantic Ocean and a violent wind storm caused a storm surge that shorted out the few subways still operating, created four feet of water standing in Manhattan and the Christmas lights state-wide were darkened. But it was a day of joy, for in Colorado Springs on that day, during a gentle snow fall, Jesus II was brought into the world—at least that was the official line and more than a few eyebrows were raised when newspapers blaring gaudy headlines announced a resurrection and did so on the very day of the birth. But few people were skeptical as a tired nation reveled in the joy of the news, not questioning the timing of the event. Despite the stated purpose of the return of Jesus II to earth, the nation quickly forgot that this swaddling was to become the spiritual leader of the world but, in the manner in which all melt before the precious gift of a child in their arms, the child became to all Americans just what it was, a precious nursling, a bundle of dependence that siphons the tenderness and caring out of even the hardest human beings allowing them to become the humans they are capable of being.

In an anteroom of the huge AGM complex, an elated Jerry Faretheewell and a smug Paul Link met informally for the first time—although they had formalized conversations many times before—while awaiting their appearance in a televised interview to discuss the sensational event of the day. "This is a glorious day for all Christians," Reverend Jeremy began, "a culmination of all our hopes and dreams in a dreadful world and the beginning of a glorious new era."

"How is your daughter?"

"She came through the thing very well and she is ecstatic over her accomplishment."

"Did she actually get to see the child? I know the child is to be put into the growth chamber immediately; but did she get to hold him?"

"Actually, they allowed her to hold him for quite a while but, the brave soul that she is, she gave him up. She knows that is for the best." Then pondering to himself briefly, the reverend said, "I think that it was a beautiful act of God to resurrect His son on Christmas Day—it means so much to Christianity."

Link did not respond, but standing aloof, smiled to himself.

Frowning a bit, the reverend reiterated, "He was born of Christmas Day after all—that couldn't have been by accident."

Link only smiled. Then, as if to change the subject, he said quietly, as if repeating a rumor, "Have you heard about H.L. Houten?"

"No, not at all, what happened?"

"He was committed to a mental institution. He had become very irrational, was saying some bizarre things and there was even a report that he was suicidal. So he is currently undergoing evaluation but it doesn't look good."

"I thought," the reverend mused, "that such a glorious thing would be a therapeutant for all of us; I mean, why would he become disturbed at such a wonderful time?"

"Maybe it was just because he expected a more important part in bringing the baby into the world—perhaps he just felt left out," Link said with a wry smile.

"Such a tragedy. He did so much but even then what he brought to the world through his work should have been gratifying enough—why should anyone expect more?" the reverend asked.

Link added, "I know that he was extremely disappointed in the response in the Middle East. He thought that the burial cave would become a shrine and that masses of people would make pilgrimage to it, but it never happened."

"Why do you suppose that never happened?"

Link was silent for a moment and then said, "I think it is because most Christians believe so intensely in Biblical prophecy and when it doesn't happen just the way it is stated, they do not accept it as fact."

"But most of the world has accepted the return overwhelmingly. Why not the Christians and Jews of the Middle East?"

"Surprisingly, many of the people rejoicing are secular along with some sects out of the mainstream and they are so desperate for a solution to the incredible problems facing the world that they would believe anything that might bring a solution."

Then the reverend said, "I feel empathy for Houten—it's unfortunate that he is unable to appreciate his accomplishment."

"That's the price of ambition, sometimes we are never satisfied and I always knew him to be driven and perhaps too ego-involved and when they led him away he kept saying, 'what have I done, what have I done?'"

"What does that mean?" the reverend asked.

Link responded, "I think what he meant was the old feel-sorry-for-me routine, you know, to cynically ask what one has done to bring such treatment upon oneself."

## THE LEGEND OF SUSEJ

"Maybe he was questioning his discovery and subsequently bringing the baby into this world."

"Don't be silly," Link said. "He was in it for what he could get out of it and it just didn't happen—he couldn't just be a part of the Christian family and accept it at that."

"Well, I will pray for him and his recovery."

Dr. Emmit Verill, doctor of biology at the University of Chicago, a thin, pale, middle-aged professor with a seemingly no-nonsense attitude, had received a special grant which would allow him to observe the rapid growth procedure at the Accelerated Growth Module at Colorado Springs for the entirety of the program. He was not impressed one way or another when he arrived at the module having seen the module silhouette an incredible number of times on newscasts or the endless documentaries shown on the subject. Verill was beginning to have doubts as to whether he even wanted to be part of the project, so overwhelmed was he with the superabundance of copy on the subject bombarding the airways. Security clearance had been the main hurdle for approval to the protected area, and to his surprise he found out, during his interrogation for security clearance, that the NSA had records which included some of his high jinks as an undergraduate student at Yale University, behavior that had no malicious intent or political objective but was more in tune with the old-fashioned quirkiness typical of fraternity play and that offended no one at the time; even the most somber professors saw no harm in it. His most heralded outrageous act of frivolity, for instance, occurred during the unveiling of a statue of the virgin Mary at the university, for when the shroud dropped, it revealed, in the lap of Mary, a young Emmit Verill, clad only in a huge purple-polka-dot diaper, kissing and throwing rose petals to the exuberant crowd witnessing the event. Years later with the memory of that fiasco still in mind, a happening that actually brought more pride to the university than a rare win over their traditional football rivals, coworkers and fellow professors could not believe that Dr. Verill was one and the same man, so serious and dedicated to academics had he become. But Dr. Verill survived the disquisition and received security clearance. During a long cat-and-mouse interrogation, the NSA inquisitor, who took himself quite seriously, was on the verge of being abusive when Dr. Verill, nearly exhausted, offered that he was tiring of the whole process and that he had little further interest in pursuing the matter, at which point the agent began to back off and replace his aggressiveness with a more arbitrative demeanor.

Once cleared, Verill proceeded to the AGM where he was met by a Dr. Levitts who was assigned to escort Dr. Verill through the facility, answer any questions and then take him to the quarters that would be his for the duration of his stay. On entering the complex, Verill first saw the above-ground chambers and his initial impression was that the structure must certainly have been low-budget—stark and Spartan as it was—but then entrance into the underground revealed state-of-the-art laboratories, medical facility, communication center, computer facility, kitchen, cafeteria and various staff offices. The doctor's purpose of being there was to observe the proceedings and report daily to a center at Johns Hopkins University where the information would be prepared for dissemination to scientific institutions throughout the world. The process of gaining the assignment had been quite contentious for Verill as the Congress had been united against such an interloper in the AGM program, preferring instead that the communication center handle all information released to the public. But the majority of workers at the module were scientists and they were adamantly opposed to processed information as, in the six months prior to the arrival of the cloning subject when the AGM was being tested and evaluated, the scientists found those in the communication center to be cold and unfriendly and thus, it was obviously assumed that they were programmed ideologues. The Congress was forced to approve a compromise allowing Verill's position of scientific information officer to function but only after a supervisor's inspection of the communiqués and with the assurance to the communication center that their reports would receive no such scrutiny.

Dr. Verill was profoundly impressed with the ABM and the assembled staff; in fact, he had never met, in all his years in the scientific community, such a homogeneous and blithesome group, and with none of the religious baiting that he had come to expect. Instead, they were dedicated scientists and, as scientists, they had no inquiry or pronouncements regarding the objectives of the program. Dr. Verill was shown to his quarters and was advised that in the morning he would be taken to the main computer room where the clone was being observed by television and electronic monitors and he consciously began to prepare himself for an event that might be emotionally overwhelming. While Dr. Levitt chatted about the lifestyle and camaraderie at AGM, Dr. Verill gave a cursory glance at the written material supplied to him by the doctor and saw on the outside cover that the AGM program had been funded and planned by the federal government five years hence. He could not help himself when he inquired how the federal government could finance a program of such magnitude and of such specific purpose several years before the archeological discovery in the Middle East. Dr. Levitt was vague and suggested that maybe the program originally was meant for another clone, to which Dr. Verill responded that the government was adamantly against cloning philosophically so it seemed hypocritical of the government to finance scientific experimentation of something they were politically opposed to. Dr. Levitt, a middle-aged, tall, thin man, seemed agitated by the dispute but finally, resigned to it, said, "Look, this tremendous program is a God-send, most of us here were working part-time, if at all. This is a guaranteed five-year stint and then who knows where it goes from there. The money for the program has been allocated and as hard as times are these days, that is a pretty good assurance for the immediate future. And, look around you at the people here, they are contented because they don't have to worry, at least, for a while. So, yeah, we all wondered at first how they put together this program so fast after the discovery in Israel, but we sure to hell aren't going to question it."

At dinner that evening, Dr. Verill made instant friendships and liked those he would be working with—it was the most spontaneous, witty and outgoing group he had met since his college days. He sat with the group well after dinner drinking coffee and talking about trivial things—it was the grandest welcoming he could imagine. But he noticed a small group sitting apart from everyone else, staring intently at their plates as they ate, and without conversation. He was advised that they were the communications staff—they sent daily reports to the media on the progress in the program but it was "obvious that they don't trust us—and we don't trust them either," said one of those at Dr. Verill's table. "They are just a bunch of super-religious freaks." The small group's isolation from the main group was disconcerting to Dr. Verill who, as a life-time member of a Methodist congregation, had always rejected the argument that Christianity and science were at odds with each other. This was the one serious perplexity that he could see at the center and he knew that it would have an ongoing negative effect.

That night, Dr. Verill rested well considering he was in an unfamiliar bed and as he had been energized by the upcoming activities in which he was to be involved. After a quick breakfast and what he thought was an unnecessary wait, a Dr. Stevenson led him into the computer room—known as the command center—at 10 AM sharp. It was the fourth day since the infant's arrival at AGM. As he walked through the room, Dr. Verill oriented himself by feel and quick side-glance as to direction and to keep himself from walking into work cubicles, chairs or electronic equipment as, like a rank conscript, as his attention had been drawn to the televised images illuminated from a coterie of some thirty sets mounted on a single wall, he searched for that first, quick impression of the child. But his mind was unable to project the images into comprehensive form—he simply did not know what to look for or what to expect. Once seated preparatory to an indoctrination by Dr. Stevenson, Dr. Verill had a moment to study the electronic image in front of him and Dr. Stevenson, in appreciation of that special moment and its discovery, gave Verill the time without interruption.

It was not a moment that Dr. Verill would recall in the future with any flourish. What he saw was the Amah Simulate robot, laboring over the baby in herky-jerky fast motion, her presence obscuring the child from view. Other than that there was not much to see as the doctor was not familiar with her actions or the functions she was involved in; that is, other than that she was performing the duties of a mother and was doing so in a different time dimension. As a reporter for the scientific community, Dr. Verill would be oriented in all phases of the command center. All the personnel in the center were medical doctors or bionic scientists which included eighteen individuals on two twelve-hour shifts monitoring every heartbeat and all vital signs of the child as well as a meticulous inspection of the robots and their function. The screens would go dark four times in twenty-four hours, representing night-time in the child's time dimension each lasting about two hours, and during those periods of time the center's team would review sections of the previous period, videotapes and audio soundtracks, in slow motion for evaluation. Dr. Stevenson explained that the growth chamber had been sealed after placement of the child inside and that barring a serious medical emergency would remain unopened and it was emphasized that many of the attending simulates were capable of sophisticated medical procedures; and, even if they were not, they were very capable of complying to instructions from a command center physician. According to Dr. Stevenson, perhaps the most important operator in the center was one Dr. Nuse Ai Allha, who controlled the physical aspects of what was essentially a time machine, a position which required constant survey of changes in time weight or space and, as Dr. Stevenson explained, he was currently in the process of computer adjustment of the growth chamber in order to overcome gravitational warp to maintain homeostatic equilibrium.

In explaining the function of the growth chamber, Dr. Stevenson isolated one television monitor and directed it on a 360-degree sweep of the chamber for Dr. Verill's observation, revealing on one wall thirty not-in-use monitors, draped like new suits on hangers flat on a wall where they were conveniently out of the way. The chamber currently employed only two monitors, Amah Simulate and a cooking robot who worked in a extravagant kitchen processing prepared food on a constant basis. The rest of the monitors, all of very specific function, would remain inert until their time of task was at hand. These monitors included playmates, teachers, instructors, counselors, father, a robo-psychologist, a linguist, two peer companions of impeccable character, four jack-of-all-trades and two physical instructors. To Dr. Verill's surprise, the tour revealed that the chamber actually had two floors—the upper one with sides that sloped inward to form a ceiling, the bottom sloping downward to form the floor. The bottom room contained common furniture as one see in any apartment, row after row of books and exercise equipment such as treadmills, free weights and weight machines. The floor also contained electronic games and computers on the belief that a child at the beginning of the age of exploration would suffer deprivation due to lack of living space and therefore would need constant exposure to the virtual reality that would give him a sense of freedom and discovery, this at about age four, or at about ten months in the chamber's artificial time dimension.

In response to a nagging curiosity Dr. Verill asked Dr. Stevenson, "How did we know that the child would be male? I haven't heard a single person mention it or ask the question and yet it seems that the sex of the child was always assumed."

Dr. Stevenson, slightly jolted by the unexpected question replied, "You know that's true, no one ever thought the child would be a girl—everyone just assumed that it would be a boy. But then again, what difference does it make?"

"It doesn't make any difference in my view but I noticed that the toys and clothing in the chamber were for a boy and I know that was set up before the birth, or even conception."

"It may be that the Christians were calling it a boy from day one and since they seemed to believe that it was God who was bringing Jesus II back to earth that it most surely would be a boy."

"I suppose that it is a non-issue but it would have certainly upset many people's thinking if it had been a girl."

"Well, yes," Dr. Stevenson mused, "even though it is a boy, my question would be what if the child was highly independent and unlike Jesus in any way, in other words, did not fit into the mold that is expected—we are talking about genes here and they can be unpredictable."

Dr. Verill agreed, stating, "I would challenge the whole concept of bringing a favorite Son back as a clone, in itself it doesn't make a lot of sense. Even if the Son of God could lead us, what assures that we would follow Him, particularly if what he advocated was distasteful to our current leadership."

"I disagree with that. Recent demographics suggest that an overwhelming majority of Americans ascribe to the fundamentalist philosophy and a surprising high percentage have strong faith in this project and would probably follow without question."

Dr. Verill thought for a moment and then sarcastically said, "What if the new leader demanded that the first-born son of every family be put to death?"

"I shudder at the thought," Dr. Stevenson responded, "but I don't think that is a possibility."

"Well, I hope not," Dr. Verill added, "but the problem for me is that I have seen inane things happen under the control of churches. I am in this program because I was given the assignment and I was willing to be an observer because, despite the fact that the thing does not seem plausible, I did not want to miss out on the cutting edge of a new scientific origination."

"It's interesting, when they were recruiting for this project, their initial goal was to hire only scientists with a strong fundamentalist Christian bias but they found out that there were few available who had the qualifications to work in the program."

"But it seems to me that everyone I talked to in the program is Christian," Dr. Verill interjected.

"No, what I mean is the extremely radical Christian—these people all have faith but in my thinking, they are reasonable and their belief will not compromise their work."

Dr. Verill thought a moment and then said, "You know, I think that this whole program is suspect. Just think of the gigantic leap from the discovery of human remains whose identity was never really documented to a high-tech research center run by professional scientists that ironically legitimizes that very questionable discovery."

Dr. Stevenson was quick to reply, "You were not here in the beginning. It was unbelievable—the pressure from the newspapers, churches and the administration was absolutely overwhelming, and if the scientific community did not go along, then everything would be put in jeopardy—all the money for research, university grants, future projects and even college scholarships. The pressure was so intense and then when the Congress legitimized the deal, all objectivity was lost. And, of course times are so hard economically we were practically forced to go along."

"Perhaps when this plays out something positive will come out of it like reform to keep the government out of scientific study."

"I doubt it."

Dr. Verill settled into a routine as an observer and as such, he had the freedom to move within the command center at will, interviewing fellow scientists and analyzing data. From the start, it appeared that the project would be uneventful as the monitors did their functions exceptionally well and the scientific staff seemed to be nothing more than onlookers. Even the pediatrician responsible for the child continually found the child's growth normal and other than inducing prescribed growth hormones into the baby at regular intervals, there was little concern. Ironically, the most active workers were not in the command center but those who worked with the chamber itself supplying nutrition into a food supply system almost constantly and the sanitation workers responsible for removing disposable waste from the chamber, both of which were accomplished through tubes. Meanwhile, Dr. Verill's observation was growing so mundane that he began to write human interest essays about his fellow workers; similarly, national newspapers found so little to report daily, they did likewise to keep readers interested.

After the third week, Dr. Verill actually saw the child in its entirety during a bathing session for the first time. The Amah Simulate had always seemed to block the view of the child in bending over him or cuddling him after a meal; but now the child could be seen and that gave new meaning to an otherwise bored staff. After that exposure to the child, and others over a short period of time, Dr. Verill concluded that there was nothing remarkable about this child other than the fact that he was growing at an extraordinary rate and although those in the staff were advised accordingly and had prepared themselves for the growth that they would witness, each shift change began with the shock of the unexpected; that is that the child was larger and better developed than the preceding day.

At the conclusion of the first six weeks Dr. Verill reviewed a psychiatric evaluation of the cloned subject by a Dr. Schulter, who described the child as very pleasing, calm and responsive according to slow-motion tapes that he had studied and neurotransmitter data. The child smiled a great deal and made eye contact with the Amah, and he cried rarely and usually that could not be described as troubled. The doctor went on to say that the amygdala—the core of the brain that processes primal emotions—was not burdened down with fear or irritability and therefore could adequately fuel curiosity, passion and laughter, producing a very emotionally healthy child. By the third decade of the century, chemical neurotransmitters, which change predictably with a patient's mental state, had become widely used as valued mental markers of a patient's thinking process, the body fluids taken from cerebral spinal fluid, blood plasma, serum or platelet and urine, a procedure that became an important evaluative tool which could not only predict disorders but accurately foresee a healthy mentality. In addition, the AGM program in itself provided a remarkable strength to the child in its developmental life methods. He pointed out that in the American culture, children are instructed in and taught as many negative factors as they are positive factors and thus anxieties, stress, phobias, disassociation, sociopathic features or self-alienation are learned behaviors in a country that believes that its children are being raised properly. "In projecting ahead," the doctor concluded, "this individual will be incapable of deceit as nothing in his upbringing would create a conflict that necessitates deception—even little white lies to avoid hurting another's feeling would deviate from his emotional persona. Assuming that if everything goes as it is, when the child starts adolescent maturity, this sense of honesty will be a cornerstone of his self-identity, autonomy and independence. Furthermore, as he appears to be developing into a very gentle and sensitive person—even at this young age—he will be skilled at pacifying those who would otherwise be stung by his honesty, but beware those beguiling individuals he confronts over their recalcitrant dishonesty. And, at this time I will step out on a limb and say that he will have an uncanny ability to see deceit in others and this will cause him great stress in his lifetime but at the same time, he will attract a dedicated following."

Then in the next few weeks a remarkable thing happened: a dedicated, intellectually tough-minded crew of professional scientists gradually became emotionally connected to the child they only saw through television monitors and he became important to them and they could not separate their work from their emotional involvement with him. He was a beautiful child with an inner comeliness that transcended all the electronic apparatus and they came to love him. When the child had been in the program for a year he had become a joy to behold, and the scientists, uplifted by their relationship with the child, united in spirit and knew a new purpose in their lives. They all rejoiced when the child exhibited normal sleeping patterns—an obvious offshoot of the child's innate calmness—a concern drawn from their own personal experience as parents, and the cause of that elation was not that their work would be less complicated but the simple compassionate consideration for what would be an easier time for the child. The amah, programmed as an attachment parent, was a co-sleeping adjunct that would breast-feed on demand, cuddle and caress intimately and curl up with the child in bed. This amah that had enthralled the center's employees so passionately upon first observation, now drew their praise as the consummate mother and because of her expertise, the child was secure and happy and did not experience colic, thumb-sucking, sleep problems, tantrums or any other perplexities that so typically distress neophyte parents.

The operation at AGM became a labor of love for those directly involved in the child and his environs and there was, in fact, a tendency among the employees to become overprotective and to overanalyze his growth and vitality as all, it seemed, in their own way, became doting parents. When the child had matured in appearance to about age ten in the second year at AGM, he began to exhibit feminine traits which was largely ignored by the scientists but was worrisome to a communication center concerned as to how that would be perceived by the Christian coalition. Furthermore, as he matured, the child showed little interest in the traditional interests attractive to boys but at an early age was appreciative of art and music and was drawn to anything that would enhance a sense of tenderness in him—dolls, simulated animals or gentle interaction with his peer simulates.

This tendency in the child was contributed to experimentations by Bio-Med Inc. in which, in response to the fact that ninety percent of cloning attempts resulted in failure, offered the theory that since the genes of the opposite sex were blocked from the DNA before transfer of the DNA fragment to the self-replicating genetic element for cloning, the cloned subject would lack the balance between male and female characteristics so necessary for a healthy immune system. It was noted that because of the compromised immune system, there were high rates of infections, tumors and other problems in the cloned animals before there was any attempt at sexual balance of DNA. This may or may not have produced the feminine traits observed in the boy but the scientists saw no cause for concern. Obviously, had the boy been raised in a normal environment, he might have become a target of abusive comment and slur, exacerbating his characteristics into something crude and unnecessary. Because of the Bio-Med Inc. influence, in preparing the DNA sample for Jesus II, select female plasmids were incorporated into the mixture by the scientists after previously successful experimentations. As the boy matured, that became a non-issue, particularly with the psychiatrist's report stating that the boy had appropriate traits and was "masculine but yet was not afraid of his feminine side and he was forceful where force was appropriate, strong when strength was called for but was gentle and compassionate when that was warranted. In fact, I have never observed a more balanced and pleasant human being." Very judiciously, the communication center kept this information from the media.

The scientific staff was mesmerized by the rapid growth changes in their progeny, the changes occurring on an almost daily basis if not on shift-change basis. By the beginning of the third year of the program, all simulates were involved in the process and even the Amah Simulate was still active much longer than originally programmed as it was the opinion of the psychiatrist that he needed her for emotional support despite that she no longer took part in the actual upbringing; she seemed to always be in the immediate background but at times hovering over him or touching him tenderly on the arm or face. But the pale blue growth room of the AGM was increasingly crowded with the scurry of tutors and instructors and because of the deprivation of space, it was known by all that the amah's active days were numbered.

Then one day, the staff director, on a recommendation of the psychiatrist, placed the dear amah on inactive status. At the end of the shift, she simply turned toward the simulate container wall, dutifully walked slowly to that wall, head down and shoulders slumped, and upon reaching the place where she was to spend her remaining days, she turned, raised herself up and clasped herself to a gaff, and then dropped her head to her breast and she hung in still isolation as if in effigy. The staff observing her gasped at the sadness of her retreat, yet her actions were no different from any other simulate going to inactive status. But there was a profound eeriness about it and a numbed staff could only feel a deep sense of pity for this forlorn and abandoned robot mother. It would make one wonder, at that point, if the perfectly rational electronic brains of the computer-robots could somehow become emotionally connected to their human peers, leaving them weak and vulnerable to crises within themselves that they are incapable of rectifying. During the early part of the twenty-first century, scientists attempted to unravel the mysterious cognition of the mechanical mind, having recalled on numerous occasions, that under questioning, robots would make what appeared to be meaningful eye contact with the scientist, seem thoughtful in a mode not programmed by their creator and reply in soft expressive terms. The scientists of the AGM now understood that conundrum. There were reassurances that their amah could be reactivated if necessary but all knew that was not going to happen. It had been reasoned that Jesus II, now an adolescent, was too occupied with his studies and would not miss his simulated mother. But staff reviewing slow-motion tapes noted an occasional disconsolate glance from the youth toward his amah and that was usually followed by a short period of thoughtfulness—he loved her and he always would.

## THE LEGEND OF SUSEJ

By the time he had reached the earth-age of fifteen, Jesus II was proficient in Greek and Hebrew as well as being functional in all the romance languages. He could recite the Bible in full and fully understood the tenets of all the world's major religions. He could read at an amazing speed and would read three books in an evening or twelve books in a day by earth time-dimension. He did not, however, show any interest or aptitude in science or mathematics although functionally he would have scored significantly above the national average for his age in those subjects. But more importantly, he was intellectually curious, was exceptionally wise for his age and seemed to possess incredible insight into human behavior and the inner workings of the human mind. However, if there was anything that impressed the science staff, it was the boy—almost a man—himself, as there was something about him that defied description, an awesome quality that connected him to all with whom he came into contact. It could not be simply explained as charisma—it was deeper than that, for there was a glow from those gentle eyes that penetrated into the soul of all with whom he interacted, even casually, a visage that could even be observed through the twisted images projected to the staff by camera.

The impact of the demise of the Amah Simulate was felt with great apprehension among the staff in the computer room, for they had witnessed how the amah was inactivated, callously, many of them thought, and although she was only a robot, they felt despair for her and they knew very well that one day the end of their mission was coming as well, so thereupon, all resolved that they would cherish each day as if it were the last while accepting the finality of the project and their part in it. Jesus II was growing at a rate faster than had been anticipated and would certainly reach his full growth potential before four years were up. He had grown to five feet six inches and weighed one hundred and forty pounds. He was in excellent physical condition and had good muscular definition. He possessed high cheek bones, beautiful olive skin, had a flawless handsome face except for a slight hook in his nose and he allowed his hair to grow long—his personal preference. Unpretentious to the end, he dressed causally in tee shirt and when chilled he would don a poncho—he liked the simplicity. Of course, the dominating feature of his appearance was the projection of his personality and how he touched people, even people he could not see, and in that personality there was a palpable that transcended all interaction, all antagonism and all ideological discord.

As the day the young Jesus II would be released from the AGM approached, the scientists became increasingly ambivalent in their feelings toward their young progeny and the program that had brought him to be. For they were elated for him in his achievement of completing AGM but at the same time they condemned the theological hierarchy that would now take him away for them, and that hierarchy, to the very last day, to the chagrin of the scientists, would dictate that very thing—his last day. For it was their instruction that he would be "resurrected" on Easter Sunday as if that had been ordained by God, and as monumental celebrations would take place on that day all over the world, and medics had agreed that the youth was in such excellent health that a day or two either way would hardly be concern and thereupon they fell into the collusion of that unknown cabal in the shadows behind the scenes.

But surely that last day came. The scientists could no longer argue that it would be premature to release Jesus II for he was an impressive specimen and it seemed, the whole world was ecstatic in anticipation of His return and thus, the growing global pressure was overpowering and could not be resisted. On his final day, the youth was taken from the growth capsule and placed in a decompression chamber in the earth-time dimension where he would remain for a minimum of twenty-four hours depending on placid results of the monitoring of his adjustment and overall condition. The scientists all were able to recall, with the same basic observations, the shutting down of the dervishes in which they related they had never been aware that they were audible; yet, as the low moan of the devices diminished as they wound down, the scientists became cognizant of the sound, which then died as the great machine came to a stop and all was silent.

As Jesus II was completing his last twenty-four hours at AGM, an assemblage of twelve men had gathered outside the AGM complex. They were the entourage of Jesus II and would never leave his side for the next year or however long it took for the youth to make a complete adjustment in moving from the AGM to the earth's time-dimension. This entourage, as they were called, would be his protection, first responders in case of medical complications and his evaluators. Personnel from AGM described them as cold, unsmiling and impersonal, and even their subsequent interaction with Jesus II was indifferent. They all wore three-piece suits and subdued ties. One scientist said that they caused him to recall the early days of the government's inquisition and surveillance of all suspected terrorists during the Middle East wars when agents would scan crowds with narrowed eyes and contemptuous accusation. No one seemed to know who these brazen men were but it was correctly assumed that they had been hand-picked by the evangelicals.

## THE LEGEND OF SUSEJ

At the end of the designated twenty-four-hour period in the decompression chamber, the pressure was disconnected upon the recommendation of staff doctors and Jesus II emerged from the chamber disheveled but in good spirits. After an interim in which he composed himself, he presented himself to the clinic inside the AGM medical facility where he would be given one last physical and once that process was completed, he stood poised at the entrance of the spacious computer room where he had been monitored for the first three and a half years of his life and there before him, standing in awed silence, were the two shifts of scientists—thirty-six in all—who had worked with him so diligently and to whom he felt a deep sense of gratitude. He moved forward and they, in return, stood motionless, experienced social animals who suddenly were incapable of the most basic courtesies. They were all stunned by how small he appeared and yet there was an aura of power about him. Nurse Ruth O'Connor recalled later that at that moment he looked so handsome and she wanted to hug him. But Jesus II was not a hugger; instead, it became his trademark to grasp a person's right hand in a handshake while pressing his fingers to that person's upper right arm so that he could hold him at a distance by which he could look into his face as if to look into his eyes to see his very soul. Thus, he went around the room to each and every man and woman, taking his time to the chagrin of his entourage, treating each individual as if he or she was special, and much of the conversation was surprisingly trivial but revealed that he had an amazing knowledge of culture and human nature and the time he gave the staff was something he needed as well for, although he had never met them, he knew them, he knew them and felt their presence and like his precious amah, they were essential to his well-being. Even the unflappable Dr. Verill was smitten by the youth and when his turn came to both greet him and bid him farewell, the doctor who had been used to terrorizing students in his classes with devastating wit and invective, suddenly could not stammer through a simple sentence and blushed so openly in front of colleagues he would not forget this most embarrassing time of his life. But Jesus II, always aware of the language of the mind, read the doctor's discomfort and assuaged his strain with, "I want to thank you for your work, you have been very important for me—I shall never forget you."

Then it was suddenly over and he bid goodbye to his scientific friends and turned to join his entourage. He paused at the flood of light shining in through the door, seemed hesitant and then proceeded out into a world waiting for him. The door slammed shut and in the darkened AGM hallway there was an anguished silence and the scientists stood in wonder at what had just occurred and even the doubters had to reconsider their skepticism.

# Fifteen

If the first three and a half years of our precious Savior's new life on earth was pleasant, the year that followed was ugly and contentious. From his first day upon leaving the AGM, he felt uncomfortable with those of his entourage as, despite his remarkable social skills, he found that he was unable to dent their tough exteriors and develop any rapport with them, a very frustrating turn of events for a young man who had engaged in social interaction so easily—addressing all, whether doltish or luminous, as equals—during his formative years. So to circumvent these uncomfortable encounters, he immersed himself in his studies and episodes of meditation.

The second problem facing our young man was a developing and increasingly worrisome health matter. While in the AGM, he had been sheltered from illness by the sterile environment of the growth chamber and to prepare him for life of the outside after his release, he received artificially induced antibodies to build his immune system to counteract the effects of foreign substances or organisms he would encounter in the general population; nevertheless, the fact that he had been shielded from the prevailing illnesses of society left him vulnerable to many infirmities as many of the antibody matches administered at AGM did not coordinate with what was rampant in society. It was noted that shortly after leaving AGM, he experienced sore throat, occasional chills and muscular weakness. As the AGM medical staff continued to monitor him, they were able to prescribe injections of synthetic DNA to boost the effectiveness of the innate immune system and to be administered by a nurse traveling with the entourage. He also complained of chronic tiredness, a new experience for him, and it seemed that each ailment tailed off into a new ailment but, fortunately, he was never hospitalized or even spent a day in bed. AGM doctors were unworried, stating that these health problems were expected and were quite normal as the youth was making an abrupt adjustment to a new environment; he was quite naturally developing and strengthening his immune system. As it turned out, after much concern, they were correct.

Being of active mind, Jesus II spent the dreary hours of recuperation reading extensively. He had reluctantly accepted the concept that it was necessary for him to be in a transitional phase for a year after the AGM program was completed and although he found his entourage boorish, he treated them with kind warmth and interest as was his nature with all humans, but it frustrated his senses to explore the nuances of these people but then see little good in their being. He tried with the patience of a saint to invoke communication and unlock the mysteries of their purpose and existence but he was unsuccessful and that brought him near to despair. But his greatest shock was yet to come and then one day, he requested a copy of *Why I Am Not a Christian*, by Bertrand Russell, and his request was not only denied but the resulting incident report met the judgment of the Evangelical Society of America where it became a concern of almost scandalous proportions and caused not just a few of the evangelical dissidents of the program to suggest that perhaps the young lord needed a comeuppance. However, when questioned regarding his request, young Jesus II unapologetically explained that as a student of religions it was his intention to study all religions and all argument regarding both pro and con sides of the issue and to study them in depth and that, he felt, would be expected of anyone expecting to fulfill a leadership role in the spiritual world. The argument worked and he received his book, but the damage had been done and he felt great remorse that he had been mistrusted and his integrity questioned by clandestine emissaries who always seem to hang back in the shadows silently prying and spying upon imagined incursions upon ecclesiastical doctrine.

Upon leaving the AGM, the entourage spent their first night in a motel in Colorado Springs. Jesus II, inexplicably exhausted that first night, had an undisturbed sleep and felt refreshed in the morning when the group enplaned at the local airport in a private jet for his new home in Memphis, Tennessee. He sat forward on a window anticipating the wonderful spectrum of flight and he recalled the many times that a writer or even he had used flight as a metaphor and now he would understand more fully the analogy. He sat by himself and then an entourage affiliate, James Martin, maneuvered himself into the row, lurching and clawing his way to the seat next to Jesus II where he dumped himself abruptly without comment. Jesus II did not respond, expecting another muted individual who, at best, would respond to any inquiry or attempt at conversation with single-syllable gutturalism. But unlike the others of the entourage, Martin was different as his behavior had been modified by the fact that he was older and more self-assured. All other members of the entourage were young, menacing in appearance, intense while on duty, very professional and personally distant. Martin, however, had been assigned to the group as an experienced security agent who would have steadying influence on the others. He was nearing fifty and although he had once been slim, aggressive and arrogant like them, experience and reality had compromised many of the imagined absolutes of his world and over the ensuing years he had developed an ability to understand the intangibles and make intelligent compromise. Not that he had turned his back on the authority that he represented—he did not—and he remained a staunch defender of flag, the presidency and the cross, but the weariness of duty had softened him and he was now at least open to random possibilities.

Martin was the first to speak and asked rhetorically, "How can a man as young as you know so much as to be considered a leader of a great nation?"

Jesus II replied, "It is not what I know but a time-honored method of discovery."

"Discovery?" Martin exploded. "If you are the one that you are supposed to be, then you would be complete, inundated with the Truth—there would be no need for discovery."

"That's the most serious pathology of our culture," Jesus II answered, leaning back satisfied that he had finally found one who could converse. "We have traditionally looked for leaders who could only repeat the tenets of the status quo and the prevailing ideology as if they were being led, not leading; but, if it were really that simple, we would never pursue change or seek wise men."

"But we have many wise men. Don't you think that we listen to them?"

"Many distressed men will change their religious faith but not their minds and they call that enlightenment. But they are not wise, only opportunists."

"So from whom does change come and how do we know them?"

Jesus II answered, "C.G. Jung once said, 'As any change must begin somewhere, it is the single individual who will undergo it and carry it through'—so it begins as a germinal thought in one flickering microsome of time, in the most vulnerable receptacle—the human mind—and then, through the mystery of probability, flourishes and its eventual value becomes relative to its acceptance."

"So what is this great method of enlightenment of which you speak?"

Jesus II answered, "It is as old as mankind. The Buddhists speak of losing the Self and to accomplish that they suffer self-denial through pain, hunger, thirst and fatigue. But I believe that is false and that one must not lose the self but give up the trappings of culture that prevents one from true enlightenment which is then accomplished through self-understanding, and once one is shed of the biases, moral platitudes, restrictive doctrine and judgments imposed by culture, one can seek true enlightenment. In fact, it is the flight from the pain of life that becomes an escape and leads us on a path in which we avoid the truth."

"But how do we choose which of the wise men who should lead us?"

"Have you ever watched a maple tree drop its leaves in the fall? As you watch you will see large numbers of leaves fall downward into the wind and then each will twist and turn on an angulating zigzag course to the ground; but, if you watch long enough, once in a great while you will witness one beautifully constructed leaf drop straight down for a short distance, catch the breeze and then as if purposely directed, fly a clean course at a slight angle and it will be so aerodynamically constructed that if will waft through the stiffest wind undeterred to a landing far from its mother tree. This analogy can be seen in all species and it is of those exceptional ones that we turn for leadership. But remember, there are those who seek a specific truth and then there are those who seek the truth."

"But how do you recognize a seeker of truth and not a specific truth?"

"Your own naturalist Henry David Thoreau wrote, 'It is easier to sail many miles through cold and storm and cannibals than it is to explore the private sea, the Atlantic and Pacific Ocean of one's being.'"

"But the clerics say we must follow religious doctrine."

"They can have the hymns, organized prayer and collection plates but I prefer the rectitude of the natural world. I am inspired by what I don't know and once awakened I will experience a thousand lifetimes of limitless incertitude and I will be drawn by the unknown that is beyond the understanding of practical reason and dogmatic escape and in anticipation, I feel the wild bird of anticipation flutter within my breast."

"The rectitude of the natural world?"

"Why do you think that poets use so much reference to nature. It's because it is the one thing in our lives that is constant and true—nature cannot exist in a vacuum of lies– it must always be true or it would not exist, and poets are seekers of truth."

"You repeat utterances from many sources. Can it be that you can recall everything that you have ever read?"

"Hardly, I only recall that which touches my soul."

Suddenly the jet engines generated a pre-takeoff roar, startling the young Jesus II. The plane then began to taxi slowly at first, paused, made a tight turn and then started down the runway. Filled with awe, the young man leaned forward in the anticipation of his first flight but the sense of power necessary to lift the metallic bird to flight was almost overwhelming to him, and that along with the roughness and jarring of the plane on the runway caused him to wonder if something were not terribly wrong and then, just as quickly, the craft bumped into the air and there was flight. Pressed to his window, he was awestruck by the experience and thrilled at his first glimpse of the planet from the air. Meanwhile, Martin sitting back in his seat stared blankly ahead. The plane climbed steeply, leveled off and then made a slow turn south and young Jesus II was able to admire the beauty of earth as the dowdy residuum of civilization quickly blended into the landscape. Like a child, he gloried in this beauty all the way to his new home in Memphis.

During the plane's final approach to Memphis, the airport was shut down by a huge throng of Christian zealots and curious onlookers who came to view their idol despite the fact that the flight had been secret, even to the military. Upon being advised by loudspeaker that the flight had been diverted, the crowd, estimated at half a million, stormed the field, became bellicose and rampaged through the terminal destroying anything in their way and rendering the airport inoperable for several weeks. Information on this tragic turn of events was withheld from young Jesus II, who undoubtedly would have been greatly traumatized that such demolishment would have resulted from his arrival at the airport.

Upon landing at a private corporate airfield, Jesus II was still ecstatic over his flight, something that he wanted to share with all who had traveled with him but all were long-time flyers and for them the thrill of flying was of the past and they dutifully tromped off the plane ignoring their exuberant young star. Two taxis took the entourage to the new home of Jesus II, the several-million-dollar mansion, The Holy Graceland, which had been donated to him in the name of the Southern Baptist Convention which had given him the estate, formerly the home of a twentieth-century rock-and-roll singer who shook, rattled and rolled his way to temporal fame, but by now long forgotten.

At the mansion Jesus II was shocked at the extravagance of the place as so simple was he in taste and so limited was he in pleasures, he did not understand the ostentation or elegance as it related to his needs and aspirations. As the entourage unloaded in front of the mansion, members of the group peered at him smugly looking for any indication that he was pleased if not overwhelmed by the beautiful place which became his just by his being who he was. But he remained expressionless as he surveyed the mansion, its grounds and the hotel—the Heartbreak Hotel, an obvious commercial ploy—just across the street. As he moved slowly toward the great mansion, he came face to face with one Bernard Bouregard, who was to be his host at the mansion, standing between two stone lions and two metal benches that bordered brick steps on the approach and who possessed an outgoing if overly flamboyant personality, greeting the new king with such aggrandizement as to embarrass one of such benign disposition. Bouregard was an average man in height and weight and even in an elegant three-piece suit he appeared to have the shape of a sack of potatoes and his face was fleshy and shapeless with a flapping triple chin as well. But he had a glib talent and seemed unperturbed by his protégé's lack of response to him.

The two proceeded past the four two-story stone pillars that bordered the entrance and then through a magnificent mahogany and stained-glass door with a Christian motif into the main hallway beyond which was a collection of rooms featuring a gold and plum color scheme throughout the mansion coupled with gaudy chandeliers that might have given an interior designer indigestion. Jesus II walked slowly through the mansion floors ignoring the incessant babble of the attentive Bouregard, who was trapped in a well-rehearsed history of the mansion. If the original designer had an overall plan of decoration it was long lost in the design of individual rooms that appeared to have no concept of fitting into the grand design of the place but apparently responded to a designer's ambition to treat each room with specificity. As he mused slowly through the establishment, Jesus II came upon a small performance theatre where, at one time, private concerts were presented to selective audiences. In revamping the theatre, the architect replaced a wooden floor with marble at incredible cost and on the stage sat a huge golden throne-like chair embodied with Christian symbolism. Apparently, the architect envisioned a young Jesus II sitting in that great chair pontificating the wisdom of his devotion to mesmerized followers of his faith, the throne giving authoritativeness to that sacred presentation. Exhibiting an uncharacteristic playfulness, Jesus II climbed onto the throne and sat spryly deep into the seat and pretended to mouth an address to his followers; and, in that overdone pietistic insigne he seemed a pathetic scrawny figure incapable of such magnificent bestowal.

Then Jesus II descended to the main floor and turning to Bouregard uttered to him in soft tones, "Why is it that you exhibit so much gold in the interior design of this place? I mean, like, furniture that might be beautiful in its natural state has been gold plated, there are statuettes of gold and I note that all picture frames are golden, there are golden drapes, every conceivable thing that could be gold, is."

He answered, "Gold is the great symbol of wealth, an indicator of the success of the Christian religion and, bringing gold to the feet of a great king has always been the purpose of a king's subordinates."

"But a man's symbol of triumph can also be his failing."

The smile gone from his face, Bouregard answered, "The success of which I speak is a result of our beliefs, if others do not accept our faith, that his their failing, not ours."

"On the other hand, gold as a symbol is shallow, as shallow as golden paint, for beneath that paint lies the truth and the truth sans gaudy symbolism can be ugly. What I have read about your society and the little that I have seen of it, tells me that beneath that ostentatious wealth, you cannot house the homeless, feed the hungry or provide medical attention for the sick and wouldn't those concerns be Christian concerns?"

With his corpulent chin fluttering noticeably, Bouregard stammered, "We have offered, implored earnestly and solemnly, pled openly, opened our hearts to all believers and yet, they have spurned us and hastened their own demise."

"In other words, gold has become the symbol of your failure to reconcile mankind to the goodness of Jesus himself. He rejected the money-handlers, the greed and the ostentation of accumulated wealth. He understood that for mankind to exist peacefully, there must be a balance that sustains all equally and fairly and the rich man was only a detriment to that cause. This mansion is unnecessary to me as one who eats and lives simply. It is a showcase—nothing more. You have failed to achieve the very thing you sought—spirituality."

"But," Bouregard argued, "we have done nothing more than follow the teachings of the Bible and we believe in the inerrancy of the scripture."

"I have read that your clerics have stated that 'We will subdue the earth to the greater glory of God,' and at the time you have crudely sought purification of your denomination and in doing that I believe that you have confused ecumenism with political power."

Stunned, Bouregard was speechless. It was never this difficult before, all he ever had to do, he always had thought, was feed back to the believers what they wanted to hear—and do it with feeling. Why, he wondered, was this person so different? He had never been exposed to a dissenter before. Clearly, Bouregard and Jesus II were of different worlds; Bouregard of the practical real world of contemporary society which ironically, exploited the inherent needs of mankind, and Jesus II, of an otherworld which sought the keen intellectualism of spiritual exploration compassionately seeking to redress those innate needs. Stung by what Bouregard felt was a rebuke, he immediately responded by aloofness and adjuration as, unable to make even fleeting eye contact with the young lord, he took on the appearance of a coltish fledgling who would pout his way to the safe haven of close-mindedness. But Jesus II would have none of that as he felt that every individual had the ability to discover in oneself that which he never knew existed and once moved from the shadows of one's own limitations, one could come to know a part of himself that he never realized existed. Thus Jesus II proceeded to charm Bouregard with honesty and intellect, even asking at times for his opinions on things, most assuredly trivial things, to which Bouregard would respond with giddy response while the two of them assiduously avoided anything that would bring contentious confrontation. Although Bouregard never saw where all this was headed, he also failed to recognize any slow progressive changes within himself.

Once settled in at the Holy Grace, Jesus II spent many hours, his throat wrapped in flannel and his person reeking of the pungent odors of liniment, roaming the huge place and its environs and, as always, he was amazed at its size and ostentatious adornment. He particularly liked the chapel in the woods but his favorite place was the meditation garden. There he spent many hours despite fever or chills, in deep thought but seemingly never in prayer for he was not given to praise another nor ask for the bestowal of privileged considerations. For there in the garden, he was truly alone and the solitude and serenity gave him freedom of thought and it was after such sessions that he would emerge in radiating grace.

Of the entourage, the medical doctor in charge of all medical decisions was one Dr. Clarence Sorenson, a displaced Oklahoman who had attained a high position in the Southern Baptist Convention unrelated to his profession. A tall straight man about fifty, he was attractive to women, spoke with a soft Oklahoman accent and had the smooth pervasive personality of an avowed con-man. He was rigidly orthodox and would argue endlessly on religious matters with coercive dialectic. His first medical alert with Jesus II came one morning when there were complaints from the young lord of acute pain in the kidneys. Dr. Sorenson sought relief for the patient in prayer which he performed with rather melodramatic fervor. Jesus II characteristically went along with Dr. Sorenson's celestial appeal to a medical problem, standing erect with his head bowed while the doctor in earnest prayer knelt before him. By midday the pain was more intense. A second prayer ensued. By the end of the day, Jesus II, in even more pain, suggested that he perhaps needed a second opinion. At that point, Dr Sorenson prescribed an antibiotic and within the hour the pain has subsided. An embarrassed Dr. Sorenson apologized and added that perhaps they needed a miracle and that was what he had prayed for, to which Jesus II responded that "miracles are usually a result of our lack of understanding of probability. When a situation appears hopeless but comes to a happy conclusion, we immediately think in terms of a miracle. But many medical problems are psychosomatic and as we don't understand that in the terms of causation or probability, the situation may not have been that serious and the solution, unknown to us, was relatively simple. But where we understand the pathology and have a practiced response to it, it is silly not to deal with the malady as we know it." Dr. Sorenson did not respond.

But of all the aberrant characters to grace Holy Graceland, Lester Scroggins was by far the most outrageous. As the prime mover in the evangelical effort to instigate a church-approved mandate to allow the special cloning project of Jesus II, Scroggins had used his extraordinary powers of ecumenical persuasion to urge his followers to impugn their own moral high ground on that subject for what he term "a higher good," and now that the effort had been successful and bore the fruit of a so-called "new Beginning," he believed that he was entitled the benefits of that jubilant happening. He was not beneath reminding those in decision-making positions that he had the backing of some twenty-five million Southern Baptists as well as the president of the United States and his expectation as a dividend for his contribution to that glorious event was to be as close to the young lord as possible at all times so as to make him—Scroggins—the second most important person in the universe and thus establish his legacy in history.

Toward that end, Scroggins took up a room at the holy mansion whereby he would have daily contact with "my protégé" as well as a dictatorial part in the planning and scheduling and accordingly, Scroggins kept up his grueling speaking engagements but included the youth in all of them, which gave him stature as Jesus II was never to speak or be spoken to during his period of earthly adjustment, and that gave the false impression that the young man was following Scroggins from site to site in order to hear him speak. On orders from the entourage, Jesus II was not to directly be in contact with anyone not of the entourage, was to grant no interviews nor were any comments or other sounds from him to be recorded. When he went to Scroggins' gatherings, he was one of a large group that would sit on-stage and there he would remain for the presentation, silent and expressionless. Despite his innocuous role in the affairs, when he came into view of the audience Jesus II was always greeted with a gasp from the audience and once he was seated, all eyes remained on him for the duration of the presentation. Quite unintentionally he had dressed in an appearance that caused him to stand out as he wore a long white vestment over his thin body having removed golden emblazons from the garment, and his hair, now between blond and red, hung in loose curls to his shoulders. Thus he was a very imposing sight and, inadvertently, distracted many of the listeners from Scoggins' intended message.

It was the belief of young Jesus II that he hated no man and disliked no one. But distrust and curious skepticism was something else. When he met Scroggins for the first time, he was confused as to why this man had a following as a religious man. In Scoggins he saw soulless eyes, a condemning personality and with an indomitable will, he appeared irritatingly ego-driven and harboring deep resentment and anger. He could not help but notice that Scroggins seemed to look at others without sight or feeling. It all appeared one giant act as nothing was real and no one, either Scroggins or those with whom he associated, responded with empathy or compassion. This would be a difficult time for young Jesus II. He felt obligated to comply to those who gave him so much support and the opportunity to further develop, but in Scoggins he found that he could not converse nor mutually explore imponderables of intellectual inquiry that all of mankind faced in those dark days when religious denominations seemed to be retreating into themselves in a world faced with incredible chaos. It was not his character to harangue the witless Scroggins and he was above attempting to destroy him in any way. So it was, in the remaining year of his earthly adjustment, that he again turned to his books and his meditation and thus deepened his spiritual and intellectual growth unimpeded by a distraught and irrational world.

Reverend Scroggins, inspired by his own performance with the young Jesus II in attendance, became overly ambitious in the deliverance of sermons and, accordingly, increased his schedule to a withering pace, dragging his young protégé along on his sermon trail, thus exploiting the youth who drew, by his very presence, incredibly large crowds of the curious and faithful. During his tour, Reverend Scroggins' favorite sermon, which he pontificated at least twice a week, was a dissertation he titled "The Reality of Competitive Exclusion" in which he presented the hypothesis that although the world's population had reached an excess of nine billion, demographics indicated that the numbers of people available to be reached by religious missionaries and proselytizers were shrinking dramatically because of the high number of religions that had become competitive in the drive for new followers in an atmosphere of religious competitiveness. Because the evangelicals were the largest religious group in the world, believed in the inerrancy of the Bible and as they remained dogmatic and unyielding to blasphemy, they saw themselves as the true believers and the intractable benefactors of Christianity which gave the following a profound exclusivity among all religions of the world and, in a sense, made them not only the envy of the world but the target of all other religions. Thus, Scroggins contended, it was the duty of all evangelicals to act in a common mission for the recruitment and conversion of new members but, also, to purify the church within itself and expose all not intransigent in their belief.

Of course, Jesus II sat through all these presentations, stoic and expressionless with no outward indicators of the stress and inner turmoil he felt from this bombast and, as he felt most assuredly, his passivity during these sermons was seen by others that he agreed with the stated premise. Those who studied his face during these sermons could see no indication of dissent in the youth and probably made the safe assumption that he agreed unequivocally with the ideas expressed by Reverend Scroggins. But Jesus II felt a great appreciation for those who had helped him and provided material and emotional support in that year of his earthly adjustment and it was not within his ethical standards to disrespect or castigate those who had so graciously supported and nourished him. So he held his thoughts within and he meditated on those very issues and he studied the people and their shields and he retained those thoughts which he assimilated into an encompassing whole. He kept to himself the intellectual inconsistencies, the moral contradictions or the egocentric self-promotion involved in the movement. For now, he would hold his tongue. But he knew that his day was coming.

Although playing a passive and non-committal role as a member of what was turning out to be "Reverend Scroggins' entourage," Jesus II grew spiritually and intellectually through his prolific reading ability as well as his choices of reading material. This in conjunction with his chronic health problems and his study of those problems and their remedies brought him to reject that absolute concept of right and wrong or good and bad as he came to see all aspects of the world as a part of a harmonized interaction in which everything, no matter how diminutive or seemingly unimportant, played a dynamic part in the all-consuming balance necessary for telluric stability. The young lord learned through some brief interaction with staff members to keep his emerging views on the world and the environment to himself as a few terse comments by him had raised eyebrows and subsequent conversation revealed to him that the information had been passed on and it was information that those of biblical orthodoxy could not tolerate. So when he read Rachel Carson's *Silent Spring*, an environmental exposé from the 1960s and when casually asked about his interest in the book, he passed if off with his usual riposte that he wanted to understand all arguments on each issue. Nevertheless, he typed Carson's conclusion to her book, without identifying the source, and taped it to the inside of the door of his room in the mansion. It said so beautifully: "The 'control of nature' is a phrase conceived in arrogance, born of the Neanderthal age of biology and philosophy, when it was supposed that nature exists for the benefit of man. The concepts and practices of applied entomology for the most part date from that stone age of science. It is our alarming misfortune that so primitive a science has armed itself with the most modern and terrible weapons, and that turning them against the insects it has also turned them against the earth."

Jesus II was bothered by what he had read and he had to ask himself if the Bible used the reference "subduing the earth" as a metaphor, was it a common reference used by a primitive people frustrated by their desperate struggle for survival against a relentless and hostile environment or was the use of "subdue" a word of the era not used with the finality of annihilation as implied in the contemporary use of the word? But, he concluded, the modern usage without considering original intent is what matters here. So Jesus II could not comprehend that a people would deliberately destroy the very thing that sustains them, and that begged the question of the infallibility of the Bible itself. Did not such passages, Jesus II reasoned, expose the ignorance of the times. He knew at that point that the preservation of the earth and a call for all to cherish and respect that entity would be the cornerstone of his prophecy.

But as fate would have it and although he had placed the Carson quote in an obvious place as a reminder of man's assault upon the earth and did so quite innocently, he was surprised when the following day that none less than Reverend Scroggins confronted him with what he perceived as a blasphemous attack upon biblical prophecy and his misunderstanding of the relationship between man and the earth. Jesus II stared at the reverend with arched eyebrows in an inquisitive look of disdain but did not answer but most likely was thinking, *My room? My sanctuary? You invaded my privacy and judged my contemplations?* The two men stared at each other for a few seconds and departed without word. Jesus II knew at that moment that he could no longer take for granted any intellectual freedom outside of evangelical doctrine. He did not know just what action the evangelists could take against him but it would not be improbable considering their zealousness that they would be prepared to diminish his role in the evangelistic scheme of the political world. He regretted that as it threatened the freedom of thought necessary to meditate and understanding the spiritual unknown and that left him one of two choices: one, to diminish his capacity for spiritual understanding by acquiescing to dogma he did not agree with or, two, convince the entourage quite circuitously of his agreement to their tenets while in the quietus of his own mind to continue to pursue those lofty explorations of the meditative mind. Of course, he chose the latter, but not without critical introspection as he felt profoundly hypocritical and a traitor to the cause of intellectual curiosity but he saw it as a calculated necessity in order that he not jeopardize his mission to the people of the earth. And yet, that depressed him, for intellectual honesty had been the cornerstone of who he was. So although he remained basically quiet in his demeanor, he did release tidbits of false erudition and quite surprisingly, Reverend Scroggins appeared satisfied and, in his own mind, felt that he had accordingly changed the direction of human history.

Those last few months of the adjustment year were tenuous for young Jesus II, who felt the crush of a frenzied citizenry when he went out into public and, when closed to the mob, he could hear desperate pleas for miracles and healing and for mercy on the sick, homeless and hungry. The crowds became so unruly, even at scheduled religious events, that control and order were unenforceable and the young lord's presence at those affairs had to be judiciously curtailed. That was not with regret for Jesus II, for the whole matter of touring with Reverend Scoggins had become a jumble of confusion and misinterpretation. But physically, he was feeling better—the sore throats, chills, fever and ague seeming to disappear as his immune system strengthened and he yearned for his freedom from the restriction of the Holy Graceland mansion where he was a virtual prisoner in a compound surrounded by hundreds of National Guard troops. And then one day, Reverend Scroggins approached him and asked him to prepare a speech for his debut before an expectant and exuberant public at the Omni Christian Center in Atlanta on Easter Sunday and cautioned him that twenty-five million Southern Baptists would be listening. But Jesus II knew that the whole world would be listening.

## THE LEGEND OF SUSEJ

The entire world seemed determined to be at the Omni Christian Center for what amounted to the christening of the new Jesus. The city was in a hopeless traffic deadlock three days before Easter and everything in the city had come to a standstill as the population, multiplied several times, reveled in glorious anticipation for the coming out of the spiritual leader. But in addition, the poor, the infirmed, invalids being pushed in wheelchairs, the addicted, the homeless, and every type of malcontent or psychotic imaginable traveled, sometimes hundreds of miles, on foot to hear or view their new savior. The city, at the last minute, set up loudspeakers throughout the city so that the masses could hear the words of Jesus II and in that way defer the masses from inundating the Omni and, again in a last-minute rush to accommodate and control the vast numbers, organized the masses by sectioning off roads and passageways whereby Jesus II would travel so as to be physically seen by his worshipers and in that way satisfy their need to have at least some type of tactile contact with him. The event had drawn people of every aspect of religious fervor from the sanctimonious to the profoundly soulful deep believer, and the demeanor evident ranged from giddiness, boisterous reveling, stoic posturing, those deeply moved and the outlandish behavior of those loudly exhorting their followers or chastising nonbelievers. But over all there was a great feeling of joy as those great masses took on a celebratory ambiance. But in addition to the great numbers hungering for a rebirth of religious dedication in the country, there were those who came not as devotees to ecclesiastical reformation but as mere observers, some skeptical, others open to unexplored truth, but all hopeful that there could be a new enlightenment; and then there were the groups of blatant nonbelievers, Satanists and devil worshipers who wished to cause disruption or the serious agnostics or atheists seeking to exhort their own beliefs.

Easter Sunday morning dawned sunny and brilliant and the crowds, held waiting in anticipation for several days, gained a new energy as the time of the appearance grew short. The appearance of Jesus II was scheduled for two in the afternoon, but the tour of the city before the great crowds would begin at ten in the morning, representing a laborious four-hour ride for a youth who had no great love for crowds of people and who was so self-contained that he had no desire to try to impress or inspire others. The truth of the world, he felt, was within the capacity of all of us as individuals, but to impose a permanent truth on the many had never prevailed nor would it ever prevail. The young savior's entourage, led by several ominous-appearing military vehicles manned by solemn-looking Chinese troops, proceeded narrowly in the center of the streets of the parade route, the crowds pressing inward to almost touching the vehicles despite hastily put up restraining ropes. In the bright weather, Jesus II could be seen sitting in the rear of a last-minute commandeered convertible, sitting next to a waving and ecstatic Lester Scroggins. Jesus II sat motionless except for an occasional wave—he had been asked to wave continually—to an unknown individual with whom he had unintentionally made eye contact. By contrast, Scroggins was in constant motion and never seemed to tire of the attention. As the vehicles would turn down each street, the crowds, previously excited and noisily anticipating the savior's arrival, would fall silent with awe as he passed and then he would only occasionally hear praise of him, an oath, a proclamation of faith or, very rarely, an insult. The whole thing was quite ridiculous, he thought.

Despite the fact that he had never spoke publicly, Jesus II was unusually composed prior to his inaugural before the world and after suffering a dizzying foray through the frenzied streets of Atlanta. Turning down Martin Luther King Boulevard, the entourage began the final leg of the parade and here, the crowd was more spontaneous, organized and presented a histrionic response that resembled the ovation that a returning football team might experience after winning a world championship while the malleable Reverend Scroggins was so swayed that he rose to his feet and welcomed the adulation with open arms. Jesus II remained passive but resolute. His time had come.

The early-arriving crowd at the Omni Christian Center sat passionately as if joyful that the affair was late so that they might sit even longer before a spiritual realm never before witnessed by mankind, as it was to each one, one's own moment in history, so they sat there, not in anticipation but in dedication to a new higher authority, in ecstatic rumination. The crowd, estimated at one hundred thousand, consisted of the crème de la crème of Christian Evangelism, all plumed out in their refinery, the most elegant clothing, with the women in their pompous Easter hats, glimmering gold and jewelry and with various ornaments of Christian symbolism; but they were not entirely the only advocates in attendance, for among them were the religiously disenfranchised, the dispossessed and recusant believers seeking a new understanding.

In the interim before the start, the crowd projected a controlled murmur, not loud or chafing, the product of the masses' whispered conversations spurred by the anticipation of the moment. Then quite suddenly figures emerged from the curtains on the right side of the stage, walking in a group to the table, chairs and microphone at the center, and among that group Jesus II was easily identified, a slight figure in flowing white robes, long golden hair bordering a pale handsome face, his personal inhaler hanging loosely from his neck. Needless to say, all eyes were on him and he appeared almost nonchalant to the mass of worshipers. After the appropriate prayers and hymnals, Lester Scroggins was the first to rise to speak. And speak he did and whatever his intentions were in that rambling speech it was lost as the congregation seemed mesmerized by the very presence of Jesus II, who sat quietly with folded hands while listening intently to the feverish words of Reverend Scroggins. Then, almost before anyone expected, despite the longevity of the Scroggins speech, Jesus II was introduced. Women and men gasped as he stood to approach the microphone, women fainted and young girls squealed. He appeared before the microphone and his first utterance, regarding a housekeeping matter, revealed a beautiful masculine voice but high in tone and a voice carried effortlessly, contrary to his own seemingly frail appearance. He proceeded to quickly discuss other minor issues and each smiling comment by him was received with spontaneous laughter.

Then came the time of great hope and expectation and the masses in attendance leaned forward in anticipation of the first words of the new savior. Standing straight and staring fixedly over the heads of those inspired faces in the front rows, he began: "I come here today in great anguish, for over the past year I have traveled this land and I am greatly dismayed by what I have witnessed and by scientific reports regarding the environmental health of the land and I address you specifically on this issue because you represent the politico-religious base that has set and implemented social policy for the last thirty years and therefore, I must ask you directly, what the fuck have you done to our beautiful planet?"

When those words were uttered, seven women in the first row simultaneously pitched forward in dead faint onto the floor in front of their pews with such perfect timing that one might suspect that they were all responding on cue. Throughout the now anguished congregation the most common response was eyes widened and mouth agape as if one had witnessed a horrible accident but also among the responses were the hands cupped over the ears, head buried in hands, index fingers penetrating the ears, eyes narrowing to a thin slit with mouth pursed tightly, violent shaking of the head and the always popular tightly shutting of the eyes as if to say that "this is not happening." Of course, there was a surprisingly large number, dispersed throughout the center, who did not respond at all, probably because they were not paying attention or simply did not understand what was being said. One visiting Englishman in the first row turned to his older brother, held a cupped hand to his ear and asked, "Wad de say, Reggie?" Reggie responded, "I cannot repeat it." Reverend Ezekiel Nostrom, in attendance and sitting stiffly erect as if in judgment on the young lord, suddenly became even more erect, his face a mask of piety as he judiciously surveyed those around him. The scene had turned into one of anxious ambivalence but everyone remained in their seats.

Then Jesus II began to speak again, "I speak to you thusly because you are the powerful of this country, you are the movers and what you have accomplished or failed to accomplish falls directly on your shoulders. You have, for example, forced the enactment of federal law banning the defilement of Christianity in any manner and in doing so you have expanded the expression 'defilement' to include non-acceptance of your faith by others who did not agree with you and it appears to me to be an incredible abuse of power that there can be people imprisoned because of their religious beliefs or their lack of religious beliefs. Why this is an issue to me is that if you can exert such power and influence to enact such mischief then you certainly have the power to accomplish great goals and preserve the earth and thus mankind. How can you put narrow self-interests before the welfare of mother earth? There currently are one hundred species disappearing from the earth every day and they can never be replaced. The seas rise every year and are inundating the land and the salt water invasion is destroying cropland. Large populations of former coast-line dwellers are moving inland to already overcrowded lands. Storms have become increasingly disruptive and in the resulting food shortages, we are able to feed only our wealthy. Health care in this country is non-existent and the masses of impoverished, homeless and sick are simply written off as being unworthy. And I am sure that you can rationalize this as God's will or that God will provide. But that is an incredible assumption that God is guiding everything but what if he created the earth and set it in motion and thereafter took no active part but left it to man to take care of the planet. Then we have failed Him miserably. And, like the priest and the Levite in the biblical story, you choose to ignore such abomination."

Denominational members looked to their church leaders and when they saw a nod and a head motion toward the exits, they dutifully arose and moved down the aisles en mass for the doors. As large contingents began to move, the noise level in the great center began to rise until even the penetrating voice of Jesus II was difficult to hear as church members began to speak frivolously of unimportant things as intended defiance to what they did not want to hear and cries of "Satan" and "The Devil," could be heard repeatedly.

"Let me give an example" Jesus II continued, "of our blatant disregard for the environment and its pending disaster. I am sure that you all are aware of the collapse of the so-called farm belt that stretches from South Dakota to Texas and which has been dependent upon the Ogallala Aquifer which at one time had enough water to cover the entire United States with one and a half feet of water and irrigated one-third of the nation's crops. Thirty years ago we were warned it was being overused and that as a result of overpopulation and exploitation, it was the fastest-disappearing aquifer in the world. And now it is gone. There was no planning, no control, no restraint on human activity and now it is gone and millions of rural and urban people are without livelihood.

And, not only are you unmoved by this great tragedy, but many of you seem to have been unaware that such disaster was pending—how could you be so ignorant? Is this what your religious doctrine begot? Has your rejection of science that you thought threatened biblical literacy closed you mind to the reality of possibility? And now you desperately seek a way out of a calumnious situation, not examining the facts of the matter, but by the inaction of rejecting the very dilemma that you face by ascending to a peripheral level of thought unrelated to the true world."

By now the masses of worshipers had thinned, disseminating to the exits in steamy lines leaving row after row of pews unoccupied. Yet, there were individuals and pockets of individuals who not only stayed but applauded the thoughts being expressed. Outside, in the parking lot, a gritty unkempt forty-something man had returned to his automobile, a rusty white-colored twenty-year-old sedan with Tennessee license plate and covered with biblical references and with the epitaph "Kill Lucifer" draw in crude letters by paint brush on the hood. The man, in an extreme state of fury, began shouting unintelligible utterances and then opened his vehicle, produced a Winchester rifle and announced that he was going to "kill the son of a bitch." He was subdued by several security personnel who later reported that the man resisted mightily and had "unnatural strength."

Jesus II continued: "I come to you not as one with a vision; I have no message from God; I have no sacred mission; I am not a prophet and I cannot heal or create miracles. I come to you only as one who has the same abilities and possibilities as you have and that is the ability to perceive, understand and apply ourselves to the task of saving our world and in doing so, save mankind. Your holy books speak of salvation and redemption and that is commendable, but you are accomplishing just the opposite with your obsession with religious orthodoxy. We must free ourselves from such imprisonment and each of us uninhibited by evangelical restriction go onto a spiritual quest. We cannot assume that all that is known is only what is acceptable and that which is new and previously unimaginable is somehow evil. I implore you to explore that which is above and beyond what is known while at the same time applying your humanity to the sorry conditions of the world. "

Reverend Scroggins by now in the center's private parking facility, was in a furious mood and suddenly reversed himself and stormed back into the center to confront his fledgling. Upon reentering the center, he was confused to hear sparse cheering in the arena which by now was near empty. The speech Jesus II had just concluded and with the look of one who might be asking himself "what now?" he stood talking to one of his few remaining admirers of the congregation when Scroggins cut in, "You really blew it. There is a time for candor but not with the masses. You have just lost your integrity, you've lost the backing of twenty-five million people and now, thanks to your stupidity, you are nothing—nothing—and you are through. You will never survive this and I doubt that you are who you claim. I see in you Satan and you will be destroyed."

Jesus II without anger or malice, quietly reflected for a moment and then said, "Lester, I am not of your world, I am a simple man, my joys are simple and I see no value in materialism. I have observed you manipulate and trick others, and not for a good reason but for yourself and whatever advantage you can garner. I cannot believe that you are a man of God and one of the things that I reject is that you use your God to serve you rather than you serving your God. I don't know where this will take me but I do know that I belong with the people that I love. I am sorry that I have caused you pain and stress and I hope for you in the future. Perhaps someday you will experience a real enlightenment and come to understand the spirituality of the natural world and then, perhaps, you will be at peace with your God."

These were meaningless words for Scroggins, whose entire definition of words within the English language were his definitions that fit into his own philosophical domain and that, by themselves, simplified his world and its complications. In one swift demarche, Jesus II had gone from saint to satanic sinner in Scroggins' eyes, and for Scroggins, it suddenly put the whole matter into logical perspective for it explained the incongruities between the two men and the constant departure of the young man from the tenets of the Evangelical Christian faith and comfortably put those dicta into the realm of Satan. And Scroggins thereby conceded that he had not been fooled but in the name of peace had accepted a brethren despite an inner voice that was warning him of an evil conspiracy. With that rationalization in mind, Scroggins calmed and now with a new sense of purpose and mission he left the center resolved to enlighten the world of this incredible deceit.

Suddenly Jesus II was alone on the stage but as he descended the short stairs to the main floor, scattered appreciators approached him and silently touched his cloak, smiled into his face or spoke gently to him. They knew. No matter why they had come individually, they had witnessed something resplendent and they knew that from this time on, they would follow this man. But as he walked from the arena, Jesus II realized that he had not only emancipated himself from an equivocal congregation but in doing so he had lost any means of support for himself and that now he would be left to his own resources. The very next day, the Southern Baptist Conference put a motion before the federal court to have Holy Graceland reclaimed by the church under a legal contract stating that the ownership of the mansion by Jesus II would be null and void upon the evaluation by church elders that the young savior was not complying to church doctrine, had made blasphemous statements or, was simply insane. Reverend Scroggins took the matter a step farther a week later when he went before the nation on federal television to advise of the great Satan that had been revealed among us. In a brilliant sleight of hand, Scroggins portrayed that he had been suspicious all along and did so with such exertion and, as it seems few listened to what he was saying anyway, he appeared entirely believable in his assertion. During the speech, he used the expressions Satan, satanic, evil, Lucifer, devil, diabolical and others of similar definition ninety-six times in a short speech. It was as if Scroggins was born again for he now had a new mission—the elimination of the evil one among God's people and the reaffirmation of the evangelical doctrine. In concluding his speech Scroggins said tersely, "He came to us as the Lamb of God but we recognized his evil game and we exposed him for what he is, the antichrist, and it is hereby ordered by the authority of God that he will hereafter be referred in name as Susej—the evil one."

One hot humid day in August of that year, on Interstate 95 in North Carolina, with the traffic congested on all four lanes in both directions and the heat shimmering furiously over the cement roadway, on the debris-littered roadside, a boy in tattered and besmeared white tunic trudged wearily north-bound, alone and unnoticed by vehicular travelers. He sweated profusely and his body was wracked with the wheezing and hacking from the extreme heat and ubiquitous pungency of burnt automobile fuel. His gait was agonizingly slow and labored but there was a binding determination about his effort. For a youth to be walking the freeway in these hard times was not an unusual sight, but on this particularly sultry day most pedestrian travelers would have been in seclusion in the shade waiting for a cooler time of day. But the youth trudged on. Then he came to a confusing intersection, a freeway veering off to the right with very limited traffic. He chose to leave his current path and follow the new road to the right knowing only for sure that it was northerly. But as he walked, traffic became increasingly light, most of it veering off on side roads until at last, he was walking the road totally alone. What he had inadvertently stumbled onto was an unfinished freeway that had been abandoned due to lack of funds. The youth did not discover his mistake until he had traveled some five miles where he came to a confusing uncompleted interchange with another freeway and which abruptly ended his progress. There was nothing left for him to do but turn back to the original Interstate 95.

Then in a corner composed of cement and steel girders, he spied something huddled on the ground. It was a dog and not a very impressive one at that. It was small, extremely thin, white in color with a black circle over its right eye and obviously stressed, its breed anyone's guess, dropped its head and shivered in fear despite the heat as the boy approached, but when he picked it up and held it to his chest, it whimpered and then snuggled. "I guess that you are now my responsibility," the boy mused. "I can't very well leave you here." The dog, probably abandoned or its master had expired, had made the same mistake the youth had in taking the new route under construction possibly in an effort to avoid the bump and clatter of the interstate, and once on that road to nowhere, continued ignoring side exits until it ended in the place where the construction had been halted those many years ago and so he found a hidden spot among the girders on the cement flooring and there he remained for several days without food or water. So the youth, packing the shy canine, returned the five laborious miles to the interstate and reconnected to his northern trek and after a short while he lowered the dog to the ground to see if he would follow, which he did, short skimpy legs in frenzied little steps. They both had made a commitment and now all they had was each other.

The two labored on into the night and sometime after dusk entered a small town nestled along the interstate. After asking directions the youth found a community house that provided food for homeless people in the industrial section of that berg but unfortunately, there was a closed sign on the door indicating that they did not feed after eight in the evening. The youth knocked despite the sign with the hope that house could afford some handout. A large elderly ham-fisted man with a bull neck and bald head answered the knock. He obviously was of serious demeanor, a rugged individual who had done it all and seen it all and with the appearance of one who had been toughened by a hard life, was prepared to send the youth away but as he stood there with the door ajar, he stared at the boy and his face softened slightly. Perhaps he had recalled himself in a similar position years before or just maybe he saw something in those soft gentle eyes that was unusual for these hard times. He bade the boy welcome and sat him at a long table which he was in the process of cleaning. "I think we can scrape something up for you," he said. Then the man spotted the dog next to the boy. A sign on the wall firmly stated, "no dogs allowed." But the man was not one to give in to rules or regulations he felt were unwarranted or unjust—he had always been driven by what was by his inner feelings.

So the boy and the dog were fed, the boy eating meagerly despite his impoverished condition while the dog lapped everything put before him in a saucer on his chair. Once the meal was finished, the man sat down with the two after providing the youth with a cup of green tea which he savored greatly. "I see that you enjoy the simple things," the old man said, referring to the tea.

"I find tea very relaxing and it gives one pause from the problems one faces and that gives a time to reflect and reorganize the mind," the boy answered.

"Where are you two headed?"

"New York City."

"New York City? Do you know that that place is flooded eighty percent of the time? That the subways are inundated, that there is limited electricity and that crime is out of hand—I mean, like there is no police protection? It's not a good place."

"I'm going to live with the Mole People."

"But why, what do they have to offer you?"

"From what I have learned they will accept anyone willing to work and they believe in freedom of the spirit and that is worth any risk that may be involved. Besides, they are dedicated to good works, the betterment of all and saving the planet."

"Let me ask you—what skill do you have to offer them?"

"You may laugh, but I honestly don't know, but I think I have people-skills if they can use that."

"I am sure you do." The old man smiled. "Look, we have a pantry out in the back and it has a cot in it—sometimes I stay there at night. I wanted you and your little buddy to stay there tonight and then in the morning I'll be the first here and I'll give you breakfast and you can be on your way before anyone else gets here."

The next morning the boy and his dog were on the road refreshed from a good night's sleep and two meals. The old man gave them a large kerchief on which all four corners were tied with a common knot and contained sausage, cheese and bread. "Look, I hope you don't mind, but most of the food we get is stale. Homeless people get used to that and I wish I could give you something better but this will hold you over," he said looking into the depth of those noble eyes. The boy graciously said goodbye and then the old man sighed as he watched the two walk toward the freeway that would eventually deliver them to New York and thought, *Perhaps there is hope for the world after all.*

# Sixteen

A new president of the United States was inaugurated in January 2033. His name is not relevant. He was an exact duplicate in appearance, manner and political manipulations as the previous president—and the one before that. His first official act was to honor the First Chinese Infantry Battalion which had just returned from the Long War in the Middle East where they had fought for ten years, distinguishing themselves for bravery and dedication to freedom. They were offered citizenship as compensation for their service but most declined.

American military forces had been removed from the Long War as their presence in the Middle East had created restlessness and hatred among Arab countries for the US and, as a privatized army, they were too expensive, and therefore were replaced with Chinese troops serving under the American flag as security forces. However, under CIA direction which used the new technology of the SpyInvader computer which was able to select those among the population who would, in the future, develop a predisposition for rejection of the status quo and be violent, the Chinese clandestinely sought out certain suspect individuals and secretly annihilated them. This unexplained and seemingly senseless slaughter infuriated the population which formed an insurgency of such dedication as had not been seen in many years. The wrath of this insurgency fell on the hapless Chinese soldiers, who although well-trained for conventional warfare, were totally inexperienced in combating the guerilla tactics of the Middle East. But they were valiant and the Chinese commanders, under the leadership of the Americans, cheerfully saw the situation as an opportunity for advanced combat training. It would have seemed a golden opportunity for a country for the use of a nuclear bomb—everyone it seems had nuclear capability—but since all governments in the Middle East were totalitarian, oppressive and facing popular opposition, the presence of Chinese troops instead gave those governments political legitimacy in the form of their threat.

The first legislative act that the new president was to sign into law was the Global Identification Act, which would extend the National Identification system to include everyone in the world, representing a sensational technological breakthrough which not only would put every living individual on a computer database but would also include personal information on each which would be gleaned by nanotech computer informants crawling over the globe like golem spiders. The information would in appearance seem harmless and non-consequential but would, in actuality, supply critical information as to one's religion, political leaning and what evangelicals referred to as one's "emotional stir-pot," that is, a previously undetected tendency to act against "the public interest."

The second legislation the new president would be signing into law was the Christian Purification Act, which in essence would outlaw all sects or religions not in compliance with Evangelical doctrine. The body of the law including a rider in reference to the individual known as Jesus II and ordering that he was to hereafter be referred to as Susej, the evil one, as he "had come to us as the Lamb of God but that was a deception in that his actions became traitorous and blasphemous" and it was subsequently ordered that a warrant for his apprehension and arrest be issued by the attorney general. However, even though the federal government had processed the evil one from his conception to his adulthood, they had failed to get a definitive photo of him, had failed to implant a microchip in him and for unknown reasons, SpyInvader was unable to identify or locate him. Thus, the youth became public enemy # 1, but as the streets of all cities were teeming with disenfranchised youth without resources, drifting the streets without hope or purpose, the number of vacuous arrests was astronomical. The whole affair took on a comical aspect when the attorney general's office in issuing an all-points bulletin could not put upon itself to describe the youth as physically resembling the popular concept of Jesus as that, by its very act, would be blasphemous.

The third legislation signed by the new president was the Assault Ministry Reform Act, which essentially said that all lawyers hired by federal agencies would have had to complete their law degree at Liberty University or, at the very least, have received certification of theological compliance from the university which stated that the attorney was qualified to preach the gospel and confront others on issues of moral default. The law became necessary, the legislators offered, after years in which Liberty graduates were placed in positions as aides, counselors, advisors, prosecutors and judgeships and had done such a marvelous job in those categories that when non-Liberty lawyers challenged them there was such upheaval that it was felt that only Liberty lawyers could be trusted to carry on the task of facilitating the government.

The fourth legislation signed into law by the president was the establishment of a federal television program featuring Reverend Lester Scroggins, who would appear daily for an inspirational message to the nation. All other programming would be curtailed during that fifteen-minute time period which was presented in the evening just before prime time. It was to become an exercise in redundancy as the good reverend had a lot of energy and tons of words, but no nascent ideas. Nevertheless, the purpose of the presentations seemed not to be their content but their emotionalism. Cynics referred to the enduring spectacles as the "daily rant."

The least of the new president's worries was the State of the Union address, which would be presented as those before; that is, ignoring the negatives of governance while making far-reaching and magnanimous promises for the future, a time-honored technique used by every modern president with the exception of a president who had five years previously varied from the common script admitting serious problems within the government and offering a radical concept of a new spiritual leader leading the country out of the abyss. Furthermore, this president was completely comfortable with things as they were, was not, as he reasoned, the government, the legislature and the Supreme Court more unified than any time in history? Had we not weeded out all the dissidents, malcontents, anarchists and radicals that did such disservice to the smooth function of government? And, had we not eliminated all the social programs designed to make individuals dependent upon government and in doing so forced them to rise up and be responsible for themselves and those who perished as a result were simply an unworthy drain on the economic system? An unchallenged assertion by the president was that rampant minds are a threat to the sanctity of Christianity and the stability of our culture; and, although at one time it would have raised the ire of any patriot, that offering was now repeated so often that it seemed to have won popular acceptance.

Despite the myriad problems facing the United States, the president seemed preoccupied with trivialities, not to mention demands made by foreign individuals of political power and prestige who used the disadvantageous position the American government had now found itself to promote their special projects. An Arab sheik demanded the right to purchase 5,000 acres of a national monument for a ranch; a Chinese businessman wanted to buy a major league baseball team so that he could fire the Japanese center fielder;

an Indian developer insisted that low-cost housing in Honolulu be demolished so that he could build high-rise condominiums which would bring economic prosperity to the area; a Turk, living in Phoenix, Arizona, wanted all species of Chiroptera destroyed by insecticide as he had a phobia for vampire bats; and a Japanese businessman requested that the name of San Francisco's China Town be officially changed to National City. The president responded by granting all requests after ostentatious debate projecting the appearance of a concern for national security and emphatically to only grant such requests upon receiving something of equal value in exchange which actually amounted to little or nothing at all.

The president, as was revealed in his State of the Union address, did not have a great concern for the wretched condition of the economy or its twin nemesis, the apocalyptic state of the environment. Economically, the national debt was approaching forty trillion dollars, the government regularly defaulted on payment to the debt, foreign governments who owned property in the United States as collateral now found the property valueless and, for the first time, the United States was on the verge of becoming a third world country. At the same time, the polar ice caps had melted almost out of existence, thousands of animal species were extinct or threatened, the nation was unable for the first time to grow enough food to feed its people and the country was beset with problematic weather on a daily basis, impeding even routine living patterns. The United States Weather Service reported that global warming had increased two degrees—past the point of no return—in this century but the president quashed the report and issued a directive to all media that inclement weather was to be reported as "normal patterns" and the rise in global temperature was not to be discussed. The president's disregard for these serious problems within the nation was singular—he believed in Armageddon and that the events unfolding before the world were the signs of that great upheaval on the planet.

The president's belief in Armageddon went back to his childhood, a childhood that had been so bleak and forbidding that it rendered him into an almost psychotic state of mind which he learned, over his adult years, to disguise behind a superficially charming demeanor, the public or even his close friends not being allowed to view the moments of his high anxiety, although, had they been alert they would have witnessed, during his private time, relentless fidgeting or constant scratching to burn up stressful energy. The president's mother had been incapable of nurturing and in the early perplexities of motherhood, she would wring her hands in frustration over her inability to control a son she felt was already out of control, and as she lacked any modicum of patience, she felt she would lose her mind. And then she accidentally discovered that the youth had an abject response to fear and quite simply she was able to control him in that manner. But she did not stop with simply controlling his behavior and she created fear stories which she embellished all out of proportion, and what she found that even amazed herself was that she enjoyed invoking fear into her son and she subsequently developed a hedonistic joy in twisting the blade, often proceeding to go far beyond what was necessary for simple control. The youth lived in sheer agony over the fear being projected into his life, but as his mother also abhorred his anguished and disconsolate personality, he accommodated her by transpiring to classical sociopathic charm. Of course, he had to deny his dark side in order to believe that he was everything good and it was therefore an amazing accomplishment that he never recognized his own evil-minded tendencies, even after shoving a firecracker up the rectum of a frog and blowing it to pieces.

In the second week of his administration, the president called for a meeting of his cabinet which included the newly approved position of Secretary of Religious Matters, a position to which the Reverend Lester Scroggins was appointed. The meeting was arranged as a sort of a free-floating opportunity for the members of the cabinet to explore their thinking and pick each other's minds on matters of public policy and political problems facing the administration. From the beginning the president appeared unusually candid and worried, exhibiting vulnerability that none of them had ever witnessed before. In his opening remarks, he expressed that "Over the previous two administrations we have had the most efficient and cooperative government in history and during that period of time we have accomplished much. But what is of concern to me is that despite the fact that we can legislate anything we want as we see the necessity, things are not going well in the country and there seems to be little that we can do about it. For example, our party has banned abortion, put the science of creation in all schools, outlawed homosexuality, created a strict moral code for all legally identified citizens and we have forbid the teaching of evolution, we have removed all obstacles and restrictions on economic growth; and yet, we are broke, badly in debt and foreign countries are making payment demands on us that we cannot meet. But we do have the ability to legislate any action that will redress the issues facing us."

The cabinet had never known such unsophisticated frankness during their tenure and were stunned into silence. Then he continued, "As you all know, we put a lot of faith and money into a young man who we incorrectly viewed as our spiritual leader for the future and that turned out to be a fraud by the devil and although he appeared to be the real entity—the savior of humanity—we must acknowledge his evil intent and understand that the uncontrolled mind is a direct threat to a stable government and his attack upon our government and all that we believe revealed his essence." The cabinet mumbled their agreement.

Then in the following silence, Reverend Scroggins spoke thusly: "We are on the verge of Armageddon. All the signs are there. This moment has been prophesied in the Bible and is now upon us and there is no retreat, no going back to another time and it is our God-given obligation that we respond to it as the Lord intended us to do. In the last two years we have had a mega-tsunami in Seattle, a gigantic earthquake in Los Angeles, a series of level-five hurricanes in the Gulf states, a drought in the Midwest and staggering ice storms in the Northeast, and all this long after our ability to come to the aid of the victims had all but dried up. I must say that anything less than a Christian response would be blasphemous and would put all humanity in jeopardy. We have been backed into a corner by the forces of Satan and we must respond to that challenge as true Christians.

"I need not remind you that Armageddon was a gathering place about twenty miles east of Haifa where the great battle between good and evil was to be waged. But it is more than that. It is not a place at all. It is an event and it will happen when all the kings of the earth meet to take collective action to persecute God's chosen few. And they will be led at this time by a fallen angel named Susej who has followed Lucifer. And those evil forces will be led by two leaders who will create miracles to deceive the people into a false system of religious beliefs and they will invade the Middle East under the pretense of bringing peace.

"In that treacherous time before the great battle, the seven lost plagues—the vials of wrath—a series of catastrophic events will occur and each will be announced by the sounding of trumpets warning of the danger they impose with the final trumpet blast gloriously announcing the return of Jesus Christ to establish his rule. The first five vials of wrath we have seen—the grievous sores upon men, the seas red with blood, the rivers and fountains red with blood, the scorched earth, darkness and unbearable pain. And then the sixth vial, in which voices of spiritual destruction are released on the people by a false prophet—Susej—who claims to be an end-of-time prophet.

"And at that time will come the seven trumpets and voices from heaven will say, 'The kingdom of the world are become the kingdom of our Lord and of his Christ and shall reign for ever and ever.'

"And those opposing kings will see Christ coming out of the clouds to beckon us and they will call him the antichrist but he will call on us as his chosen and the battle will come and he will establish his kingdom here on earth and we will follow him. As Daniel said, 'And in the days of those kings, the God of heaven will set a kingdom that will never be brought to ruin. And the kingdom itself will not be passed on to any other people. It will crush and put to end all these kingdoms, and it will stand to time infinite.'

"Gentlemen, I must announce that during the past week, I have repeatedly had a vision and that vision calls on me to be the seventh trumpet and I will announce the return of our Jesus Christ to earth."

A stunned cabinet and president sat blankly. Had this been ordained from the beginning? Why was there no alternative to the current crises? They had conceded so much and so easily along the way. They never spoke out but that would have been blasphemy and they knew that careers could be ruined.

Alexander Wainright, the secretary of the treasury, downcast and disheartened, sat silently and thought back some twenty years before when, with great trepidation, he had cast an aye vote as a member of the House of Representatives for a bill in which it would become law that anyone seeking public office must believe in a supreme being and later that bill was modified to definite supreme being to be that of the Christian definition. *How did it get this far?* he asked himself. At the time the time of the vote, Wainright, a Christian, worried that the bill was a violation of our basic freedoms but he reasoned that in the face of the intimidation and threats to the dissenters that if the advocates were placated this one time they would be satisfied. But not so, for in a rapid succession of legislation, the banning of a homosexual lifestyle, outlawing abortion, the removal of anti-Christian books from schools and libraries, the ban on teaching evolution in schools and other such measures, all options were removed from the government and there would be no retreat from the current course. Wainright wondered why he had not spoken out but the answer was all too painfully evident.

Then the secretary of the interior, a pasty blonde with a shapeless face, blurted out, "We should catch that antichrist son of a bitch Susej and nail him to a cross as retribution." There was mumbled consensus of agreement from the cabinet.

Scroggins continued, "In my vision Jesus will beckon to us from the clouds and we will join him to do battle against the antichrist, but you may ask how will we accomplish that? In my vision God has called on us not to be passive but to initiate an approachment with the Lord and in doing so to demonstrate the resolve and determination necessary to not only reconnoiter with him but to defeat the forces of evil. Toward that we must look to the resources that have blessed our being, given us by the great God Almighty, a fact that we can now recognize for its purpose. Specifically, I call on the chosen to mount the various space vehicles that have been placed in their disposal and we will reach space and enter orbit and then in a glorious flash of hallowed light we will reunite with the Savior preparatory to our indomitable army's triumphant return to the throne of the world and conquer the antichrist. Jesus will thereupon establish a kingdom that will rule all of the earth for ever and ever. We have the money, power and the resources to do this and anything less would be inefficacious and cowardly."

The blood in Wainright's face seemed to drain away and within, he felt incredibly cold and empty. *This is what it has come down to? We have so alienated ourselves from the rest of the world that we must commit mass suicide?* he asked himself. But to stand up now would be counterproductive. How could he now claim that there were contradictions in the Bible, that much of it was metaphoric, that we could not risk all-out war on a narrow interpretation of the Bible or that the Bible had been written by men of many contrasting beliefs and, the obvious question, why then had he not spoken out before? Even if he did raise a protest, Scroggins would use it against him and return to the you-are-with-us-or-against-us rhetoric of the past thirty years and then would surreptitiously claim Wainright to be a follower of Satan. And the rest of the cabinet did not share Wainright's concern, for quite spontaneously they rose to their feet and cheered Scroggins' proposal. Wainright then sadly reflected on an old poem that the great statesman Winston Churchill had memorized as a ten-year-old and which came to mind in the dark days before World War II when British foreign policy seemed to be adrift and now seemed appropriate:

Who is in charge of the clattering train?
The axles creak and the coplings strain;
And the pace is hot, and the points are near,
And sleep has deadened the driver's ear,
And the signals flash in the night in vain,
For death is in charge of the clattering train.

The president leaned back in his chair smiling broadly, for in that instant he felt a sense of relief, of peace, for the chaos and turmoil of the day were not relevant any longer. *Of course,* he thought, *this is the way it was meant to be. This is all part of God's grand design and all the problems that we have faced just do not matter.*

The president returned to the Oval Office a changed man, as if the weight of the world had been lifted from his shoulders and his attitude toward subordinates became mawkish and condescending. The decision had been made and now there was no turning back, for Scroggins in his presentation had hit the sensitivity that had made the president so vulnerable in the past and once the onus had been relieved the president responded as if he had experienced a great unburdening. It was not unlike a dispirited individual shrouded in the gloomy dungeon of melancholia who sees his only way out as doing away with himself and who then, with suicide as the final solution to the unsolvable, becomes enigmatic to others as he displays a consuming blithefulness.

The White House was immediately alerted to the new scheme, a plan that would call into play all the resources available to the president but which would not be available to the common man, whether of the chosen or not. Such discrepancy would have to be dealt with in a sagacious manner for the division in the country was precarious and the appearance of preferential treatment could be disastrous. But that was the problem always encountered in reality; those who had earned their status, wealth and prestige were inevitably in a position to benefit from any governmental project—it was a fact of life and those left out, nonbelievers most of them—would feel discriminated against. So under White House direction, the media would have to handle the matter delicately.

Of course the administration would have all the resources of the US space program available to it as it had been decades since the public had ever challenged government use of public funds. Furthermore, there was so much wealth in the religious community that there was no doubt that many of the followers could make orbit, particularly since many of them already owned a Leer Space Explorer, the small space plane which could reach orbit and had been quite popularly used on family outings during the previous decade. The government plan that was eventually drawn up would include one hundred and forty-four thousand of the chosen to be represented in the government contingent. Individuals would be welcomed to go as they wished through their own resources. The overall plan was one of expansive bureaucratic accomplishment and received few complaints from the legislative or judicial branch of government. One member of the House of Representatives, not on the approved list to orbit because he had once been critical of the ruling party, was allergic to the smoggy air of Washington, DC, and in preparing to present his case to be included in the trip, began coughing so badly that he was never able to speak.

Within two months' time the plan had been formulated and all was set to go. Military spacecraft and NASA experimental craft had been readied and modified for human occupancy. Ten sites were arranged for the takeoff of some thousand space vehicles, all to be launched on the same day. The day of launch would be unknown and would be determined by Reverend Scroggins, who would sound the seventh trumpet when he received a vision of Christ appearing in the clouds.

Public reaction to the tentative launching and the battle of Armageddon was of disbelief and ridicule. Nine thousand people were dying every day in New York City because they could not breathe or afford inhalers or respirators to implement their breathing, and yet few believed that there was any escape from pollution. Furthermore, there was great fear among scientists that the mass exodus would further deplete the oxygen on the planet and might even leave a dead planet. The president dismissed such concerns as scare tactics and stated that the mission to defeat the antichrist was far more important and worth the risk. Any anticipated insurgent response from the public was discounted almost immediately as a public used to an unresponsive government felt powerless to alter their fate.

# Seventeen

During the thirties of the twenty-first century, the wealthy of the Untied States became the elitists that they had strived to be in every sense of the word. A ternary ruling class composed of church, corporate business and military, they represented a government that was formulated to meet their own needs and upon achieving that through legislative action that ignored the principles of democracy, over the decades they developed a rhetoric that was an antithesis to their actual being as they unabashedly continued to speak in praise of the basic freedoms but acted out of self-interest. It was always a mystery to scholars of the day how the three separate governmental entities, seemingly so contrasted in philosophy and purpose, could amalgamate so well, but undoubtedly that was explained by the fact that they needed each other to fulfill their missions. But a look into the workings of the three components found that despite the differences one might expect in each, many of the important leaders were quite compatible as if all leadership was drawn from the same operations pool. In one example, a famous infantry training commander had the same flair for religious emotionalism as any evangelist preacher, often preaching in a resounding voice on some training battlefield while, at the same time, he was a major stockholder in a mega-corporation. His multi-faceted resume was impressive.

But what really upset the scholars of the time was that these self-styled elitists seemed to have no awareness of the chaos and disruptions that plagued the planet. In fact, the marks that they gave the current president and his administration over the previous decade were extremely high. Polls and questionnaires to these people revealed that they were either in total denial or were woefully out of contact with the realities of the day. They did not recognize the degradation of the environment as a concern despite the fact that cursory exposure to the media would have made a daily deteriorating condition evident to them. When given a list of problems facing the country, they ignored those not affecting them but were emphatic in pointing out those issues that might directly or indirectly affect the business climate they were personally involved in. In addition, throughout the elitist government there was an apathetic disassociation with the chaotic events of the day as there was a prevailing faith that God would take care of "us" without any consideration that it was the "us" that created the problem in the first place. One statement repeated all too often in Congress when approving a substantial increase of the national debt level was, very ironically, "We will not have to pay it off anyway because Armageddon is coming." Why individuals focused on the final battle against Satan were apathetic toward the issues of the day is perhaps something that only the religious can explain.

But it was not precisely evident that all non-governmental society was isolated from the government as there were various institutions and businesses dependent upon government cooperation that needed to conjoin with the money source and therefore complied to governmental positions. The Harvards, Yales and Standfords of the higher education system, like other foundations that were dependent upon federal funds, became prime adherents of the elitist government. Whereas these universities had previously served an array of constituents, they found that only the elitists could pay the exorbitant costs now necessary to produce top-quality scholarly advancement. These universities had become research universities but inevitably, like anything caught in the web of something larger and more powerful, that research became less and less faithful to the principles of conscientious inquiry but more fitted to expected results. As universities are fanatically hierarchical and structured education for undergraduates a long-forgotten dream, they tend to morph into the same inconsequential bureaucracy as the government that they have learned to emulate. But the importance of the prestigious universities remain for they are a sure upward step for any elitist youth so disposed and become an expedient recruiting ground for a government that wanted to maintain the philosophical consistency of its employees.

Apparently no one had ever warned the elite class to be careful what they wish for. For their wildest dreams of power and enrichment had been fulfilled as they had wealth far beyond what they had anticipated—but it still was never enough—and this all eventually came at an unmitigated price. For if the elite class was anything it was isolated. The separation between the classes had become so pronounced that the rich and the poor were easily identifiable in public and the lower-class hatred for the wealthy became so profound that the elites were unable to venture out on a public street for fear of assault. The elitists justified their position in society cynically and referred to poor people as "God's trash." Nevertheless, the cost of security in a bifurcated society was astronomical and then not necessarily reliable. Wealthy individuals would not dare venture on the street in anything less than an armored limousine and then they would often be victimized by roadside bombs. They essentially became prisoners in their own homes or estates and many of the wealthier resided on man-made islands or on security cruise ships. During the thirties, shopping malls for the wealthy sprang up throughout the nation, malls that guaranteed protection and were aesthetically designed for the tastes of the wealthy. In addition, there were sections of each city that were sealed off for the rich only, including the prime parks, beaches and other recreation areas. But those in jeopardy in such a disparate system were those who were only marginally wealthy and thereby could not afford the expenses of security or were not welcomed, because of lack of achievement or recognition, in the safe country club havens that protected the rich.

But if the wealthy or the near-wealthy felt threatened in their existence on earth, they always had one sanctuary and that was Lunar City, a rebuilt space station on the moon's surface, only two seconds away from the earth by radio waves. Lunar City was originally designed and built during the second decade of the century as a staging area for space flight to other planets. It made economic sense as the energy for a space vehicle to lift off from the moon is one-twentieth that needed to lift off the from earth, and a space vehicle fired from the moon does not burn up earth's precious oxygen. Furthermore, refueling rockets from the moon would also be cost-efficient. Unfortunately, after the space station had been in existence for less than five years, funding was cut and the station prepared to close and was put for sale, a surprising announcement. But many privately owned spaceships were venturing into earth's space at that time and it became apparent that private excursions to the moon would be an enterprise of the near future. Then an evangelical organization, "Bound for Rebourne," bought the station for a stepping stone into space and the planet Rebourne, the earth-like sphere where it was theorized that man could reestablish himself and his kingdom. The project lasted only a few years and then when space science failed to produce the highly sophisticated technology essential to space travel to the Andromeda system—although many suspected a change in theology was instrumental to the shelving of the project that caused the program to fold.

But in preparing for that mission, the evangelicals made some brilliant innovations for living on the moon which allowed their workers to reside quite comfortably in moon capsules without the necessity of encumbering space suits. The capsules were thick-shelled structures half buried in the moon surface and could easily shelter the inhabitants from the temperatures that would range from -250 degrees F to +259 degrees F in a single day. The process of living on the moon made necessary daily flights from earth as the station was completely dependent upon supplies and, as the station grew, living structures became larger and more comfortable. In one amazing innovation, large silos were constructed to capture the moon's extreme heat and then sealed as the temperature dropped so that individuals could drain off the retained heat to warm their capsules. Smaller silos were filled with oxygen from generators from which supply lines led to individual capsules. But when the project was to be abandoned, there were surprisingly many who opted to remain, a similar phenomena occurring at the experimental space island Alpha a few years before. Those remaining cited the quiet and uncomplicated lifestyle of the moon as the main attraction for them to continue to reside at the station.

Seeing the possibilities of a financial bonanza, several gambling corporations from Las Vegas purchased the moon station for the establishment of the Lunar City Project in which it was planned to build a city for ten thousand people and with a mega-casino that would attract the wealthy who sought to escape the confines of an earth crowded elbow to elbow with the shimmering hordes that threatened the tranquility of the elite's leisure time and solitary lifestyles. The casino, named Diana after the moon goddess, mostly underground in order to avoid the constant pelting of cosmic rays and micrometereorites, became a small city in itself and was connected to lunar hotels and individual capsules by extravagant tunneling. The project was an instant success; an advertised guided "walk on the moon" became an important draw appealing to the American spirit of achievement to a promotion that emphasized "our culture of exploration." The dangers of such activity presented a challenge to the adventurous who would venture out in a guided tour to walk among the craters and twisted ridges in their state-of-the-art NASA spacesuits that gave them protection against the violence of space, the solar radiation and ultraviolet light, charged particles from the "solar wind" and the astroplemic "star scars" and it was to become such a prestigious accomplishment for the few and as a cherished mark of honor, some even including it in their resumes. The Mole People were quick to pick up on the phenomena and dubbed the elitists as "the Moon Walkers."

## THE LEGEND OF SUSEJ

Diana was everything a city would be and included a church, the First Baptist Church of Lunar City, the minister being R. C. Simpson, the emphatic helmsman who led the evangelistic campaign denouncing scientific claims of global warming by emphasizing that the symptoms of the warming were in reality the first signs of Armageddon and by denouncing science itself as inaccurate and contradictory. Simpson did not have the charisma of a Lester Scroggins and therefore did not become a daily television feature, but he was rewarded for his work against global warming that had worked so prominently to the benefit of a beleaguered federal government by being named pastorate of the Lunar City Congregation. Simpson fit quite comfortably within the lifestyle that was Diana in that his own previously denied addiction to gambling went unnoticed.

He had been head of his church less than a year when one outrageous night he heard a great swelling cheer in the casino main room and, while waiting for a call on a roulette wheel, inquired as to what event had caused such a momentous response, was advised that the space station had just been notified that the federal government had recognized that Armageddon was imminent and, upon the return to earth of Jesus, the greatest battle would commence. It became a time for great celebration on the space station.

Simpson, a small wizened man of sixty-three, immediately pushed away from the roulette table and proceeded to the Diana Cocktail Lounge to celebrate the impending great battle, and as he imbibed of red wine he basked in the glow of that great coming event, congratulating slaps to his back shook his body. It had happened just the way the Bible said it would—the new world order, a planet in upheaval and now, Armageddon. He sat there surrounded by acquaintances he did not really know but who knew of him and shared his joy of the moment. He watched their warrior posturing and their battle cries and the old tired clichés that followed man into battle over the ages. He observed, when they removed their outer garments when the excitement and heat of the occasion brought them to be overheated, that they lacked muscular development, were thin and emaciated with distended stomachs, not individuals one would want to share a combat experience. But they were enthusiastic and, as members of the ruling class, their enthusiasm would carry forth into the battle. Then slowly Simpson felt the euphoria of the occasion slip away and after about twelve wines, he drifted into a enveloping numbness and he thereupon very politely excused himself from the noisy rabble, explaining that it had been a long day and he needed his rest. This seemed to be happening more and more during his drinking binges, his descent to a level of numbness and then inevitably, depression.

He made his way to his private capsule, a small twenty-by-forty single room which was all an unattached man would need and he proceeded to the room's only window at the far end of the hovel. The window was inches thick to keep out the heat and radiation but was designed to allow accurate imagery and he sighed as he saw the same trying white-hot glow of the unchanging lunar days of uninspiring vacancy. Somewhere out there about one hundred and fifty miles away on the floor of Mare Imbrium—the Sea of Crises—was the International Space Station where diligent Chinese space workers were preparing a space flight to Mars. Sobering to the edge of depressive reaction, Simpson wondered when did America lose its sense of adventure, its sense of exploration and the pathfinder spirit? *What happened,* he wondered, *that we have been so caught up in the unimportant battles of daily life and the distraction of feckless debate that we are now unable to aspire to the high dreams of the human endeavor as we had in the past? And how did I get to this pathetic place?*

Then he heard the cry of a loon in his mind and was taken back to a still lake where that plaintive sound came across from the far side where a green-black forest crowded out the shoreline as that lonely cry chilled the soul, for it was here that he had experienced the inner peace and spirituality in the Canadian wilderness. He was very young then and raised in a rigidly religious family, he wanted to become a great minister in a great church and he wanted to embellish the world with the values of Jesus. But things did not go well as he developed for he was not charismatic nor was he a great speaker. Years were wasted when the best he could do to remain close to the church was to offer his service as a volunteer preacher. Then unexpectedly, he found a position researching and writing political-leaning essays in the new politico-religious movement of the twenties and it was then that he knew that he had a talent that was a value. Religious magazines were extraordinarily popular in those days and he learned to write with an overly academic flair that sounded intellectual but was written in such sophisticated ambivalence that the layman would accept its premise but professionals would not get anything other than vague postulates they were unable to challenge and then, in the final paragraph he would make a concluding statement combining an inviolable version of political reality and church doctrine.

But even during Simpson's work to deter global warming ideology, an evil he called a liberal conspiracy, he never returned emotionally to that lake in Canada. So his work on global warming brought him the grand reward of being stranded in this weeping little room on a rock in space, for then, even his church brought him no clerical or emotional rewards, his fluctuating congregation dutifully in attendance at his sermons while their alcohol-numbed minds dwell on the contrarieties of the gaming table. Now, after all this, now at the end, why has he belatedly remembered that beautiful place in a Canadian wilderness in a thought that had remained buried in his memories like a tarnished gold nugget imbedded in the drifting sands of the shallow current of an old meandering stream. Too late in life he had tears. Too late in life he was able to see through the shallowness of the politico-religious manipulators. And too late in life did he realize that he had been robbed of his humanity. Now he was at a dead end and sadly, there was no last chance for redemption.

    The high prairie of western Nevada was a land bypassed by our ancestral pioneers who saw little value in the desolate scrubby hills. Years after the first explorers passed through, mining became the principal economy but little else ever developed until the modern era dependent upon gambling. But the experienced farmers leaving the prairie states of the Middle West knew instinctively that the waterless land was not arable for any type of agriculture, and even the last resort of growing grass hay on land that was marginal. Not even cattle could thrive on such pitifully poor soil and the sparse grass that grew there. There had been a time when experts from the university tried to poison the low-lying sage under the assumption that to rid the land of the sage meant that grass would grow and replace it. But that did not happen; instead the seeded grass did not come up, the soil became arid even in the spring and the constant wind blew the little topsoil there was into the stream beds and the canyons. So the project was abandoned. But despite its agronomical shortcomings, that wild place was a Godsend for the wild horse that seemed to have the perfect place—beautiful rolling hills of sage of no value to man.

    Josh Moreland had lived in western Nevada all his life and had no desire to live anywhere else. He had been an honor student in high school and although offered the opportunity to attend an Ivy League school on scholarship, he declined so that he could remain in his home state and maintain a simple way of life. He attended the local university and received a degree in accounting. In appearance, Moreland was quite striking; he was six feet, well proportioned, with a rugged face and an athletic build. But what was most remarkable about him was his gentleness. Very soft-spoken, he rejected sports in school as he disliked team competition and its vagaries; he did however, participate in gymnastics and diving and excelled in both and he rationalized those activities as not being competitive as one vied against oneself in those sports. He eventually became a certified internal auditor and worked on contract for several firms which involved a great deal of travel. Approaching thirty years of age, he was now considering a family and was engaged to a girl whose parents ran a tourist business in Virginia City.

On this day, Moreland was motoring up the interstate highway to Reno having just left Bridgeport, California, and he looked out at the expanse of land, the blue-grey monotonous sage that never seemed to change, but that is what he liked, the stability, the consistency of simplicity—it fit his personality and he felt secure and at home for there was no pseudo-drama of grass dancing in the wind or sun-splashed hillsides or seas of wildflowers. Instead, this was western Nevada where there was little change but a satisfying permanence and he worried not about the ever-expanding encroachment of civilization. As Moreland loved Nevada, he also had a deep sense of pride that wild horses have existed on those plains for decades and that they were wild and unfettered and Nevada had become one of the only places on earth were a species could run free without peril. And yet, there was a concern, for unconfirmed reports hinted that plunderers were taking wild horses from other areas of the west in violation of state and federal law and there was a suspicion that the laws were just not being enforced by a government unsympathetic to the wilderness cause.

Somewhere out there on those high prairies to the east, wild horses were meandering through the gentle canyons and small valleys, unaware of the faraway chaotic world of man, the foals frisky and mischievous, the mares attentive and the stallions alert and restless. He remembered only seeing them on one occasion and then they seemed strangely like their domestic kin as he recalled them trudging single file along a long abandoned dirt road, with an occasional snort or grunt. He had expected something more romantic but nevertheless, it thrilled him to see them in this natural wild state. To the west lay the magnificent Sierras where from their lofty height the mountains dropped down to the prairie in only a few miles, so abruptly that an east wind off the prairies would be cast upward to such height that in that place gliders would set world altitude records. But because of that abruptness, little water flowed eastward, most being diverted toward the Sacramento Valley to the west, and therein was the reason for the isolation of the Nevada prairies—the scarcity of water.

In thinking about the horses, Moreland remembered an old Indian account of the first coming of the horse to the west. It was called the night of forwardness. It said:

"There once was a tribe of people who lived in a valley surrounded by three great mountains. They were a joyous, resourceful, loving people and their natural beliefs sustained them very well. But they had to journey many days to a lake that supplied them with fish and then they had to smoke the fish before the long trip home. Once, on that long walk with their fish, they came upon some beautiful animals that snorted and ran ahead of them. At first the people were afraid but afterward they could not stop thinking about those animals. So they returned to that place but could not find the animals. Then in the fall, they saw many of the animals and of many different colors. Many months later, after both the people and the animals became used to each other, the little ones of the herd and the little ones of the tribe began to interact and it became evident that a bond was being formed between them. Tribal elders, in a meeting regarding the animals, gave permission for the little ones to mount the animals and ride them. It was done in good fun and with gentleness and it allowed the little ones to go forward and see many things and a great loyalty was formed. The people began to change because the animals gave them new opportunities and the animals became sacred. The people realized that achieving a bond and trust with the animals was a lifetime goal and it made the people more gentle and thoughtful. Even today, once in a while out in the brush and sage one can hear the gentle voices of the past—a snort, a whinny, a soothing sound."

As Moreland proceeded north, the land flattened out a bit but otherwise remained the same, the road straight unlike the southern portion which followed a meandering stream. It was here, somewhere south of Carson City, that he first saw the truck, a fifty-three-foot Kenworth cattle truck on the shoulder of the road, partly in the roadway, and as he sped passed he was shocked at what he thought was blood flowing from the bed, oozing from under the door. He stopped, turned around and proceeded back to the truck. There he encountered the driver, a huge man with bull-like shoulders, a crew cut and the face of a bar brawler. The driver was inspecting his truck preparatory to transporting his merchandise to Reno when Moreland, who had suspicions as to what that merchandise might be, exited his auto to inquire about the blood flowing from the truck bed.

"I'm hauling wild horses, we just rounded them up. The blood is from a colt that fell down and the other horses trampled the dumb son of a bitch," the driver replied.

"Why are you rounding up wild horses?" Moreland asked.

"People are paying a good price for horse meat these days and they are no good to anyone otherwise, so we slaughter them and butcher them for meat."

"How many horses do you have in the truck?"

"Got about forty."

"Sounds crowded," Moreland replied.

"Don't matter. They're going to be slaughtered anyway."

"How did you round them up?"

"ATVs, trucks, horseback and helicopter. And we chased the dumb son of a bitches for miles. Some of then even ran over cliffs and fell a long way and we could hear them screaming."

Concerned, Moreland asked, "Did you put them out of their misery?"

"Naw, the stupid bastards did it to themselves, we just let them be—screw 'em."

"How far did you chase the rest of them?"

"For miles, until they couldn't catch their breath and there they were all wild eyed and the stallions fought us to the death. But we shot all of them down. The dumb bastards, didn't they know we were superior to them? This group here kind of gave up. They made it easy on everyone so we just drove them here and loaded them over there," he said pointing to a loading chute in a large corral about a hundred yards out in the adjacent field.

Moreland remembered an account of a slaughtering, an image that he was unable to forget through the years. It described the slaughter of a shy young mare that had been prodded into a funnel-like chute onto the cold slippery floor of the slaughterhouse and there her depression turned to sheer terror. Her senses told her that something was wrong but being the shy animal that she was, she only stood trembling, urinating on herself. Then an attendant brought a retractable bolt full force down on her skull, shattering her skull, a process that was repeated until she went down. While in withering convulsions but alive, a sharp hook pierced her leg and she was hoisted upward, her head dangling to the floor, pain and terror possessed her and then a huge blade sliced her throat and her life's blood flowed onto the floor.

*That is not going to happen with these animals,* Moreland vowed to himself.

The driver continued to inspect his truck while Moreland walked slowly back to his auto. He leaned on the vehicle in deep thought them opened the door and removed a jack handle and turned back to the cattle truck. As a child, Moreland had been his mother's joy as he brought home every abused, abandoned or strayed animal he found. He had been a loving child close to his family and when in high school and college, he volunteered for social programs for the poor and he worked tirelessly on wildlife issues. He had never hurt anyone in his life. That was about to change.

Moreland walked up behind the driver of the truck and, using the jack handle as a club, he swung the handle in a horizontal arch so as not to penetrate the skull but to hit the driver with a hard glancing blow on the top of his head. The driver straightened, swung around to face Moreland, gave him quizzical look, took a step toward him, dropped to his knees and then fell forward on his face, unconscious. Finally, Moreland had the presence of mind to look for traffic and seeing none, drug the unconscious driver to the side of the road which had a steep enough slope that passing autos would not see the body. The truck was still running and as Moreland mounted the vehicle he was thankful as he did not have a clue how to start the vehicle. The road to the loading chute was to the rear of the truck so he attempted to put the truck in reverse but could not find the gear. Instead, he found a forward gear, perhaps compound low, and proceeded forward, then turned left in a wide arc turning across the roadway to the opposite side of the road where he continued turning to bring the vehicle back across the road and onto the dirt road to the loading chute.

But first he had to go through a locked gate to the fenced field and, unable to find a key to the lock, he pushed the vehicle up to the gate, pressed on it briefly and then accelerated slightly. The gate groaned and then sprung open. Placing the truck in front of the loading chute, he once again sought reverse and then as if a gift from the animal gods, he found reverse on the right, down and outward. After much grinding, the truck lurched backward, moving toward the chute. After a pause, Moreland opened the rear doors to see the frightened animals panic away from him. He then opened the corral gate to the miles and miles of blue-green sage that was the world of the wild horse. He returned to back the truck until he abutted the loading chute and although the truck remained a little askew, there appeared ample stability for the horses to cross down the chute into the corral. But they did not come out and his voice was not reassuring to them. Frustrated he kicked noisily on the front of the truck bed to scare them out but there was no response.

Then quite unexpectedly a shy mare poked her nose out the opening, smelled the air and walked almost casually down into the corral, out the corral gate and disappeared into the sagebrush. A stallion followed her. Then there was a sudden rush and all the animals were out of the enclosure that meant sure death, once again on their beloved prairie running free, heads high and manes flowing.

Moreland then ran the truck to the edge of a slight precipice, started it rolling downhill and jumped out as it gained speed. The Kenworth started to tip, then righted itself, caromed off a rock and then smashed into a dry creek. Not much damage but he had made his point. He returned to look in on the driver, who was groaning and apparently coming to consciousness. Moreland left the driver, who probably would have little more than a headache from his encounter with the jack handle and would soon need the assistance of a passing motorist.

Back on the road, surprisingly, Moreland felt no shame, guilt or compassion for the driver. That was a strange experience for him for he never thought himself capable of hurting another human and could not really envision himself doing so. But he felt no emotion in this instance and was not sure why. Obviously, the driver was a vile despicable coward but Moreland had always concern for others despite their faults. That night in Reno, he slept well.

In March, 2033, Mrs. Daniella Thompson of Mt. Vernon, Illinois, received an unexpected letter from her brother, Edward M. Worthy. Worthy usually wrote to his sister once a year and then his communication was invariably brief and included Christmas salutation. Mrs. Thompson opened the letter with apprehension fearing for her brother's welfare so unusual was any missive from him.

The letter was as follows:

*Dear Daniella;*
*You are probably surprised to hear from me it is so rare that I write; but, I think that this will be of special interest to you, particularly in light of the heated debates that we used to have over religion. New events that will be described have brought a new prospective to me on the subject or, at least have made me reconsider some of my previously held ideas.*

*Last evening, I made my usual Thursday trek to Kingdom Hall in south Philly for my therapy groups for drug-dependent persons. I was early and was doing some group planning with a co-counselor when a man known by the Hispanics as Jesuscristo Dos—and to the Evangelists as Susej—entered the hall with a group of street people. You have undoubtedly heard of this guy as he has been in the news a lot. It's a little freaky to hear of a guy on the six o'clock news and then a couple of hours later, see him in person.*

## THE LEGEND OF SUSEJ

*He came with no fanfare, no trumpet overture, hallaluyas, ritual, ceremony, falling on the knees, shouts of joy or anything of that kind. He just walked in quietly and sat down. He was casual as were those with him and they treated him as they would anyone else. And, I might add, they looked like street junkies, homeless, just plain thugs. We understand that they hid him out as he is wanted by the feds on a warrant for blasphemy. They were all totally at ease, there was no nonsensical banter, forced conversation or theatrics as one might expect. He was a brother.*

*Physically, he was quite small—not a bigger-than-life person that you might expect. His face was Middle Eastern but that might just be my bias. He was not handsome but then he was not unpleasant looking either. His hair was short but not styled and appeared to have been cut with sheep shears. His hair was reddish, thin and he had a receding hair line. His nose was a little prominent but his outstanding feature was his eyes. They were black, soft and incredibly gentle and when he looked you, it was as if he were looking right into your soul. It was as if he brought every nefarious thing that you ever did out of the unexamined unconscious. But despite that he was open and frank and very easy to converse with.*

*When Jesuscristo Dos spoke his eyes carried the most wonderful animation and even in discussing very trite things, one was drawn on every word. He had humor and he smiled a lot. But what impressed me though was that despite his notoriety, he was in no way intimidating. I cannot remember when I have been so comfortable with anyone.*

*I learned from others that he was in transit to New York City and because he was sought by police, had to practically walk the whole distance. But people were feeding him, providing him with shelter and protecting him. His only steady companion is a small mongrel named Adler. Sometimes at night when he slept in doorways, the police, not realizing who he was, roused him out and kept him moving. "Not in our city," they would tell him. But he accepted that with good cheer and harbored no ill-feelings. Normally, I would be concerned for his safety on the streets and the crime rate is so high but, I am told, even the thugs respect and protect him.*

*Shortly after his arrival, I had to attend my group and I was fearful that I would lose contact with Jesuscristo Dos. But when I returned he was still in the hall, his people hanging on every word. I noticed that he was not drinking wine as I would have suspected but good old American coffee with its usual thirty percent residue of stems, leaves, trash and insect parts.*

*Then I listened to that soft voice and looked into those intense eyes and I felt an awakening—a glow, and it was quite euphoric. I listened to him for over an hour and I will tell you one thing and that is he is no imposter or phony. I have been around for too long and I don't think that I can be fooled. This man is real. It is against my grain to believe in the spiritualism that he advocates but I am certainly reevaluating myself and my beliefs. There is so much logic to his positions—for example, he rejects orthodox religion but advocates spiritual exploration by the individual unimpeded by doctrine dictated to him by others. We are all unique individuals and each of us must find our way through our intellect and the spirituality of all things. What also impressed me about him was that he doesn't preach, sermonize, dictate or lecture—he only tries to establish an atmosphere for spiritual exploration and self-understanding. He expresses possibilities and allows the listener to discern for himself as he says that each of us must find our own way. Also, he is a good listener.*

*As for his beliefs, I can't say that he is a Christian and let it go at that—it is much deeper. He obviously rejects the dogma that restrains human development. He doesn't describe God as one would a man but rather he sees God as the supreme intellect that created the universe and has made it continent upon humans to participate in that world as equal but subordinate parts and having said that, we must conform to what is necessary to maintain the earth to the benefit of all living things and future generations. But he says that the message has always been that but over time myth has betrayed that message.*

*When Jesuscristo Dos left I was in a state of exhilaration and even with that limited contact with him, I will miss him. I believe that he has changed my life for the better and now, for the first time, I can accept a religious belief and still be myself. I feel whole once again.*

*Love, Ed.*

Daniella never responded to Worthy's letter.

# Eighteen

"Your eleven o'clock is here," came the voice over the office intercom.

"Give me a few minutes," answered Ian Petrovich, space travel consultant for the Interspace Travel Corporation located in an old dingy building overlooking the Bay of Fundy in St Johns, New Brunswick.

Petrovich looked at the clock on the wall. Quarter to eleven. He had fifteen minutes to catch his breath so he sat back stiffly in his orthopedic chair attempting to relax with his eyes closed. But somehow the effort only seemed to aggravate his stress, making him more conscious of it.

This malaise had been going on for several months, or at least that was when he became aware of it—the persistent fatigue, feelings of vagueness, irritability and the persistent sore stiff muscles. He rejected a doctor's suggestion that he suffered from depressive reaction as he did not feel depressed but simply, he felt nothingness—as if he was not there; after all, was not depression when you felt—well—depressed? But as a behaviorist, he knew the symptoms and genesis that created stress, but his effort toward stress-reduction—yoga, stretching, exercise and meditation had all been futile. He resisted prescriptions that he viewed as quick fixes but sought health remedies that brought no relief. He physically attempted to relax individual muscles, first his fingers, then the wrist, followed by the forearm and arm but to no avail and the muscles at the base of his neck were like boils and too painful to touch.

Petrovich had worked for ITC for five years. He was originally from Labrador where all the family men before him—his father, grandfather and great-grandfather—had been fishermen and he had always thought that he would follow their footsteps. But the seas were dead and the fisheries closed. So instead of fish, the New Age ingested pills, caps, powders, dietary supplements, soy, tofu, anti-oxidants, wheat germ, succulents, interlineal cleansing formulas, power diets and mega-vitamins and their sewer systems showed the evidence of a cultural addiction to organic self-medication.

So Petrovich found work in Nova Scotia and then when ITC opened one of its seven offices in St. Johns, he was interviewed for the position and hired. The St. Johns office was part of a joint US and Canadian program by ITC to process clients for interspace travel, and the choice of the office site was an attempt to improve employment opportunities in an economically depressed area. The original program was developed to make available to travelers space shuttles to the planet Rebourne and the unsuccessful claim that, as an earth-like planet in the Andromeda Constellation it was claimed to be life-supporting and therefore would be a new start for mankind on an unspoiled place. But the planetary research was unproductive and space travel premature and planning was scrapped. Nevertheless, once the project and been authorized it could not be stopped and despite the failure of Rebourne to materialize as a viable alternative to life on earth, other options were explored and within months space hotels, space islands and the very popular Lunar City were being developed, and the opening up of NASA by the US government to big business was a boon to space development creating the possibility of human travel to other planets or space islands as well as previously unimagined possibilities.

Then, as the air quality and environment deteriorated on earth, many of those having made the first primitive explorative flights found space hotels quite livable and requested permanent residency in orbit. Thus the new government urgency became "space—our greatest resource." This was embellished by government infomercials which advocated such travel as a "celestial odyssey." This was a natural phenomenon, a god-given solution to the inhabitants of a dying earth—a natural event—according to the advocates of the profit-driving space program—and it was now emphasized that national economic resources should prioritize its budget to concentrate on space exploration so that the new pilgrims could settle in a new world and human life would continue to flourish.

The plan was met with much enthusiasm—although knowledge of the project had been withheld from working-class people—the opportunity to make money became so obvious that the program began to grow exponentially. Originally, in anticipation of the "new start" of Rebourne, many want-to-be space pioneers began to compete for occupancy on yet-to-be-built orbiting space hotels where they could reside while awaiting transportation to outer space. But with the collapse of the Rebourne dream, the idea of space hotels sprung up and actually seemed to the more logically minded that it would represent a first step in a reasonable one-step-at-a-time approach to the mysteries of space exploration. Thus came the birth of the Lunar City Project and the Alpha and Beta Projects. When the moneyed classes began to fill the still-uncompleted Alpha, the Beta Space Island Projects began accepting applications for residency. Meanwhile, the firing of space shuttles to supply workers for construction of the two island hotels had been a drain on an already depleted earth atmosphere—an ironic twist to a self-fulfilling prophecy.

But suddenly everything had changed for now the quest for passage into orbit for the start of Armageddon dominated everything. The demand for space was phenomenal and ITC employees, despite their feelings regarding the veracity of such adventure, were instructed to process the applications and verify financial ability to pay without compassion—it was business as usual. The bargain-basement Armageddon space trip would be simple. The spaceship, very fundamental and basic in design, would be fired out of the earth's gravitational pull, gain a speed to achieve orbit and then remain in orbit until its occupants connect with their savior, who would then guide them back to earth as a great army to fight the antichrist. Once the space vehicle was in orbit, the obligation of the contractors would end at that point while some of the more expensive vehicles would return automatically to their point of origin while the cheaper models would simply be left adrift. There was an immense surge of applications for the most inexpensive flights to orbit but few applicants qualified financially. Despite the fact that the overall plan lacked logic and had not been thought through by those smitten with zeal for the concept of Armageddon, the demand was immense.

Petrovich glanced at his watch. It was eleven sharp. He had gained nothing from his rest other than delay from that which he did not want to face. He rumpled his shoulders and they were even stiffer than before and the muscles in his neck stung. He hoped that his clients would not notice the deep circles under his eyes. He took a deep breath and called on the intercom for his eleven o'clock appointment.

It was a family of five, the Norman Johnson family of Van Nays, California. They shuffled in as a unit and sat in unison without salutation waiting for Petrovich to speak. The Johnson application requested two passages, one to Space Island Alpha and then a second one for orbital flight to Armageddon when the seventh trumpet sounded.

Petrovich opened the family file. The father, forty-one, was wealthy, the owner of a construction firm and he was well educated. His wife, a homemaker, thirty-eight, was quiet but attentive. The two gave no clue as to their relationship. The children included a boy, sixteen, a girl, fifteen and a girl, five.

The first part of the interview was what Petrovich hated the most—explaining what they already knew about the program and the deception of not telling them what they did not know. In a practiced voice that sounded too rhythmic and monotonous to him, he went through the routine and expectations of what living on Alpha would involve. In reassuring tones, he explained the daily schedule on Alpha and he emphasized that they would be living in a biologically perfect environment.

But what he could not tell them was that they would be confined to the standard living quarters for a family of five, a forty- by fifty-foot module. Leaving the family area would be limited by schedule and there would be no freedom to roam the island as all inhabitants had to be coordinated in the hermetically sealed controlled environment. A public address system would advise families of various activities aboard the island but that was limited by time restrictions and the family would be confined to their quarters most of the time, not unlike laboratory rats. But, of course, the ITC procedure manual instructed the travel agent not to discuss such "mundane" settings.

Mr. Johnson, through the interview, appeared confident and controlling. His family on the other hand, was passive and stoic. He was undaunted in his decision on relocating in space and he believed firmly in the literal biblical prophecy of Armageddon. A fundamentalist Christian, he had a rigid upbringing himself and had been taught to never question the theology. Furthermore, life on earth had become intolerable to him, the problems facing the nation insurmountable and the threat of the antichrist were becoming overwhelming. In addition, his two oldest children suffered from chronic and debilitating allergies and life on a space platform with its purified environment would be more tolerable than life on earth. Both Mr. and Mrs. Johnson suffered from lung disease, the most common ailment on earth, and both felt hampered in their daily routines by the personal air supply units which they carried constantly with emergency oxygen supply.

During the interview, Mr. Johnson maintained the same professional demeanor, Petrovich assumed, that he did as owner and operator of his construction company. He was always brief and to the point in comment—everything predictable but much of it unnecessary. But what were his unconscious feelings, Petrovich wondered. He was so sure of himself, so sure that what he was doing was right for his family. He was utterly without trepidation—there was not even a hint of incertitude.

Then in an instant, Petrovich saw something in Johnson not there before. Had it always been there? It was a look, a harried pause, the chimerical glimpse of another possibility. In that moment his intensity dissipated and the look was disconnected from current conversation and it was as baleful a perspective as one might suspect of the insecurity of one looking at the earth for the last time. The unexamined life had led to this one irrevocable moment and even as self-assured as one could be, there was hesitancy—perhaps it was a cry from the soul.

Petrovich used that moment to jump ahead in his presentation whereas at the end of his interview he would ask if there were any doubts or reservations regarding the program. But Mr. Johnson had caught his own inner weakness in that moment, reestablished his austere persona and assured his interviewer that he was firm in his commitment.

To Petrovich's observation, Mrs. Johnson was dutiful to her family and obedient to her husband and she seemed to be going along passively with her husband's plan. But that was to the casual eye, for when Petrovich paid closer attention, he noticed that she gave her husband a reassuring tug on the sleeve of his arm to give him emotional support and then when he made one of his authoritative-sounding pronouncements, she would pat him on the back approvingly. Petrovich wondered if she sensed some hesitancy in her husband not apparent to others. Was it possible that as passive as she appeared, could she have been the motivator here? Did she need to constantly prop her husband up lest he falter and be swayed by second thoughts?

And what about the children compelled to this space odyssey? The son's only concern during the interview was whether there was a soccer league on Beta to which Petrovich gave the ITC-approved staid answer to all similar questions, "We seek to provide all recreational facilities and opportunities."

The oldest daughter, adorned with make-up and garish jewelry, wore ultra-tight clothing and appeared indifferent to the interview and seemed emotionally distant from her family. Her only concern was whether there would be boys her age on Beta. She was assured there would be.

Petrovich casually turned his attention to the youngest daughter, a tiny thing with long, black hair shrouding a doll-like face which was perhaps too flat and her eyes too large but features that one day would give her face a special uniqueness. But those eyes were troubled and considering her body language, particularly her wary reactions to her father's comments during the interview, it was obvious that she had been paying attention to the discourse and that she was strong-willed and made up her own mind about things. In her lap, the girl held a simple rag doll of corduroy, homemade perhaps by a grandmother and probably her most cherished possession. Her name was Jana and she demanded attention and would not be denied. She looked up at Petrovich with intense eyes and asked if she could have a kitten on the space island. The procedure manual gave Petrovich some latitude on that specific question and he lied, "Maybe." When her eyes dropped, he added, "Let's hope so."

Jana gave Petrovich a long look as if undressing his psyche then lowered her head to fondle her doll with focused intensity. She frowned as she did so and Petrovich knew that her thoughts of him were not flattering. *Since when did five-year-old girls think so intuitively?* he wondered. More importantly, he knew that the rag doll was her link to some safe comfortable place or person, whether imagined or real. Then a slight tremble of her lips gave her away—she was afraid.

This was the time for family members to come to her and hug her or, at least, for one to comfort her by a tug on the sleeve or a kind word. But none did. Petrovich understood then that the little girl was alone, a victim of a family of ego-driven high expectation and achievement but with little or no regard for loving or caring relationships. He wanted, at that moment, to swoop the little girl up in his arms even though he suspected that she was feisty and would resist. Nevertheless, he reasoned, she needed the affirmation and was smart and therefore after a token show of hostility, there would be secret understanding and appreciation. But, he just could not be unprofessional. *God, how I hate this job,* he thought.

The remainder of the interview was to address financial eligibility issues and an explanation of the time-frame for application acceptance and scheduling of the actual flight to Alpha. In the meantime while waiting for a flight to be scheduled, the Johnsons would be obliged to stay, on call, at ITC's pre-flight space hotel in St. Johns as were all Alpha travelers.

Upon conclusion of the interview conference, the family rose, almost automatically, and moved quietly toward the door; with the exception of little Jana, who always seemed to have her own little twist to everything she did as she seemed to pause to say something to Petrovich. But before she could, her mother grabbed her by the arm, pulling her toward the door. Jana then took her mother's hand but continued to turn herself sideways so as to maintain eye contact with Petrovich which she did with an enigmatic not-quite-a-smile smile that penetrated Petrovich like a laser. Not looking where she was going Jana bumped the door, eliciting a gruff response from her mother who, yanked her sideways and then twisted her through the aperture. The last impression Petrovich had of the girl was as she was being led away by the hand, her head straining backwards, her eyes riveted on Petrovich in a last supplicating effort. *What have we done to this kid?* Petrovich thought.

The family was gone and obviously, their application would be accepted. They could easily afford the space flight and their reason for going and the family's dissolution were irrelevant—those were personal matters and of no concern to ITC.

Petrovich looked at his watch and realized that the interview had scarcely lasted forty minutes. He wondered if he had short-changed them, if he forgotten anything essential to the flight or if he had rushed through the interview because he was uncomfortable with the family's apathy and apparent indifference toward one another. But if he left now, he would have an additional twenty minutes for lunch and he desperately needed the extra time. With slow deliberation he straightened his desk and then reported to his secretary that he would return at one o'clock. He took a breath of oxygen from his personal oxygen supply unit and slipped out a side door to the elevator. Once on the street, he headed in a southern direction for Irma's Café just two blocks away but then suddenly deviated. He had decided that as he had spare time that he would go home for lunch, a surprising decision considering that his apartment was two full miles from his workplace. Later, a taxi driver remembered a fare to the address.

Well into the afternoon of that day, ITC secretary Nancy Neusome sought Petrovich on the intercom to announce the arrival of a client for a scheduled meeting. There was no answer from him and it suddenly dawned upon her that Petrovich had not returned from lunch, checked the attendance board or called in. She contacted other staff but received no information as to Petrovich's whereabouts. He was simply not available. The client was then rescheduled for an open hour later in the afternoon with a different agent. As for Petrovich's absence, it was shrugged off despite that the behavior was unusual for him and the supervisor was certain that in the morning Petrovich would have a reasonable explanation, considering his integrity.

The following morning Petrovich failed to report for work and by 10 AM there was concern. Ms. Neucome called his apartment by telephone but received no answer. Alarmed, the ITC supervisor contacted the St. Johns police department but they were unable, by law, to start a missing persons investigation for twenty-four hours after the person was reported missing; however, out of public relations courtesy, they agreed to send an officer to the Petrovich apartment unofficially.

At approximately 2 PM, Officer John Bradley attempted to contact the missing employee at his residence, a modern two-bedroom flat in an apartment complex inhabited by young working singles. The officer, upon approaching the apartment, saw a light on inside but received no response from his knock on the door. In trying the doorknob, he found it open. There was nothing noteworthy about the living room so he proceeded to the kitchen. There he saw that it was very neat and clean and at the table was a half-eaten egg sandwich, a full glass of milk and an uneaten donut. Almost unseen as it was so inconspicuous was a crumpled piece of paper which when unfolded said in large crude letters, "I can't take it anymore—I got to get out."

Concerned, Officer Bradley moved gingerly toward the bedroom cautiously fearful that he might make a grisly discovery and, finding the door ajar, pushed it gently open. Inside, the light was on and Petrovich lay on the bed on his back as if he were resting. Then Officer Bradley saw the blood.

According to the official report, Petrovich had entered the bedroom with a cup of tea, drank a portion of it and then, considering how immaculate the bedroom was, may have, as a last act, straightened the room up a bit. Then after a brief period of time, he drew a nine-millimeter handgun out of his nightstand, put the barrel to his right temple and ended his existence on earth.

# Nineteen

Linda Lafevre had been up since 5 AM when the knock came at the front door. As usual, she was readying the center for the day, warming the assembly room, starting breakfast, making beds and being sure that the older residents, upon rising, would tend to their personal hygiene. It was unusual for anyone to call so early in the morning so she approached the door with cautious inquisitiveness, opened it to slightly ajar and then slid it full open to reveal a handsome boy in soiled white tunic accompanied by a small dog. She knew the boy immediately.

"I knew that you would come," she said softly. "Come in." The boy entered while his dog, later identified as "Adler," made an impish entrance on busy little legs that carried him as if he knew where he was going, descending two steps onto the tiled floor to a couch where he bounced up, turned around to lie down and then look up as if to say, "I'm home, when do we eat?" The boy laughed at the impertinence.

The woman and the boy seemed to know each other intimately but there was no way that they could have ever met. She took him to the stove in the center of the large room where he could warm himself. It had been unseasonably cold and warming oneself was one of the simplest pleasures one could enjoy. "This is an interesting stove. Where did it come from and what is it that you burn in it?" he asked.

Pausing on her way to the kitchen area, she answered, "Ironically, it originally was a cauldron used by a junkie to mix chemicals but we have a welder who put legs on it so as not to scorch the floor and a ventilation system and as funny looking as it is, it works quite well. We burn pellets made from waste products which we make right here, and since there seems to be incredible amounts of waste lying about, we have an unlimited supply of pellets."

She brought him some tea. "We'll be having breakfast shortly." Then she added in a serious tone, "What are we to call you? Jesuscristo Dos? Jesus II?"

"Just call me Susej."

"But that is what your enemies call you," she said.

"The people of the world are too divided now. For me to have a name for those who support me and another for those who are against me would further divide people. I will accept the name that they give me as part of their problem and not mine and perhaps one day when we all come together, the insult that they intend will become meaningless."

Just at that moment, Darius Celosi, a new member and the recently deposed CEO of Bio-Med Incorporation, entered the assembly room, saw the boy and in suspended awe stood mute and uncertain until he dropped to his knees before him. Susej responded strongly, "Don't do that to me. Get up. I am just a person like you—no more, no less. If I am in any way different from the rest of you it is probably because I had a pure education—despite the intentions of my mentors—and because of that I am completely objective and have no implanted biases or emotional hang-ups from their pathological teachings. So I implore you to treat me as one of you."

Celosi hesitantly introduced himself. When Susej inquired how he came to the center Celosi told the story of how he had been the CEO of the world's largest biological-medical corporation but that he had been replaced by a younger brilliant man and was asked to fill a lesser position but that same week his father died in New Mexico. He had failed to see his father for several years because of the demands of his position and then suddenly when the old man passed, Celosi knew tragically that the demands put upon him had caused him the separation from his father. "I was shocked," he mused, "when I was relieved of my position, but not as shocked as I was a week later when dad died. I thought that if I was successful in my profession everything else would just fall into place. But it is not like that at all—your family is everything—a job is just a job. So I refused to go back to the corporation."

"That's the way it is in life—you either learn gradually, one day at a time, or you learn in one swoop and the latter can be catastrophic when it catches with you by surprise," Susej replied. "But how did it come about that you ended up here?"

"I was suddenly on the streets and nowhere to go—which is an unbelievable situation if you have been used to a high lifestyle. Then I heard about the opening here for a bookkeeper management position overseeing those we call bell-ringers who are people in the underground who move information by word of mouth because the feds monitor all electronic communication. So to protect ourselves we don't communicate anything that can be used against you. The bell-ringers are incredible people with photographic memories and carry messages around the country. Their identities are unknown outside our system and the system itself has never been breached by spies because spies are so different from us and so obvious to us. Anyway, I lost a job that paid a cool half million a year and took one that pays room and board plus reciprocation credits. But I am happy now and feel that I am a part of something important. It has been such an awakening for me to come here as I carry great guilt in my heart for my failure to take care of my family but that is the way of corporate business—actually come to believe that their course is the only course and that anything you need to do, no matter how degrading or devastating to other people, is all right and all ethics are forgotten."

"You said reciprocation credits?"

Celosi answered, "We disdain money as an evil. We are not purists on that—there are some cases where you have to pay or receive money, but in theory money is the primary source of evil. So, if on your job you overproduce or work long hours, you receive credits—based on trust—and it all works out quite well because our needs are so modest."

"That is quite commendable," Susej replied. "I learned in studying our culture that the internet computer system was the biggest hoax ever perpetuated on the American people. Somehow they got people to believe that it was necessary to advance civilization and improve the economy and people got hooked on it. But it is remarkably inefficient and time-consuming, plus it is used for so many nonessential pursuits. But more serious was the fact that instead of learning from computers and then carrying on their lives independent of computers, our children and ourselves became like one with the computer and we have a situation where the human brain has morphed into a computer-like cerebrum incapable of unbiased objectivity or creative thought. We have become computer zombies."

Lafevre laid out a table with modest breakfast with tea or coffee. Eight members of the center seated themselves and it was quite comfortable with easy banter and much laughter.

As it was Susej's first day at the center, Lafevre explained the history and current use of the building that housed the assembly room. The room had originally been built as an antique-gift shop in the business district of Staten Island. The room itself was round, quite large and originally designed to accommodate garish displays and to supply the need for buyer movement within the display area. The center oval area was tile and now contained a large heating stove surrounded by numerous cots arranged in a semicircular pattern. The room was bordered by a wood floor, two steps higher than the tiled oval and was originally used for access for shoppers and staff. The room had twelve windows, all high to not allow outside vision but to allow light to enter. Fortunately, the center was located on some high ground and never incurred high-tide flooding that dominated much of the city. To the rear of the assembly room were two doors that led to what was formerly a small mall but was now used as work rooms. The original building possessed a high arched ceiling but when it was damaged in a storm, the ceiling was lowered and became a simple flat structure that rankled against the basic design of the place but was more practical in saving heat in the winter.

The breakfast occasion was so enjoyable to those assembled that they found excuses to delay their projects for the day and Lafevre quite easily rationalized that this was a special event and they all deserved to further enjoy the reception of Susej. Then, as had been expected, Ivan Davis, who had been called away early in the day for a counseling session, returned to the wonderful surprise of the new guest and, hopefully, new member of the clan. Davis was obviously enraptured by Susej but did well to contain his enthusiasm in that first meeting.

Susej, in noting an English accent and the appearance of a well-educated and cultured man, inquired of Davis as to his background, to which Davis replied, "I was educated in my home country and after a career in London, I was offered the position of rector of the Saint Thomas The Apostle Church in Los Angeles where I served for many years. But we were a very liberal and socially active church and when I spoke out against the religious dictatorship of the administration, they took offense and eventually one day I was giving a sermon that I thought was actually rather innocuous and I was arrested. At first, I did not think that it was too serious—just a form of harassment. But they made an example of me and I was sentenced to eighteen years in prison for blasphemy in a trial that was a complete farce. However, after eighteen months in a minimum-security prison in California I was released on the appeal for clemency by the United Kingdom and upon my release I was ordered never to preach before a church congregation again. I guess I could have defied that order and become a martyr but I think that I can do more good here."

"And what do you do here?" Susej asked.

"I use my education in psychology and religion to counsel members of our neighborhood who request assistance because of social or emotional problems—the demand is almost overwhelming—it really keeps me hopping. And in counseling others I can share spirituality with them and in that way lead them to God."

"But that doesn't violate the administration's order?"

"Actually, no. The wording is such that I just cannot appear before organized groups. Besides, they really do not know about this. They have written off what they call the Mole People, that is, the people that they claim live under abandoned buildings and scavenge like animals. We just do not matter to them and they do try to monitor us but they certainly do not know about our organization or the sophistication of our developing culture."

Susej liked this man and knew that they would be friends; and then, thinking what Davis had said, asked, "Was this developing underground society one of planning or did it accrue naturally as things developed?"

Davis answered, "By grace we have been saved by our faith but this is not of our doing; it is a gift from God."

"I would dispute that," Susej said.

Wha…?" Davis stuttered.

Susej continued, "You are obviously quoting from Ephesians 2:8; but I say, God set the universe in motion but he does not play any further role in it. He is not a super egoist who expects everyone to praise Him and rewards those who do and punishes those who do not. To the contrary, the gift that He has given to man is the gift of an inquisitive mind, the ability to reason and evaluate and the ability to be spiritually creative. The very problem with those who oppose us is that they grew tired of spiritual exploration—or were never exposed to it—and decided to take the easy road and fell back on hackneyed synopsis. And then they worked harder on solidification of their base membership and all the wonderful spontaneity of mankind was lost."

Davis fell silent. Being preached to was a new experience for him and he covered his embarrassment by changing the subject. "What are you planning to do here?"

Susej said, "When I was traveling north, I stopped in a small town in Pennsylvania and in a small commune there was a man suffering from acute myocardial infarction, or at least, that is what the county nurse said. She gave him a shot of morphine and left him to himself. He was scared to death even though relieved of the acute pain so I told him to take a deep breath and, as he exhaled, to feel it, to feel himself becoming relaxed, and then, instead of forcefully drawing air in, to wait for the body to draw air in on its own. In that way one knows the body is functioning and then one can relax because it is not necessary for him to concentrate on breathing. Then I had him sink into the bed and just sort of float on the mattress and appreciate the feel of natural breathing.

"In addition, I perceived this man not to be suffering a heart attack as such but he seemed to be of a highly stressful personality and I surmised that he was actually having a stress attack. So I discussed with him his background and it appeared that he had unrealistically high aspirations and no way of accepting anything short of success in his endeavors and so he was in a constant state of stress and conflict—a virtual time bomb.

"Within minutes the man had relaxed and everyone in the commune thought that I had performed a miracle. But I told them that there are no miracles. The word miraculous might apply because by definition it means 'as if by miracle.' That makes sense, but actual miracles just don't happen—it is usually just a question of probability.

"Anyway, after that incident, I began dealing more and more with healing in the holistic sense; and I knew that by creating a healing environment both internally and externally I could facilitate healing and particularly when the pathology is emotionally based. I knew that I had the persona to engender the healing environment but also I wanted to include healing skill so I studied the healing touch, music and sound therapy, relaxation modalities, guided imagery, meditation and self-care intervention."

"But I heard that your main area of concern was restoration of the environment, not holistic human healing," Davies interjected.

Susej answered, "They are one and the same; at least, by method. The technique of healing that I would apply to humans I would also apply to the environment. In healing the years of environmental degradation and neglect, we must create an environment both internally and externally of care and love and, most important of all, we must apply ourselves to learning the unknown configurations of the universe but, at the same time, we must understand that like the human body, the earth has the ability for self-healing but that is dependent, like humans, on an environment conducive to healing. All things have the potential for self-healing but must be in a friendly environment to overcome the pathology they face.

"What we must accept without skepticism is that all things are interconnected and therefore dependent upon each other and that what is detrimental to one species or one substance of the earth indirectly affects us all, and that nature attempts to teach us, if we listen, to the equilibrium essential for the survival of all of nature.

"In other words, the simple basic substances of life speak to us and it would be simple to therefore assume that all things tangible or intangible have a vested interest in how we treat the total environment and that all could talk to us if we could understand how to listen. This is where the spiritual creativity of humans must come into play. We must come to understand from all things, through our spiritual creativity, what we can do and cannot do in order to continue their existence of the earth which will assure our existence as well. Understanding the spirituality of substances is not that difficult. In presenting these photographs to the public, it was astounding how many indigenous peoples responded so emphatically to it. They spoke of their ancestors who said the same thing about water and other natural substances and the ancients related that there was a spiritual aspect to water and that we must therefore preserve our water resources and all other things that speak to us.

"So, what I am saying here is that we must treat the earth with the same love and care that we would in healing or medically treating a loved one. Of all the medicines, there is none with more healing power than love."

Lafevre sadly observed that "scientists have for many years told us that we are past the point of no return—that the earth is too far gone to be saved. They say it would be too expensive or even that our efforts to overcome pollution or waste products would damage the earth at a faster rate."

Susej replied, "I have studied responses from many scientists on this topic and there were so many on each side, I had a friend run them through a computer en masse with the intent of finding if there were any biases on either side. What we found was very sad. It said that those who felt that trying to reclaim the earth would hasten the end substantially and the best thing to do would be to try to live with it were all associated in some way with the ruling triad. Those who said that we should make a major effort toward environmental salvation had no such associations.

"But just imagine the impact on the public! A professor from Harvard submits a report approved by the administration for publication in all newspapers which says that attempting to save the planet would be a colossal waste of time and money and that total destruction of the earth would not occur in our lifetime. Compare that to some unknown professor from Illinois Normal who offers a counterargument that the earth has an amazing ability for self-healing and that it has begun the healing process—through storms and weather pattern changes, occurrences which are perceived by many to be part of the problem rather than the solution."

Returning to the group with a new pot of coffee, Lafevre asked, "To change the subject a little, you seem so gentle and pleasant and yet, at your coming out at the Omni Center you used profanity and in doing so blew the whole thing apart. I must ask, is that a part of your character that we do not see here?"

With a wry smile Susej answered, "Of course, the subject I was addressing was the same issue—the environmental degradation of the earth and man's seemingly deliberate part in that destruction. But I was angry and I needed to shake them up. Of course, it didn't work in the way that I intended. I apologize for the profanity but not the anger. There is nothing wrong with appropriate anger directed at social or moral wrongdoing, but anger because of a personal affront is inappropriate. Anger is within all of us but interestingly, the most gentle of people are capable of outrageous anger if provoked by circumstances but it is those who constantly project anger and at the same time are totally alienated from understanding the cause and effect of that anger who are the dangerous ones. I understand that after Omni, there was fierce ranting from the pulpit of the churches all over the South against my effort to awaken them but, at the same time, there was the beginning of thoughtful discussion on the subject among objective peoples."

"Well, then," Lafevre said, "what about the claim that you are anti-religion and that you do not believe in the literal interpretation of the Bible?"

"I don't believe in politically correct Christianity, the paraphernalia of priesthood, that spiritualism can only be found in the institutional church or that the purpose of faith is to perpetuate human ambition. In the beginning when a religion is born it is of good intent and is related in purpose and content to the lives of the people creating it. But if it proliferates and becomes institutionalized, its purpose of being becomes itself. Then money, organization and insensible ceremony become the dominant characteristics. What I believe is that each of us must find God in our own way through spiritual exploration. But that cannot be done by adults who as children were brainwashed into a specific belief system and therefore are not capable of intellectual inquiry. However, there are those incapable of such advanced thought because they are lacking in the ability; those are the ones in need of established religion, and I applaud that, but I would just hope that established religions were more in step with the spiritual needs of the individual follower rather than the needs of the church.

"As for the literal interpretation of the Bible, let me say that Jesus challenged that very thing—he was a rebel whose values came from within, not from commandments chiseled in stone and, as for the contradictions of

Bible, when Jesus died on the cross, did he die screaming in pain or was he composed as some versions claim? Versions on that vary."

Then came the inevitable question as to His position posed to Susej on the hot issues of the century—abortion, gay rights, the use of contraceptives, Darwinism and physician-assisted suicide, but Susej interrupted to quickly close the subject saying, "Most of these are personal decisions and others outside those directly involved should mind their own business. It seems to me it is immoral to attempt to control the behavior of other individuals through the auspices of religion. As for Darwinism, God created the universe and gave man the apperception to appreciate the beauty of evolutionary change. It is fact, accept it, arguments to the contrary are delusive."

Then an unfamiliar voice from the group asked, "Do you believe in eternal life?"

"I think," Susej said, "that the original writers of any religion recognized the great capacity of life to renew itself but that continuation of life was perhaps deliberately confused with the concept of eternal life in the individual. The founders of organized religion knew that people had a great fear of death and that if they promised eternal life through a belief in their doctrines then they would gain acolytes and converts. The irony of this is that once the individual matures, the prospect of death is seen as a natural part of the life process and is not feared."

The group had grown very serious and although now very intense, they were not uncomfortable. Nevertheless, Susej wanted to break away from that mood and so he began to tell the stories of his travel on the road to New York City and he saved his favorite for the last.

According to Susej, a man in a British-made automobile broke down on the freeway in North Carolina, tried to start the vehicle and when he was unsuccessful sat behind the wheel in a state of agitation, swearing as loud as he could. Susej, who was walking past the vehicle with Adler, stopped, walked over to the vehicle and put one hand on the hood asking, "What seems to be the matter, sir?" The man who recognized Susej from newspapers was obviously very uptight and intolerant of failure, replied, "I can't get this British son of a bitch to run." Sesuj contemplated that for a moment and then said softly, "Oh, you have a problem with the queen, sir?" The driver laughed uproariously at the comment and that relaxed him and then after a few seconds, he tried again and the car started right up. Susej laughed from deep within in concluding the story and said, "As he drove away he thanked me and said that he thought I had performed a miracle."

Susej then thanked the small gathering and stated that he planned the beginning of his undertaking to restore Gaia, the totality of life on earth, here in New York City because of the remarkable people that lived here—"they can become the beacon of the world." He referred to the fact that although the city was awash during high tides and the subway system not functioning, many New Yorkers remained in the city and in doing so showed great resolve, dedication, resilience, innovation and even humor. "And nature's healing process has commenced already; although many of you complain of the poor quality of the air, positive changes have begun despite that the money-lenders are still in charge. For instance, for many decades, the small species of birds that migrate only at night were drawn like moths to a flame to their deaths by the lights on towers and skyscrapers of the city and the bird-kill was enormous but since the city can no longer afford to light those buildings, the bird-kill is inconsequential. At the same time, since only elitists can afford to fuel their cars, there is very little consumption of fossil fuel and with alternative fuels coming more in use with other alternatives sources of energy, volunteer scientists tell us that the pollutants in the atmosphere have diminished and the so-called ozone hole is closing. We must understand that the world will continue, but it is up to us if man is going to be a part of that world. Otherwise, the earth will go on without us, returning to a state of a billion years ago when it was composed of bacteria, algae and simple multicellular plants, and the rebuilding process will commence anew but without us."

So it was the beginning of something new but without fanfare or ceremony. The family of the center worked well together and they were supportive of each other, the gossipy meddling typical of the common workplace was absent so strong was the dedication and commitment to cause. Then suddenly, the spring which had returned like an old friend, gave way to summer with its stifling heat penetrating the center where air-conditioning was a thing of the past and a high humidity doubled its effect. Although law enforcement had never come to the center to question the whereabouts of Susej, by agreement, his name was never used and he moved about like an ensconced phantom, unacknowledged and unnamed by his partisans and those that they served. Even in dealing with those whom he healed, there was the implicit understanding among the poor that all should be cautious lest their champion be exposed but that was a simple task for they had long been used to the mental devices of covertness in order to avoid the cynical encroachment of government in all affairs affecting their lives. But Susej maintain a more sophisticated concept of the matter as he felt that the government needed him as an enemy but not as a martyr and that they would never touch him even if they knew where he was.

Despite the heat and poor air quality, the summer was one of joy and the projects of the Mole People progressed while the fortunes of the presidential administration deteriorated. The hours were long but that was due to the acceptance of the need by those employed at the center—a commitment to cause contrary to individual reward. Darius Celosi, upon completing his daily managerial duties, began to lecture in the community on matters pertinent to the principles of this new social movement and to his surprise came to understand that he could communicate and had compatibility with the lower class, the very people with whom he previously had disdain for.

One placid evening in August when the family was discussing the events of the day, the door opened to allow the gentle surge of cool air from the Atlantic and all members sitting about a table with their tea, coffee or bottled water, an old lady stepped to the threshold and rapped politely on the door frame. Her name was Mildred Howard. At eighty years of age, she was tired and disheveled from a long walk in the late-afternoon heat to the center. Once inside the assembly room, she identified herself as the widow of Chester A. Howard, once a prosperous businessman in Manhattan. Upon his death about five years before, she explained, she was left with a sparse bank account but no steady income as the government received most of his inheritance through a process of questionable legality. Mrs. Howard's situation had deteriorated so badly that month that she was unable to feed herself and as a last resort, she learned that she might receive aid from what one fellow described as "the woo-woo people who lived in an old gift shop on Staten Island." She learned the address and proceeded to Staten Island on foot.

At the center, Mrs. Howard was fed, was given a bath—a very rare occurrence—and then as exhausted as she seemed, she was offered a bed but she garnered energy anew and, fed by the casual vitality of the group, became revitalized. She was an incredibly sweet old lady, modestly educated but for years was waited on by servants and developed no skills or knowledge of her own. She brought smiles to the faces of those at the table for she was a classical example of cultural conflict; her perception of the conversations was that of a person limited by imagined experience that gave contrary meaning to even basic words. When someone spoke of the poor, she immediately thought of those filthy ignorant people who were beneath her and who her husband deplored. When the political party that her husband despised was mentioned, she immediately envisioned evil manipulators. But those at the table were gentle people and no confrontations on discordant issues were forthcoming.

The group liked Mrs. Howard immensely despite her opulent background by both birth and marriage. They saw her as a childlike despite that she felt tremendous knowledge and power over others and nature and emphasized that during her developmental years and after her marriage to a wealthy man, knowledge and power became an inflexible ideology, and although her role in the marriage was a subsidiary one, she remained steadfast on her inherited beliefs. Had Mrs. Howard remained consistent with her upbringing and marriage she would have lacked the perspective to understand the Mole People—to her they were a blight. But now, whether she liked it or not, she was one of them.

But what was to bring the most unconceivable change in Mrs. Howard was her great attraction to Susej, whom she found to be overwhelmingly fascinating and, being elderly and not held to any standards of propriety by a group that saw her as "eccentric," "adrift in senility," or "coquettish"—although some of her associations might have said the same things when her husband was still alive—she unabashedly placed her own chair next to Susej, interrupted others to converse with him and fondled his shirt sleeve constantly. But Susej saw the sweetness within the old lady and responded to her in an amicable manner. Strangely enough however, although her attraction appeared physical as she could not keep her hands from Susej, she actually listened to him and her comments and questions became increasingly relevant to his discourse. In the days following that first meeting, the two appeared extremely close and although there was no great awakening for Mrs. Howard, she was beginning to navigate in bits and pieces toward the philosophical peripheries of the disenfranchised and poor. And in one troubled moment, her sweetness and gayety was missing and she revealed to Susej about those dreadful days after her husband died when she was captive in her huge silent home without food or contact with other humans and her situation became so deprived that in total despair she walked out the home that had been her security for decades and into a world of which she knew nothing.

If Mrs. Howard was a favorite of Sesuj, she was also cherished by the clan. She was given a permanent bed and employed in the center's daycare program, located two blocks from the center. She did not exactly fulfill an essential position at the program but her presence was uplifting and particularly with the children her influence could be felt as she made over each and every one as if they were all special—an attention that was a new and enduring experience for many of them and prompted many to wonder to themselves why this warm and affectionate woman never had any children of her own.

## THE LEGEND OF SUSEJ

One day after her shift, Mrs. Howard felt the gentle rays of the sun on her face and decided to take a long way back to the center with a walk through adjacent neighborhoods and, walking in a circuitous route, planned to intersect with the center at the completion of her walk. But even during her long trip to Staten Island, she had not seen anything this bad. She first encountered a deceased female, brusquely shoved off the sidewalk where she had died and left to lie on a dusty plot of dirt that had once been fertile lawn. She saw a forty-something man suffering from lung infection lying prone on a sidewalk, attempting to absorb the heat out of the cement to warm his chilled body even on this warm, pleasant day. She saw drunkenness—and they were the better off. She saw naked and filthy children. She saw prostitutes so ugly and worn out that she wondered what they could possibly charge for their services. Then there was a young woman sitting aside her front porch, her face blank with despair, her legs apart with her dress above her knees, unconcerned that she was exposing herself to the world. She was shocked to see individuals urinate in gutters or defecate in their yards. But it was the children that really devastated her, facing a slow death in a society that no longer cared of their fate. She saw a naked little boy, with a swollen gonad hanging lifelessly halfway to his knees. There were children incredibly dirty, disassociated from those around them and so hungry that they had no interest in children's games and felt no affection or care from parents who had a long time before given up. And she saw the fighting and the sexual acting out in public.

Totally dismayed, Mrs. Howard became disoriented and erratic in her course, desperately changing direction several times in order to find her way back to the center. Finally, she flagged a taxi, a rare occurrence in that day and age, and after a surprisingly short drive, was back at the center. The center staff was able to scrape enough coins to pay the fare from a kitchen drawer where they had accumulated without purpose as the coinage possessed so little value to those who questioned the integrity of a monetary exchange system. Upon entering the center, a silent and tearful Mrs. Howard proceeded to her bed where she plunked herself on the edge, her hands clasping her face as she bawled unashamedly. Susej went to her, gently pulled her to her feet and as she sobbed he hugged her as blurted into his chest, "All those years I lived in affluence and I didn't even do a full day's work—ever. I didn't know that there were people who were living like that. I could have done something. I could have helped at least some of them—particularly the children. I just didn't know. I was ignorant and I was kept that way."

Susej understood her pain and despair. He saw those same sights every day. So he consoled her as best he could, but he knew the reality; that she had been living these many years under false assumptions and in her world, people like herself, whether by design or without intention, lived above the struggles of the common people and all other living things, without compassion or concern for anything other than own gratification. Susej knew that her day of reckoning had come and that she would never recover and because she was so clearly of the autocratic class and now, with her discovery, she would carry the burden of guilt the rest of her life. He attempted to bring peace to her through the rationalization that there was no intent by her to hurt or deprive others, that she was, by her very circumstances, a victim of the Ubermensch mentality that devitalized the lower classes and that she had been kept subservient to that cogitated belief which dominated her education, upbringing and adult comportment. But she knew. She had failed the simple test of compassion and to not see the obvious had been foolish and the result now burdened her with its full force for had she seen to become part of the effort to overcome poverty, it would have brought forth the person she was meant to be, for that was her secret anguish all these years—that she had an identity crisis and desperately wanted to find herself. But now the opportunity was lost forever—or so she thought.

Mrs. Howard thereafter always implored Susej that more must be done to overcome the suffering. She proposed that soup lines be set up and that the center go into the impoverished communities and physically make the changes that would improve people's lives. Susej patiently explained that assistance without expected obligation of the recipients would accomplish nothing and that those who receive aid must be part of the program with the understanding that they believe in the system and contribute through work or other contribution. He emphasized that growth of the system would be low due to the very nature of a belief system; that is, one in which members develop a sense of community, love of their fellow man, the balance of all living things and a willingness to submit one's soul to the common good.

"Submit," Mrs. Howard said in ironic tone. "If only it were so easy. Let me tell you a story: I grew up on a farm in Western Pennsylvania and in that county in those days they did not allow hunting or shooting by law. Everyone complained about the foxes raiding the chicken houses and ravaging small domestic animals but because of the anti-gun law there was nothing anyone could do and the foxes began overpopulating. Then the community took action and one Sunday after church they formed a great circle of people in the county and began moving with a lot of loud noise toward the center. The noise was atrocious, eerie, there was chanting, humming, cowboy yells, profanity, laughter, even the name of God was repeated, and at first the foxes, confused and agitated, moved ahead of the people but then the circle closed in on them and they became frightened and finally they were trapped and were beaten to death. I remember one small boy was given a club by his father and told to "be a man" and the boy beat a baby fox senseless. I was horrified but my father told me it was good. I had no opportunity to submit or reject what was going on—and these were pious people! I held this inside of me all these years and now I grieve as if it happened yesterday and there is nothing I can do to amend for what happened there. And the people said, 'they are only animals.'"

Susej grasped Mrs. Howard's hand and said quietly, "The longer love of all living things is denied, the more painful it becomes at the time of its discovery. Fortunately you have experienced the truth and you have turned away from institutions or organizations that besmirch Christianity and therefore, you will not receive part of their plagues. But that does not ease your pain but your pain will ease only as you endeavor to show the love that marks true Christians."

"But these people were Christians—how could they do such a thing, particularly to the defenseless?"

"Because they were false Christians. Even two thousand years ago they spoke twisted thoughts about Jesus and they publicly declared that they knew God but in reality they disowned Jesus by their very words; that is, pretending to follow Him but willfully and persistently rejecting his teachings."

"But," she said, "I have heard them say that you are not a Christian."

Susej countered, "I accept no organized religion but I know that Jesus was the most extraordinary man who ever lived. But the Christian organizations would astonish Jesus today and until we reject the 'system of things' and Christians become loyal to the things that he taught and walk in his paths we will never know the truth and have love among ourselves."

During the next few months, Mrs. Howard demonstrated significant emotional changes as observed by those in the center with whom she worked. There seemed to be a new inner peace within her and she knew now that she could love her deceased parents without inner constraint and that she could forgive "the great fox hunters" of the bygone era as the "system of things" and its advocates had used every unrighteous deception in the advance of their sinister agenda and thus the hunters themselves were fooled. Sadly, she understood that the failings from two thousand years ago were being repeated and she knew that Susej faced the false accusations as had Jesus.

Nevertheless, she had found her peace and believed that in the "final days" true believers would come together and that gave her tranquility. Before Christmas 2033, Mrs. Howard died peacefully in her sleep at the habitant of the Mole People. Her last act was to will her vacated house in Manhattan to Susej; a futile act in the sense of monetary value but an effort that would eventually prove to be invaluable to the growing community of true believers.

# Twenty

The old Howard home stood ominously before the group from Staten Island, a four-story Victorian mansion, stark, mysterious and foreboding, the sole survivor of a one-time affluent neighborhood that had fallen on hard economic times and the ravages of violent weather. The house had been built in 1905 in economically robust Manhattan and became the nest of the Howard clan for some twelve decades and was the center of the Howard financial empire. During the twentieth century the house was remodeled and upgraded on several occasions but when the last Howard monarch died, the old place, left to his widow, deteriorated.

As the group stared up at the place on a dark dreary day, in the upper windows they could envision apparitions standing back from the windows, peering down at their intruders through macabre eyes murmuring in repetition, "Don't enter here." For a brief instant, a drape seemed to have been disturbed. Was it the wind or an edgy imagination?

With nervous laughter the group approached the old place, an elegant house actually—faced with brownstone, a stoop leading to the entrance and preceded by weathered and slightly warped stairs bordered by brass-fitted banisters. Because of its size, the house had been crowded forward toward the street leaving little or no room for landscaping. The door, not weathered as was much of the exterior, was an elegant teak with panes of colored glass forming a semi-circle configuration just above eye level and was probably a last-decade purchase from a big-box outlet but sorely did not fit the regimen of the original architectural intent. But the door slid open easily and the pack entered and came to view an interior of high ceilings and windows, a grand staircase on the main floor, a beautifully maintained wooden floor—amazingly pristine after all these years—brass fittings on display everywhere, typical of its day, all a tribute to the style of the affluent.

As the group explored the house, each story exploded in light as the group moved upward and, in the group's imaginations, apparitions moved upward and away from the advancing light until they hunkered in their last source of concealment, the attic turned apartment that was the fourth floor, and here, harboring the resentment of whatever injustice had befallen them in life to cause them to be smitten with acrimonious outrage at those who played no part in the wrong, they made their last stand until even that secluded space was invaded and although it was poorly lit, they resisted the light and then with a shriek retreated into the shadows of their despair. The house which had been so moribund a few minutes previous became alive with light and the boisterous joy of the Mole People in the midst of peeping discovery. The furniture had for the most part been removed but of the occasional pieces left behind, Susej upon entering what had apparently been a board meeting room, discovered a huge beautifully finished antique table and as it was a good twenty feet in length and extremely heavy, it had most likely been left as too difficult to move. It was here that future meetings and planning sessions that might effectively change conditions in the world would be held. This was a godsend.

After the death of Mrs. Howard in December, the group refrained from going up to the old house in Manhattan out of respect for the woman but there was no People's Center in Manhattan and this was the perfect chance to open one. So on the first of March a group of eight from the Staten Island center took an ethanol bus into New Jersey, up the JF Kennedy Boulevard to the Lincoln Tunnel and a dash under the Hudson River to Ninth and Sixth and then a short distance to Hudson Street and the Howard Mansion near the now defunct Stevens Institute of Technology. Linda Lafevre was thrilled at the prospect of relocating in Manhattan as this would put her in proximity with her beloved Central Park as no longer would she be faced with the tedious bus ride through Brooklyn and Queens, crossing the Hudson twice to arrive in Manhattan—the park would be accessible to her daily.

The month of March was spent preparing the Howard House for occupancy and the initial planning phases of expanding their program into the new boroughs, Manhattan and the Bronx. Darius Celosi opened a counseling center to the public and was almost inundated by sign-ups the first day. He called in an old friend, John Buckman, to aid in the project. Ivan Davis went into the community and found two abandoned offices to use for evaluating and treatment of the emotional and spiritually distressed. All the while, idle individuals in the community were organized and put to work up the rubble of badly damaged homes in order to use the space for gardens, and the wreckage of many of them was delved into for any material that could be salvaged to be used for the construction of greenhouses. Organization of the community was expedited by the cooperative mood of people going without the necessities for so long. At the Howard House, Susej found that a huge building directly behind the main house had been used for a garage and storage area and was so large and accessible and as increasing the food supply was the most immediate necessity, he made plans to set the space up for canning a storage of raw food supplies received from upstate or the once-a-month arrival of food from the Midwest.

But Susej's main project was to assimilate into the population and present to them the moral beliefs and spiritual devotion essential to restoration of the planet and reformation of human dignity. He would be the first to admit that there were many alienating and intractable philosophies in the world that would resist any transforming belief. Nevertheless, he felt that the goodness in man was innate and that we all recognize what constitutes goodness even though for psychological or sociological reason we resist that recognition, inevitably we all will come to understand that the very survival of man and the earth is dependent upon acceptance of a belief system that will bring man and the planet together into a common bond. So Susej disappeared into the impoverished crowds to do the very thing that he loved—communicate with the masses; and there was an amazing irony in that and that is that, during that first week that the Howard House was opened, it was that week that Susej became number one on the FBI's most wanted list but by the very fact that he was among people who supported him and his whereabouts was constantly unknown—he slept here and there among the poor—and those who were beginning to follow him would protect him at all costs.

He continued to believe that the federal government did not really want to capture him—it was all a ruse—because he became the enemy they needed. But in one amazing turn of events, a junkie trying to beat a local drug charge told authorities that he would "give up" Susej if charges against himself were dropped. But the junkie's information was based upon assumption and that is, he saw this young man among the poor in Manhattan and he put things together, his looks, personality and dress, and thought that he looked like Jesus. So two young police officers were put on the trail of Susej and when they did contact the most wanted fugitive in a crowded vacant lot and they had the task of identifying him. Their flyer on the subject had no photo, of course, but there was a sketched drawing of the proposed Susej in which he looked vaguely like the standard composite of Jesus but was years older in appearance than Susej and had a hard evil look to the face in the drawing. But what really confused the young officers was the description that was included in the flyer including that the "fugitive has an evil appearance" and one of the officers actually inspected Susej for horns. In addition, it was reported that the fugitive might change images "as he has the ability to assume many different apparitions" in order to fool the unwary. When the officers demanded why he did not have a federal identification number, Susej explained that he had been a poor boy, had not been born in a hospital, had not attended public school and had never worked and therefore had missed any opportunity for federal identification. The officers eventually dismissed Susej as a useless derelict not worthy of their time. The informant was rearrested and in a near-coma from a recent mega-hit of mixed ingredients was transported to the borough jail with new charges for drug possession and false reporting.

Susej enjoyed interacting among the masses, particularly in old Harlem where he found an amazing affinity for reality and meaningful discussion. His favorite time and place became the community center where the Howard House fed the homeless and derelicts that had come for a desperate meal and, afterwards, full and relaxed, they would sit for hours and talk among themselves or with Susej. He loved their openness, their humor and that they had given though to the meaning of their own existence. But what excited him even more, when he tested them, was that they were receptive to his philosophical convictions—not that they accepted without contention but they responded in a way that was typical and special to the inquisitive mind and there was no outright rejection of his beliefs that would alienate future acceptance. He also discovered that during the great book purges by the government, the people had saved important books which they stored for the future in a long-abandoned vault that was above the high-tide waters that periodically washed over the land and it was only opened on the occasion of secret arrangements and the books themselves were considered the community's great treasure.

In his ventures among the poor, Susej knew them not as followers but as equals, fledglings in the intellectual world but of famished minds that would eagerly feast on the erudition of the world they did not know, and although he felt that one day they would follow, he now knew the reality that they were naturally skeptical and of prior learning experience that held them back from self-exploration and spiritual inquiry. So he was careful to take it one step at a time and knew they must first develop trust and until they did that there would be no social or spiritual growth. He would tell them, "You must trust yourselves for everything that is accomplished through human interaction is accomplished first through trust and all the good qualities of personal worth—intimacy, responsibility, autonomy, love of others, and eventually wisdom—is dependent upon trust. So it is, one stone upon another. And trust begins with self-trust—if you cannot trust yourself, then you will never be able to trust another. That is how you develop confidence in trust—by trusting yourself. So throw out the mind games, it all has to be real now, throw out those little white lies that you claim are designed to not hurt another's feelings and throw out any deceit used to gain an advantage over another. And when you do this you will feel an affinity for others and your existence becomes real."

Unfortunately it was not all that easy. For Susej was surprised to feel a high level of trust grow within the community and they began to communicate on a higher plane but the expected interactive growth did not come and then he came to realize that much of the trust that developed was based upon the people's commonality, that they spoke the same local dialect, felt the same anxieties, suffered common troubles, saw racial and ideological differences in others and had always bonded together in the threat of the outside world. It was time for them to interact with those of other communities and come to understand that all humans are basically the same and that the perceived differences are just a way for the exclusive mind to disguise itself. That led to a new method for Susej—the teacher was himself learning the lessons of social communication—and it was essential that different communities explore each other in mind and spirit and although there was great hesitancy at first, it became a project that inspired the people and began to bring them together.

Susej so loved to be among the people that he often wandered far afield at night to strange places at unthinkable hours. In doing so, he dressed like much of the local people which usually included, during the summer months, simply jeans and a t-shirt. His reputation preceded him by word of mouth and although he would be the last to admit it, he was developing a following among the poor of Manhattan, even in those districts he was yet to contact. Those followers referred to themselves as Susites and were particularly receptive to the notion that their spirituality was within each of them waiting for discovery and that there was no necessary reliance upon archaic scriptures, commandments in stone or ambiguous interpretations and that there was no use of fear or guilt to perpetuate the belief, only love and understanding.

So it was one night that Susej visited an abandoned basement garage that was being used to house the Harlem Community Project, a locally organized group that received food supplies with expired dates provided by a major supermarket to feed the homeless. That part of the city had experienced over fifty percent unemployment for over three decades as there were actually individuals in their thirties who had subsisted a lifetime on donated food, as inconsistent as that may have been. The basement was small and aggravatingly uncomfortable at feeding time as everyone was crowded together and it seemed damp and chilling, even on summer nights because of its cement construction and, despite that it had been scrubbed out and chemically treated several times, retained the penetrating smell of motor oil.

As Susej spoke to a group of young people in sort of a spontaneous give-and-take session, he spied an elder man sitting by himself in a far corner by himself. There was something familiar about the man that drew his interest. In concluding his discourse with the group, he excused himself and approached the man who was drinking coffee after a meal. Susej noticed that the man's hands trembled intensely and that he had deep sorrow in his face. Upon sitting opposite the man, Susej introduced himself and looked into a face that was all too familiar—the heavy lines of age, once overweight, the sudden loss of weight sagged his face badly, there was the hollow expression of despair, lifeless eyes that focused on nothing and the appearance that all hope seemed gone. Physically, the man was big-boned but shockingly thin which his shabby over-sized clothing failed to hide. Susej, in his gentle way, put the man at ease.

"My name is Paul J. Link," the man said. The name meant nothing to Susej. He continued, "I am from Chicago. I was the CEO and primary stock holder in Mega Media Inc, the largest media corporation in the world."

"So how did you get here?" Susej asked softly.

"Well, this is totally ironic—you won't believe it but I was instrumental in the project to have the bones of Jesus transported to the US and then be cloned so I have followed your story as it developed from the beginning." Then after a pause, he said, "I now admit that I manipulated a man into unethically reporting false information about the bones and their genesis and so I ordered our media to report favorably on the project and in doing so we deceived and deceived—the whole thing kind of escalated and all kinds of higher-ups got involved until the president himself needed it to cover a failing administration. So I was accused of fraud although I was never charged with a crime but then the board of directors of Mega Media dumped me, so to speak."

"Who was the man you manipulated?"

"It was a Christian-slash-archeologist named Houten, but all he needed was a little urging," Link answered.

"But if he was an archeologist, wasn't he responsible for the integrity of the dig?"

"He was, but he was so ego-involved in that he wanted to be famous for having found Christ's bones that he crossed the ethical line. But the problem is that I recognized that in him. I had seen it so many times in business transactions and I knew that he would cave in if I nudged him a little. And then afterward I had no pity for him when he went back to being a nobody. I don't know where he is today and I am genuinely sorry for that."

"Sometimes lessons learned come too late in life to make a difference in behavior but you should have gained peace of mind at this point because of your acceptance of your culpability in the matter even if you can't make amends," Susej said.

"Well, it doesn't ease the pain but I guess I got what I deserved," Link replied.

Then Link thought and said, "I didn't think that you would accept me and then—believe the luck—I ran into you in this unexpected place."

"Actually, that is not true, I don't look down on you because you have learned from your experience and you are remorseful. I think that I would not respect you if you had experienced all this and then refused to accept what you did and for whatever reason. I cannot believe you did what you did for religious faith but for the prestige and power it would bring to you."

"Sure, that's obvious," Link conceded, "although at the time I believed it was faith driven because that is what I wanted to believe."

"But you weren't the only one involved in the deception were you?" Susej asked

"No, surely not, but they made me the scapegoat to cover themselves. The president was very angry because it made him look so bad so they really went after me. I just hope that God can forgive me. I don't know who you are or not who you are, but I find you the most noble person I have ever met."

Susej responded, "I am who I am, no more no less. There are those who still think of me as the clone of Jesus but when I say something contradictory to what Jesus said, then they attack me and listen to me no more."

"I wish that I had your candor."

"Truth is not a singular thing—it is always accompanied by valor. If there was no threat or intimidation in telling the truth then we would all be truthful. But it is not that easy and many individual characteristics come into play because so many have an interest in not hearing the truth and much of an individual's candor is developed as a child and the responsibility for telling the truth becomes rooted in character or willingness to stand up to consequences."

As Link spoke with Susej, his face brightened and his eyes came alive—he had never felt so comfortable with another person and felt that he could say anything and there would be a gracious response. Then his voice took on a serious tone and he said, "The loss of my corporation wasn't the only thing that went wrong. After that, my savings and cash accounts were seized by the government, I lost my home, my wife divorced me and then I had a massive heart attack. After I got on my feet, I was broke and without friends so I just drifted around and eventually ended up here. But, in a way, I feel better about things—the lack of pressure and trying to constantly be one step ahead of everyone, you know, it is like being pursued by the devil and it's with you all the time."

Susej spoke, "From what you have told me I would assume that you have expertise as a writer, editor, publisher…"

"Yes."

"We have room for you. We really need to get our message out, at least on a weekly basis, and we have an abandoned print shop with presses and although the equipment is dated, it is workable. It would help us draw our program together and give people an identifiable reference. We would like you to come and work with us."

"I would be honored."

So Susej traveled by foot through the five boroughs of New York City constantly spreading his word and providing healing to those he could. He became well-known and the Susites grew in number. But always, his home was the Howard House, a place that he grew to love.

The people who knew Susej by sight were many and of those, no two seemed to have the same description of him, undoubtedly a fact that would have confused law enforcement had they been actively seeking him. Some women saw Susej as extremely handsome while others saw him as plain. Some men were drawn to his masculinity while others thought him effeminate. But once he began his discourse, appearance became unimportant as what prevailed were the penetrating eyes, the depth of his sincerity, the genuineness of his candor and the strength of his beliefs. If his personal appearance was beyond consistent description other than long curls to his shoulders—not an anomaly of the day—and a boyish presence, he became quite identifiable when, one day, he commenced to wearing a loose cotton robe, called dichdasha in Iraqi, and he so dressed in that attire thereafter. The incident that brought about the abrupt change of clothing from back-street New York to one-time common wear in the Middle East was one of the deep mysteries of his young life despite that his life had been recorded, evaluated and analyzed from his conception probably more than any other human on the planet.

The incident was one of those rare occurrences that invades one's life unexpectedly seemingly without reason. Susej had just returned to the Howard House from an exhausting two days of travel in Queens and as he slipped past the kitchen he could hear the rattle of silverware and the hum of gossip and then as he passed the living room, the television, on to take advantage of a couple of hours of electricity in a city of sectional blackouts, blared the news of the day. Unconcerned of the news—Susej had little time for government news as he considered it not factual—he proceeded to his room glancing at the screen indifferently just as there was the televised flash of a street scene from Baghdad as had been typically shown for the past three decades to reassure the public of the government's noble efforts there. What he saw quickly gained his attention as, in that street scene was a group of Iraqi women and in the midst of the group was a young woman, wearing a common burka, and she touched something deep inside Susej, penetrating his psyche and shaking his solemnity. He took pause and then in the span of three seconds, she was gone—forever.

Who was this girl and what did she mean to him? He had been drawn to her instantly and he knew that somehow or someway he knew her. A long-lost relative? But how could he not know who she was. His life had been so capsulized that it was always open to easy inquiry and there would be little chance of anyone, particularly one of such a perfectly formed face, escaping his survey. That night in daily group, Susej described the woman and the impact that she had on him. The questions from the group were varied. Was she a relative? Once a lover? Susej had no answer but he believed that the explanation was deeper than that and maybe it was nothing more than an intense mnemonic device that brought back an event or relationship from a previous existence.

That night Susej dreamed of the girl—he disdained calling it a vision. Visions were getting a little too common—and he saw the same shape of the face as on the television except that in the dream she was smiling and talking to him intimately. The dream was short and gave no clues to her identity or her relationship to Susej. When Susej shared his dream experience with others there was a tendency among many to contemplate that the mysterious girl was Mary Magdalene, but Susej rejected that, stating that we did not know if she was even from a bygone era or perhaps that she was now alive.

Susej knew that this was an opportunity to make something more out of the dream and to perpetuate his beliefs, but that was the same shoddy performance that he had seen so many times before and that it would have to be based on what one wanted to believe rather than what evidence there was for any belief. He chose to have her remain his endearing mystery. But what it did do was draw him into a sense of history and to his roots for, as the birth product of a scientific laboratory, he had no roots, no history, no genealogical connection with the past, and that is the one thing that this girl brought to him—the feeling deep within himself that somehow he belonged to the culture of the Middle East and that this girl came to him from long ago to touch him and bring him back to his genesis. That was not what he necessarily wanted to believe but what he felt and he knew that it was necessary to believe this so that he could become a complete person.

So thereafter, Susej always wore his dichdasha and became recognizable on the streets of the five boroughs by his garment and now he had a sense of identity other than that imposed on him by a feverish society. He would never forget the girl on the screen and the mystery of her and how tragic it was that she had no knowledge of him or the impact that she had on another soul thousands of miles away.

During the first few months of Susej's existence at the Howard House he had grown deeply concerned over the Christian Virtual Reality movement which was gaining momentum among nonbelievers as well as followers of the Christian faith be they of the Christian right or the liberally minded. It was all a result of a seemingly innocent move in the first decade to bring new members into the churches with their flagging numbers by appealing to the cultural phenomena of the times. Thus drummers, guitarists and keyboard artists replaced organs or a choir. The intent was to lift churches out of the humdrum of prosaic ceremony by bringing celebration and joy to the services with dancing, clapping, happy music and dancing instead of kneeling. Many services were performed in abandoned neighborhood theaters and some extreme groups met in closed sections of taverns attended by scantily clad cocktail girls, which was justified by modern-thinking elders based upon the result that such methods brought in new membership. The Evangelical churches became even more tradition-bound but when the new mega-churches began growing at an alarming rate, the conservative churches relaxed their standards and gradually gave way to less traditional services and churchgoer's attire. Nevertheless, the Baptist congregations continued to solidly be the largest religious group in the world maintaining their political clout.

But the net result of the time was that although the overall number of Christians increased significantly, there were many splinter conceptions and there became deep divisions within the faith. Many pragmatic clergymen took advantage of the new movement and broke from their established church giving rise to a spectacular array of anomalous beliefs. Of course, the net effect of this was that the Christian faith was weakened and lacked unity and direction.

Then came the proposal by the federal government to clone what was believed to be the DNA of Jesus, recovered from a dusky cave in Israel and that reunited the faith to its core and brought new hope to not only Christianity but to the world and the old struggles of the worship wars were forgotten. That became an inspiring time in Christianity and the church was united and even the poor and the homeless felt a sense of hope and revival. Then on one grey Sunday morning in Atlanta the myth of communion was shattered. Jesus II was revealed as a fraud and was quickly ordained by the Evangelicals as "Susej, the evil one" and the hope of a world yearning for peace was dashed in an instant. And after that unfortunate occurrence the church began to splinter but now on even more controversial terms, an instability that even threatened the seemingly inviolable Evangelical Church.

Then, almost as if on cue, the massive void that had existed in Christianity was pulled together dramatically by that most unlikely of contemporary cultural phenomena, the computerized Christian-oriented virtual reality games. In the absence of theological direction, what had started as a computerized chimera, developed into a serious mind-set in a society that had difficulty distinguishing reality from fantasy. It all fell under the general heading of computer games called "second life" and really caught the imagination of the disenfranchised believers when multiplayer games gave Christian followers communal acceptance. Initially, the games were quite banal, only appealing to the more insular believers as the early games usually centered around the graphic character of Jesus who roamed over the landscape in a series of guileless adventures which tested the player's moral consciousness and, if the player was to participate successfully without being zapped into hell, he would have to accept the code of the Christian belief. This belief system was realistic in the beginning until opportunistic ministers saw the possibility of programming their own particular theological slant into the games. That created a plethora of games bearing serious philosophical differences challenging the basic concepts of Christianity but eventually, possibly due to the sheer numbers of participating players and their religious leanings, the Evangelicals emerged as the dominant philosophy and with that right-wing authoritarianism emerged stronger than before.

But the number of Christian players in those early days rarely exceeded twenty million a day, a rather low number in the virtual reality world, and to stimulate growth of the industry, an appointed board of Evangelical clergymen called on their churches to hire a business advisory group to recommend programs to make the Christian alliance more competitive and to create more collaborative instruction methods emphasizing conservative Christian values. Additionally, in order to appeal to the young, programs were developed, featuring intense adventure and constant danger. The first of these was a game titled "The First Crusade" in which Pope Gregory VII took the initiative of a crusade against Islam and in which Jesus was transformed from benevolent peacemaker into punitive warrior, a depiction of his personality that followed him thereafter throughout all subsequent virtual reality programs. The crusade game was highly popular and based on sudden rapid growth in interest by the public, was immediately followed by the "Second Crusade" and the "Third Crusade." All these programs carried the same theme and that was that the alliance with the supernatural and eternal life under the invincible banner of their general—Jesus—must prevail.

To Susej this was a considerable threat to spiritual acceptance and logical analysis of truth. Although in his travels he never met or talked to any of those involved in second world reality, stories of their existence persisted and he felt that their consciousness would be impenetrable. In reports it appeared that many of them were virtual zombies, spending incredible amounts of time on their computers and in some extreme cases, some were actually bodily removed from their computer stations and hospitalized for malnutrition or dehydration. Apparently to many, the world had become so threatening or beyond understanding that they found refuge in this fantasy world where they were comfortable and the world as presented to them made sense. But social scientists and medical persons found that the large majority of them, although not subject to extreme deprivation caused by their involvement, were so imbued with the autism of the contrived themes of virtual reality that they had significant trouble functioning in society and were totally resistive to any intervention into their private world. It was this inability of them to respond that so worried Susej for it had been his indomitable belief that anyone exposed to the truth in the context of their own psychological incompleteness would experience the enlightenment of being.

The Howard House turned out to be a blessing for Susej movement as not only was it accessible to the five boroughs of New York City but had even easier access for pilgrims from all over the nation through the New Jersey city of Hoboken, just across the Hudson River. Furthermore, the location of the fine old house near the once-famed Times Square, now the darkened hanging gardens of electricity, was symbolic of the decadence of the failed society and economic system as well as the gloom of a failed orthodoxy. The eager young advocates of the new truth, believers in overcoming the constraints of a canonical society and to whom the words "freedom" and "self-evident" had new meaning, flocked to the once-great city in search of their salvation. At first, Susej held meetings in Greenwich Village, Harlem and the various parks of the boroughs, but as the numbers increased, the meetings came to be organized on a time schedule and were invariably held in the expanses of Central Park. And then, as the winds of change became a deafening tumult, the exigency of that moment in time became all too apparent, bringing forth indescribable energy within the new believers. Susej toiled long hours and to appearances he grew gaunt but never weary and then, with the entire movement working with a new urgency, it took an intractable faith toward destiny.

Susej's life—as little as he actually lived there—became complete when a retired priest, Jonathon Neuhaus, came to reside there and which gave the Howard House a strong Christian base as no other religion was represented in the house and that, despite that Susej strongly advocated the assimilation of all religions and the tolerance for unorthodox ideas, gave the residence a Christian bias. Neuhaus, approaching old age, possessed a worn wrinkled face with intensive eyes, and his body, although thin and slightly stooped, was shapeless. He had received a PhD in philosophy from Creighton University and then found employment as a writer for the Institute on Religious and Public Life in New York City where he remained for some twenty years, terminating to join the People's Center after he became disillusioned with the direction of his life as he had spent so many years entwined in the lofty patois of analytical philosophy and the extenuation of the Catholic faith but had made precious little difference to the common man. Now, Neuhaus reasoned, he had come to the time in his life that he must go forth and carry his message to the common man, so desperate and without guidance in their dilemma of deprivation and despair. He had been inspired toward that course by underground printed accounts of Susej who obviously was giving so much to the world without personal remuneration.

When he first came to the center, Neuhaus was put to work in the garden, the greenhouses, and as canning season had just commenced, he slaved long hours with the women involved in the old garage processing foods for canning.

But it was the intention of the center that Neuhaus would be placed in an outreach program as he certainly had expertise in counseling and dealing with social problems considering his impressive resume. Then when Susej met Dr. Neuhaus he was cordial but restrained as he had little use for those theologians who pontificated on a meritorious level but toward their supposed flock were pretentious, arrogant and unapproachable—an unfair assessment, perhaps. Both men were politely restrained at first, avoiding the onset of any philosophic argument that might quell a positive relationship and then gradually they relaxed and spoke of unimportant things, but that would not last for in both of them there was a curiosity that would move them both toward eventual discourse.

Then quite unexpectedly they launched into a philosophical discussion about the nature of truth. Neuhas had initiated the discourse by a casual reference to "the truth" which Susej could not let go unchallenged, so tired had be become of that reference meaning that doctrine was abiding and unamendable and which inevitably led to close-mindedness on issues essential to the evolution of mankind. After a robust repartee that accomplished no insight in either man, Susej finally conceded that he would need a definition of "the truth" for clarification of either man's position. Neuhaus responded by defining the issue as the truth of doctrine and that in the triumph of Christianity, Christ showed "the way" in which the church would supply crucial doctrine regarding the ultimate truths and that those basic truths were humanizing and provided the orientation for a life of faith. And, in his explanation, Neuhaus—perhaps unwisely—offered that those who reject foundation or the truth of doctrine are, in effect, afraid of the truth.

Susej responded to Neuhaus' statement by saying that to the contrary, those who reject doctrinal truth are not afraid of the truth, but as the ultimate truth is yet unexplained and discovered, mankind must be open to all appeals to reason. Each individual must seek God in his own way and it is essential to humanity and America that we honor the individuality that is necessary for self-exploration. Furthermore, such inquiry is an indispensable help in communicating the truth or lack of in gospel and that by encouraging philosophic inquiry we may encourage the truth of Christian doctrine and, to question the validity of doctrine is akin to self-critical analysis in the individual in which the individual through such exploration will only improve his being and become stronger.

Neuhaus then contended that the gospel has stood up to the test of time and that is based upon faith as an undeniable truth and that it is foolish to say that whatever we cannot explain or provide evidence for should not influence our lives. "But," Susej countered, "the analytic tradition will eventually provide evidence to the foundation of Christianity, but we would be remiss not to seek discrepancy and inaccuracy in that faith and evidence to this point if put in the context of a time-frame is that Christianity has constantly gone through amendment in the face of scientific discovery. The current antagonism between religion and science is a very dangerous thing and I think that Christianity in itself is strong enough in theological concept to withstand any threat to its existence."

At this point in the discussion, Ivan Davis entered the room and observing the two men sitting opposed at the dinner table and the scene illuminated by a single candle and upon hearing the last statements of the argument said, "In regard to his break with tradition Descartes said that 'in this way I should better succeed in the conduct of my life that if I built only upon the old foundations.'"

Upon suddenly being overwhelmed by what he perceived as a two-on-one attack, Neuhaus drew back and then restructured his debate tactic, resorting to high-sounding rhetoric steeped in the abstract as he emitted such theoretical terminology as "transcendental Thomism," "abstract universality," "The Cappadocians," and "Continental Rationalism," to which Susej responded, "Wha-ut?" while Davis just shook his head and departed for his cot in the main sleeping area, tired from a day of administering the poor.

Nevertheless, the contention was healthy and out of it Susej and Neuhaus bonded as the debate engendered no ill feelings or resentment; in fact, both men felt energized by the confrontation and it was to become a regular affair as Susej felt that such debate brought out the reflective aspect in himself and he needed such philosophical examination to test and affirm his convictions. Even in his long days in the American polyglot boiling pot of ethnos in the five boroughs, Susej would hasten his step homeward, anticipating the nightly disputation with Neuhaus, a needed and indispensable contingency at the Howard House.

During that spring of 2032, young people, lost and spiritless, flocked to New York City, a city ravaged by Atlantic storms and its transportation and delivery systems marginally disrupted, where there existed a young prophet with whom they could identify as a spiritual leader and a liberator of a despotic and oppressive hierarchy. They came to knowledge of his existence not through the internet, computervision or written communication but through word of mouth which scampered across the country on the awakening wings of involvement and revelation and in this way appealed to a disheveled youth culture of rebelliousness, the requisite to question and that dared to dream serendipitous thoughts. They even began developing their own arcane language which they jokingly called Susejish, a jumble of seemingly incoherent expressions designed to keep their calling insular and protect their prophet from outside intrusion.

In that spring, New York City seemed to come to life through the outside influence and the People's Program began to grow exponentially. Susej preferred that his teachings be before relatively small groups where he could make personal contact and emotionally touch his adherents with intimate interaction. But the practicality was that the great numbers of followers made it necessary that most of his teachings be held in Central Park where even there the sheer numbers became overwhelming. Furthermore, as many of those spiritually impoverished youths were eager to move into the program as active participants, the organizational needs demanded an assembly-line organization to place and organize the new adherents into work programs for the common good. Thus, it became necessary that Susej appoint four disciples, Darius Celosi, Ivan Davis, Dr. Neuhaus and Paul Luftus, to disseminate his teachings into an articulate belief system for good works. In return, each disciple need appoint two adherents who must be strong believers in Susej's faith and necessarily include an understanding of the environment as the core center of all existence, the spiritual connection to the natural world being essential to man's spirituality. In accepting those requirements, the four disciples requested that Susej appear before all twelve disciples, once they were all chosen, and present his beliefs.

Thereupon, it was determined that the disciples would assemble before Susej one week prior to Easter for that purpose.

# Twenty-One

A few days before the day of Susej's great revelations, a storm surge ravaged the city with its low points receiving as much as four feet of water, but the water quickly receded to be followed by an extreme inversion layer, inundating the city with grey pollution while the great Atlantic lay vapid like an African desert and high humidity made the chore of returning the water-logged city to function an uncomfortable undertaking. When the disciples assembled for the meeting on Sunday one week prior to Easter, they all suffered from congestion, many being so ill that it was suggested that the aggregation be dismissed, but Darius Celosi quickly pointed out to them that working-class people had no such option and if they failed to show for work, they would be summarily replaced and that since this group represented the working class and its people it would behoove them all to suffer through their infirmities stoically.

Without any more discussion, they assembled in the second-floor boardroom at the beautiful rich mahogany table that had seen many years of fiduciary tricks and strategies of the grisly headhunters of entrepreneurship and their one-dimensional approach to human materiality. The boardroom was devoid of furniture other than the long table although modern printed paintings—modern in the twenties and including Picasso's *Three Dancers*—hung on the walls but were barely visible in the weak periphery of the illumination of six candles that were in a line down the center of the table. The twelve sat stiffly at first, wheezing and snorting with an occasional nose blow. Then Susej entered the room and very softly proceeded to one end of the table where he sat down gracefully with a broad smile and trivial banter. The group relaxed and then, as if by command by an unseen force, their various afflictions seemed to dissipate.

"Let me say at first," Susej began, "that I am not a guru, or a saint, or the Messiah, I am not a genius, or a savior—I am just like you, a simple man. I make mistakes but because I am self-critical, I learn to correct myself and thus improve myself. What I would like to present to you this evening is not chiseled in stone and it is not immutable. It is merely as I perceive the world and how we can change it for the better, at this time. As followers I do not expect you to accept my opinions without question but there certainly is the common ground which originally drew us together and so I would assume that our message to the world would subscribe to the same basic principles.

"If I were to give my thought a name it would be Gaia, the totality of life on our earth and in that totality of life there is a spiritualism that pulls life together in one common effort and that in that spirit there is the power of self-healing. In our culture, we have set out to destroy anything and everything that does not fit into the human plan for subduing the earth and shaping it to our materialistic desires. Toward that end, we have actually attempted to wipe out whole species that did not figure into our purpose of making the earth easy and convenient for us. Thus, we have tried to eradicate invertebrates without understanding that invertebrates can live without us but we cannot live without them, as without their contribution to balance we would not last six months, nor would the birds, mammals and fishes which would be followed by the plants to extinction, then the vegetation and the soil would decompose until there would only be simple multicellular plants. But even then the earth would eventually return to an ancient state of a hundred million years ago and would begin to gradually rebuild. So the earth would survive, in a different form, but we would not. And this is the eternal life that we strive for; that is, the continuity of the life of mankind himself but not the individual who dreams a fantasy of ever-lasting life.

"We must ask ourselves if there is evidence that this spiritualism actually exists within the natural world or as many religions believe there is a chasm between man and the natural world and that man has no interest in preserving the natural world as there is no connection between the two. But researchers believed that there were hidden messages in water and those messages proved not only that there was a spirit within natural substances but that the message carried was one to perpetuate a healthy environment.

"The researchers, using dark field microscopes, took photographs of microscopic water and found that pure water when frozen produced beautiful crystalline forms while polluted water photographs showed incomplete asymmetrical patterns with dull colors. He took the experiments a step farther and found that music by Bach, Beethoven and Mozart gave forth beautiful images while heavy metal music gave dull, shapeless forms. Even the feeling behind words were reflected in water as 'love' and 'gratitude' produced beautiful forms while negative words gave ugly forms. Because of this, the researchers emphasized that parents must use beauty-engendering words with their children so that a child may develop as beautifully as pure water and that those children will become citizens of the natural world and its environs. In his many presentations around the world, tribal leaders and descendants of indigenous peoples applauded the concept, saying that was exactly what their ancestors advocated in that we must preserve the water and keep it clean and through the years many prominent physicians have said that clean water is the only medicine you will ever need.

"Along that line of thinking, physicist Erin Schroeder theorized that living organisms have the ability to create a 'stream of order' within themselves and thus direct seemingly formless masses of molecules into functioning beings. And, we know that subsequent studies on other natural components have shown us that trees scream internally when a chain saw is put to their bark for cutting and that even ground vegetation blushes violently when being cut back. In our culture, we contend that there are good and bad animals, there are good insects and there are pests, there are useful plants and there are those that we designate as weeds, but the good and the bad are interconnected and essential to each other for the survival of the planet.

"God has called on us to take care of His earth and He has demonstrated unwaveringly that the relationship between man and the earth is one of interdependence. Man cannot exist without the earth in its current form—they have risen together. Yet for the earth to continue to exist as a life-producing entity it must have the same purity of its existence that has endured for millions of years. But for that very thing to happen, it is essential that man inhibit his encroachment upon the planet by self-restraint but man has never shown such self-restraint. We know that animals have a mechanism of self-restraint when necessary to assure the continuation of nature's balance. For example, when there is an overabundance of rabbit prey, the predatory coyote will reproduce prolifically, but when the numbers of the prey become low, the coyote offspring will be substantially lower, and this is not a conscious decision made by the predator but is a result of the unconscious spiritual entity that exists in all of nature—except for man, whose ambitions have apparently extricated him from the natural process.

"What man has done thereafter is to cherry-pick his values and activities while expressing his advocacy of the 'common good,' and, toward that end, he will make symbolic gestures toward good works. The market economy has noted that an increase in population and the degradation of the environment bring increased profit—for now. Therefore, there is no attempt to curb population growth or follow a course of good environmental health. But no problem, for instead they make much of their Christian values in helping the poor or starving. So when the Congress approved a fifty-billion-dollar program to deliver genetically manufactured grain to the starving populations of South Africa, in one swoop they addressed Christian morality and brought multimillion-dollar profit to the bio-tech food industry selling food to a third world country, food that was unacceptable for health reasons in advanced countries; and, while the food was being loaded for shipment, within two miles of the loading dock millions of people are starving. Yet, the economist feels good about his Christian act and his profit.

"We must therefore turn away from any institutions or organizations that besmirch the teachings of Jesus, who condemned the money lenders that now use Christianity to promote their money-making schemes. To do this, it is essential that we practice self-denial, that we empty the mind of all images, explore the self and the fabrication of culture and then determine a new self and purpose of life. But in doing that, we must always move on the edge of uncertainty, never rely on dogma and seek our own truth.

"Remember never to study knowledge for the sake of knowledge but seek a useful purpose in study and that one must always be sincere in learning. There should not be a preconceived purpose in learning but the purpose will emerge from the learning itself.

"Be on guard of too much cleverness in your presentation.

"Also remember that knowledge can be communicated but not wisdom. Teach inquiry and the individual will listen to his inner self and reveal truths. It is essential for you to create an atmosphere of self-exploration and not ask a follower to adhere to the tenets of your belief. If you follow this rule, he will naturally follow the right course. Jesus said, 'you will know the truth and the truth will set you free.'

"All men must work and produce something but should be cautioned regarding management of money and remember to remove all cultural trappings. The importance of any economic system is that it must involve all of the community and if it fails to do that then it will assuredly fail itself as the market economy has failed. What we advocate is that if all contribute in a single community then they develop mutual love the community will coalesce.

"Do no harm in the name of good works. Many are those who make great amounts of money in their lifetime and then in their last days to gain redemption spend great amounts of money of noble causes, but remember you cannot buy your way to salvation and you are accountable to the totality of all your works, not just an exerted effort at the end.

"Steal no food. To eat gluttonously while others in your community go without is tantamount to thievery.

"Ancient man lived in the spiritual bloodstream of nature and when we gave up the traditions that came from nature, we gave up our humanity. Now we must reconnect with nature.

"Deal leniently with others but, be strict with yourself.

"Christians have long advocated that the devil is real—as if a real human being. And it goes that Satan observed man from the beginning and ascertained that man was created with a spiritual need and thus the devil learned to cleverly exploit this need and the Christian asks how does he do this? The orthodox answer is that the devil feeds mankind religious untruths and these truths, in the context of religious scripture, are contradictory and confusing and therefore, it exists then that many religious teachings are devised to misguide people and accordingly, the Bible refers to Satan as 'the god of this system of things' who through this method has blinded people's minds. So the Christian calls on God's word to safeguard you from being misled.

"Therefore, it is attested that man's spiritual inclination has caused him to explore the unknown, which has exposed him to another of Satan's deceptive devices, spiritualism, and we must ask, how does man handle such affront? According to doctrine, it is stated, by turning away from those who 'employ divination.' Satan was the perfect angel, it is claimed, who gave us a desire for self-exaltation, and he awakened in Eve a desire to be like God and thus, the defense against Satan's appeal is humility. Although I praise humility in mankind, this is where I have to disagree with the Christian philosophy.

"What has just been expressed, although Satan is described as human in appearance and interaction, is that this is a metaphor for the malfeasance in each of us. The fact is that we must understand that there is good and evil in each and every one of us, and each of us, in our own way, must explore our weaknesses against the background of the good expected of the individual in society and learn to purge the evil from our soul and this is only done by understanding the cause and effect of the evil-producing factors in each of us. But many religions ply upon those weaknesses in order to advance their own religious agenda and in such case the individual becomes helpless in the face of mentors who express a confusing array of scriptural passages that are designed to have the individual follow the religion's way but giving no consideration for developing the individual's intrinsic strength.

"What seems to be the center of all religions is the overpowering fear of death that seems to possess most people and which causes them to accept outrageous pronouncements by their clerics who do not attempt to mitigate those fears but instead use them to exacerbate those very fears to promote their own faith. But death is a very natural phenomenon every bit as much as birth. It is sensationalized in the young by exploitive religions which draw upon this fear to reinforce the tenets of the religion. On the other hand, if an individual follows the steps of maturity and upon reaching the state of senescence, the elderly phase of life when one has a need to nourish and care for future generations, the fear of death disappears and the person becomes quite comfortable with the prospect of death—but it must be remembered that is achieved through self-understanding and a connection with the spiritual and natural world.

"Jesus spoke out against war and toward that end, he discouraged his followers from becoming political as politics invariably leads to conflict. Accordingly, political Christianity almost always becomes militaristic Christianity with Christian clerics giving blessings to the military. There are military historians who praise war as necessary to the advancement of civilization and as self-serving as that might seem, those historians fail to consider the loss of tradition and culture and they never ask themselves if what we have become was really worth the struggle. There is actually evidence that historians claim has some validity in that several conflicts such as the American Civil War or the English Civil War of the seventeenth century brought extended peace and prosperity to those two countries, but one must ask if long before those conflicts had those warring factions come together as peacemakers willing to love all men and accordingly compromise and concede conflicted issues it would not be hard to imagine a greater benefit to mankind.

"Let me say in conclusion that there is no doctrinal way to achieve a relationship with God. It can only be done through your own exploration and subsequent enlightenment, for God is different to each man and each in his own way. But, whatever one deems as the perfect deity, God is of Gaia and those truths necessary to preserve the world. Similarly, each of us has a different concept of truth for each of us perceives differently. This is, of course, a most debated topic in Christianity and few Christians accept that truth is relative to the individual. Yet, we have a government in America that maintains that their truth is the only truth and to perpetuate that, they have brainwashed, sought control of whole electronic systems, made compliance foods mandatory in our diet, rewritten history, exiled protesters, murdered dissenters, installed secret police, bribed politicians and maintained complete control of the media and all written material. They have destroyed democracy and replaced it with what they deem the perfect political system and yet, it is on the verge of collapse, so therefore, after its collapse we must rebuild our world, commit to environmental restoration, work together in a common goal and accept the best values of all religions and the commonality of all ethos. We have no other choice."

The next morning, the half-light of dawn finds Susej walking, with his little Adler, head high and proud in quick cadence, on the dike road around the west pond of the Jamaica Bay Refuge, a bird sanctuary within the city limits of New York City near the Kennedy Airport. In the distance, he sees a garbage scow on the Atlantic after having emerged from the East River followed by a circling, screaming flock of herring gulls frantically seeking to fill their cravings for human refuse. An early fog is lifting to reveal a grey day and then, unexpectedly, a gentle breeze eases in from the ocean. Susej walks deep in thought, and then is joined by Ivan Davis. The two walk in silence for a while. They observe glossy ibises, a rare bird on the edge of extinction. They see ruddy ducks perform their courtship rituals, and then there are snowy egrets and greater egrets and black skimmers, silently stalking fingerlings in the shallows. The early morning breeze gives them all respite from the choking pollution, so thick in the city but on the edge of tolerable in the refuge.

Finally, Davis speaks of the night before. "Your presentation was excellent and I think that your Gaia will attract many like those who love Jesus as well as many nonreligious people who see the value in what you preach. But the very rigid doctrinaire folk will resist you to the end."

Susej answered, "Gaia, as nature, depends upon all coming together and all working for the common belief. The rigid folk will resist, of course, but they are bringing about their own demise, so I don't worry about them. That is what we are observing in this country at this time in our history. Despotic forces are inevitably self-destructive in the long run. Now we see those exploitive forces reaping what they have sown. They have been so caught up in their inflexible beliefs that they continue to force those beliefs upon others, but at the same time are incapable of introspection or creative thought."

"But even if they join you," Davies offered, "there are things that they will never give up—like creationism."

Susej countered, "But creation is of the here and now, and we are all a part of the supreme experiment and this is not really debatable; but think how thrilling the revelation of a moment could be when we get first glimpse of a creative moment and how unfortunate it would be if the limitations set by parochialism prevented such discovery."

Then Susej went on, "This is comparable to the debate on truth. Conservative Christians have dichotomized that issue into 'their truth' verses 'no truth.' All truth to them lies in religious scripture but since there are many religions there can be no absolute truth. On the other hand, I believe that the ultimate truth is in the undiscovered and that we are always on the edge of new discovery. We see creation every day but the conservatives believe God created earth one time and thereafter there was no change—only permanence- and since he created earth it is that His earth that must be in accord with His way, which is, of course, their way."

Davis listened intensely to Susej and then asked quickly, "People will say, regarding your stance against war, that if there was a pending situation which indicated a need to act aggressively, but if you denounced such action, you would be 'unrealistic' or 'naïve.'"

"Yes, of course, it would be viewed as unrealistic or naïve, but that is because there is no short counter to war other than war itself. Gaia implies that a war is preventable many years before as individuals in society must act in good faith for the welfare of all and not for individual advantage. We know, for example, that even in times of a very emotional situation that the majority of people oppose war, yet we have war foisted upon us by the emotionalism of the few who have something to gain by the conflict. We know that the majority of combatants are incapable of killing a human in war but still, the few prevail, and that is because we did not act in a humane way in dealing with the adversaries or we had a lack of understanding and devotion to good works for many decades or, perhaps, even centuries.

"In the Bible, God appointed David as the future king of Israel and then David's friends urged him to do away with his enemy Saul, but when the opportunity came, David refused, stating that he would do everything possible to soften Saul's attitude toward him, but other than that, he would not intervene, for God had previously appointed Saul as king and it would therefore be up to God to remove Saul from the throne."

"But," Davis countered, "David's example is an extreme example because when emotions run high and a real or supposed threat is imminent, people would not listen to David's explanation."

Susej responded, "But that is exactly the problem, as a people we have, through our lack of faith, allowed a situation to deteriorate until there is no other action open to us and then we react violently. And one of the ironies of the war mentality is that those who are advocates of war seem to be the most fearful among us—they are not brave as they would have us believe. But this also contains a vital lesson for Christianity. If there is a debate on war, then certainly there would be other issues debatable within the church that would be unsettling to the congregation; but, just like the issue of war, we must be faithful to our belief system and not look for the quick fix but understand that we will be rewarded for our patience and integrity."

Davis responded by saying pointedly, "But is it not always the goal of religion to determine an ultimate good and evil?"

"Traditionally that is so," Susej answered, "but unfortunately, it is never quite that singular. Truth can be evasive because times change and circumstances change. There has been a movement within this country to denounce science because science brought up too many issues that were contrary to religious teachings, and I think that it is detrimental to society to give faith more value than knowledge, particularly when clerics cannot agree on Biblical history. Furthermore, because religion has created a separation between faith and science and since the established system provides for common welfare, a robotic system takes on a life of its own and thus we allow our culture to dominate nature with impunity and we even dismiss the government's atrocities as banal or necessary."

"But," Davis mused, "how do we deal with those individuals who advocate that which is not to the interest of a religious society?"

"Humility. We seem to traditionally acquiesce to the powerful, the wealthy, celebrities or the famous as if we owe our allegiance to them. Eve was possessed by evil thoughts by projecting a proud, selfish longing to be like God. But the faithful needs to reject such blasphemy by silent protest. We know that God will reject such ambition but we must not allow societal mischief in the meantime. If we comply with our faith, then the result will be genuine happiness, and the humble appreciate the simple pleasures available to us like stirring conversation, the spectacle of bird-watching, a cooling rain in one's face on a humid summer day, unexplored places, the thrill of serendipity, classical music and meditation when one feels peace. God is in each of us but it is necessary that each of us find him in our own way."

"You make it sound so simple," Davis said.

"No, it is not simple, but we must understand that we can achieve whatever we need. But it is simple if we have the will and intellectual inquiry to take action that will bring needed change. I firmly believe that there is only one ultimate truth. This year a woman challenged me by asking if I read the Bible, implying that perhaps I had not. I did not answer her but I said that it is interesting that the two of us are philosophically and spiritually in agreement but both of us achieve that point in life through different methods, and does that not indicate that there is a simple truth we can all realize in our own way?"

The two walked in silence toward a water barrier while Adler, meandering in a busy disjointed course, unconcerned of the conversations of the two men, was certainly caught up in the seriousness of his own exploration. The sun, by now at a high trajectory in the sky, gave forth a diffused light. It had become a most pleasant day but by now the birds had become less active and their songs less continuous. Susej remembered seeing warblers, vireos, flycatchers, rose-breasted grosbeaks, tanagers and several migrating species he did not recognize. "It has been a good day," he concluded. But, he knew that the birds' numbers were declining and their general health was poor.

Then on the ocean side of the levee, in a patch of grass, Adler became very excited and the two men proceeding to the spot came to see that the mutt was playfully pawing a young mole. "Apparently the high tide flooded its hole and it is seeking refuge in the grass," Susej surmised. Then he bent over and picked the youngster up. At first it squawked and resisted but then when he held it to his chest and cuddled it, it curled up against him.

"Look." Davis said, "he is responding to your touch, he knows that you are not a threat and that you care for him."

"We can have a relationship like that with all living things," Susej said. Then, upon examining the animal, he observed, "At first he looks freakish but when you think about it, he is a beautiful animal. He is so specialized to what he does. The sensitive neurotransmitters in his snout and whiskers, short stubby arms with sharp claws for digging, huge sensitive ears and his beautiful short-cropped fur, show that he was created for his special environment. And, you know, like any warm-blooded animal, he responds to touch and affection."

Susej and Davies found a grassy area on high ground away from the water and proceeded to dig a hole with improvised sticks and placed the mole in it and covered it with dead weeds to shield the animal from exposure. He immediately began to burrow.

"Perhaps," Susej stated, "this is allegorical to the Mole People and how they are perceived. They were initially viewed as a strange-looking people who lived underground and the elitists had disdain for them, but when you get to know and understand them, they are a beautiful people. And the same is true for this magnificent city. When you have an overview of the city, you see flooded subways, empty streets and the dark, silent ghost towers of the past. But those towers, dead and empty as they appear, are the beginning of the new age. In the lower floors, new believers are creating a new basic economy not dependent on selling what is eye-catching but what is essential to survival as those first few floors contain food-processing rooms, storage rooms and shops to create elementary needs—and they are constantly inching upward as we expand. That is an attestation to the indomitable spirit of man that directs him toward Gaia."

Davies said, "It has been passed down that Jesus trained the shepherds of his flock. You do not seem to do that. What is the difference?"

"Trust," Susej answered, "but other than that there really is no difference in our respective approaches if you examine what has been said. When John and Peter stood before the Sanhedrin, they were viewed as 'ordinary' because they had no rabbinic training in the study of scripture. But Jesus knew his disciples as effective teachers and that they had high moral and spiritual standards. Jesus felt that the ability to teach gave one the high possibility of inspiring followers. He reasoned, rightly, that the ability to teach cannot be taught but is a gift. Furthermore, let me say that I am pleased that of the twelve chosen disciples, six are women. I find that women, because of their gender, are extraordinarily gifted in communication as they tend to be open, are caring and compassionate and have no fear of the truth. They have been shut out of the various male-dominated churches for over two thousand years and at this desperate time in our history we cannot afford to squander their abilities."

"But," Davis offered, "what I don't understand is this: I studied hard for several years at a prestigious university to become the rector of my church in Los Angeles and how could I pass on all the great theological writings, the scriptural interpretations and the doctrines of the faith if I were not so educated?"

"Because," Susej answered, "it is really much simpler than that. The only things you must do to receive devotional sanctification is praise the Creator, be one with nature, do good works, love your fellow man and all living things, do no harm and put the welfare of your family and community before your self-interests. It's just as simple as that."

"So, that's all there is to it?"

"Not quite," Susej said. "Once one becomes active in Gaia, he will be expected to bear the burden of saving our mother earth and that will be a lot of work. In our culture we have allowed the system of things to carry us and without question. In exchange for that we have had an excess of leisure time as we sought out that which was easy, fun or entertaining and in doing so we have lost our vitality as a people. But the earth maintains her vitality, and that vitality is now energized in reshaping the planet into something that will ensure her survival but not the survival of mankind. We must now reconnect with our mother and return her to the state in which man can survive."

Their day coming to an end, the two men walked in silence and then Davis asked Susej coyly, "If you could have anything you wanted, what would you wish for?"

Susej answered without hesitation, "A perfect cup of coffee."

# Twenty-Two

The president was having a bad episode during the week prior to Easter of that fateful year when the future of the world would be determined by incalculable events. He had grown tired of waiting for that grand vision of Christ's return to earth as promised by the Reverend Scroggins, a promise that had alleviated much of his anxiety as it conjectured an end to the insurmountable problems that had befallen his administration. But in these last few weeks, despite White House and media reports that the economy was good and that the administration was competent and successful, persistent reports from underground sources indicated a much different story, citing glum statistics regarding the general outlook for the country and predicting that a comatose government was on the verge of collapse, not the result of adversarial governments but simply that the current administration would disintegrate from its own incompetence. The president, of course, saw the threat not from worldly governments but from the satanic forces of the antichrist, and if the savior did not return soon, he feared the anarchic rabble would rise up and create even more devastating chaos than those which already existed. He shuddered at the thought that as the treasury was empty and as all American armies were foreign, the country would be unable to defend itself, he would be summarily relieved of the presidency, a hysterical nation would turn on him and, he imagined, there would be the usual beheadings that are always counterpart to insurgency.

Sitting rigidly at his desk, the president flipped the intercom and was told that he had an interview with his cabinet in thirty minutes. He put his head in his free hand for a second or two and then said, "Give me another forty minutes—just advise them accordingly with my apology for the delay." Then after a few seconds added, "Please send in Jejune."

Jejune was a product of Martel Game and Video Corporation, an advisor-counselor robot made available to high-profile businessmen and politicians that was developed after extensive psychological research with the objective of building the esteem of professional people experiencing adjustment difficulties in their emotionally challenging work. The president had used Jejune for several years intermittently but more so within the previous year. Personal advisors attempted to dissuade him from the use of the robot altogether, but he had tired of his aides' subjective honesty and had permanently turned to Jejune, Lester Scroggins and a couple of quirky little advisors who always had their finger to the wind. Physically, Jejune looked very human and always presented himself in a three-piece suit, properly groomed and with a perpetual smile. It was not the smile one would expect of an artificial being like the classic female body builder with a surrealistic smile before a hyped-up muscle audience, but it was relaxed and casual, giving forth a feeling of easy-going realism.

The robot entered the Oval Office and, walking with the coordination of an actual human being, proceeding to the chair in front of the president's desk and seated himself, quite smoothly—for a robot- and once seated, he even crossed his legs. "Jejune," the president began, "I am quite disturbed because I was expecting Armageddon before now and if it doesn't happen soon, it may be too late for me and the country. I think that the time is right but because of the delay it is causing many Christians a great deal of stress."

Jejune pressed forward, engaged internally, there was a soft whirl from within and he spoke: "…patience is a virtue…there is always calm before the storm…but the truth will be told…time is a necessary evil…and time hangs heavy…"

"But," the president said anxiously, "I worry about the legacy I leave."

Jejune spoke: "…you will be all things to all men…with the dreams of Morpheus…uncharted seas…then a moment of truth…you will become all of what we survey…"

"There are those who criticize me for my belief."

Jejune spoke: "…must play the devil's advocate…a red-letter day…you will reign supreme…but you must separate the sheep from the goats…"

Feeling better but still worried, the president said, "But I fear that the dissenters will create anarchy in the streets before the coming."

Jejune spoke: "…sour grapes…only fools rush in…take up the cudgels…cross the Rubicon…throw caution to the winds…eternal reward…"

Then the president said, "The Satanic one, Susej, is the leader of the antichrist movement and although he has been quiet in the past, he is gaining followers and much attention in the underground media and frankly, he is becoming bothersome and we don't know where he is."

Jejune spoke: "...agonizing reappraisal...hear the lion in his den...moment of truth...fat is in the fire..."

"But I am averse to stirring up the unwashed if the arrival of our savior is imminent."

Jejune spoke: "...goes without saying...eyes of the world upon you...epoch-making...more sinned against that sinner...but keep profile low..."

The president said, "Of course, these Mole People are underground and very difficult to locate."

Jejune spoke: "...you must face the music...time to take the bull by the horns...in one fell swoop..."

Relaxing and at last at ease, the president said, "I will feel better when this is all over, the Christians rule the world and there is peace."

Jejune spoke: "...like a bolt out of the blue...opportunity knocks...but will be grand and glorious...then it will be all over but the shouting..."

"Hallelujah."

"...God be with you..."

The president thanked Jejune with sincerely felt gratitude and dismissed him. He sat back for a moment, took a deep breath and feeling relieved, smiled to himself and dialed the intercom to have his cabinet assemble in the Oval Office. The meeting was congenial with much spinning and all reports presented were positive. The subsequent meeting eventually turned to menial banter, the atmosphere giddy and the conclusion at the end of the session was that there were no dire situations that needed to be addressed. Then, although the president was never to be interrupted during a cabinet meeting, with a single exception—that exception was received from Reverend Scroggins—Scroggins was put through immediately to the president. The cabinet was thereupon dismissed and after several minutes of jocularity and posturing, the office was vacated and the president took the call.

From the first utterance from Scroggins, the president could hear the elation and, accordingly, he knew that that meant the coming would be soon. In a screech, Scroggins announced that he had the most wonderful dream, one of Christ returning to lead the true believers in the battle against the antichrist. "It was a most beautiful vision," Scroggins portrayed. "He came through the clouds, his face huge and all-consuming, and He made eye contact with me—direct eye contact as if to say that I was His messenger and that I would lead with Him in the great battle that lay ahead. It was a wonderful experience and he ordered that all true believers were to meet him in space of Easter Sunday when we will assemble for that last battle."

The president felt great joy at the statement by Scroggins and he thereby knew that his patience and perseverance had paid off. "This is the greatest moment in the history of mankind. It is fortunate that we have planned in advance and have our ten launch sites ready and available and we now have three days to travel and prepare for our launch into eternity."

"Yes," said Scroggins, "we will fire into orbit en masse and then await His coming and when you see Him as I did, you will be awestruck. Today, I plan to give the first of my radio messages addressing the coming and then I will repeat the messages the next two days. That message will basically be instructing the believers to enter the gates of Heaven through the portals of space travel designed by the godliest among us, and now we can boast that the whole purpose of space exploration has come down to this moment justifying our faith in that field of scientific research."

"This is a glorious day. A day ago, I was fretting over the incursion of that imbecile Susej and those flocking to his cause and now we will be able to teach the son of a bitch a lesson."

Scroggins responded, "He's just a pipsqueak—in over his head. Imagine, he advocates that he can rebuild society just through the so-called innate goodness of man while rejecting the tenets of the scriptures. That is pretty weak thinking, and those poor pathetic souls that follow him, are they in for a rude awakening."

The president and Scroggins rattled on for a few minutes, each too excited to make much sense but then that did not make any difference as neither man was listening to the other. The conversation ended as each announced that he had much to do.

The president sat back. His stress had left him, to be replaced with a flood of jubilant emotion. He needed this time to himself to enjoy the moment and to anticipate the coming triumph. "Glory to God," he shouted. Then the intercom suddenly startled him.

The receptionist advised him that an R. Todd was calling on the president's private line but advised, "I am not familiar with that name. Does he have clearance to use your number, sir?"

Without answering her question he said, "I'll take it."

A voice said, "You alone?"

"Yes."

"I've made arrangements for your dominatrix to meet you at the usual place at eight o'clock tonight."

"I'll be there."

The president hung up and said aloud, "God, what a day—it just doesn't get any better than this."

Over the months, Reverend Scroggins' noontime radio performances on the government station became one of increasingly boorish exhortations that waddled in Christian sentimentality and neoconservative ideology and offered little relevance to life for those outside the evangelical political base. But on the Thursday of Easter week, the usual aplomb of Scroggins was enhanced by a new energy and strength of presentation as he announced to the whole world his remarkable vision of the night before and what that vision would mean to the future of the human race. He repeated that he had often spoken to God and that God had promised the imminent return of Jesus and then, on that glorious night, Jesus appeared before him and spoke directly to him. "And Jesus was angry," Scroggins offered, "as he is extremely distressed over the deteriorating condition of the human race which he contributes to the forces of the antichrist, and this man is not the Jesus of the worldly wimps, but a punitive Jesus who will gain vengeance on the forces of evil and return His people to their righteous place in the Kingdom of God. He has thus ordered that all true believers mount their space steeds and ascend to the heavens where we will reconnoiter preparatory to the great battle that lies before us."

"We are on the threshold of a new world, a world promised to us by God. The governments of the world have failed mankind despite that fact that God made the physical world perfect for mankind and now those governments will pass and they will be replaced by God's Kingdom led by King Jesus Christ and his 144,000 heirs resurrected to that new kingdom.

"And when that new order comes to fruition, our planet will become alive with lush vegetation, colorful birds, splendid animals and warm-hearted people and the meadows and mountains and rivers and seas will rejoice. And during Jesus' reign, Satan will be restrained; wickedness, violence and warfare will be no more; there will be an abundance of food on our tables; no one will suffer illness; the effects of aging will be reversed; loved ones who have passed away will rise from the dead; and, most importantly, we will be able to worship the only true God.

"So, I call on you, in the name of Jesus Christ, on Easter Sunday to report to your designated Resurrection Launch Site where we will all be lifted off to orbit or sub-orbit flight to meet our Savior. We have made conscientious plans for this day and with God's help, we will complete our mission and win His blessing. God be with you."

The Scroggins message was repeated on Friday and Saturday and brought great excitement to his followers but great consternation to Christians of more probable beliefs who feared that a disastrous result would not bode well for Christianity. Meanwhile, Susej and Darius Celosi were south-bound from city center on the Hudson River Bike Path for a neighborhood meeting when they got the word that there would be a mass exodus into space by some Christian sects the following Sunday to welcome the return of Jesus and to fight the antichrist. Susej sadly shook his head and said, "I grieve for them, they go to nothing and they leave nothing—no good works, nothing to benefit the earth or mankind—it will be as if they were never here except for their destruction."

That evening, the Committee for American's Twenty-first Century met in a hastily called emergency session to discuss and plan action for the expected events that would come from Reverend Scroggins' vision and the administration's expected course. The CATC was in its twenty-fifth year as the secret domestic and foreign policy makers behind the government although the philosophical roots of the organization—the ambition for world domination—went back another twenty-five years. In actuality, the committee's board, composed of twelve billionaires, controlled the administration, the president taking direct orders from the chairman of the committee, a fact that was repeated in rumor but always vigorously denied by the government. The president's religious faith, particularly his belief in Armageddon, had always bothered most members of the committee but since the president had used religion so effectively in his election campaigns—they thought it was a ploy and that he did not really believe what he espoused—they had tolerated it, but now it was coming to a predictable conclusion.

The chairman of the committee was shaved-headed and steely-eyed, one of those nondescript unidentifiable faces always in the shadows of government and power. As a young man, he had been thin and somewhat effeminate but in later years when he matured he gained weight, looked like a bigger-than-average man and he developed some incondite traits of masculinity such as talking out of the side of his mouth, facial grimacing, an aggressive almost barking countenance when speaking and an irritating simulation of a professional wrestler by stilted hands held in constant macho poses whether he was writing with a pen, holding a cell phone or drawing on a chalk board.

In addressing the committee, the chairman spoke thusly: "You are aware, I am sure, of the recent events and the impact all that will have on this nation and our committee. Since we have all planned for this day we are prepared to take action to continue our cause. In going into space, the president is essentially abandoning the nation by removing the government and it can be expected that radical anarchists will immediately take over.

"But there is nothing left here to fight for. The country has been bled dry and is now of little use to anyone. Foreign armies cannot be trusted to keep the peace and there is no law enforcement. So the anarchists are welcomed to it. We safely have our money in foreign banks and homes in our favorite places. The remaining financial powers of the world recognize us as the rulers of the world and its rulers we will be.

"There are those who say that the followers of the man called Susej will inhabit and change the country and that his movement will spread to other countries. But they are a pathetic undisciplined mob with no power, money or plan—why, some of them cannot even afford inhalers (mocking laughter). They seem to think quite erroneously that simple faith and belief in a cause will bring them together and give them an effective method of governance. But they will fall easy prey to the nihilists who have no interest in their idealism, or those pathetic creatures scrounging through the debris of a shattered city for daily survival will have no time for them, or the psychopathic street gangs that find reward and pleasure in mayhem will victimize them.

"As for us, we have accomplished what we set out to do. We have given this nation to perpetuate pure capitalism and in doing so, we have eliminated all taxes except for the poor who must pay for their own preference for a poverty lifestyle; we have eliminated public education so that money will not be wasted on those not able to be educated; we have wiped out those pesky social programs of the New Deal that squandered money; we have developed a ruling authority of the wealthy who because of their accomplishments obviously know how to rule; we have opened all 155 of our national forests to economic development—my god, did they really think we could waste those resources on recreation?—and, we have, among other things, prevented senseless environmental projects which we have determined are not relevant and, in doing so we have insisted that the proper role of science be to improve the profit system and not to squander their time with idealistic misconceptions.

"Now we will all retreat to our chosen paradises where we will keep in daily contact via the Internet for updating, new information and to make governing decisions. The three other major countries in the world, China, India and Saudi Arabia, accept our role as the supreme rulers of all mankind and they understand our power and will comply to our dictates. The world that we leave behind was inevitable. The countries that are no longer able to support their populations are numerous but that situation is one of the natural order. Man was designed for this very thing. As dominant species of earth, he has used the earth for empowerment, and the loss of other species was part of the plan that brought environmental changes that were predictable but necessary. We are the great rulers—we were meant to be and that was a fact from the very start. So we now go our separate ways but will always remain enjoined to rule those miserable malcontents we leave behind."

The day before Easter, a New England millionaire named Aristotle Diplomatica departed hurriedly from New York State to yacht club at Newport, California, where he moored his fifteen-million-dollar pleasure craft, *Reagan Express*. Diplomatica had purchased a used space exploration craft used by NASA for orbital research and as a devout follower of fundamental Christianity and the neoconservative political philosophy, was planning to ride into orbit on Easter with others of that belief. Upon arriving in Newport, Diplomatica hired a helicopter, had it follow behind his boat and then once at sea, he set nitro-charges on the ship, departed from the vessel via the helicopter and watched as the yacht was blown to bits. He just could not bear the thought of the poor trash remaining behind invading his boat and living on the craft while he was fighting with the army of Jesus Christ.

On that day, church attendance in the country soared, the national mood being solemn and introspective as even the non-religious were awed by the faith and dedication of the believers. Adding to that anticipatory drama, those clerics most known for their verbosity were surprisingly mum at this time of great expectations; instead, participating in perhaps the most heartfelt ruminations of their careers while holding deep respect and admiration for those going aloft to fight the great battle. The day seemed almost overwhelmingly a day of national worship, a state of being that clerics would have liked to have accomplished but not as a result of the current circumstances. Unintentionally, the nation was temporarily drawn together. Old animosities were forgotten and even the most cynical were drawn to the human family, filled with compassion and admiration for those willing to risk so much for their cause. It was a brief time in the history of the country, a time when the communion of its people could have overcome any obstacle to their survival. But as one previously poison-tongued adversary of the religious right lamented, "We'll dress them in mourning."

That night, the president and his staff assembled preparatory to the trip to the launch site at Cape Canaveral where they would stay in the Space Shuttle Inn. Accompanying the president would be sixty-one U.S. Senators, a majority of the members of the House of Representatives, six Supreme Court justices, various aides and advisors to the president, the entire presidential cabinet, the Army chief of staff and an imposing group of businessmen and influential millionaires and billionaires. Launching would be scheduled for ten in the morning on Easter Sunday. There were ten official launch sites but uncounted were the thousands of individuals owning recreational sub-orbital space vehicles who would be launching from private residences, public parks or vacant lots. As the president was leaving at a late hour, an ubiquitous radio journalist from government radio, the eclectic Harry Pubicus, asked the president if he had any last words before his departure. The president replied, "We have gathered a faithful congregation of men, women and children out of all nations and tribes and peoples and tongues uniting them under the headship of one flock and when we return under Jesus Christ in war against the institutions and organizations and peoples that have besmirched and defamed Christianity over the past two thousand years and then God will execute His judgment upon them and He will bless us, the true believers, and reward us by returning our earthly paradise, and the earth's meadows and mountains, its trees and flowers, its rivers and seas will be renewed. Our globe will be alive and the whole world will become one as Eden, and man will thereafter follow in the steps of Jesus. Let Armageddon commence!"

Then, almost as if an afterthought, the president bowed his head and said, "Let us pray:

"St. Michael the Archangel and Mighty Warrior of God,
Defend us in battle; be our safeguard against the wickedness
and snares of the devil. May God rebuke him, we humbly
pray. And do thou, O Michael, O prince of heavenly host,
by the power of God, cast into Hell Satan and all the evil spirits
who prowl about the world seeking the ruin of souls.
Amen."

It had been several weeks in which the resurrectionists had time to prepare for their flight into the heavens but on that historic day of leaving the earth, last-minute engagement was hectic and confusing. Huge mobs of onlookers and religious supporters assembled at the ten locations but were surprisingly muted and solemn in their response to the activity before them. Binoculars were the order of the day as spectators scanned every detail of the drama being played out before them. One newspaper columnist recalled watching a young family dutifully marching toward their spacecraft, the father, stern and proud, had two tykes, barely old enough to walk, by a hand, and the child one right side, a girl, had her eyes on those and she passed stumbling slightly as she proceeded forward, her eyes wide and innocent. *What was she thinking?* the journalist wondered. *Was she looking for reassurance? Intervention? Or was she just a trusting soul filled with idle curiosity about those around her?*

    The crowd had gathered at dawn and although nothing of import had occurred in all the time before the liftoff, the mass was drawn to the scene as if watching a complex and emotionally provoking stage play. And, even as the time of departure neared, the crowd maintained its hush, giving only slight response to the tense anticipation of liftoff. Then at Cape Canaveral at ten sharp, the presidential spaceship, *United States Spaceship One*, a converted Nova generic type rocket, four hundred feet in length, with all the social luxuries afforded to the wealthy, fired up. It stood for a few seconds as if refusing to ascend and then, by the time that its sphere area was blanketed with swirling fumes, it began to lift slowly but steadily. This vehicle, once considered too dangerous to have anyone within fourteen miles of its liftoff site, had undergone technological improvements at the president's bidding and would be the symbolic beacon of freedom and liberty as it soared into the sky—sucking precious oxygen out of an already oxygen-depleted planet—and disappeared above the clouds.

    The president's departure was followed by blastoffs from all ten sites, all in outmoded space exploration vehicles purchased by billionaires who had considered spending a weekend in orbit elegant entertainment, an activity that went well with the current conception by the wealthy that the earth itself was foul and dirty and that their deliverance lay in the profusion of space exploration. But at the same time, there was the younger crowd of entrepreneurs, understanding the realities of space and spacecraft production who invested in the new concept of Siamese Twin spaceships whereby two separate halves of a single craft were joined at takeoff, one vehicle powered by rockets and upon reaching a speed of six times sound, there would be separation, the first section returns to earth and the second half obtains orbital speed by jet engines as it is still in the atmosphere. Once in orbit the single twin maneuvers by small rockets. The young adventurers found the twins relatively inexpensive and of high performance.

    All the morning and into the afternoon, the firing and liftoffs continued but the areas around all lift sites were so obscured by the toxic fumes of the early flights that nothing could be seen as the thick haze from the ground reached unto the low-lying clouds to make a solid sheet impenetrable to the eye and thereupon, the choking crowd began to dissipate. At the cape, one of the last of the ships to cast skyward, unseen but envisioned by the crowd, was apparently privately constructed and so poorly conceived in its construction that as it climbed heavenward it would cease firing, spurt a bit and then catch on and fire again. This happened repeatedly for several seconds and in the crowd's mind there was a poor pathetic middle-aged space explorer want-to-be wearing a New York Mets baseball cap desperately steering a small garage-constructed cone roughly resembling a 1920s version of a rocket with a variety of used rocket motors for propulsion. After the final firing, there was thirty seconds of silence and then, in the distance, a crash. That brought laughter from the departing crowd.

While the wealthy dabbled in spaceships that could obtain orbital entry, the marginally wealthy invested in what came to be in the '20s, a sub-orbital vehicle craze that exceeded any fad in history. It came at a time when the earth was considered by many, a despicable place unworthy of human existence and with that, came the flight to Lunar City and the space islands in orbit, and during that era, there was the opportunity for young inventors to develop inexpensive space vehicles unable to obtain the speed necessary for orbit but because of their availability would interest a large segment of the population. It was in that intense time that Galaxy Inc. and other sub-orbit spaceships like the Leer Space Explorer came into being.

Galaxy Inc. developed a line of sub-orbitals after early experiments were successful and when the experimental crafts were opened to transport individuals into the outer atmosphere for a twenty-minute experience in weightlessness for a fee of twenty thousand dollars a trip, the industry grew beyond expectations. Galaxy came out with the top of the line in their Galaxy Starsearch vehicle which carried seven passengers, would be ferried to 55,000 feet by a tow craft and then a dovetail of exhaust by the turbo-jet engines propelled by liquid nitrous oxide would rocket the vehicle to 368,000 feet and it would continue to climb for a full minute at that trajectory after the engines shut down. After about twenty minutes of weightlessness, the nose would begin bobbing downward and thereupon, a hands-off reentry would commence.

At first, the vehicle would be free-falling, a very scary experience and, in addition, the pilot was locked out of the controls which were now on computer pilot control. The vehicle would plunge straight downward until molecules collected and upon being compressed by the wings would begin to slow the craft. When the vehicle eventually developed a glide path, the passengers would be reassured. Thereafter, the computerized navigation system returned the vehicle to the site from which it had taken off and the pilot's single obligation was to make a landing in the glider-like vehicle.

When Galaxy began to mass produce the Starsearch, the management picked up the old Henry Ford sales approach used for the Model A, exhorting that there would be a Galaxy in every garage and it seemed for a while that that very thing would happen. Every weekend, the sky would contain thousands of Galaxies, or other makes, in various stages of ascent or descent. It seemed that every teen in the land had hands-on access to a sub-orbit vehicle and all dreamed of being space explorers or space vehicle inventors. So it was not unexpected that on that fateful Easter Sunday morning that the sky was full of sub-orbitals determined to become part of the Savior's great army, and Lester Scroggins had encouraged that very thing as, on his last radio broadcast on that morning, he assured all that in his reoccurring vision, the Savior appeared to him from the clouds and the clouds parted and He embraced all those who came to Him and from those He formed his army.

But of that vast array of Galaxies and the like which inundated the skies that Easter Sunday none produced a more enthralling impact upon passengers than the one that carried the Reverend Jeremy Wheeler of the River Falls, Missouri, South Baptist Church. For Wheeler, it was the first flight of any kind in his life and it goes without saying that the experience was almost overwhelming to this gentle man who had always led an ascetic lifestyle; in fact, only on rare occasions even he left the small berg where he had been born and lived his whole life. But this momentous occasion drew him from the safety and comfort of his environs and led him to make this incredible journey into the heavens to do battle for his lord. What a near seventy-year-old man could offer as a warrior was never thought out by the good reverend, who only knew in his heart that he had to answer the call to arms.

Wheeler had been an only child born to a single mother out of wedlock. Since the conception, Ms. Wheeler had a bitter disdain for sex and conveyed that bitterness to her son. She wanted him to be a minister and prepared him, as much as she could, for that endeavor. For the boy himself, he could never remember wanting to be anything other than a man of God. His mother was able to scrape up enough money to put the boy through church schools. As a result of his persistency, Wheeler was eventually given a position in the Falls River Church and that subsequently appeared to be a good choice as this soft-spoken gentle man developed an enormous appeal to the parishioners and was effective in his sermons. Superiors often grumbled that Wheeler was "untough" or was "too willing to listen to a sad story" but his reputation within the church attendees was well-established and he was a permanent fixture among a congregation that believed they could not do without him. But when the call empowered Wheeler far beyond what any had thought him capable, they could only applaud this brave little hunched-over soul who knew explicitly why he had been put on earth.

On that Easter day Wheeler proceeded to Spaceport, New Mexico, and there, for the first time in his life boarded a flying machine. The anticipation itself was almost overwhelming to him even before the vehicle had been towed to the takeoff site, and by then perhaps Wheeler had set a record for the quality and quantity of prayer emitted from one person in such a brief time. A simple takeoff caught him breathless and just when he thought he could not take any more, the vehicle shot straight upward. The tow to fifty-five thousand feet was laborious and slow to other passengers—all clerics—but to Wheeler, their progress was a shattering experience. Then the turbo-jet engines fired and he felt as if his heart would leap out of his chest and during the next minute of ascent he was certain that he was suffering a heart attack. But eventually the craft leveled off and Wheeler began to feel the first indications of weightlessness and with that, he seemed to have forgotten his purpose and instead of concentrating on seeking his Savior, he became enraptured in the experience itself. Looking down, he could see, as one Russian astronaut described it, "the endless face of earth," outlined by the cobalt blue of space, and he felt a cosmic consciousness—the most profound spiritual experience of his life. Then, total weightlessness and with it, rapture, and he murmured over and over, "It's all true, it's all true." The flight lasted fifteen minutes before descent began.

It had been an incredible day. Thousands of spaceships ascended the earth and an uncountable number of sub-orbital craft among them, but despite that, by percentage the number of Americans cast into space on that day was infinitesimally small. It seemed that the entire nation was under the toxic clouds of the liftoff and resulting poor air quality, already a national disgrace which caused thousands of deaths each year from lung disease and other infirmities. Before the day was done, church fathers were claiming the day a success, the most historic day in human history, and it was shouted that the earth would soon be purged of the antichrist.

Late in the day, in Space America, the station set up for the media to observe the spectacular launchings, Harry Pubicus asked a NASA official, "On which craft did Lester Scroggins ascend to the heavens?"

"He didn't go."

"He didn't go?"

"No, it seems he had a bad head cold."

"I see," said Pubicus, silently damning the fact that he allowed that conversation to be heard over an open microphone.

By early evening, the sky was full of Galaxy sub-orbitals and other makes winding downward on the slow circuitous glides necessary to bring the crafts down to their landing sites. Little was said by those advocates that had dared to seek the heavens to connect with their Savior. The faces of those landing were expressionless but in their eyes there was a deep confusion, the result of the unexamined life or lack of an open mind for the possibilities of existence. But even at that, there was no denial of deep-seated beliefs; there was no questioning the static mind or the implacability of their logic. For them, there had to be a cogent explanation. Surely they had failed due to a misunderstanding of their mission and how to accomplish it. Surely, that was it! Scroggins had misread the sign. Sub-orbital flight was not sufficient to connect with the Savior. Orbit flight was necessary, for only those who could put such spacecraft into the sky were acceptable. They were the real elitists, the top of God's hierarchy, and upon meeting with Jesus they would return with Him and reunite with all those having made a vain attempt to meet their Savior.

Sometime after night fell, the peripatetic Susej and Darius Celosi moved slowly up the Hudson River bike path toward the Howard House after a day of preaching and counseling in southern Manhattan and, about two miles from their destination, they were met by eight of the people from the house. It had become a ritual that when Susej was returning to the home, a group of residents would venture in the direction he had taken and at a time he was expected to return to greet him. It was not planned and originally occurred spontaneously. And it was not for protection or to relay information or advise of pending problems—it was simply a matter of the joy of the moment that they felt in greeting their inspirational leader. On this occasion, Linda Lafevere was the first to Susej, throwing her arms around him and holding him in a long embrace and then there was much talk and excitement as the group discussed their day. Little Adler, lost in the melee, found his master and then with LaFevere grasping Susej's hand, the entourage continued north.

At that moment, the sky overhead began to clear—a rare occurrence—and with it a fresh breeze came up and on its wings came unusually clean air and the members of the group bounced their inhalers to their chests. "Ah, the winds of change," Susej said. "What a marvelous gift on such a beautiful night." Then their attention went to the sky as from the east they saw a herd of star-appearing objects moving at a slow, steady pace to the west across the ebon space and of that pack, one ultra-illuminated star stood out. "That must be the president's spaceship. He is leading the pack," Celosi said.

"Or bringing up the rear—it's all a matter of perspective," Susej retorted.

"How long are they prepared to stay up there?" a voice asked.

Celosi answered, "A long time. They can even hibernate if they have to. They have plenty of food it they have to wait it out. But the point is, that is irrelevant. If Jesus was returning to earth in a vision, then it is He who is calling his followers together, but He wouldn't do that and have them just sit up there. It would necessarily have to be precisely planned."

"Not only that," Susej added, "the longer that the president is up there waiting for the call, the more he will be perceived as having failed. It would be very humiliating for him to return a failure. He just couldn't do that—so he will wait it out."

"Maybe he ought to go to Lunar City—he has a lot of rich friends up there who could take care of him," said a voice.

"Yeah, well, he would be surprised how easily your friends will turn their backs on you once you are out of power," said Celosi.

Susej said, "We must show them compassion and understanding no matter how this turns out. That is one of the traditional problems with mankind, once one has failed in his endeavor, loses power or has been politically defeated, we turn our back on him and then surprisingly, he will rise again, if he can, but with vengeance. And, as for Lunar City, space travel and the materialism of the wealthy, when the economy has collapsed, all those things will disappear and they, like us, simply go back to basics."

"But what if they are right and this is the beginning of Armageddon?" a voice asked.

"That is fine if that is the ultimate truth," Susej replied. "We are not here to force our beliefs on others but to discover the truth, and if this venture works out as they think it will, then we can accept that. But that is precisely the objective here. Man has a very short time here and therefore we must come to understand the ultimate truth. What I fear is that in failure, rather than change their thinking the evangels will look for justifiable explanations and that would be most unfortunate because we no longer have the luxury of beating a dead philosophy or ideology just because we are comfortable with it. But what happens here tonight will go a long way in determining the future path to be taken by man."

"My concern," injected Celosi, "is that as our government is in space we have a political vacuum in this country and you would certainly think that there would be some political force to step in and take over. I mean if not political movements in this country then China or India."

Susej said, "I don't think that is a concern. The despots have run their course and there is nothing left. What political movement or country would want to step in and take over an impoverished nation? What would they gain? China and India are plunging ahead with their rigid ideologies, ignoring the obvious signs of destruction that they themselves are creating and adamantly enforcing the very policies that will eventually destroy them. Why would they want the added expense of running a poor country unable to support itself? What we have is what the evangels and neoconservatives have accomplished and there is nothing left."

Celosi asked, "But if there is nothing left what can we do that other powers cannot?"

Susej answered, "The world will eventually go back to a primitive time several centuries ago. That will cause unbelievable dislocation and many deaths. But as we have seen, those who well-intentionally offered solutions have done so with plans that included society pretty much as it is now, in other words, with the same disregard for mother nature. Actually, we have two things going for us and they are that we know that we can produce our own food and we have unlimited labor. The one thing that is unsure is whether we can bring all peoples together in a common effort and under one spiritual fidelity."

"But with our ability to grow food and labor to process it, we still couldn't feed the starving people of the world," a voice injected.

Susej said, "That is right. We cannot save everyone. But to try is a mistake Christians have made in the past with their missionaries and food and medical programs to the impoverished. They changed nothing—there was never any long-term effect. They could praise their followers for good works but it actually appeared that they were only proselytizing. We are unable to feed the poor of other countries but what we can do is be successful within ourselves and demonstrate how they can apply the same methods to save their own civilizations."

Ivan Davis at that point queried, "But where does God enter into it? It seems irreligious."

Susej said, "Every man has God in his heart but in attempting to collar large numbers into a given religion we accomplish just the opposite, that is, confusion.

For example, if you take two men, very much alike and of the same religion and general background, and you ask each to describe God in his own words and, despite their common world experiences, their descriptions of God could be incredibly dissimilar. And yet each man is driven by the same religious doctrine.

"What we must instill into each man is the idea that God is a part of each of us but in each of us God is unique as we are—that's the beauty of it. But don't be confused. That does not mean that you are God but that God is in your heart. And from that God we derive the meaning of life, our self-esteem, the need to perform good works, a love of goodness and nature and a love of all living things. But with it there are awesome responsibilities like acceptance that there is no eternal life, that you cannot stand above your brethren and that the greatest achievement in life is to obtain senescence, the psychological need to nurture and care for future generations—there is nothing beyond that."

Celosi said to the group, "That sounds like Susej a few hours ago when he was addressing a street gang and after that confrontation I think that he can find peace through negotiation with any group or belief."

"What happened?" asked the group impatiently.

Celosi answered, "We were approached by a notorious street gang, the Eastside Cripps, on the bike path. My immediate response was to run like hell. But Susej engaged them in almost casual conversation and for a minute they were so accepting of him that I thought he was one of them. He just connected with them and I knew from their reaction that they admired and trusted him and despite their first protest and claim that we did not have a right to exist they listened to his explanation that we were all alike except for our individual histories that set us on different courses and that as we are all of the same family we must reconnect. They hugged him when we parted and said that they would contact him at the Howard House."

The conversation was getting heavy while the group felt that now was a time for joy and celebration. They were just two blocks from the Howard House but did not want to go in for the night so high were their good feelings and enthusiasm for the future. So they loitered about on a scraggy street corner lawn that had once been the pride of a family's landscaping effort and they talked about trivial things in giddy conveyance. It had become a beautiful night, the air was fresh and blown by a gentle breeze, seemed to be oxygenated, and the night sky was clear, revealing an incredible number of star images moving in steady tempo through the sky toward the west.

# Twenty-Three

The morning after that momentous Easter Sunday broke clear and brilliant, the first time in over eight years that the sun could be seen in New York City. There were children eight to ten years of age who had actually never seen the sun except when it was filtered through rare thin clouds or the black-grey smog of industrial pollution. But this morning the sun appeared, optically large, emitting rubescent rays that bathed the world in a rosy glow. It would be an inconspicuous observation to one having experienced the diurnal stages of old sol, but to someone as new to the natural world as even Susej, the experience was awesome and by its very occurrence seemed to portent a new world. In addition, a high tide had been expected and it was assumed that most of the city would be flooded again; yet, the tide raised only slightly as there was no accompanying surge from the restless Atlantic. Weather experts were unable to explain the phenomenon.

Susej, up before dawn, put about to organize a meeting in Central Park for the following day, notification to be by word of mouth, but on such short notice it was doubtful that many would be in attendance. Nevertheless, he set his followers out to pass the word that he would speak of a shining new day and new world order. In that prelude, the usually diffident Susej was a flurry of activity, giving instructions, organizing groups and project areas and plotting out organizing tactics. So changed was the man that Linda Lefevre elbowed Darius Celosi and exclaimed, "Look, our boy has grown up."

In the effort toward organizing, Susej spoke with authority, had a new forcefulness about himself and walked with the posture of a great leader; in fact, he appeared taller and larger and what brought about the transformation, whether he saw opportunity in the political vacuum or he saw the breaking of a beautiful day as the sign of a higher authority, we may never know. But what he did emphasize clearly was that he expected that the poor, the homeless, his own followers, the sick and the wounded—the generally disenfranchised—

make a mass exodus to Central Park the following day and gather in optimism and hope in an experience of spiritual renewal.

But even on that first day, a movement toward Central Park commenced as individuals and small groups moved steadily in the descending dusk toward the new heralding. Small groups morphed into larger groups, each with its own purpose, each with its own consciousness, varying from those filled with the awe of adulation, those giddy with inexplicable expectation or those marching along grim and solemn in martial lock-step. Then late in the night, they stopped along the highways for rest, building campfires where they huddled and drank their bottled water and freeze-dried food, setting bedrolls in neat tight circles on the hard blacktop, and they bonded together and sang, "Amazing Grace" and "Where Have All the Flowers Gone?"

The next morning, the sun rose in a clear sky but more brilliantly illuminating than the day before; one could almost hear the trumpets announcing its arrival as the first rays tinted the desolated cityscape with a subdued red eventually giving way to a golden mantle so intense to eyes as yet used only to darkness that one was forced to squint or look away. It was from its very inception a remarkable day and with its opening, long forgotten were the orbiting stars of the previous two nights, visual evidence that a government had abdicated but as there had been little tangible evidence that the government had functioned viably, it was of little concern to the common man whether there was a government or not. In those first few hours of the second day, the few remaining opulent families remaining behind the great Christian air-lift, packed up and left the city, destination or future resources unknown, even to themselves.

As the sun rose, the crowds pressed forward clogging the great highways, a restless surging of anomalous groups displaying banners, flags, signs portraying sometimes outlandish exclamations; there were jugglers, frisbee throwers, musicians, roller-skaters, skateboarders and they sang hymns of every religion. They consisted of the homeless, flushed from the ruins of this once-great city, "squats" living in abandoned homes, office buildings, sealed-off skyscrapers, even those who had invaded the most exquisite high-rise apartments in the city and included longtime residents who had somehow remained in the city they loved. Gradually, the groups meshed into a solid teeming sea, moving ever more slowly as they converged with other human seas. They crowded across the Queens Bridge; they pushed up Fourth Avenue and Flatbush Avenue to cross the Brooklyn Bridge; they pressed up J.F. Kennedy Boulevard from Staten Island to join those from Elizabeth, Newark,

Hackensack and Jersey City and would eventually cross at George Washington Bridge; they moved up the Gowanus Expressway past the Buttermilk Channel; they crowded south along the Henry Hudson Parkway from the Bronx, Mount Vernon, Yonkers, New Rochelle and White Plains; and then they merged onto Park and Broadway, their massive numbers allowing only stubborn entrance to Central Park.

They had gathered without an announced time of the event and yet, they stood in patience and good cheer surrounding an ancient wooden platform once used by the rock group Nirvana during the height of the youth culture. Then without fanfare, Susej suddenly walked among them but they did not crowd him, holding back as if by order to allow him to pass at will through the assemblage. He acknowledged them, not as a conquering hero but as a peer with the same common goal as they. He was dressed as they did, a simple blue t-shirt, cut-off Levis, running shoes and a baseball cap. He touched some fondly, spoke to a few and smiled at all, moving in a circuitous route to contact as many as possible. Some followers wept, others doffed their hats and many attempted to touch him; but when some poor acolyte dropped to his knees, Susej admonished him, demanding that he rise and thereafter "bow to no man but respect all men." The event had been without organization but with the advent of Susej, the milling throng suddenly stilled and became orderly.

Susej knew that his speech would be short and despite the emotional impact it hopefully would have upon the masses before him, a short presentation would not satisfy the energy of the assemblage anticipating complete emotional fulfillment. Therefore, he set the stage for his own presentation with a polished rock band, The Enlightenment, that played and sang in spiritual resonance but without specific religious reference. The band, which had practiced nightly at the Howard House for several weeks, had been hand picked by Susej, who felt that their presence would inspire feelings but not confuse with religious symbolism, and for their part, the band did illicit a smooth, even rhythm before the gathering and brought them to a mood of anxious anticipation.

Then in a precise act of timing, Susej in sensing that the gathering was approaching the edge of indifference in the band's continued performance, signaled a halt and the band ended with the planned final song, "Let There Be an Awakening." The group hushed and then Susej decorously approached center stage and the huge crowd roared its approval but when he raised his arms, they quieted. His first utterance was one of welcome but, more importantly, all were amazed that this man, so small in stature and without a microphone, could convey his message so succinctly, not in an overly masculine voice of high volume but a high-pitched voice that penetrated to the edges of the masses before him as if his voice were designed to do that very thing. The response from the crowd was shattering but yet, when asked for silence they responded immediately. The affair was turning into a gigantic love match between this diminutive orator and the great mass of followers that had come in hope and reverence seeking to absolve their despair.

Susej began, "In the past nineteen centuries Christian belief has specified four last things: Death, Judgment, Hell and Heaven. But what has been obviously omitted is the word 'earth.' When we read through modern Christian teachings we find reference that our world is destined to disappear; that the Kingdom of Heaven is apart from the world we know or that the earth will be destroyed. Yet, the scriptures told us that the earth would one day become a paradise for man's everlasting benefit. The scriptures told us that the righteous will possess the earth and they will reside forever upon it and that a lasting paradise is part of the divine purpose. And on the Sermon on the Mount, Jesus promised the scripture that says 'Blessed are the meek, for they shall inherit the earth.'

"But biblical scholars deny the true meaning of these statements. How do they do this? Merely by saying that reference to 'the earth' is simply symbolic, that the earth reference as the kingdom of the heavens was, to them, a symbolic use of earthly values to explain their own interpretation of scripture. Also, for other scholars, the promised land, Canaan, was only to be taken in the spiritual sense and represents the kingdom of God in terms followers could understand. So what, I must ask, is so difficult about the simple and direct language of the scriptures as when God said, 'The transformation of the earth into a lasting paradise is part of the divine purpose.' So what is complicated about that and why are these scholars so quick to dismiss the physical earth from God's promise?

"When Jesus railed against the money-leaders, it was one of the most completely comprehensible acts ever reported in his life and one that should have established the most important tenet of the religion. The fact that he showed rage, this gentle man who rarely showed anger, should have been a flag on how important this issue was to him. Yet, we have chosen to ignore it or even worse, interpret its meaning falsely. Had the ancient businessmen taken his action to heart, they would not have relied upon money provided to them by men seeking a profit but instead would have developed a system based upon their faith in which they would earn their own capital to finance their own schemes. That would only be good financial stewardship. But the act of lending for the purpose of receiving lucrative interest rates, not to mention power over others, was too difficult to resist and once set in motion was impossible to resist. Once ingrained in economic development, the power behind the money became more important than religious faith and it became indispensable in civilization's economic life. Once money-lending had become enmeshed in society, the churches became silent on the issue and the practice grew exponentially and money-lenders became the power brokers and political movers in society. And that defies the specification that the righteous themselves will possess the earth but instead we have an earth defiled and degraded by the rich and powerful.

"It would seem reasonable that the moral test for religious affinity would be righteous behavior rather than material possessions. But the churches became part of this grandiose scheme as their connection with the wealthy assured the churches' prominence within society and in fact, books have been written projecting the idea that the achievement of wealth be proof of one's place in heaven. Yet the incredible injustice and inequality within our society goes on without protestation. And we must realize that there is no end to the economic demands on the economic system. What was a satisfactory profit yesterday is marginal today and corruption and overdevelopment rule the day.

"Well, now I say that they have had their day. They have had their wars and they have exploited the earth and its people and there is now nothing left to exploit and they have left a denuded planet and all the while we admonished them on what they were doing to the earth but they said that it would be too expensive to save the environment, that we could not afford it, as if it were some aesthetic project and nothing more. And now we have nothing.

"Imagine, if you will, what modern society would be today had we complied to early religious expectations. Not just Christianity but any religion. Just imagine if we had shown theological restraint and that we progressed no faster in our economic and social expansion than we could pay for at the time. Imagine if you would, a world in which there was only a billion souls or more and in such a world no one would go without, there would be enough space for everyone and the natural environment could exist and we would learn to live within the tenets of nature. If we had just stated a purpose for growth and expansion rather than satisfy ourselves with the explanation that it was simply our god-given duty. So now we have overpopulated the land, defiled the earth and polluted the environment and all for lack of planning.

"But I ask, how much profit is enough? And can these people really believe that they do no damage, that they deserve what they earned, and when they transgressed upon other peoples is it just the natural order of things? During those nineteen centuries of exploitation there was no planning for societies as again they believed that the direction of growth would be a natural one and we needed no planning. They used science to promote their advantage yet when warned by science that they had gone too far and given back so little, they rejected scientific research that warned of red flags in their behavior. And these same people who insist through their political ideology that every individual must show responsibility also claim that they are merely following God's plan and therefore they are not individually responsible for what has taken place.

"There has been a tendency within modern society to forgive and forget injustice and atrocities. Too often our people have said that we should forget what had occurred and just go on with life. But that was never true in primitive societies where it was realized that failure to take action for an outrageous antisocial act would allow that act to reoccur. In any society there must be collective guilt to right injustice and unfairness and thereby we must incorporate into our thinking a realization of all the nuances of behavior that contributed to the eventual act. To blame the government in charge at the time and then let it go at that is to underestimate cause and effect. Ethnic cleansing cannot be solely blamed upon the current leader as racial hatred begins at the lowest level of society, among the most inept and mundane individuals, those who are frustrated by life but take no responsibility upon themselves but blame other ethics or races and their bitterness remains unchecked by intervention or educational effort. Thus it will grow to the point that any politician ambitious to come to power will endorse the hatred and become part of it whether a sinister value he actually shares or not.

"Our belief is that we must return to an earlier phase of human development and for three reasons: one, that we must build society from the ground up; two, because we lack the resources to do otherwise; and last, to save our precious planet earth. To do that we recognize a need to reconnoiter with science and incorporate their research with our struggle for enlightenment rather than be selective regarding what we want to believe or what we want to reject. Our quest, which we beseech you to join, will prepare us for stewardship of the earth and will require that each and every one of us be involved in the spiritual exploration of the universe.

"So come with us on a journey of restoration and spiritual discovery. We do not ask that you accept or follow specific doctrine but that you remain open to all possibilities. We pray that you will join us and live like Coptic monks in a simple lifestyle, experiencing only the basic pleasures and unite with one's God. Monastic life is rigorous both physically and mentally, but it is rewarding. In addition, there will be endless exhausting labor as we must return to the earth much of that wasted by useless activity. There will be no reward for such labor other than the hoped-for restoration of our earth but certainly that is a worthy goal. You may object that such a lifestyle is boring and unchallenging but the human mind is well capable of attuning itself to unpalatable situations and in the process finds delight in the simplest pleasures.

"We have chosen New York as the city for this great movement as I believe that this is the new holy city and that the world will emulate what we accomplish here. Once we demonstrate that our belief is workable it will spread across the globe. In our quest, we cannot save everyone but we can set a course for survival. Much of the work we will do will appear trivial and unnecessary but always keep in mind the seven gifts of the Holy Spirit: wisdom, understanding, counsel, fortitude, knowledge, piety and discovery of the unknown. The earth can no longer suffer the consequences of an ideologically split-level world. We must unite.

"The congressional doers have long advocated comprehensive legislation in all of their actions. They have constantly proposed a complete package in each legislative act which included a final solution to the problem they were addressing. But it never worked out that way. Perhaps they were unaware of their own secret agenda. We cannot actually do any more than a first step, a first phase before we can proceed one step at a time, for the outcome of each step may provide unexpected results. Our first step is to unite in spiritual accord and without that there will be no further progress and we must learn to love each other and cast off no man."

Then after a pause he added, "And with that first step, we must all learn what it is to be human. And, in challenging the adventure of exploration and creativeness, we thrill at the flutter of the wild bird in our breast.

"So I call to you of all religious faiths as well as atheists, agnostics, pagans, doubters and nihilists to join us. There is a place for you. Come join us on this spiritual and intellectual adventure."

Then Susej ended his sermon to a great roar with, "We are the meek," and, raising his arms added, "and we have inherited the earth."

So it came to pass. The governments of the world collapsed as had the economies that supported them as the result of the depletion of natural resources on which they were so dependent. But as those governments collapsed one by one, there was surprisingly little apprehension by the governed who had never in their lifetime received any benefit from the various governments that they supported. Instead, they had increasingly learned to survive on their own; a fact that allowed them to accept the tenets of Susej, the great prophet and visionary from the Middle East who inspired the masses to recognize their greatest asset; that is, their intellectual curiosity and their role as an integral part of the natural environment. For the people knew all too well that the myths of history had allowed the senseless destruction of the environment and that every man must now toil to overcome the burden of that destruction. Thereafter, the people of earth became a classless society, held together by common necessity and they came to understand that they were in fact wealthy once they accepted the simple pleasures that abound upon this beautiful planet. Meanwhile, on clear nights, hundreds of gleaming stars sped across the open sky in the measured pace of orbital flight, a sight that brought beauty to the eye but caused the masses to lament the ghastly possibilities that might befall those wanderers as, over the next few months, one by one they flickered out leaving mankind with only the attenuated hope that each had, in his own way, found the peace that he sought.